The Symbolon

Book Two of the Sibylline Trilogy

To Dael & Maelyn

love

Del. J. Col

A Novel by Delia J. Colvin

www.DeliaColvin.com

Firefly Press

The Symbolon
Published by arrangement with the author
All rights reserved.

Paranormal Romance Saga

Can love defy fate?
The Symbolon is the passionate second novel of *The Sibylline Trilogy* that weaves Greek mythology with a modern tale of eternal love!

For 3000 years, Alex has dreamed of a life with his symbolon, his mortal soul mate. But when they approach the ancient council of immortals for approval of their marriage, they discover that sinister forces object to their union. Soon, they are faced with terrifying threats, including a devastating separation that neither may survive.

THE SIBYLLINE TRILOGY
a love more enduring than life...than death...than destiny.

For contact information: www.DeliaColvin.com
Or E-mail DeliaJColvin@gmail.com

To my symbolon—my beautiful husband,
Randy Colvin

Your love, support and extraordinary
enthusiasm
for this story is why it is!

It means more to me than words can
express—and so do you!

I love you!

∞

Delia J. Colvin
AUTHOR OF THE SIBYLLINE TRILOGY

CONTENTS

Symbolon: Noun [sim-boh-luhn]
Origin: Aristophanes as discussed in Plato's Symposium
1) Soul mates.
2) Two halves of a whole, never complete until re-united.

Love is not love,
Which alters when it alteration finds,
Or bends with the remover to remove:
O, no! It is an ever-fixed mark,"

SHAKESPEARE SONNET 116

CHAPTER 1
653 B.C. Carrara

Alex stirred sleepily and opened his eyes. He shook his head in mild amusement; even in her sleep, she needed to possess him! Kristiana was lying naked, except for the long crystal that was strung on a leather cord and permanently bound around her neck. Her soft body, with its delicious curves, straddled his, as her arms and legs wrapped around him in ownership. She was beautiful, he had to admit. Her curves, along with her sexual appetites, were intoxicating, taking him to pleasures he had only previously imagined.

To have lived his long existence without the secret knowledge of a woman...and then to feel Kristiana alive in his arms, and to make love to her, was extraordinary! It was a welcome distraction from the previous 500 years of extreme loneliness and devastation that had been his life.

Mani and Melitta had been right; it wasn't good for Alex to spend his life mourning. Cassandra was dead and gone and nothing could be done about it. Alex was immortal and would live forever…and his soul mate, his symbolon, was gone.

If, in fact, he would live forever, he had to find something more in his life! As Mani said, Alex had been gifted with immortality for a reason. Still, it struck him as unjust that he should have survived the drowning. Over the years, he had continued to believe that the gods would smile on him and bring Cassandra back…somehow. But now, it really was time to find some way—impossible as it seemed—to move on.

Melitta told him that the first step to a new life was to find a distraction other than Cassandra. He *had* tried. But it seemed that any activity that didn't include thoughts of her was wrought with a never-ending grief.

Once, he went an entire year without sculpting or painting her. He had kept his mind engrossed in the precarious task of climbing the great mountains north of his home. This was an enterprise that should have occupied his mind completely; but several times, during the night, despite his exhaustion, he had caught himself beginning to draw her face in the ground.

He almost held his breath as he counted down the final days of the year. On the last night, he didn't sleep. He sat perched, waiting for the sun to crest the mountains. Then, leaving behind all of his supplies, he ran—possessed by the need to see and touch the paintings and sculptures that were all that he had left of her.

He wondered what was wrong with him. How could a woman whom he barely knew, except for his visions of her, and their brief time together as children, affect him even after all these years? But thankfully, because of Kristiana, thoughts of Cassandra had become only a dull ache in his heart. He worked to shake off the melancholy that had become his constant companion over the years.

Trying to convince Kristiana that he was not the man for her had been a challenge equivalent to convincing a hungry lioness that a bleeding lamb would cause her indigestion. Once her sights were set, she persevered regardless of the cost! He knew it was a tremendous hardship on her to be married to a man who seemed only capable of loving a memory, but she felt certain that she could make him love her one day. And her physical efforts were certainly proof of that, he thought with a wry smile.

Kristiana's long bronze hair spilled over most of her face. He brushed it back, noticing the occasional gold strands from their time in the sun. The honeymoon had been fairly brief— only a month—too short from her perspective, too long from his. Alex was not an idle man; and now that he was married, rendering artistic representations of Cassandra was no longer appropriate, so he struggled to find his worth.

Still, Kristiana seemed happy and her insecurities were reasonable considering that he was still obsessed with *his* Cassandra. During their first sculpting lessons, three years prior, Kristiana had tried to get him to sculpt someone or something else. He had explained to her that he was there only for Cassandra, and if Kristiana wasn't able to help him with that, he would find another tutor. With the sizable remuneration he was paying her for her services, Alex knew that Kristiana could not afford to turn him down. He was certain that she had been hurt, but she needed to know the truth.

It had never been his intention to lead her along, and he often thought that he should have refused to marry her. But after that early June evening, he had agreed; not out of the joy of new love, but to resolve her desperate need for him and his desperate need to have something in his life other than grief.

Their courtship, if it could be considered that, had begun recently, after three years of Kristiana's constant flirtations. She had asked him to join the townspeople at her home to celebrate the sale of one of her sculptures. When he arrived, it was evident that he was the only guest…and her dress suggested that no one else was invited. Alex decided that he should leave. But she begged him to stay. Of course, he knew that she had not invited anyone else. The men and boys in town would have flocked to her if they'd been asked. Kristiana had offered Alex a drink and he sipped it. When she began to dance provocatively, he told her it was time for him to leave. When Alex stood, he realized that he was incapable of walking. That was all he remembered.

The next morning he awoke, stunned to find that they were both naked in her bed. Kristiana arose, almost covering herself with a blanket, and spoke of Alex's promises and seduction the night before.

He knew it was all a lie, but watching her—despite his headache—he felt something other than grief. It certainly wasn't love. He knew she was not to be trusted. There were rumors around Carrara that she could cast spells and Alex had suspected that her interest in growing and blending various herbs was not purely medicinal. However, it was the first time in 500 years that he had been distracted by other thoughts.

He felt a touch of exhilaration at the possibility that he could enjoy life. And, frankly, he was flattered by her efforts. Within minutes, Kristiana's brother burst through the door—no doubt to witness the impropriety. Paolo stomped through the room, insisting that Alex had taken advantage of his poor sister and demanded that the pair marry. Alex had difficulty containing his snickers at her brother's sanctimonious shock, seeing how Paolo was known for his legions of sexual exploits! Although Alex was quite certain that nothing had happened, he ensured that there was no further question of his conduct while they discussed what the future might hold.

Despite his attempts to convince Kristiana that she should

marry someone else, she had no doubt that he would eventually love her. Perhaps she was right. It wouldn't be the same as his love for Cassandra—a connection and love that he could only have with his symbolon. But perhaps he could have something that, it appeared, he could never have with Cassandra—a life.

Even after the wedding, Alex's obsession continued to be like a burr under the saddle to Kristiana. During their honeymoon, she had insisted on seeing Morgana, his home. He knew that despite what he had told her, she expected far more than the simplicity that he preferred…and he *had* warned her! She had been shocked to find the simple shack that had been built by his father. Of course, he had fortified the structure with more modern enhancements, but Kristiana was stunned into a rare silence to see its contents; almost every open space was occupied by Alex's artworks of Cassandra.

Still, he felt that Kristiana had handled it better than expected. She had merely asked what he would do with them now that they were married…and refused to sleep there. And she did that all without breaking a single thing, Alex recalled with relief! Before leaving, she asked him if he would torch the shack along with his tributes to Cassandra. It had never occurred to him that Kristiana would want his centuries of work destroyed. Alex had tried to reason with her and hoped that she would understand that this was his life's work. But in truth, to destroy it would be like losing Cassandra again, and *that*, he could not do. To maintain their marital bliss, Alex had agreed that they would return to Carrara and build a home that would be more to Kristiana's liking.

Watching her sleep, Alex realized that, even now, she appeared to be scheming. Then she drew a deep breath and stretched, pushing the long clear crystal around her neck into him. He reached over to move it and she jumped up, now wide awake, her eyes alarmed. She snatched the pendant from his

5

fingers and then, seeing his surprise, she relaxed and gave him a sensual smile as her mouth moved to his.

∞

Alex hadn't expected to like the tiny Etruscan village, but Carrara had grown on him, as Kristiana had. The discovery of the extraordinary white marble—heralded as the finest in the world—had changed not only his fate, but that of the residents of Carrara, as well, as it created a major industry for the sleepy town.

It was still early when the sun slowly rose over the mountains. In Kristiana's studio, Alex watched as the light shifted dramatically through the various hatches in the ceiling, capturing the white dust that clung gracefully to the air and coated everything within yards of the building with its mystical sparkle, including Alex and Kristiana; transforming an otherwise drab room into a magical place.

"Why are you striking it there?" he asked, amazed at Kristiana's adeptness with the hammer and chisel.

"Watch!" she ordered, without taking her eyes from their position on the glistening white stone. The chisel sat angled on the delicate face of her sculpture. Alex held his breath as the hammer gently tapped on the marble and the piece broke away perfectly, leaving what would become the delicate chin of a woman.

The room held numerous works that Kristiana had completed recently, but had not yet sold. Most of her sculptures were of women that rose, arms outstretched, from the sea. Her work was a marvel to him in that is was ageless and appeared to be effortless.

Noticing his expression after her last tap, she signaled for him to come closer for another lesson. "As I tell all of my students," she quipped, seductively placing Alex's hand on her chest, "you must feel the cut in your heart first before you cut with your hand." She pulled his arms around her. With Kristiana, he could almost imagine what it would be like to be happy.

"But you must practice! I never see you practice anymore," she scolded, softly. An unfinished work sat in the corner. Neither Kristiana, nor Alex, had the nerve to move it. The face could be transformed into someone else, but he didn't have the heart for the work anymore.

Analyzing one of her works, Alex said, almost distracted, "You need the marble more than I do." It wasn't a complete lie. He had told her that he would go up the mountain to select and purchase more marble—it gave him something to do. He envied Kristiana with her passion of creating art for the sake of creation. His only artistic goal had been to see Cassandra again; Alex had no desire to create other works. He knew that his hands and heart knew only one subject. So it was better not to sculpt at all.

She rose, facing him, with a mischievous smile, and turned his palms toward her. "To be a great artist you must have the marble in your veins." She placed his hands on her hips, covered in white dust. He smelled her hair and felt her curves. "But we will begin with it on your hands."

He kissed her lightly and offered her a rare smile. Then pulling back, he said, "I need to leave now, if you wish me to return this evening."

Until then, he had been concerned that too much time away from her would cause his mind to wander back to Cassandra, causing his pain to return. But now, after a month of togetherness, he knew that he needed the time to himself. And Kristiana needed the marble.

She sighed. "Tonight then." She kissed his neck and

pressed into him to seal the deal.

∞

The narrow dirt road wound its way through the village of Carrara and then up the hills to the marble quarries. Alex could see the serpentine pattern from the numerous hairpin turns up the precipice. Although he recognized that his seeming immortality kept him safe from most of the hazards of the roads, he still preferred his own two feet, as opposed to a cart or horse. Flying marble and ox were constant companions on those roads so he walked, gladly paying the price for delivery.

From the village, he could see Kristiana's brother, Paolo, directing the crew on the construction of their new home, a veritable palace, which she had decided to name *Bella Vida*— Beautiful Life. It was good to see Paolo take an interest, as it appeared far too easy for him to get into trouble.

With a friendly wave, Alex wondered what Paolo and Kristiana would be scheming while he was gone—perhaps an additional wing for Paolo's pursuits? Alex shook his head in amusement. Paolo was a few years younger than he and tended toward self-indulgence. With the olive skin of the Easterners, and the blue eyes of the Galts, Paolo was striking and the responses that he received, particularly from women, tended to support that viewpoint.

To no avail, Alex had spent a great deal of time attempting to instill humility and ethics into Paolo. He was, like his sister, high-spirited and singularly focused on whatever was occupying his attention at the moment, whether it be the virtue of a new conquest, or plotting to increase his wealth. Still, outside of the Trento family, the family of oracles on the other side of the country, Paolo was his closest friend and Alex tolerated his antics, knowing that Paolo did have a good heart…besides, now they were brothers.

With the town behind him, Alex turned off the road to cut through a field where the wild flowers sprung up toward the sun and framed the base of the marble mountains in yellow and deep blue. Arriving three years earlier, he had climbed across those mountains, seeking a famous sculptor; a teacher. He had been attempting to capture his memories of Cassandra for centuries—her as a child, her looking at him, her sleeping, her and the visions that had dominated and preoccupied both of their lives. He constantly clung to his memories of her, while attempting to create something new. But he needed a new medium. When he realized that painting would never be able to capture her spirit, he began experimenting with bronze with amazing results. However, once he had seen the white Carrara marble, he had to learn to sculpt with it!

Stepping through the deep field he brushed his hands over the soft blossoms, and then abruptly sensed the ocular flickering, both a gift, and a burden of his destiny…a vision. Already, he knew that this was not a minor vision regarding wealth or other relatively unimportant issues. It had been over 500 years since he had felt an impulse this strong! Alex's heart dropped into his stomach as he realized it was like…his visions of Cassandra.

The flickering formed a circle in his range of vision. Soon, it would obscure his view and his ability to walk. He felt a slight trembling, as he suddenly became desperate to see her beautiful face again. Just as suddenly, he felt his chest tighten in dread, terrified that a vision of her from the past would send him reeling back into that nowhere land where his grief ruled. Still, to think of seeing her face…he felt his heart rate climb as he closed his eyes. Then the thought occurred to him, causing hope to germinate—*what if she had come back?*

Immediately, Alex realized the error of his thinking. The

vision could be of Kristiana's safety. Then he shook his head as the corners of his mouth turned up momentarily. He would hate to see the fate of anyone attempting to best her! Kristiana was a woman of fire…she was well-known for her adept handling of a dagger.

Giving into the inevitability of the moment, Alex slid to the ground, as the kaleidoscope effect overtook him. He placed his head in his hands, closed his eyes, and looked…

The breeze gently caressed the tall grass as two women moved along the trail.

His heart leapt! It was Cassandra! But not a vision from 500 years ago—her clothes were more modern. *She was alive!* He choked as his heart rushed to his throat. Then he remembered Myrdd's instructions: Pay attention to the details! Alex pushed back his emotions and watched. *Oh, to see her beautiful face again!*

She was wearing a Roman toga and her brown curls were tamed in a long braid, with tiny tendrils that escaped around her face and neck. He noticed that her eyes were no longer the extraordinary shade of oracle blue that they had been; though they were still breathtaking, with the deep blue framed by her dark lashes.

Furrowing his eyebrows, he wondered for a moment if this vision was some kind of trickery. But he immediately disavowed that thought, in what he realized was a desperate attempt to believe that she could come back to him.

A fast moving cloud moved over her, creating a momentary shadow. Then he heard the soft resonance that he loved above all others, her laughter—beautiful and joyful. He breathed it in, attempting to make it a permanent part of his soul. He had forgotten the sound of her voice.

To see her face after all these years was surely a gift from the gods…or a curse. His only desire, at that moment, was to take in the vision of her. But he knew to protect his heart, he had to force reason into this new reality. Cassandra had died. He had watched her body disintegrate until Mani had insisted that he bury her. This could not be real—but Alex watched, just the same.

Habit forced him to determine time in the vision; it could be only a few years away. She looked to be sixteen, he decided, as he wiped the tears of joy from his face.

She was walking with another young girl, possibly a servant, who ran ahead to the river. It appeared to be the Tiber. Cassandra stepped into the crystal clear water to cool herself.

He tried to guide his glances, feeling that he was peering on a private moment—betraying her. But he could not. As usual, the vision would dictate.

From a bend in the river, the servant girl was talking to someone. A moment later, Alex saw the servant, face down on the now blood-stained bank of the river, out of Cassandra's view.

Alex involuntarily sucked in a deep breath; he couldn't bear to see Cassandra harmed again! But he forced himself to pay attention to the details—he heard Myrdd's wise council from the past; the old man who was the first oracle, and Alex's mentor. "Where is it, boy?" Myrdd would ask.

It was obviously summertime; the vegetation was a deep green along the river. There was a hillside ahead; a stone building peeked from behind the trees.

Hearing the footsteps in the water, Cassandra turned and smiled. Then, seeing something out of Alex's view, her eyes became suddenly wary as she started to back away toward the shore. The water was so clear Alex could almost see a reflection. Then he saw the struggle, and the flash of a dagger.

Easily controlling her, the attacker skillfully drew the dagger in a fine line across Cassandra's throat. The loss immediately caused his gut to wrench. He watched as the red line on her neck rapidly widened, while Alex choked in pain. He saw the horror of realization seep into her eyes…and then he felt the enormity of the loss of his symbolon renewed in his soul.

The murderer carelessly dropped his beloved in the river, and the film that coated the water parted, allowing a clear view through the water of the face that he adored. She stared blankly upward, as red ribbons of blood streamed around her. His Cassandra was dead…again.

∞

Once the violent sobs and retching had ended, and the shaking had subsided to a point where he could see something other than that final vision of her, Alex stared helplessly at the sky analyzing and reanalyzing every detail. Was it now? Did it already happen? Was she alive? Was there any possibility that he could change it?

Then he remembered—Kristiana! *How could he tell her?* But there was no choice!

∞

The ground moved by in a blur, as he rode on one horse, while leading a second. He would arrive in Rome, nearly two hundred miles to the south, by midday, if he rode all night and only stopped to water and feed the horses.

Kristiana had taken the news as expected. He had broken her heart—though she knew no outlet for negative emotion other than rage. Alex didn't have a chance to talk to Paolo, though he was certain that Paolo would insist on a physical battle to defend his sister's honor. Alex had no intention of

12

fighting Paolo!

As the sun set behind the hills to the west, Alex tortuously replayed the scene in the vision, searching for clues; he remembered the clear water as the murderer approached, and he scanned for anything that might be a reflection. Then his thoughts jumped to that last awful scene, with Cassandra's eyes staring up at him. The water was clouded with debris...a fine mist that prohibited any reflection.

Suddenly, Alex's eyes narrowed in thought, with the realization of the incongruity. The debris in the water floated on the surface, but it wasn't there before the murderer approached—*the murderer had tracked something into the water*. Alex drew in a deep breath and ran it again. There was something familiar about the debris. Was it pollen? No, he decided, pollen was yellow and this was white. Then he noticed something that had escaped his attention before—because it was something that had become a part of his new reality; a crystalline sparkle on the water. His eyes narrowed...was it Carrara marble?

CHAPTER 2
Present Day—Morgana

Asleep in a T-shirt and pajama bottoms, Alex struggled. Valeria saw the signs of another one of his nightmares—his tense movement and sweat-drenched brow, the rapid breathing and near-words. In fact, they had occurred almost every night since her return home from the hospital. He would refuse to tell her about them, saying it was all "old news," but she wished that he would talk to her.

Camille had said it was to be expected; he had spent eons fighting very real threats to Valeria's existence. How could that all be forgotten in the few months since what they had termed, optimistically, "the final battle." In her mind, it was akin to calling World War I, "the war to end all wars." It simply begged to be proven wrong. But she would keep her sentiments to herself. Alex had been through enough!

She had finally recovered from pneumonic plague and the near drowning; though not in twenty-four hours as she would have if she were the same as the rest of the oracles. On the bright side, an MRI at ten days revealed that the massive lesions in her lungs had completely healed! The doctors, stunned by the results, said it should have taken at least eight weeks for her lungs to heal, and asked for another MRI. Mani had halted those discussions fairly quickly. However, she still seemed to need a lot of sleep. Mani had warned that, although the lesions were gone, pneumonia was still a very real possibility due to the weakened state of her lungs.

Still, they all clung to the dream that she was now immortal. She had survived the curse that had killed her over numerous lifetimes on her twenty-seventh birthday. Valeria remembered the moment when Tavish had asked the question that was on most of their minds. Could the curse have been delayed a year? As soon as he let the words slip from his mouth, she could see his regret. The flash of terror in Alex's eyes had been almost more than any of them could bear. Tavish was crushed!

Despite the fact that he seemed like a big, tough Scotsman, she had discovered just how sensitive he was that day. He slowly kneeled in front of the leather sofa where Alex and Valeria sat, with what she was certain were near tears in his eyes.

"Laddie..." He drew in a breath, then continued, "Lass...I dunnot know what causes me mouth to ramble on without thought!" Then he stopped as if he was afraid of his emotions. The whole room sat speechless, no doubt trying to find the right words to erase the fears and hurt that had just been released.

"Tav, it's all right," Valeria said. Leaning forward while clinging to Alex's hand, she stroked the side of Tavish's face. In response to her touch, Tavish pulled back and dropped his head as if ashamed of himself.

Camille jumped in. "Tavish, we all know that you were

simply talking through what was going on in your head and that you don't really believe that it's a possibility. Isn't that right?"

Swallowing, Tavish nodded and rose.

Finally, Alex was able to push his fears back and speak. "Thankfully, we no longer need to concern ourselves with curses." His arms worked around Valeria in a way that hinted of his fear that his love might not be with him for the eternity, they'd been promised.

Still, all indications were that the threats had been handled and that she was now immortal! It also seemed likely that they had rid themselves of their enemy, the immortal Aegemon, who had probably placed the curse to begin with. And Valeria's eyes had returned to the unique oracle blue color that was really just multiple, extraordinary shades of blue. It was still a shock for her to see them every time she looked in the mirror.

In addition to that, Mani had tested Valeria's blood before and after the final battle and discovered that on both tests she carried the DNA of an immortal oracle. The question was, did she only have that DNA this lifetime, or since her life as Cassandra of Troy? And based on the DNA, why didn't she recover as an immortal might? Needless to say, there were a lot of questions that didn't appear would be answered unless Valeria became sick or started to age.

Aging was the other question. Had she already suffered her Prima Mortis—the first death of an immortal that would stop the aging process and identify her Achilles' heel? If so, was her Achilles' heel the plague, drowning, pneumonia, hypothermia, or high fever? They might never know the answer to these questions. She laughed and said that she had decided to steer clear of all of them…at least for a while. But as much as Alex loved that she was happy, he simply didn't have the ability to find any humor when it came to talk of her possible mortality.

Over the past few months, with all they had been through, Alex and Valeria had grown even closer. As he continued to struggle in his sleep, she brushed his face and whispered his name. He always had that moment when he took a harsh breath—as if a door had closed and he seemed to be wondering which world he was now in.

Then his arms would find her and cautiously, as if she might disappear, they would move around her with so much longing, that she could almost feel his eons of pain. It always brought tears to her eyes. But she tried to hide it from Alex. Especially today!

"Hey," she said, gently stroking his face. "It's okay. Everything's okay." His breathing slowed as he clung to her tightly.

Finally, he relaxed and pulled her into him affectionately. He took a deep breath, trying to cleanse himself of the memories, and brushed her hair back from her face.

"Are you kidding?" He smiled, but the nightmare still clung to him. "It's way more than okay!" He pushed the smile to his eyes. "I'm marrying the woman of my dreams in just a few days!" And then she saw that the dream was now behind him. It was always a marvel to her how he could do that!

Cocking her head to the side, she thought about asking him if he wanted to talk about it. But seeing his spark back, she didn't want the worry to return to his extraordinarily beautiful face.

She pulled his left hand into hers, in a move that was now familiar to him, and began tracing the continuous loops that formed a triangular mark on the back of his hand between his thumb and forefinger.

"Tell me about it again," she said, as she pressed her

mouth to his hand.

"It's our unique mark; the one that is *only* for you and me. This particular shape is called a triquetra or more commonly, a trinity knot," he said, his voice still sexy with sleep. "Apollo gave a special mark to symbolons…soul mates, if you prefer," the corners of his mouth turned up in the way she loved, "so that we would know our other half."

"But our mark is more significant," she said, her eyes focused on his.

Alex brushed her face with his free hand, as his eyes glowed with love. "Yes. Most of the marks I've seen appear fairly arbitrary. But ours does seem to have particular significance." They laced the fingers of their left hands together, in a need for more closeness.

"I do think that Apollo could have made it easier on us and placed mine someplace more obvious," she joked, and then lowered her brows. "Alex, do you really think I have our mark?"

"Absolutely!" he said, and then glanced down toward their hands. "But…you know, I have *never* needed a mark to know that we belong together!"

The sun flitted through the windows; he smiled as he pulled her head down to his and kissed her sweetly. With her face still inches away, his eyes filled with playful joy. "Besides, I was thinking that searching for your mark would give me something *else* to do," he drew a quick breath, "on our honeymoon!"

It was the first time either of them had mentioned the honeymoon, and what occurred in her body at that moment was a reaction of a previously unknown magnitude that both shocked and thrilled her! She felt an electrical charge that forced her heart into high gear and revved her internal engines. He responded by running his hands down her spine, as his mouth covered hers.

Then, just as suddenly, he sighed and rolled her onto the bed next to him. With his voice husky from sleep and desire, he drew a deep breath and muttered, "Just a few more days…"

Shaking it off, Alex offered her a cursory glance and a smile before jumping up. "Coffee?"

She pulled up on her elbow. "You need to ask?"

"Good point!" He grinned.

"I'll shower, while you make the coffee," she proposed.

She went into the bathroom and turned on the water, and while the temperature of the water warmed, she peeked into the great room. "So, where exactly are we going for our honeymoon?"

"You're just going to have to wait and see," he said without turning his head from the task at hand. But she could see the hint of his smile from her angle.

She pouted. "But you know I don't like surprises!" He turned to bring the coffee pot to the sink on the marble island. Now facing her, he began filling it with purified water.

"Yes, *I do* know that." He winked. "And as you well know, I did share that with Camille. But she has insisted." He raised his eyebrows innocently and shrugged. "I am, therefore, sworn to secrecy."

This had become a standard line of question and answer between the two of them. Because she was still looking at him expectantly, he sat the pot down and cocked his head to the side. Leaning his arms onto the counter, the corners of his mouth turned up in a mischievous smile. She attempted to match his expression, except her eyes widened in expectation when he began to snicker…which always caused her to giggle, effectively ending the stand-off. As he went back to the coffee-making, she went back to the bathroom.

Stepping into the warm shower, she realized that it was

useless—she had been trying to get it out of both of them for months now. Despite the fact that he said it was Camille's secret, Valeria knew that a part of Alex was anxious to surprise her. He seemed to live to please her!

Camille, being very organized about things, had come by daily with a very long list of details from colors to flowers. Valeria hated to admit it, but it was kind of the best of both worlds; she didn't have to plan the wedding or worry about the results. She just had to show up to what she knew would be just what she would have wished for…and then marry the beautiful man who was well beyond anything she could have ever dreamed up. Tears of joy formed at the thought of how very fortunate she was that he had found her…and loved her. She blinked back the tears as she stepped out of the shower and wrapped herself in the rich Turkish towel before heading into the bedroom.

To her surprise, Alex was sitting on the edge of the bed waiting for her, holding her coffee cup. He normally avoided being near her when she wasn't fully dressed. Especially fresh out of the shower—the temptation was just too great! She gave him a brief quizzical look before taking the coffee.

"Here you go. Just the way you like it." He winked.

Sipping the coffee, rich with cream, she sighed, "Hmmmm!" Taking advantage of his sudden mood, she leaned in just enough to kiss his neck. "Thank you!" She smiled seductively at him.

Then she noticed that he was looking at her with…*that look*. With a hint of embarrassment, she posed. He let out his beautiful laugh that always lifted her heart and she started for the closet.

"Hang on!" He grabbed her hand and pulled her back to him.

Carefully moving the coffee cup behind his back, she

leaned into him. He wrapped his arms around her amorously, running his hands over her shoulders and down her back. Stunned and excited, Valeria wished she could get rid of the full cup of coffee in her hand and lunge at him.

She reasoned that perhaps he was feeling more relaxed because the threats seemed to be gone and they were actually going to be married in only a few more days! She was breathless...and still holding her cup of very full coffee—perhaps that was his plan! Then Alex released her.

"Wow!" She raised both eyebrows, attempting to hear her voice over her pounding heart. "Where did that come from?" she asked breathlessly as she gently pulled her cup from behind his neck, being careful not to spill a drop. Her responses to him were always such a wonder to her!

He smiled and took a deep breath. "I just want to be married to you!"

"Well, now." She leaned back into him, and said softly, "*That* is an amazing coincidence!"

∞

She sipped her second cup of coffee as Alex laid out his jeans, T-shirts, and shorts onto the bed. Camille had informed her that she only needed to bring comfortable clothes and the rest would be supplied. When Valeria tried to argue that Camille shouldn't be spending money on clothes for her, Camille replied, "Oh, don't worry! I'm sending the bill to your fiancé—he can afford it!" Alex had smiled a perfectly contented smile and kissed her neck.

There were only a few things she knew for certain. First, it would be in Greece—unless something had changed in the past couple of months; second, they were going to request approval for an immortal marriage from the Ancient Council of

Delos, a secret society of immortals; and, lastly, that Weege, her closest mortal friend from Manhattan, wouldn't be able to join them. That was disappointing, but she understood. That's what happened when you worked in corporate America.

Camille had very quickly become Valeria's best friend and was taking the Maid of Honor role. She was quite a planner! Although there truly were far more details than Valeria cared about—and she knew the wedding *would* be nice—but it was her marriage to Alex that she desperately wanted and was most interested in.

Pulling her suitcase out from the closet, she remembered the last time she had seen it. It was the night that she had gotten up the nerve to declare her love to Alex. That had been a monumental moment for her! She was here with Alex because she had found the courage to tell him that she loved him!

She smiled, remembering her confusion about his love for Cassandra. It seemed so obvious now that he had been trying to remind Valeria that she was his symbolon—the reincarnation of Cassandra. At the time, her insecurity had kept her from being able to see that! Not that her confidence had taken giant leaps forward. But being with Alex, and feeling wrapped in the warm cocoon of his love, had changed things for her. The world had become a brighter place full of hope and wonder! She realized that she hadn't fit in with her previous world because it wasn't *her* world. This was her world! Here, in their beautiful cottage north of Trento.

From the time Valeria had left the hospital, she had tried to talk Alex into just sending for a Justice of the Peace so that they could be married and enjoy *all* of the pleasures of marriage…and so that he didn't feel that their life together was quite so fragile. But obviously, it was important to Alex to treat this marriage in a manner that honored the vision that had carried him through 3,000 years. She also suspected that the sweetness of the vision of their wedding night was a dream that he desperately desired, and was willing to wait for.

As she packed her toiletries in the bathroom, she glanced at Alex who had just pulled his sports bag from the closet. "So, do I need to be nervous about this council thing?"

"Not at all!" He sat down. "I hope you don't mind, beautiful." This wasn't the first time they'd had this conversation. He pulled her onto his lap. "Besides, I would like you to have the experience."

She recalled the story that Alex had told her. Apparently, Apollo had selected a secret and sacred location for the council meetings and presented that location only to Cassandra, the last oracle, Myrdd, the first oracle, and Aegemon, a priest. Apollo and Cassandra had even recorded the laws of immortals, though Valeria didn't remember any of it.

"I understand…I guess. You want our marriage to mean that we are truly together *forever*." Valeria leaned her head on his shoulder. "To me, you are forever, no matter what anyone else says." She smiled. "I do understand that you've waited much longer than I have for this. But I still don't understand why this council would even care!" She kissed his cheek and then rose to continue packing.

"Look at it this way," Alex said as he began rolling his T-shirts and placing them into the sports bag, "when an immortal marries a mortal, that union is short term—basically, it is similar to dating in terms of commitment. The immortal is with the person for such a short period of time that there is no requirement to get council approval." He zipped the bag shut.

This discussion always caused her to wonder if having her declared an immortal was for the purpose of providing Alex with some validation that she would now be with him forever. Or perhaps he expected that she would suddenly remember all of her past by going to the sacred location.

He continued, "Council approval wasn't always necessary for immortal marriages. But because an immortal marriage is for an eternity, it can cause a lot of issues if there is a bad pairing. In fact, it's been the cause of several major wars."

She giggled as if he was pulling her leg. "Really?"

Raising an eyebrow, he said, "The Trojan War, of course, and World War I to name just a few. Two ticked off immortals can create a world of havoc!"

There was a concern that perhaps she was not really immortal. Was she going to marry this beautiful, sexy man and be older than him in ten years? What about in thirty years—if she was fortunate to live that long this time around? He didn't seem to care about her aging. But her ego did!

Her other concern was that even if she was immortal, what if her "clock" had been reset and she continued to age until her "new" Prima Mortis? She didn't want to be like Jeremiah, who was 147 and still ticking. Still, there could be worse things than to spend her life with the most beautiful man in the world who would never age and loved her unconditionally.

"Darn!" she said, standing in the closet. Alex looked up from placing his toiletries in the suitcase to see her walk out with a handful of crumbled burgundy knit, another one of the many Christmas gifts from Alex.

"Oh, well!" He cocked his head to the side. "Your favorite sweater will be here when we return! You won't have much need for it for," his eyes sparked, "at least for a while!"

She smiled, placing the sweater back in the basket in the closet. She wondered, did he mean that they would be someplace where it would be too warm for sweaters? Or better yet, that they would have little need for clothes? She *loved* that thought, and felt her face flush in response. Their housekeeper, Ingrid, had been instructed never to wash Valeria's clothes because it made Valeria feel ridiculously pampered; besides,

Ingrid did enough without having to worry about the clothes that Valeria could easily care for herself.

As she closed the suitcase, she watched as he zipped the garment bag that carried several tuxedos and a few suits. She bit her lip imagining him in a tux…and had to sit down when she thought of him out of the tux! Then a sudden feeling of dread overtook her.

"Alex? What happens if the council denies your request?" She could have sworn she saw his pupils flash.

"Not a problem." His smile broadened, but she was certain it was for her benefit. "The first step is for the council to declare you an immortal. With the documentation we have from Mani, that shouldn't be an issue. But really, beautiful, I don't want you to concern yourself with this! There is no reason for them to deny it!"

"Still, what if they do?" She persisted, as she wrapped herself into his arms in an attempt to halt her increasing vulnerability.

"If they decide—for some insane reason—to deny our union, then we'll be married by a Justice of the Peace!"

"Promise?" She narrowed her eyes at him.

Giving her a confident nod, he leaned down and kissed her. He knew she had a tremendous amount of insecurity regarding this council who held their future in their grips.

From where she stood, she could see the family portrait over the fireplace. Knowing that she had spent most of her existence truly isolated from the rest of the world, with no pictures even desired to mark time or relationships, the family had surprised her at Christmas with framed pictures of her with the family and then a photographer had arrived and they posed for professional portraits. It was the one thing that she would never have thought of, and the thing that she cherished the most!

Now, there were pictures of her and the family throughout their cottage. Over the mantel was the largest of the portraits. It was a picture of her with the family surrounding her. As much as the official family portrait meant to her, the candid shots meant even more. They seemed to capture the spirit of her family.

The picture of her and Alex laughing together the night before her birthday was her favorite. Then there was the sweet picture of her arm around Caleb's neck, while her other hand messed up his hair—the boy who had never before experienced human touch. The look on his face was priceless!

Valeria loved the pictures of her, Ava, and Camille—the Three Musketeers! She glanced to Alex's side of the bed and saw another one of her personal favorites; it was a picture of her sleeping in his arms. It had been taken the day that she had returned from the hospital. The day he thought would never happen! She had survived the curse and had committed to their life together. The glow in his eyes was so beautiful, that she couldn't look at that picture without feeling the extraordinary depths of his love.

Still curled in Alex's arms, they heard Lars tap his horn from up the hill by the main house—they were leaving! She smiled excitedly and went to the door. As she was about to step out, he stopped her.

"Your jacket?" he reminded her gently, holding it out for her to slide into. As she did, he wrapped his arms around her, happily holding her for a few moments.

The horn honked again. The family had taken to this system of announcing their impending arrival due to Valeria's inability to receive their non-verbal communications. She grabbed her purse and bounded out the door.

There was two inches of fresh snow on the ground that had already been cleared from the steps and the area in front of the cottage. Valeria took in the look of her beloved home with the fresh snow piled heavily on the evergreens, causing the deciduous trees to almost disappear, except for their thick trunks. The sky was a brilliant winter blue and the temperature a crisp thirty degrees.

Homer, the ancient caretaker of the property, stood nearby shoveling snow off the main driveway. Alex stepped outside, with a book in his hand.

"Val, I think I'll bring *The Odyssey*, what do you want?"

She wondered why she hadn't considered something of this magnitude earlier. They could be gone for weeks, or more...she hoped. "Uh, *Pride and Prejudice*—oh, and maybe *Shakespeare's Sonnets!*" That would keep her occupied.

Alex nodded and glanced at the old man shoveling the walk. "Grazie, Homer."

Although she had heard his name numerous times, hearing it now in conjunction with the poet, Homer, and *The Odyssey*, and then noticing the old man's ancient movement, suddenly leant itself to a new idea. Noticing her unspoken question, Alex mouthed, *What?*

She mouthed back to him, *Homer?* As Homer slowly lifted another scoop of snow, Valeria wondered how he had possibly cleared the walk so quickly.

Finding her question quite hysterical, Alex let out a beautiful, rollicking laugh, a sure sign that the old man wasn't "*the*" Homer! Immediately, the caretaker turned back around and Alex bit his lip to stop his snickering.

Homer didn't seem to notice and uttered a low, guttural, "Prego."

Lars' classic black Mercedes pulled up in front of them and the windows rolled down to reveal Lars, Ava, Camille, and Caleb.

"I'll be right back," Alex said as he returned to the house.

Valeria walked toward Lars' car. She smiled at Camille, who had her straight black hair pulled into a shiny ponytail. She was wearing a black sweater dress that set off the dark mahogany of her skin and her brilliant blue, Kewpie doll eyes.

"Hey! We'll see you there tomorrow!" Camille yelled excitedly. Then she teased, "And don't worry about a thing! It causes wrinkles!"

Seeing only four members of the family in the car, Valeria asked, "Where are the rest?"

Lars responded, "Tav and Daphne are flying down tomorrow."

Ava cut in, leaning an athletic arm out the car door. "Couldn't stand the idea of listening to them arguing all the way there!" Valeria laughed.

The front door reopened as Alex came back out wearing his down vest and sunglasses, while carrying two suitcases in one hand, a camera bag hooked around his neck, and two bottles of water in his other hand. Valeria knew she should have offered to help him—although she knew he would never have accepted it!

"Where's Mani? Is he flying with Daphne and Tav?" Valeria asked.

She noticed Alex's slight flinch. "Uh, sorry love, Mani won't be there."

Stunned and disappointed that Alex's closest friend wouldn't be there for the wedding, she asked incredulously, "Mani isn't coming?"

"Caleb's filling the bill as best man!"

The ever twelve-year-old Caleb, who was concentrating on his computer game, looked up and lifted his hand in a victory fist. "Yes! Best man!" He was such a sweet boy, and he meant even more to her since he saved their lives.

"I think Caleb is a wonderful choice." She winked at

Caleb, who still had a major crush on her.

"All right, well, we're heading out. We'll see you there!" Camille said as the car began to roll down the drive. Wherever "there" was, Valeria thought. As the Mercedes disappeared from view, Alex tossed the suitcases into the trunk of his car.

"Why isn't Mani coming to our wedding?"

"He's…" Alex carefully positioned the garment bag in the trunk, but she suspected that he was stalling. "Don't worry— we'll celebrate with him later." With that, he closed the trunk, tossed the camera bag in the backseat through the open door, and said, "Got your passport?"

She nodded, looking at her "real" Louis Vuitton bag that had been a Christmas gift from Camille—the only stipulation was that Valeria had to get rid of the "knock-off." She gave the bag to Ava, much to Camille's chagrin and Ava's delight! Not that Ava cared about style whatsoever. Still, she liked a sturdy leather bag that wasn't "frilly and feminine."

"So, are you going to tell me now? Alex, where are we going?" she asked for the hundredth time.

Giddy with excitement, he said, "Let me have my surprises!" He closed his arms around her waist and kissed her sweetly, and then suddenly overwhelmed with joy, he swung her around.

∞

The Porsche easily plowed through the snow as they wound along the drive leading to the highway and away from Morgana. Valeria glanced through the forest and appreciated the way that everything seemed to be aglow with hues of pale pink and blue. After they entered the highway, the snow quickly became a wet mess; but as they continued out of the mountains and into the valley toward Venice, the roads dried.

All the while, Alex's smile continued to broaden.

"I hope you don't mind that we didn't go with the rest of them, but I wanted to have the day alone with you. I know we'll have the honeymoon, but I really haven't had an opportunity to court you."

The honeymoon! Her face flushed just thinking about it, as that marvelous warmth shot through her body. He noticed her reaction and his mouth turned up in the delightful smile that she loved. He hadn't told her where they were going. But frankly, she would have been absolutely content to spend their honeymoon at the cottage or in her Manhattan brownstone which she had decided to keep.

In fact, her only requirement for a honeymoon was that the two of them were there alone for as much time as possible. And Valeria was quite certain that there was not enough time in a mortal life for her to express what she felt for him!

She turned away, regaining her composure. "I never mind being alone with you. It's being without you that I can't take!" With that, she was surprised to find a tear come to her eye. He gave her an inquisitive look.

"Well, fortunately, you won't have to worry about that! Beautiful, I am yours forever!" He took her hand and pulled it to his mouth. While they were still miles from Venice, he pulled off the road and into a field. Now it was Valeria's turn to give him an inquisitive look.

"I always wanted to show you Venice. So I thought we would take the morning—unless you're anxious to get 'there,'" he teased.

"Isn't Venice still several miles away?" She pointed to the southern horizon. Alex's eyes sparkled.

"You know, after the accident, you've been so weak that I wanted to wait until it warmed up a bit to do this." He drove around a hill and there was a feast set out in the middle of the field, along with a hot air balloon that was still laying flat on the ground.

Valeria's jaw dropped. She tried to find something to say, but again, he had taken her breath away with his remarkably romantic gesture. He parked and jumped out, opening the door for her. They ate a wonderful breakfast while a crew filled the balloon with hot air.

Then he took her hand and helped her into the basket. They both sipped their Mimosas as the balloon rose. Within minutes, they were over Venice seeing the Grand Canal and the Rialto Bridge. She looked down on the ancient city with its green waterways filled with gondolas, and the magnificent domes of St. Mark's Basilica with the extraordinary piazza that looked out to the sea.

"Fantastic!" Valeria enthused.

Alex nuzzled her neck. "Napoleon dubbed the piazza 'Europe's finest dining room' because of the spectacular views." She pulled his arms around her tighter.

It was so very romantic and beautiful; she turned and kissed his cheek as they landed in a field east of Venice.

"What about the car and our luggage?" she asked, drinking him in from beneath her lashes.

Just then, a boat pulled up. Alex led her to the motorboat and gave the driver instructions. She loved hearing him speak in Italian. It was just so...*sexy!* She felt herself blush. Valeria was certain that the only sound more extraordinary than Alex speaking Italian was his beautiful laugh. He winked at her and she drew a deep breath as the boat jetted toward Venice.

"You know what you do to me, don't you!" she gushed privately to him, and kissed his ear. His smile widened as he looked on.

"I'll keep that in mind!"

They pulled in near St. Mark's, crossing the bridge to walk

through the pigeon-filled square and stopping in one of the shops to get a cappuccino along the way. They toured St. Mark's and then walked back to the Grand Canal. An elegant gondola awaited them. "Buon giorno, Il Signore e la Signora Morgana!"

Stepping into the gondola, Valeria's eyes lit up at the gondolier's assumption.

"Like that, do you?" Alex said as he sat down next to her.

She leaned her head against his shoulder. "More than you know!"

The gondolier began singing Puccini, as they moved effortlessly through the canals of burnt pastel buildings. Valeria felt the anxiety that had affected her earlier drifting away.

"I've always wanted to ride in a gondola...it's so Venice, and so very romantic," she said.

"Mussolini tried to ban them."

"Why?"

"He thought they were archaic." A bit of sunlight flitted over them, as the gondolier continued his romantic serenade. Gesturing toward the gondolier, Alex continued, "Most people believe that the gondolier punts, or pushes off from the floor of the waterway. But see what he's doing?"

Valeria watched and noticed that he was gently turning the oar back and forth. Alex continued, "That method of turning the oar actually exerts less energy than that of walking."

They pulled up to a restaurant and Alex thanked the gondolier in Italian, glancing at Valeria to see if it had the desired effect...it did. He took her hand and they walked a few blocks before turning into a quaint restaurant. Again, the staff was waiting for them.

They ate a marvelous lunch and then strolled along the ancient brick streets passing an ornate building that looked like a fortress with numerous sculptures of lions. Squeezing her hand, he told her that it was known as the Arsenal, the first mass production, moving assembly line in history! In the 1400s, while it took most shipbuilders months to build a ship, the Arsenal could produce them in hours. She smiled dreamily. She could listen to him forever!

"You know," Alex said with a wink, "there is one little detail of the wedding that Camille and I agreed would best be decided by the bride." Coming around a corner, Valeria saw an extravagant bridal shop with the most exquisite wedding gowns she had ever seen. He steered her into the store.

"Alex, my guess is that these are all special order."

He cocked his head to the side and lifted an eyebrow. "They may be for others…but not for you!"

An older, very attractive woman, probably the owner of the shop, greeted them by name in Italian; while a man, obviously her assistant, rushed to get Valeria a glass of champagne. The man and woman talked while critically analyzing Valeria's figure and coloring. They made her turn around and then both smiled, approvingly. The woman gave several orders to her assistant, which he hastily executed, while the shop owner led Alex and Valeria to a comfortable lounge that had two dressing rooms large enough to be bedrooms.

They sat in a comfortable loveseat while the assistant brought back various gowns for them to look at. Alex didn't say a word while he observed Valeria's responses. The woman held out several of the lacy gowns that were beautiful. Valeria didn't want to offend her, so she just nodded in response.

As the woman was about to hang the gowns in the dressing room, Alex said, "Scusa, per favore," requesting that the shop owner give them a minute before placing the dresses in the dressing room.

"You don't like them," he challenged Valeria.

"They're beautiful!"

"But?" He raised his eyebrows. The male assistant attempted to tell Valera something, that she was certain was an encouragement to try on the dresses. Alex kindly held up a finger, to silence him, and waited for Valeria to speak.

"I don't know. They're really beautiful. I'm just not sure that I see myself in something like these gowns. We probably should have just gone to the Justice of the Peace because this big fancy wedding is just…I don't think it's me."

Alex pursed his lips and narrowed his eyes for a moment, and then raised an eyebrow in thought. "Let me try something. I want this to be fun for you!" She nodded, feeling like a pigeon in an exotic bird shop.

For the next several minutes, Alex explained to the shop owner and her assistant exactly what he was looking for. They nodded and listened, anxious to please him. Valeria thought she heard the names of several designers, but she didn't know enough Italian—or enough about designers—to determine what they were saying. She did love hearing Alex's voice though!

Valeria leaned toward Alex's ear as he finished speaking. "I think you're going to have to teach me Italian." Alex beamed and kissed her forehead.

Then the assistant noticed the blush moving over Valeria's face and down her neck. He and the storeowner both laughed and the woman made a comment to Alex that made him turn his head in mild embarrassment as he brushed his fingers through his hair.

"Do I want to know what they said?" Valeria grimaced.

He shook his head as he rolled his eyes. "Oh, it was just a reference to our honeymoon."

There was that word again! Valeria's face brightened to purple, as Alex gazed at her with pure adoration and offered a soft, enchanting laugh. She guessed that she was hypersensitive to all of his charms because the wedding night was getting so close. And frankly, he just did something to her that she couldn't explain; it was definitely beyond the physical.

Finally, the storeowner and her assistant returned with several gowns. Without showing them to Valeria, the woman invited her into the dressing room. Valeria looked to Alex for approval and he nodded.

In the dressing room, Valeria was both embarrassed and glad for the woman's assistance; she had brought her a beautiful handmade corset, which Valeria would have never been able to hook by herself. Then she tried on several dresses. They were gorgeous, much better than the previous gowns. But Valeria felt that she, as a bride-to-be, just didn't "work" in something this formal. With each dress, Alex offered a nod and said, "Very nice," while he evaluated the look in her eye and occasionally provided further instructions to the shop owner.

Then the assistant brought Valeria a simple, but elegant, silk-crepe gown with a cowl neck and a low back. She would have never seen herself in something this sexy or exquisite. But as she looked in the mirror, she felt a thrill run through her. It looked and felt as if it was made just for her.

Offering Valeria a sharp appraisal, the shop owner's eyes lit up and she called to her assistant. The assistant returned with a hair comb, pearls, and a pair of high-heeled shoes. Pulling a few strands of Valeria's hair to the top of her head, the woman hooked the hair comb and the pearls and then gave her a nod of approval.

Valeria slid on the satin shoes as the assistant opened the dressing room door to present her to Alex and she nervously stepped into the lounge.

"What do you think?" she asked.

His response said it all. Alex was speechless, and then his eyes lit with emotion. She knew at that moment, that *this was most definitely the dress!*

While Valeria changed back into her jeans, Alex purchased the gown and accessories. The feel of the jeans was disappointing after the luxury of the silk. She was thrilled at the thought that in just a few days, she would be dancing in Alex's arms, in that dress.

The shop would do the minor alterations and deliver it in two days, which was the morning of the wedding. Valeria decided that they couldn't be too far away if they were hand delivering the dress, and the beautiful undergarments. But then again, this was Alex and he would go to any lengths to make certain that her wedding day was perfect!

"Better thoughts of Venice now?" he asked, satisfied that the memories of their previous visit to Venice had been eclipsed. All she could do was smile as she leaned into him affectionately.

"So, is this where we're staying?" she asked, hoping he would now give in and tell her their destination. He shook his head in mild amusement, while his eyes sparkled with playful mischief.

They boarded the gondola and headed back toward St. Mark's. It was simply so romantic and perfect that Valeria was disappointed that they were leaving. For Alex, he had carefully planned the visit to Venice so that they avoided all of its many marinas and the hospital. She hadn't been terribly aware, due to the high fever from the plague, but for him, that memory—although she had lived—still caused him tremendous distress. And he wanted this memory of their wedding trip to be perfect!

They arrived at St. Mark's and transferred to a motor boat. Valeria heard Alex say "aeroporto." They were headed to an airport.

Of course, she realized! Of course—they were going to Greece! Where else would Apollo's oracles set up council meetings? The speed boat pulled up to a small general aviation airport. A golf cart was waiting for them. She noted that Alex's Porsche was now parked near a hanger where men were loading supplies, including what appeared to be several cases of champagne, onto a small twin-engine plane.

"Are you flying us to…our destination?" Valeria asked. She had heard him talk about his love of flying.

"Not today, beautiful! I wanted to relax and have a mimosa with you this morning. But perhaps on *our honeymoon!*"

At this point she was certain that Alex was teasing her, seeing the effect created when he mentioned their honeymoon. The corners of his mouth turned up in that beautiful smile that she loved, telling her that Alex noticed the effect again. She suspected that he hadn't mentioned the honeymoon before in an effort to keep things cool until the wedding night. But it had come up several times today—and *it was driving her crazy!*

They boarded the flight and an attractive woman in a uniform asked them in English if they would like a drink. Valeria was stunned when Alex ordered a Scotch on the rocks. He must be feeling more relaxed!

During the flight, she thought about Mani. What would keep him from standing next to his best friend in a wedding that was 3,000 years in the making? She was certain that Mani would have cancelled any engagements from Johns Hopkins. Alex hadn't even used that as an excuse. She wondered if there was something about the council that kept Mani away, something sinister that he knew. Then she smiled—her imagination was really getting the best of her! She knew Alex would never take her there if he believed there was any danger.

Besides, her experience proved this group of oracles to be highly ethical. Despite Daphne's fits of jealousy and bad manners, Valeria knew that she would never lie, cheat, or steal!

Eventually—*and it might be a long eventually*—they would probably become friends. After all, they both cared a great deal about Alex's welfare and happiness.

Still, there was something gnawing at her consciousness; something that made her feel a bit nervous about the council meeting. It was probably because she knew how important it was for Alex to get the council's permission, and also because she would be meeting the rest of the immortals for the first time. She suddenly wondered about Aegemon. There had been neither reports of his death, nor any reports of the pneumonic plague.

"If Aegemon is still alive, is there a possibility that he could be at the council meeting?"

Shaking his head vehemently, Alex said, "Don't worry about that, beautiful!" He patted her knee, as he took another sip of his scotch. "Once you try to take out most of the oracles," he shrugged and continued, "funny thing is that none of them want you in their council."

The flight landed on an island that sat on the western boundary of Greece. They went through customs and walked to a waiting limo, as their bags and supplies, which Valeria assumed were for the wedding, were loaded into the trunk. Alex was giving directions about what should be loaded where, when Valeria noticed a man several limos down with movie star good looks who was staring at her. She felt herself blush from his intense scrutiny. The man had short dark hair, and a perfectly tanned olive complexion. He was dressed immaculately in dress slacks, a suit jacket, and a silk sweater. The man smiled and pulled his sunglasses from his face, and then he winked seductively at Valeria. She glared for a moment, stunned, and then shook her head in irritation. Alex noticed and immediately placed his hand on her back, guiding her toward the open door to the limo.

Before climbing in she turned to Alex and whispered, "That man…he's staring at me."

Alex narrowed his eyes ever so slightly. He brushed his hand over his chin as he turned to look at the man; then he hesitantly offered the stranger a non-committal wave. The stranger's smile broadened, but it didn't seem to reach his eyes.

Alex climbed into the limo next to her. "Let's go," he said to the driver. There was something in his voice. He sounded weary—or worried. She turned toward him and he looked away. She thought he looked pale.

She wondered if it just had to do with the obvious flirtation coming from the man. Since she had ended her engagement to David, there hadn't been anyone else paying any of that kind of attention to her…well, except for Alex!

The man was still staring at them, though the tinted windows prevented his view into the interior of the limo.

"Do you know him?" she asked.

Staring out toward the man, Alex muttered softly, "Yes." They pulled out from the small airport as Valeria waited for more information, but it was obvious that Alex didn't want to discuss him.

The limo took them to a marina docking port where they quickly boarded a private sea taxi. As the luggage was loaded onto another boat, Alex seemed to be watching, as if to see if the stranger had followed. Within minutes, another limo pulled into the lot. Alex quickly put his arm around Valeria, issued an order to the men loading their supplies, and then, while reaching into his pocket, gave instructions to the driver of the boat. Alex tossed a hundred euros at him and the boat pulled out immediately.

The man in the limo leapt toward the dock and called out in a light Italian accent, "Alex!" and then offered an arrogant smile that told Valeria that the man saw this as some kind of game…and he hadn't lost yet. As the boat pulled into the harbor and headed to the south, away from the island, she noticed that Alex's expression was flat.

"Who is that?"

"Oh…uh, that's Paolo," Alex replied, with attempted casualness.

"Paolo?"

Nodding subtly, Alex's expression remained pensive. She was certain that there was something she needed to know about Paolo but she didn't want to ruin the mood of the evening. She decided to drop it until later. One thing was certain, Paolo was going to the same place they were, and that meant that he was also an immortal.

The water taxi took them from Corfu to the emerald isle of Paxos. While Valeria was uncomfortable being that far away from land, she found her mind completely distracted by thoughts of Alex and their wedding…and the man, Paolo.

After an hour, the taxi wove its way around a few uninhabited islands, past an ancient white monastery, and then to the azure shores of the pretty little coastal town of Gaios. Valeria leaned against Alex and took in the beauty.

He kissed her temple. "I'm sorry it's not warmer. The climate is perfect most of the year. But it can be a bit cool in the winter." She cuddled into him. "We'll use heaters for the garden wedding if we need them." The temperature actually felt wonderful. And Valeria was about to marry the man of her dreams!

The town was reminiscent of Venice with burnt pastel buildings covered in bougainvillea and surrounded by deeply green foliage. It was breathtaking! She glanced at Alex expectantly. "So, this is it?" His expression lightened up and he smiled.

"I wanted to show you Gaios. It's quite scenic. But you

look like you should probably rest. I don't want you worn out."
She saw his eyes become playful again. "Remember, we have a
wedding…and a honeymoon in a few days!" She blushed again
and rolled her eyes at him. He laughed and gave her a light
squeeze.

"I am tired. So, where are we going next?" Valeria
suspected that the plans had changed after Alex had seen
Paolo. The truth was that she *was* exhausted. This was her first
real outing since she had been ill. And although she felt great,
her energy wasn't back to a hundred percent, but she was
certain that she had enough energy to spend a few weeks in bed
with her husband!

They waited while several bags of produce and other
groceries were loaded onto their boat. As the men finished
securing the packages for safe transit, Alex turned to her and
brushed his hand over her face affectionately. "Would you like
to see where we're staying?" he teased.

"Yes!" She happily wrapped her arms him.

The boat pulled away from Gaios and Valeria found
herself watching to see if they were being followed. As they
left the harbor, the water got a bit rougher, and her hand
instinctively tightened in Alex's as the boat steered around the
island, past rocky cliffs and the occasional azure beach, finally
pulling up to a dock with several jet skis, kayaks, and a speed
boat. From the dock, Valeria could see an enormous manicured
lawn where some kind of minor construction was being done.
Analyzing the work, Valeria's heart lurched! They were
building a wedding arbor! Tears moved into her eyes. Behind
the arbor construction was an enormous L-shaped mansion,
with a large square tower above the center of the "L". It
looked like something out of "Homes of the Rich and
Famous."

"Are we staying here?" Valeria asked, astounded.

"Yes, if that's all right. It's a family estate."

"Family estate? Whose family?" She knew he was wealthy, but this was considerably more than she expected.

"*Our* family!" His eyes lit with joy as he shook his head. She took it in; the years of loneliness, before Alex, were now nothing more than a weak memory.

He sensed her emotion and hated thinking about her life before he found her. But he knew that the tear in her eye wasn't from the pain of yesterday, but the joy of today. He lifted her off the boat onto the dock and pulled her into him in a tight embrace.

"We'll be alone this evening," he said, with his voice a bit unsteady. "The family decided to stay elsewhere tonight. But they will be in tomorrow for the council meeting. Then," he took a deep breath, "I have the extraordinary honor of marrying you!" She choked, and he held her tighter. She couldn't risk her voice at that moment.

Past the dock, there was a lush green lawn, and to her left sat two white Adirondack chairs that were perfectly placed for watching the sunset, a small table nestled between them. Ten feet in front of the chairs, the grass suddenly halted, dropping three feet to a small beach with occasional rocks that sprouted from the sand and tides that lightly lapped at the bluff.

They held hands as they walked up to the house, and Valeria couldn't help but notice the massive windows on the lower level. The home was a burnt yellow with heavy white trim that looked striking against the Greek blue sky. As they neared the home, she could see the patio that looked out over the sea. It was done in flat cut stones and cement. There were more Adirondack chairs, a teak table and chairs, as well as a fireplace, a grill, and refrigerator. The interior walls were the whitest of white with accents and arches made entirely of brick in the family room and kitchen. The kitchen to the left of the entrance had a very long preparation table down the middle and a quaint breakfast area under the brick arch.

Alex guided her up some steps to the right of the entry, leading to the only room at the top of the stairs, the tower room and master suite! The room was dominated by a wall of windows with French doors leading to a private deck that looked out over the deep blue Ionian Sea. Valeria noticed a light pastel mist that hovered on the horizon. Deep green, uninhabited hills pushed into the sea, creating a magnificent view! The bedroom was elegantly furnished with light wood furniture, pastels, and overstuffed chairs. Alex led her to the closet and the lights came on slowly, displaying a closet full of gowns and dresses…and beautiful undergarments, that Camille had certainly ordered. Valeria could tell Alex was as tense as she was.

He gulped. "I'll be sleeping in the other room until after the…" He couldn't say it now…*Oh, how she loved him!* "I thought we could spend our…our wedding night here, if that's all right." He winked as she blushed again and he laughed softly, nervously. "The room is private and no one will be able to…well…" Now it was his turn to blush. He pulled his hand through his hair before continuing. "The master suite is in a separate part of the house from…the other rooms. So we'll not be disturbed."

They would make love here on their wedding night. Her heart was racing and her breathing was going through the roof.

Feeling intense emotion for him, she took his hand. "Take a nap with me." He looked at her with so much longing, but didn't move—suddenly uncertain of himself. She stepped toward him and pulled his arms around her, and then, standing on her tip toes, kissed him. She broke their embrace and took his hand leading him to the bed.

Alex stood next to the bed, his discomfort evident. Valeria

leaned back on the numerous pillows. Finally, hesitantly, he sat on the edge of the bed. She brushed her hand through his hair. "Lay down with me."

"I think I should go…" His voice was hoarse as he drew a deep breath. "I need to…Val…" He gulped.

Just then, the luggage arrived and Alex jumped up to direct that…*in Italian!* He gave a short chortle and rolled his eyes toward her. After the luggage was delivered, Alex turned to her, but moved toward the door.

"Beautiful, go ahead and take a nap. I'm going to check on some details. After you wake up, I have plans for us downstairs."

It was torture, but Valeria laid back and found herself immediately falling into a deep sleep.

CHAPTER 3

When she awoke, the room was lit by the afternoon sun casting brilliant beams of color against the walls and ceiling. She went into the bathroom and everything had been unpacked. She brushed her teeth and her hair and touched up her mascara and lip gloss before going downstairs. Noticing the height of the room from the ground floor, Valeria thought, yes, this room would provide the privacy that they would want on their wedding night! She felt an intense warmth move through her.

Downstairs, most of the lights in the house were out. A flash of light caught her eye from the window leading to the patio. She saw Alex holding a glass with ice and a golden liquid…scotch on the rocks. When she stepped outside, he didn't seem to even see her. His mind was a million miles away and he was staring out to sea with an ominous expression; something was troubling him and her heart ached for him.

"Are you okay?" she whispered.

His eyes flicked to hers as he drew a deep breath, coming

back to this world. "Oh! Beautiful! Yes. I'm glad you were able to sleep." He sounded weary.

She curled onto his lap and his arms went around her.

"Tell me what's going on," she said softly.

He tried to smile for a moment and then gulped. "You cannot imagine how long I have dreamed of this."

Knowing she needed to lighten his mood, she changed the subject. "So, it looks like we'll be married there?" She pointed to the arbor.

Alex smiled and closed his eyes. "Yes, overlooking the Ionian Sea." He breathed out with relief.

"And tell me about the plans for our...our honeymoon," she whispered, kissing his temple.

He drew another deep, cleansing breath. "I thought we would spend our wedding night here and then head off the next day for our honeymoon." *Oh, she did love that word!*

"And can I know where we're going on our honeymoon?" She kissed his cheek as her hand stroked his chest.

"Well, I have several places that I want to take you." He smiled nervously, distracted by her touch. "But I thought we would start off with someplace very special to me; someplace very...private."

She unbuttoned his shirt and kissed the side of his mouth. "And how long do I get you...privately?" she asked, lowering her voice to a seductive whisper.

Alex's mouth curled up as his eyes closed, pushing back the nightmares. "As long as you want!"

"Two weeks? A month?" He pulled back and shrugged as his arms closed around her.

"If that's what you want!" He bit his lip tentatively, and swallowed. "I was kind of hoping you would want to be alone a bit longer than that."

Her eyes softened. "You know I could *live forever* in a

world with just you and me!" She kissed him lightly. "I missed you," she whispered. "Please don't sleep away from me tonight."

"I don't know." Alex closed his eyes, torn.

She kissed him on the mouth this time and, although she had avoided touching him in a way that might start things that he wished to finish on their wedding night, something in her had waited long enough. She ran her hand down his chiseled chest, circling her fingers around the bit of hair over his heart and his breath caught. She kissed his neck as she brushed her fingers over his stomach and felt his instant shudder. He gently reached for her hand and moved it to his lips, and gulped again.

Pulling back to look into his eyes she pleaded, "Please, stay with me." She didn't know why, but she suddenly felt so vulnerable like everything was about to fall apart. Perhaps that was normal for a bride.

He noticed her apprehension and stroked her face. "What is it, beautiful?"

She needed closeness. "Come with me."

"I was going to grill some snapper and asparagus for us tonight."

"I'm not hungry for that...come with me." Alex reluctantly nodded. She rose and walked up the stairs and he followed. The bedroom was lit with shafts of sunlight, becoming more intense as the sun began its journey to the horizon, creating a mystical mood.

"I...I have something for you," she said shyly. She went to her bag and pulled out a box. "I know there will be a lot going on for the next few days. I want you to have it now."

Alex looked surprised and then took the gift. He opened it. It was a Zanetti custom watch with imbedded mother of pearl, a bronze engraving of the triquetra—the symbol of their love—and a tiny engraving with gold inlay.

"What is that…is that writing?" He glanced down and then back up at her in surprise.

"It's the saying…from the night of our engagement," she said as she cleared her throat. "It says, 'There's this place in me where your fingerprints still rest, your kisses still linger, and your whispers softly echo.'" She lovingly brushed the side of his face and looked into his eyes. "It's the place where a part of you will forever be a part of me."

He looked at her clearly moved that she had remembered the Gretchen Kemp poem that he had shared with her on the night of their engagement.

"Turn it over," she said.

Flipping it, he read, "Two hearts now whole. I love you, Your Symbolon

Alex's face was lit with so much emotion that it overwhelmed Valeria.

With his voice almost a whisper, he said, "It's…beautiful!"

"Do you like it?"

He gave a short, emotion-filled laugh. "Oh, Val! I've never…it's the most precious gift I've ever received," he choked, "next to you."

She kissed his neck as a tear rolled down her face. "Do you know what you've meant to me?" She stroked his face. "It's like you put the color into my life. You've made everything so bright and beautiful."

Alex kept a tight grip on his emotions, as he held her close, unable to speak. Almost as a cry, he whispered into her neck, "I love you."

They sat there holding each other for some time; finally, Valeria pulled around to look in his face. "Will you tell me what's wrong?"

He shook his head. "Nothing's wrong. I'm marrying you

in a few days. How could anything in the world be wrong?" But his voice bore none of the happiness from earlier that day.

Those old insecurities crept their way insidiously into her head and she began mindlessly tracing the mark on his hand that reminded her that they were meant for each other. Still, she needed to hear it. "You still want to marry me, don't you?" her voice cracked. "I mean, if you didn't, you would tell me, wouldn't you?"

"Of course!" He let out a small laugh. But she knew something was going on.

Sitting straight up, she asked again, "Please tell me what has upset you?"

He shook his head, "Nothing, beautiful. You've misread my mood." But she noticed that his voice sounded strange.

She was certain that there was something going on and, for some reason, he wasn't willing to talk to her about it. First he had decided that he was going to sleep in another room. Then, when they were about to finally make love for the first time, she felt something in him—something sad and serious—like he had changed his mind and didn't know how to tell her. Why the sudden moodiness? Maybe he really didn't want this. After all, if he really wanted to be married to her, he would have gone down to the Justice of the Peace as soon as she was released from the hospital and they would be married now. They would be sharing this room tonight! Tears formed at the edges of her eyes.

"Beautiful, *what is going on in that head of yours?*" He turned the tables on her. It was time for someone to speak up.

"I guess I'm just wondering," she gulped, "Alex, are you attracted to me?"

He let out a short, uncomfortable chuckle. "Why would you ask me something like that?"

Valeria bit her lip. She had started this conversation, and

now was the time to have it—not after they were married! "Well, because…" She drew a deep breath, and said, "Weege told me about a guy whom she dated…and he…well, he wasn't interested in her, but didn't want to tell her. Turns out he was in love with someone else but needed someplace to stay." Valeria reddened and looked down. "She said that she realized that any normal guy would…" She stopped, mortified to be having this conversation.

"I…see." There was a slight flinch in Alex's smile. "I guess the answer is that I'm just not normal."

She laughed, with a hint of apprehension. "No. You are most definitely not a normal guy." She looked down, embarrassed, and began to trace his mark. She stopped and laced her fingers into his. His fingers tightened around hers.

"I guess being immortal kind of sets me aside from the definition of normal," he said, trying to hide his hurt feelings.

Seeing the result of her comment, she took his face in her hands. "Alex…there is so much more than your immortality that sets you apart. You are the most extraordinary man I've ever met! I just want to make sure you…well…that you really are…how do I say this…attracted to me."

His eyes narrowed and he pursed his lips and then, with a slight nod, he said, "What else? There's something else!"

How did he know that? Yes, there was something else. She looked down. "All right…well, Daphne let some things slip…some things about you and…Kristiana…and your…" Alex raised his eyebrows, waiting for the rest of it. Valeria swallowed. "Well, your physical relationship."

There, she had said at least part of it. She glanced up briefly to catch his eyes narrow and the slow turn of his head in disapproval. He released a deep sigh and she could see his embarrassment. But now that it was out, she might as well finish her concern.

"Well, it's just that...Daphne said that you made love to Kristiana before you were...." She glanced down, horrified. He didn't speak. She swallowed, but forced herself to continue, "...before you were married. I guess I'm wondering if that's true."

Alex seemed stunned. "You had a discussion with Daphne about...." He shook his head again. Then he saw her expression. Valeria was crushed by his disapproval! She felt as if he was accusing her of snooping into his relationship with Kristiana when, in fact, Daphne had offered it. Valeria had not shared anything about her sexual relationship—or lack of it— with anyone! In fact, she was certain that the family was leaving them alone tonight because they assumed that they had already consummated their relationship.

"Val, what happened with Kristiana was due to loneliness. It was because I was so lonely and I believed that you were gone, forever. That's all. But I don't believe that it's appropriate to discuss certain things. One of them would be my sex life with Kristiana." He paused. "Do you understand?"

She did. Alex was always the consummate gentleman; it wasn't in his nature to kiss and tell. Still, a part of her just felt like he had told her that it was none of her business. She knew that wasn't the case, but she wanted to be able to talk about anything with him. And to her, all evidence pointed to the fact that he had physically desired Kristiana and yet was completely capable of abstaining from her.

Seeing her expression, he pulled her into him. "Let me just tell you that if you *ever* decided that...you didn't want to wait...." He thought for a moment. "I just don't think you understand how vulnerable I am with you." He took a deep breath and then swallowed.

"I wanted to make love to you the night before my birthday—the night that you proposed," she said woodenly.

"Yes. That night was a different situation. I hope you understand. I felt that if I was weak and made love to you that night that it might change the outcome of...that whole situation. I couldn't risk your life...for one night. No matter how much I wanted you. And, trust me, I most definitely want you!"

"But, why is it that you affect me so much and it...well, it just doesn't seem like talking about our honeymoon effects you at all. You just smile that...that incredibly sexy smile of yours."

"Sexy, huh?" His eyes lit in mild amusement. She nodded and he lowered his brows for a moment. "And what is it that you imagine is behind that smile?"

"You are just very calm, cool, and collected."

He let out a chuckle and his eyes widened. "Not even close!" He thought for a moment and the corners of his mouth turned up. "You may as well know." He bit his lip and his eyes narrowed. "I'm wondering...where we could disappear..."

"Disappear?" she asked, incredulously.

His face reddened. "So that I can...have my wicked ways with you!" Despite the fact that she couldn't believe it, she saw Alex's embarrassment at his confession and her whole body responded with a mass of electricity.

"No...really?" She wanted to believe him, but her insecurity told her it was easy for him and difficult for her.

Alex gulped. "In the speed boat, and then there was that convenient alley off from the restaurant...in the dress shop, I wondered how much I should tip them to leave for an hour." He paused, narrowing his eyes. "And then there was the decision, in the hanger or on the plane? Trust me, beautiful, I am no saint!" Her face flushed three shades of purple with this revelation.

He moved his fingers along her cheekbone. "And when I

see you blush, I battle my impulses and remind myself, again, that it is only a few more days." He looked up. "And then I count to a hundred and pray for good sense to kick in!" He laughed.

Pulling his hand from her face, he brushed his fingers through his hair. "And as long as I'm confessing, you should know that from the point after you healed, and I knew I wouldn't hurt you, it has been a constant battle!" He drew a deep breath. "I would truly love to have the strength to wait until our wedding night. But I can't tell you all that I go through laying in bed with you, night after night." He turned to her with increased intensity. "To imagine lying next to you here…the place where we will spend our wedding night…is more than I think…." He gulped again. "You are the most *desirable woman* I can imagine!"

"Holy…" She meant to say 'smokes' but it didn't come out. Then, nearly whispering in revelation, she said, "Wow!" She shook her head to try and make the new reality permeate her brain. It was distracting, but she still needed answers. "Alex, I know something is going on with you. I can feel it. Are you certain?"

"Oh, my beautiful, Valeria!" His voice went hoarse and was almost a whisper. "I could spend my life making love to you!" She felt that delicious flutter in her belly. "And I intend to begin proving that to you in about," he glanced at his new watch, "forty-eight hours from now." The look in his eyes told her that he meant it. "I know it seems like silly superstition, but as long as we haven't yet made love, I know that someday we will be married."

She settled into his arms. "In your vision did we honeymoon here?"

"No." He noticed the concern in her eyes and continued, "To me it's like averting a vision. If I saw a vision of you…let's say, marrying someone in Florence. And I knew it was at a particular time, and I kidnapped you—*and, honestly, I should have a time or two*—then it wouldn't be possible for that vision to be a reality. In this case, once we are married, it won't matter if that vision takes place…because you'll be my wife…forever."

Alex drew a deep breath and bit his lip. She could feel his heart pounding. "I think we should cool the conversation on the wedding night and…the honeymoon." He smiled softly.

"Well, I think otherwise." She pushed him back onto the bed and crawled on top of him. "I think I need to investigate this vulnerability that you've just confessed to me!" Laughing, he pulled her into his arms and kissed her passionately.

He rolled her to the side and pulled his head back as his jaw dropped. Raising his eyebrows, he nodded to himself. "How about a compromise?" he suggested, as his voice gathered strength.

"Compromise?" Valeria pulled herself up on one elbow.

"I don't know why I didn't think of this before!" His eyes lit with excitement. "Well, I wouldn't have, if the family hadn't decided we needed a night alone."

"Uh…okay."

Biting his lip again, he sat up. "We have our marriage license."

Oh, she liked his thinking! "Camille would kill us!" Valeria said with a new level of thrill.

"She doesn't need to know *everything* we do," he said laughing.

"Right! It wouldn't be like lying to her. And we could still go through with the wedding ceremony. In fact, the only thing that would change is that…"

"We would be married and I could stay with you…tonight."

"Let's go right now—before you change your mind!" she demanded. Alex chuckled.

"Oh, I am *not* going to change my mind on this!" He jumped up from the bed.

"I'll race you to the boat!" She ran down the stairs, with him following close behind her.

"Wear your jacket, please!" he admonished. She grabbed her jacket as he reached for the bag that held their marriage certificate and, within minutes, they were out the door.

They boarded the speed boat and raced back around the island to Gaios. Arriving in the tiny town, Alex tied up the boat and then asked about who could marry them. The man on the dock informed them that the local priest was tied up, but the mayor could do the job.

Nearly running along the beautiful narrow streets of Gaios, they both felt an exuberance that had evaded them most of their lives. They would be married tonight! He pulled her into the mayor's office. The mayor sat at a desk right inside the door. There were two chairs in front of the desk and Alex held one out for her. The mayor looked up in surprise. Alex explained that they wanted to be married now. The mayor offered them a knowing smile.

"Where? Perhaps the gardens?" the mayor asked in broken English.

"Right here is just fine!" Valeria insisted. The mayor raised his eyebrows at her and said something in Greek that caused Alex to turn his head in mild embarrassment.

But all discomfort disappeared the moment when Alex handed the license to the mayor. She could see Alex's sudden relief and sensed their combined tension lifting. Opening the ledger, the mayor began to log their information. He stopped and pursed his lips as he drew in his bushy eyebrows. The mayor turned back to face them with his elbows on his desk.

Pointing a thick finger at them, he said, "I am sorry. But I cannot marry you now."

"No!" Valeria cried. "Why? We have a marriage license!"

"Yes. But your license is not good for another two days." Reaching across the mayor's desk, Alex took the license and studied it.

"But it says it's been approved," he said, pointing to a line on the document.

"Yes, but Greek law requires two weeks. It will be two more days until I can marry you." He handed the marriage license back to Alex.

Rubbing his hand over his face, Alex asked, "Is there anyone near here, perhaps in Italy or a neighboring country, who can marry us now?" Valeria felt her throat tighten but held on to hope.

"Of course!" the mayor replied.

"Where?" Alex asked.

The mayor smirked. "Las Vegas!" Their faces dropped. "It is only two more days. My advice is to simply wait!"

"All right. Well…thank you." Alex took Valeria's hand and led her out of the office onto the street. They both tried to handle the disappointment well…and both failed.

He was the first to speak. "You know, Val, you are already my wife…in my heart." The tears welled in her eyes and she knew she couldn't speak. She pulled his arm around her.

From a bar above the street they heard Paolo's voice call out, "We meet again!" Alex sighed as if to ask, *what more must we endure tonight?* He refused to even look. Valeria suspected that Alex didn't want Paolo to see the pain in his eyes. She didn't know who this "Paolo" was, but she didn't like him!

Just then, a beautiful blonde woman joined Paolo. She brushed her fingers sensually along his chest as she whispered in his ear. Paolo pulled back from the woman, looking mildly surprised. Then, glancing briefly back down at Alex and Valeria, he said, "It appears that I am wanted elsewhere!" He winked at the woman, who giggled. He waved to them. "Ciao!" he said, as he wrapped his arm around the woman and disappeared.

Once they were back to the boat, Alex's eyes narrowed at Valeria. "Beautiful, it really is only two more days. Then we will have our eternity!" She nodded, still unable to speak. "Val, let's not let this ruin the trip! Let me grill up the snapper and let's enjoy our evening together."

That evening, they were both quiet. She sat on his lap in the Adirondack chair by the sea and sipped wine and watched the sunset. Despite his earlier insistence to the contrary, Alex held her all night in the room where they would spend their wedding night.

CHAPTER 4

Despite the disappointment of the previous evening, Valeria awoke feeling quite exhilarated. She went downstairs and saw all kinds of deliveries arriving for the wedding…the best of them was the family!

She excitedly ran down to the boat, while chairs, tables, heaters, and a speaker system were being set up. Camille jumped off the water taxi as soon as it edged against the dock and ran to Valeria and the two of them hugged like schoolgirls. Alex just watched and laughed. Even his mood had lightened up!

Camille immediately took charge. "Okay, people! I need the bride and groom, Caleb, and Lars at the house ASAP!" She started up the lawn while Valeria and Alex finished hugging everyone as they stepped off the water taxi. Camille paused, placing her hands on her hips, with a smile. "We don't have all day, people!"

Ava added with a smirk, "Well, come on people! What are you waiting for? General Camille has spoken!"

The group walked up to the house. Camille's eyes sparkled with excitement as she hooked arms with Valeria. "So? What do you think?"

"Oh, Camille, I just can't wait! And the clothes are lovely. Thank you for all of your hard work."

"Are you kidding? I've had so much fun. But you know, I do have one disappointment!" Camille glanced toward Daphne. "I like Daphne, but we don't shop together. And Ava, well, as you know, she is a mail order girl. I would have hoped that one out of three of my sisters might be a shopper!" she said with a laugh.

Arriving at the patio, Camille took Alex's hand to give him directions, but she was immediately interrupted by the sound of a chainsaw. Valeria saw a large trinity knot being carved in a log—Camille really had thought of *everything!*

"Lars, can you please ask them to take a break?'"

Nodding, Lars complied and the workers went off to lunch.

"So, Alex…where's your best man?" Alex turned around and found Caleb sitting in an Adirondack chair on the porch playing his hand-held computer game.

"Best man!" Camille was definitely in driver mode today. Caleb turned and jumped up. But by then, Ava was talking to Valeria. Camille placed her hands back on her hips. "Okay, people! We have a lot to do. But if everyone pays attention, we can be done in about ten minutes and then have lunch. Okay?" she said with mock severity.

"Lars?" she said.

"Yes, ma'am!"

"Do you have your minister's certificate to perform the ceremony?"

Lars nodded and fished through his laptop bag, while Camille became distracted with the placement of a heater. She turned to the worker. "Excuse me, but you aren't going to leave that there are you?" The worker said he didn't understand English. Camille sighed and pointed where she wanted it and then resumed her duties as the wedding coordinator.

"All right, I want the groom, best man, and minister right here." She pointed to a location off from the arbor that was already decorated with a mix of white roses and bougainvillea vines. Valeria noticed that the flowers were real and wondered how they had pulled that off since yesterday!

"Do you think anyone's going to think it's funny that I'm just a kid and they're calling me the best *man?*" Caleb let out his joyful laugh. At that, Camille relaxed and offered a contagious giggle.

"It's really just family and I think you'll do great!" She smiled at him calmly. Valeria, being the only one who could touch Caleb without being shocked by his electricity, messed her fingers through his hair and gave him a kiss on the cheek.

"So, Lars, you'll lead, followed by Alex. Caleb, you'll walk out after Alex."

Camille continued giving instructions, and then Valeria was walking up the aisle toward Alex. She felt incredibly silly and awkward. Then she looked into his eyes. For a moment, she was actually there…*their wedding day*. The day they had waited 3,000 years for. Valeria heard nothing else during the rehearsal…she was certain that Alex didn't either. They were living the dream of tomorrow. They barely heard Lars pronounce them husband and wife. A tear rolled down Valeria's face. She could see Alex's eyes glistening with emotion.

Lars was still speaking when Alex took her face in his hands and, with his voice full of the emotion he felt, he said, "I love you more than life." Then he moved his face to hers in a lingering kiss that left her knees weak.

Anticlimactically, Lars joked, "All right, well," he scratched his head, as Alex and Valeria continued to kiss, "you may kiss your bride." Hearing the snickers, Alex and Valeria looked around and then joined in on the laughter. Immediately, Camille was giving further instructions for the next day while the couple was happily lost in each other—until Lars tapped Alex on the back. "Jeremiah's here."

Alex's eyes were still intensely focused on Valeria's and the corners of his mouth turned up in *that smile*, before he drew a deep breath and, at last, broke their spell.

"Right." He glanced toward the dock, and he narrowed his eyes slightly. "Shinsu must be coming separately."

"I'm sorry to tell you this, but it seems that it is just Jeremiah," Lars relayed. There was a momentary cloud in Alex's eyes. Lars patted his arm. "It'll be all right."

"Beautiful, come with me." Alex took Valeria's hand and led her to an Adirondack chair on the patio. "Jeremiah needs to clear you before you will receive an invitation from the council. He's going to want you to give him a transference. When he sees that you have Cassandra's memories, he will permit you to join us at the council."

"And then?" Valeria suddenly felt nervous again.

"You don't need to be nervous! Tonight there will be…some things that might…that are…a bit different. We'll talk about that later. I don't want you to be frightened. But as far as the transference, just think about the subject—which is your life as Cassandra. Focus on that. Jeremiah will take your hands and you will look into his eyes. It should take no more than five to ten seconds and it will be done."

Valeria gulped. "Alex, you promised me that even if they say no, we are still going to be married tomorrow—right?"

"Don't worry about a thing!" he said.

An ancient man with dark leathery skin and a gray Afro

and beard, approached them slowly hobbling with a cane. Valeria was certain that he was less than five feet tall.

"That's the island stud?" She giggled, recalling Alex's stories of Jeremiah, including that he had the oldest body of any of the immortals and lived on an island in the Eastern Pacific where he was considered a god and had a number of young wives.

Offering Valeria a subtle wink and a smile, Alex lifted a finger and tapped his lip, indicating that Jeremiah had extraordinary hearing! As the old man finally approached, Valeria could see his bright blue eyes—not like Alex's. Perhaps time had faded them, she thought.

The old man was chuckling, leaning heavily on his cane. "Island stud!" he snorted. Valeria looked at Alex concerned. "Don't worry, young lady. I've been called far worse!" He hobbled toward her. "I'm Jeremiah, the Abatao island stud!" He chuckled again. "And you, my dear, are Cassandra."

She wanted Jeremiah to call her Valeria. But she wasn't going to say anything that could cause a hitch. "I'm sorry for the...island...stud remark," she muttered. Alex snickered under his breath.

"Young lady, at my age, I appreciate the title!" He let out a cackle and then glanced toward Alex critically. "My young friend here wouldn't mind that title either."

"No, Jeremiah, I'd prefer to be known as her husband." Valeria noticed that Alex didn't use her name.

"I can see why!" Jeremiah let out a lascivious cackle that left Valeria feeling uncomfortable. "Alright, young lady, let's get on with the task at hand." Alex nodded and moved another chair directly in front of Valeria's. Jeremiah sat down and she held her hands out toward him. The old man shook his head in irritation.

"No, no, no! YOU take my hands!" He glared sternly at

Alex. "Doesn't she recall anything?" Attempting to soothe the situation, Alex offered her a subtle wink, but she could see that he was upset.

She reached over and took Jeremiah's hands. Now nervous, she looked over at Alex.

"Beautiful, you are doing fine. Jeremiah is just a cranky old man." Alex took a deep breath and then smiled kindly at Jeremiah.

"That, I am! That, I am!" To this, Jeremiah let out another lascivious cackle.

"Beautiful, look at Jeremiah and focus." He drew a deep breath and Valeria turned toward Jeremiah. After a few seconds, it seemed as if nothing was happening.

"How about some affinity!" Jeremiah growled.

"How about giving her reason to have some affinity!" Alex growled back. Valeria was a bit stunned; she had never heard Alex sound angry.

Jeremiah cackled again, but the smile didn't reach his eyes. "Alexander, you are approaching disrespect!" There was a dangerous edge to Jeremiah's voice that startled Valeria. How was she supposed to feel anything but fear from this man?

"Alex, I don't think this is going to work," Valeria said, rising from her seat. "I don't think I can do this right."

Jeremiah narrowed his eyes and Alex interrupted again, "Jeremiah, could you please give us a moment?"

Taking her hand, Alex led her away from Jeremiah, again subtly lifting his finger to his mouth. "You're doing fine, beautiful. I want you to just relax." He said the words as if they were lines, and then glanced toward the house in what Valeria suspected was a silent communication to someone in the family. "I know you can do this." He pulled her into him and kissed her gently, as Camille wandered out, as if by coincidence. Noticing Jeremiah by himself, she walked over to him and began talking in a way that was a touch more intimate and contained far more giggles than Valeria had ever heard from Camille. Jeremiah seemed appropriately distracted as had been Alex's intention. He nodded.

"Please, oh please, Alex, let's just have a civil wedding here! Please, Alex! I have a terrible feeling about all of this!" She could feel her anxiety moving into hyperdrive.

"I'm sorry, Val," he said, his voice tight with tension. "I'm afraid there is no backing out—we are committed." Sighing deeply, he took her hands in his. "Just ignore the old goat! Try to allow yourself some affinity for him and relax. You can do this!" But she could see an increasing concern in Alex's eyes.

Pulling her hair back from her neck, she was frustrated with herself for being so weak and cowardly. This was important to Alex and if he had a father or grandfather who was like that, she would have tolerated him. Perhaps that was the key!

"All right."

He looked at her critically and then kissed her forehead before leading her back to Jeremiah. Camille was still flirting with Jeremiah when Alex returned. "Camille, if you don't mind, we have business to attend to," he said with a hint of gruffness that Valeria was certain was to convince Jeremiah that Camille was there on her own accord.

Camille gave Valeria a confidential wink and then said seductively, "Jeremiah, I look forward to seeing you this evening!" Jeremiah cackled.

Sitting down, Valeria tried to think of Jeremiah as Alex's uncle. She took his hands and looked at him. She felt something happening that absorbed all of her attention. They sat there for almost three minutes when Jeremiah yanked his hands away angrily. "Young lady, you had better learn how to control your transferences!"

Alex's jaw tightened and Valeria noticed his face redden. Attempting to soothe the situation, she placed her hand on his arm, smiled sweetly at Jeremiah and said, "Thank you, Jeremiah. I will work on it."

"I don't need your entire epic history! Now I'll be carrying that around with me! I've a mind—"

Alex broke in, "Jeremiah?"

Standing, the old man grumbled, "I can't have her testify. It would be a frivolous abuse of the council's time." He narrowed his eyes dangerously. Valeria noticed Alex's pupils flash in response to Jeremiah's allegation. Alex glanced toward the house in what Valeria was certain was another silent communication.

"Are you demanding that I withdraw my petition?" Alex challenged.

The door opened and Lars walked out. "What's going on, Alex?"

"It seems as though Jeremiah wishes us to withdraw the petition. But she has a right to be in the council." Valeria noticed again that Alex avoided using her name.

Lars said, "Yes…yes, she does. But realize that Jeremiah has an extraordinary responsibility here. And Cassandra may simply need more time until the council is comfortable. Withdraw the petition, Alex. Give her time to readapt." Lars and Alex stared at each other for a long moment.

Finally, Alex bit his lip, and faced Jeremiah. "All right. I'll withdraw my petition for an immortal marriage."

Valeria felt relief and sensed it from Alex, despite appearances. Jeremiah narrowed his eyes once more and seemed to be analyzing the situation. He picked up his cane and hobbled back toward the dock, as he muttered, "She's invited."

Halfway down to the dock, without turning to face them,

Jeremiah added, "But I will not have her waste more of the council's time by testifying."

Alex brushed his hand through his hair and then sat in the chair previously occupied by Jeremiah, directly in front of Valeria. He took her hand and pulled her onto his lap. They sat there for several minutes before anyone said anything.

"What's happened?" she asked in alarm.

"Everything will be all right now. I should have prepped you better," he answered softly, sounding exhausted.

Once Jeremiah's boat rounded the turn, Lars said, "You had no way of knowing that Shinsu wouldn't make it. We all assumed she would be here. I'm certain she'll be there tonight."

Camille arrived with a tray of champagne glasses. "Look, Val has passed the test. Let's not let that grouchy, old pervert ruin tonight! Lars, will you do the honors please?"

"Absolutely!" Lars went to the outdoor refrigerator that was stocked with champagne. He popped the bottle and poured glasses for all of them. "To our newest immortal!" They clinked glasses and drank.

"To my bride!" Alex added as he kissed her neck. Valeria noticed him pushing the smile to his eyes as she clinked his glass and they drank.

Taking a deep breath, Camille said, "All right. That's better! Now, let's get lunch and then it's time for Valeria to dress."

∞

After lunch, Camille escorted Valeria to the master suite. Camille had insisted that Alex needed to sleep in another room the night before the wedding. And although his bags had been moved, Valeria had no intention of being away from Alex tonight!

A bath had been drawn for her. "Your stylist will be here shortly. So I suggest you bathe and then put on a button-down shirt."

"My stylist?" Valeria said incredulously.

"She will do your hair for tonight and tomorrow. She can also do your hair for your going away the next day if you wish!" Camille gushed.

Valeria was simply speechless. "Uh, no. No, thank you."

"No thank you for what?" Camille laughed.

"Uh, well…the going away part. I think I will just risk the natural look on my first day of marriage." *Oh, the dream!* Valeria glanced down. "Do you think people really get what they most want?"

"*You* will!" Camille hugged her. "Your makeup artist will need an hour with you."

"*An hour!* Really, I don't know about all of this!" It seemed like a waste of effort—she would still be Valeria Mills…well, tomorrow night she would be Valeria Morgan, wife of the extraordinarily beautiful and amazing Alex Morgan. Her heart was pounding at the thought of it all—a combination of thrill and anxiety, and she wasn't sure which one was winning.

Camille went to the closet and came back with fantastically beautiful undergarments and shoes and then the piéce de résistance, her gown! It was a periwinkle, custom-made Giorgio Armani organza, off-the-shoulder evening gown with a fitted bodice, long, gathered skirt and a slight train.

CHAPTER 5

Valeria stared at her reflection in the mirror and didn't recognize herself. The dress was almost as beautiful as the wedding gown that she would wear the next day. Her hair was swept back from her face and down in a style reminiscent of Rita Hayworth in the 1940s. The makeup enhanced her eyes and lips, though it was certainly more than she was comfortable with.

"You look perfect!" Camille stood at the door in a classic, light pink gown with a straight skirt.

"So do you!"

"Your fiancé is downstairs waiting for you." With that, Camille disappeared. Valeria took a deep breath and walked to the door.

Alex greeted her at the bottom of the stairs wearing his tuxedo. She felt an intense heat run from her face clear down to her toes and then felt her toes curling in her matching satin pumps. It wasn't just the tux—which looked extraordinary on him—it was the intensity in his eyes and the smoldering in his voice as he said, "Oh, beautiful..." At once, she was pleased with the decision to trust Camille's choreography of the evening.

Taking her by the hand, Alex led her to the patio which was lit by stars and a glow from the house; it was now set with several tables and chairs for the following evening. Across the lawn, Valeria could see where they would dance. The rest of the family was on the patio all dressed to the nines. The men looked handsome in their tuxedos—even Tavish, though he was wearing his kilt! But none of them compared with her beautiful husband-to-be!

Recalling Caleb's joke about Tavish's kilt and the inconvenient breeze that bared all, she prayed for calm winds tonight. She had never seen Ava in anything but jeans and T-shirts, but there she stood in a black strapless gown, looking gorgeous.

Everyone's response when Valeria entered was nothing short of awe! Caleb jumped up, and muttered, "Holy cow!" It was the first time she had seen him look anything but happy and relaxed. The boy would not be attending the council meeting, as he had not been officially recognized as an immortal, despite the fact that he had lived over two thousand years.

Daphne rolled her green eyes, an effect purchased to stand out amongst the blue eyed oracles, and tossed her red hair over her shoulder. "Oh, for God's sake, Caleb!" she said, her British accent adding more irritation than intended.

Alex chuckled. "Hey, buddy, you're drooling!" But Caleb continued to stare. Finally, Valeria messed with his hair and Caleb threw his arms around her waist. Valeria laughed and patted his back. "Okay, buddy!" Alex said, exercising some patience. As long as Caleb had his hands on Valeria, Alex couldn't touch her. He laughed again. "All right! *Enough*

Caleb! Can I have my bride back?"

Bride! That statement gave Valeria a beautifully warm shiver. She would be his wife tomorrow! *Tomorrow!* She swallowed her emotions and smiled at Alex with adoration.

Caleb gulped nervously, his eyes still huge as he stepped away. His voice was soft, as he said, "You look like a princess!"

"Thank you, Caleb! And tomorrow night, as best man, I'll expect you to dance with me…if you're game." Caleb's eyes grew wide.

"Okay," he said shyly. Valeria was surprised by the response. She was still *her!*

"Would you all mind giving me a private moment with my fiancée?" Alex asked.

Caleb nodded and left. The rest of the family waved and said their goodbyes as they took their champagne glasses and wandered down to the waiting boats. A moment later a boat pulled out with Ava, Lars, Tavish, and Daphne. Camille sat in the other boat waiting for them.

"So I need to tell you about tonight." Alex's eyes were still lit with emotion. "Hopefully things will go a bit smoother tonight than they did earlier today. I'm sorry about that, love! Jeremiah's wife calms things down significantly, and she was supposed to be here today. But I'm certain she won't miss tonight's council meeting!

"Let me tell you about Delos." Val nodded, though she was mesmerized by the look in his eyes…and by the tux! Alex noticed and the corner of his mouth turned up. Remembering that Camille was watching, he cleared his throat and attempted to return his attention to the subject at hand.

"When Apollo was born, his mother was cursed so that she could give birth on neither mainland nor island. She found the floating island of Delos and gave birth. Apollo's father, Zeus, in gratitude, attached Delos to the bottom of the sea. In honor of Apollo, we are known as the Council of Delos. While there is an island in the Aegean Sea called Delos that is considered the sacred birthplace of Apollo, a little known fact—except by the council and a few of the gods—is that the ground where Apollo and his twin sister Artemis were born, was hidden by Zeus, and surrounded by the River Styx…in the underworld.

"The underworld?" Valeria raised her eyebrows in surprise.

"The River Styx is the river that is said to carry our dead to their appropriate location. The Elysian Fields is where the good go and Tartarus is where the evil go to be punished for eternity."

"The River Styx…isn't that the river where Achilles was dipped to gain immortality?" Valeria asked, pleased that she had remembered.

"Exactly!" he said with a smile. "But there is an issue with the location of Delos. The swift current of the River Styx can quickly carry one to hell. So we are cautious in maneuvering in the underworld. Further, there are some…interesting characters I need to tell you about."

"Okay…"

"The River Styx is also known as the River of the God's Unbreakable Oath. Because it is forbidden for any of us to betray the location of the underworld to anyone who has not been recognized as an immortal, there was an issue with finding servants for the council meetings—and the council does have a penchant for grandiose events." Alex drew a breath, not certain how she would handle this part of the information. "We use what we call dribs, creatures of the underworld." She knitted her eyebrows together in mild shock.

"At one time, we called them shofias; in ancient Greek that loosely translates to the soulless. During the 18th century, they became known as dribs, I assume it implies that there is not much left of these poor, soulless creatures.

"In ancient Greece, it was believed that the dead must have a coin left in their mouth to pay Charon, the ferryman of Hades, for transport. If the dead were not buried with a coin for passage, they wandered the underworld. The dribs are thought to be those without coins. They are also typically those who would be exiled to the fires of Tartarus. Evidently, service is a better option. So, you will see the dribs, but it is best not to address them directly."

"Then there is Erebos, who is the personification of darkness. You should not be subjected to him, but avoid him at all costs!

"Lastly, the council, as you witnessed today, has no sense of humor. Don't speak to them unless they specifically ask you a question. Answer them cautiously, respectfully…and truthfully. I crossed the line today. But we were not in a council meeting and truly there was nothing Jeremiah could do about it. Tonight, however, will be very different!"

"That's all the business for now. I don't want you concerned about all of this. I want you to enjoy yourself. It's a special evening!" His eyes glowed with love as he kissed her hand. "I have something for you." Valeria smiled shyly, he had already given her so much. "It's to go with your dress."

He pulled a small rectangular box from his breast pocket. It was sterling and intricately decorated, similar to the one her engagement ring had come in. Inside she discovered a set of earrings and necklace made from the same extraordinary Cassandra Crystal that was in her engagement ring. She remembered that Alex had told her that he had named it the Cassandra Crystal, after her, because it was extraordinary and one of a kind. The stones exactly matched the color of their eyes. He clasped the hook of the necklace behind her neck as she clipped in the earrings, her heart bursting with love for him.

He led her to the window and she saw the reflection of a stranger in a breathtaking gown with exquisite jewelry. Alex moved behind her and his arms circled around her waist, his eyes appreciating her reflection.

That's right, she was the woman whom Alex Morgan loved—his symbolon—neither of them complete until united. Emotion overwhelmed her, and tears flooded her eyes, with the cognition that she was about to have all that she ever desired.

"It's time to go," he whispered. As his breath brushed her neck, she felt goose bumps run down her arms. She turned and kissed him lightly, brushing her hand against the back of his neck as she saw a new level of love and desire reach his eyes. He leaned down and his lips pressed against hers, and she felt the heat behind his touch and the fire of his kiss as they began to meld into one…and then it ended…far too soon for either of them. She stared up into his eyes, amazed at the level of emotion that she felt for this beautiful man! He smiled back at her, a special smile…one beyond yearning and desire, a smile that said that all of the holes in his heart caused by 3,000 years of pain and loss were now filled, replaced by her love.

Taking her hand, he lifted it and brushed his lips over it, his eyes still glowing intently on hers. Then, with a sigh of deep gratitude for this moment, he turned, leading her to the boat.

At the dock, she got a good look at the strange looking boat that was waiting for them. It sat low in the water, with three-foot edges to each side. In fact, the interior of the boat sat below the surface of the sea. She noticed that the driver sat on a leather seat flat on the ground. It was no more than four feet wide. The floor was carpeted and had built in drains every two feet, with grates small enough not to catch a woman's heel which Valeria appreciated. There was a number of elegantly upholstered white leather reclining seats and walnut wood accents throughout. She noticed built-in heaters on both walls.

"We call it a trog." Alex grinned. "Short for troglodyte. You'll know why soon enough."

Alex stepped onto the boat and then lifted her onboard. Camille was already sitting in a cushioned leather seat in the rear, leaving a double seat, in the middle of the boat.

They pushed off from the dock into the moonlit sea. This time, they headed toward the north in the opposite direction than they had gone before. Valeria noticed that the water got rougher as cliffs along the shore rose to over fifty feet. The low, flat boat rocked with the current. Her heart was already pounding from her fear of the sea...and the unknown. Suddenly the boat stopped. Valeria noticed that the driver adjusted the windshield. It had been high enough to keep her hair from becoming a frazzled mess. Now it was only eight inches above the bow.

The moonlight shined on the crests of the waves. Along the coast, numerous large boulders jutted straight up from the sea. The breakers thundered loudly on the boulders and then on the cliff's beyond them. The driver of the boat sat on the floor with his legs directly out in front of him. Alex took her champagne and placed it in a glass holder.

"Beautiful, we're going to lay back. And when I tell you, I want you to close your eyes and keep them closed until I tell you it's all right." He reached to her other side and, while holding her close to his body, he reclined her seat. With the glow of the moonlight on him, he gently kissed her, and then lifted his face no more than a few inches from hers. The corners of his mouth turned up in that beautiful smile as he looked into her eyes with so much love that she knew that moment was locked into her heart forever—her beautiful Alex.

His eyes became serious. "No matter what, you must not sit up. Do you understand?" he warned.

Valeria noticed that Camille had reclined her seat so that it was almost completely flat, although the windshield still permitted them a view out the front. "I'm not allowed to see where we're going?" she asked, hearing the tremor in her voice.

"No. I just think it might be easier on you if you close your eyes…especially with your history."

Valeria felt her heart rate picking up. "I think it would be better if I watched," she gulped.

Nodding, Alex kissed her again and then reclined his own seat, while he continued to sit straight up, calmly holding his champagne glass. She took his other hand and nervously traced the mark and then laced her fingers with his, clinging tightly to it.

"Ready?" he asked. Valeria nodded as her eyes darted about, trying to focus on him.

With a nod to the driver, the engine revved several times as if timing the waves; then, with a sudden blast, they headed full speed straight for the cliffs. There were so many rock outcroppings that Valeria was certain they would hit them at any moment. Suddenly, she wondered if she would even have a life with Alex. She watched the breeze brush his hair back and he seemed to be enjoying the ride. Her heart was pounding wildly. He calmly planted his champagne glass in the holder and then, noticing the terror in her eyes, he leaned down to kiss her again, distracting her before reclining in his own seat next to her.

"It's all right, beautiful," he said into her ear. "You'll have to trust me on this. These men have never injured an immortal on this trip." The boat continued straight toward the cliffs.

"Great," Valeria muttered softly, thinking that she should

find some humor in his statement about immortals being injured. Alex snickered.

Then her eyes focused on the rock wall in front of them and the large surges…and the fact that they were about to slam into *that* wall, as she counted down to the impact. She pictured that she would be thrown from him and drown. And Alex and Camille, the two people she loved more than life, would be…

"Alex!" she screamed. He was immediately over her, pinning her to the seat, with his hand on her forehead.

At once, the engine cut and they were in total darkness as Alex's fingers stroked the side of her face. She heard the rushing of the sea and the sound of her own pounding heart.

"It's all right, love. We're okay. Just a few more minutes." The sound quality had changed dramatically. They were in a cave. She could feel the wet coolness inches from her face and could hear her own erratic breath echoing nervously between the crashing of waves. Finally, she sensed more clearance and Alex rolled off to her side, as she clenched his hands with an iron grip.

"Sorry! I didn't hurt you, did I?"

"No. I think I'm all right," she said, her voice sounding strange to her.

After another ten minutes, the boat came to a stop and she heard the driver moving. Then she heard a sound like a match being struck and suddenly there was light. She actually felt quite calm under the circumstances! Then she noticed that her knuckles were white on top of Alex's. She giggled apprehensively and then relaxed her grip; seeing the nail marks on his hands, she winced in a non-verbal apology.

The driver was standing on the ledge with a torch. He mounted it on the wall and returned to his seat in the boat.

"It's all right." Alex winked, and helped her sit up. "This is where we get off." They were in a dark narrow cave with the tide rolling them roughly about. He stepped off the boat and onto a ledge, grasping a wrought iron rail.

Camille stood. "You did better than I did the first time! They had to about tie me down! I think they heard my bloodcurdling scream for a mile!"

Alex laughed, raising his eyebrows. "I remember!"

Valeria gathered the hem of her dress in one hand, while Alex lifted her onto the ledge. Caves weren't really her thing either. Then she needed to give up his arms so that he could help Camille off the boat. They stood there in the light of the torch as the water roughly rushed by them. The boat moved slowly back out of the cave and then disappeared silently.

"We need to give it just a few more minutes," he soothed, stroking her hair. She was still shaking and he held her tightly.

"So, you said it was called a troglodyte?"

Alex's smile widened. "That's Greek for 'one who creeps into holes.' The Latin's changed the meaning to 'cave dweller.'"

"We're going to walk, so hang on to the railing." He grabbed the torch and then led them deeper into the cave. Then he stopped. Valeria looked and saw nothing but the stone ledge that continued in the direction that they had been moving. He held the torch out over the still raging water and waved it in a sideways eight several times.

Within minutes, there was a hint of light coming from the other side of the cave. Valeria realized that there was another tunnel running almost perpendicular to their path that she wouldn't have seen without the approaching light. She tried to determine how it was so hidden and then noticed that there was a large boulder that had refused to succumb to the constant pounding of the sea.

"That boulder, and the infrastructure that surrounds it, is what Virgil referred to when he spoke of the adamantine gates of Tartarus." She nodded as if she understood, but she had no idea who Virgil was.

Alex continued, "Adamantine implies an impenetrable substance—like a diamond. Frankly, I don't know what it's made of—in fact, someday, my guess is that you will probably be able to tell me." Seeing the doubt in her eyes, he winked and smiled.

Within seconds, she heard a creaking noise that increased and then stopped as a metal bridge emerged from the stone on the other side of the rushing water and then loudly slammed down next to them. They crossed the bridge and she noticed that the ledge on the other side was wider and the water in this hidden cave seemed much calmer. She peeked down the new cave and could perceive more light, and almost hear sound, when the water wasn't rushing into the cave.

A gondola rounded a turn and pulled up next to them, which was the source of the light she had seen. The gondolier was extremely pale and bald; his faded eyes and lips were rimmed with bright red. Valeria realized that he must be what Alex had called a drib! He was dressed in a tux and kept his eyes averted. Alex helped the women aboard and then the gondola moved back from where it came.

Minutes later, the water seemed even calmer. They rounded a corner and she saw that at the end of the tunnel, the cave ballooned into a tremendous cavern. As she glanced at Alex in amazement, and saw his beaming smile, she realized he must have dreamed of this moment.

As the gondola smoothly moved into the chamber, the room seemed to explode in light and sounds and smells. She was reminded of the upscale restaurants that David had taken her to in Manhattan—vibrant and bustling. The waterway split and they went to the right around what almost appeared to be an island within the cavern. Valeria beamed excitedly at her first view of the birthplace of Apollo!

Candlelit crystal chandeliers, hanging well above the festivities, dramatically draped off the fifty-foot ceilings. She noticed the waterway encircled all but the far wall, where nine rather grand chairs sat, richly decorated in gold and red. The back of the cavern wall was covered in fine silks and appeared to be where the food was coming from.

The gondolier continued toward a small landing, set less than five feet from where the guests were, with a foot bridge that crossed from the landing to Delos. The gondola stopped and Alex offered his hand to the women.

From the tiny landing where they stood, she could see over three hundred elegant guests. Appetizers and champagne were being served on trays by dribs. Alex watched Valeria to make certain that she was all right with the new surroundings. She nodded to him, as if it was no big deal—but he read her emotions better than that. A small orchestra of dribs struck up a tune. It seemed that everyone was watching her.

Still reeling from the boat ride into the cave, she clung to Alex's arm. This was the step that would lead her to her destiny...the one where she spent an eternity with the man of her dreams! Again, she felt a rush of emotion.

"Who are all these people?"

Camille laughed. "They are all the immortals that we know of up to this point; at least the ones who we can find."

Brushing Valeria's cheek with her own, Camille whispered, "I'll see you on the other side!" Then Camille quickly crossed the bridge, joining the rest of the family.

Alex was beaming. "There is an ancient tradition that recognizes our birth. We, the immortals, walk between the world of mortals and those who live forever. In order to do that, we cross a portion of the River Styx." He took her hand and led her across the ornate foot bridge. Half way across, he stopped.

"Take a look at the river." His face lit up, as she glanced into the water and then her eyes did a double take. "It isn't your imagination, beautiful, and it isn't dye, the color of the River Styx is oracle blue." Valeria smiled in amazement.

Stepping onto the main island, the room broke into applause, as a waiter brought them two glasses of champagne. The air felt cool and comfortable against her skin and, despite the fact that it was a cave, it smelled of fine food.

"Welcome to the Council of Delos, beautiful!" Alex still seemed a bit nervous, but suddenly, Valeria was feeling very much at home. She could see Tavish in his kilt arguing with someone—or perhaps it was a friendly discussion, it was always difficult to tell with him.

Tavish turned to her with a wild-eyed smile and raised his glass. "Here's tae us, wha's like us? Damned few an' they're a' deid!" He laughed loudly and clinked glasses, sloshing out half of the champagne. His face lit with his famous combination of a sneer and a smile. Valeria got the humor to it, she understood Tavish occasionally now. It was a Scottish cheer that had more meaning here with immortals. The joke of course was that there *were* very few oracles left and those who they knew were mostly dead...or "a' deid."

Alex said, "We only get together about once every five hundred years or so. So enjoy!" Within minutes, Camille and Ava arrived as Alex continued, "If you ladies would keep my bride-to-be company, I need to speak to a few people before the council meeting begins." He kissed her cheek and left.

Camille led Valeria to a table with extraordinary food. Helping herself to a few *hors d'oeuvres,* Valeria met several of the immortals. Alex was speaking to a group of people near the ornate chairs. She noticed that he seemed tense about something and was looking as if he was searching for someone.

But when he saw her watching him, his face released the tension and he winked at her.

She also noticed that the others didn't seem to have quite the same color eyes as her family.

"Camille, I don't understand why there are so many oracles here! I thought there were only one hundred, and that the family consisted of most of the remaining oracles."

Sipping her champagne, Camille's eyes lit. "Oh!" she said in surprise. "Val, they aren't all oracles. They're immortals, well, most of them anyway. There are a few oracles outside of our family." She took a deep breath. "I think sometimes we forget that you don't recall everything." Camille grabbed another shrimp off her plate and took a bite, hesitating for a moment before saying, "Sorry, I'm starving!"

"They're immortal, but not oracles? How does that work?" Valeria queried, trying to keep her ignorance from being overheard by the others.

"Well, the immortals are related to the gods. They have very different rules than we do." Camille and Valeria greeted another group of immortals with a smile and nod. Then Ava joined them.

"Val's asking about the immortals," Camille explained to Ava.

"Yeah, well, they have a bit of an attitude if you ask me!" Ava muttered. "Like they're the royalty and we're merely titled." She lifted a delicate finger sandwich from her very full plate and then artlessly crammed the whole thing into her mouth. "Hmmm!" She rolled her eyes. "Delicious! Val, you gotta try these!" Valeria laughed.

"So that must be why their eyes are a different color than ours?" Camille and Ava nodded.

"Some of us think that the immortal's prejudice against us was the cause of the purges," Ava added.

A few more immortals approached and, although Valeria didn't sense any prejudice, she did notice that they all reacted strangely to her. She asked and Camille explained that, as Cassandra, she was one of the founders of the council and so some of the immortals were probably a bit uncertain as to how to behave toward her. And others were probably a bit in awe. Valeria couldn't understand anyone being in awe of who she used to be.

Suddenly, she felt a hand low on her back that slid around her hip. It was so unlike Alex but she smiled and leaned into him, as the hand continued around her waist to just below her breasts. She found that odd. When he nibbled on her ear, she suddenly realized—with horror—that this wasn't Alex!

Valeria spun to see Paolo offering her a lascivious grin. Her jaw dropped and she shoved his hands away from her. Just then, her eyes caught Alex's stunned expression, as his face turned deep crimson as he raced toward her.

Paolo smiled at her seductively. "You look delicious, bella."

Hearing Valeria's gasp, or perhaps a non-verbal communication from Alex, Camille and Ava both turned toward Paolo. Camille's eyes narrowed in dislike.

Paolo continued, "Camille, I can see in your eyes, you have needs that are not being met." He smirked and raised an eyebrow. "My previous offers stand."

"No thank you!" she huffed.

Arriving on the scene, Alex pulled Valeria into his arms. She noticed that his hand was slightly lower on her hip than it might have normally been and she could feel that he was very nearly trembling with anger. "Paolo, Valeria and I are engaged now. I hope you will respect that."

"You are called Valeria now?" Paolo winked at her. "I believe I prefer—"

"That's enough, Paolo!" Alex interrupted.

Paolo and Alex stared each other down, for what felt like a very long moment, as she clung to Alex protectively. Finally, Paolo broke the stare as his eyes wandered salaciously down her body, making her very uncomfortable. She was also stunned to discover that her typically very patient fiancé was near his breaking point. She pushed aside her shock and kissed Alex on the cheek. When he looked down at her, she smiled and patted his chest. "It's all right. I'm all right," she said, attempting to soothe him.

Finally, Paolo shrugged smugly and stepped away. As he passed Ava, he turned to stare at her behind. "Ava, my beauty!" He shook his head lustily. Ava smiled proudly, as he sighed with evident memories of her.

Paolo continued walking away. As soon as he was out of range, Alex muttered, "I have to get back." He gave Camille a look that carried a hint of a plea.

"I'm sorry, Alex, I didn't see him coming!" Camille confided, and then with concern, "Is she here yet?"

Alex shook his head, the tension showing in his eyes for an instant. He took a deep breath and kissed Valeria's neck. She noticed that his eyes never left Paolo, who was now working his way through the crowd. She also noticed that while Camille had an expression of vile disgust on her face, Ava was actually smiling at Paolo. Finally, Alex returned to the group near the nine chairs where Lars and Tavish were waiting.

"He is just disgusting!" Camille hissed.

Ava moved her head so that she could gleefully continue to watch Paolo's exit. "Hmm! I think he's...fun!"

"Ava! You didn't!" Camille said in obvious shock.

Biting her lip girlishly, Ava said, "Yeah, it was just a nice little..." Seeing Camille's outrage, she added defensively, "Well it *was* before I married Lars, of course!" Her girlish smile returned. "It was a fun little fling, lasted less than a decade." The dreamy look returned to her eyes. "But it was fun!" Camille glared at Ava. "*What? He's fun!*" Ava justified.

Finally, Valeria leaned in. "Who is he?"

Both Ava and Camille were clearly uncertain what to say. Finally, Camille answered, "Oh, *he's trouble.*"

"Yeah. He's fun…but he is most definitely trouble!" Ava conceded.

A gong indicated the council meeting was beginning. Watching Jeremiah tap his cane, Valeria noticed that only eight of the nine elegant chairs were occupied. She also realized that her dislike of Jeremiah was now replaced with a growing animosity toward Paolo. She reminded herself that she didn't have a poker face and that Alex had warned her about the council's need for respect.

"Alexander, you have requested that this council gather for a dual purpose. We have now recognized the immortal, Cassandra. Proceed with the next request."

Moving to the front of the room, Alex addressed the council. "As you all know, I have been in love with Cassandra since my first vision of her over three thousand years ago." He glanced toward Valeria and she smiled at him. His smile was very brief, and she thought he seemed nervous. "Cassandra is my symbolon, and now that she is an immortal, we wish to be married."

The nods and murmurs through the crowd were suddenly displaced by Paolo's voice.

"I request permission to speak." Paolo glared petulantly at Alex. Valeria noticed Alex's face redden as his eyes widened with some emotion that she couldn't quite place. She saw Tavish ball his fists and even Lars seemed upset.

"Val, you don't really want to watch this. Shall we go to the ladies' room?" Camille urged.

"What's happening?" Valeria asked, feeling the tension building in the room.

"Oh, just…too much testosterone in that man!" Camille pointed toward Paolo.

Pulling on Valeria's arm, Camille said, "Let's go. It'll all be settled by the time we get back."

"I'm not leaving." Seeing Alex's expression, her eyes narrowed. "Who is that man…Paolo?"

Camille glanced to Alex in apology. "We can talk about all of that later." Valeria noticed a look in Alex's eyes that she didn't recognize. Fear? Embarrassment? She wondered why no one would tell her. But she was certain that she would know in minutes.

Jeremiah spoke, "The council recognizes Paolo."

Nodding arrogantly, Paolo continued, "An immortal's marriage is sacred, would you all agree?" A few nodded. "Alex cannot marry Cassandra. He is already married to an immortal!" Alex's eyes darted back to Valeria in what appeared to be an apology.

Certain that she had misunderstood, Valeria asked, "What does he mean? *Alex is already married to an immortal?*" Camille and Ava stood on either side of Valeria and put their arms around her protectively.

"Don't worry about it. We will simply have a civil ceremony." But Valeria could hear the apprehension in Camille's voice.

Jeremiah nodded. "Alexander, do you have a response to this charge?" Alex glared at Paolo.

"Yes, Alex, I have been asking for a response for centuries. I'm certain *everyone,*" Paolo glanced at Valeria, "would like to hear it!"

Sudden realization struck Valeria. "Kristiana was *an immortal?*" Camille nodded and patted her shoulder.

Brushing his trembling fingers through his hair, Alex tried to gain control of his emotions and his voice. "There were no rules regarding dissolutions when Kristiana left. She has been gone for 2,500 years. The marriage is now dissolved by her absence."

"Alex deserted Kristiana! My sister has been missing all these years and his efforts have been only to chase another woman. These are unforgivable and adulterous actions! Further, this woman, Cassandra, has been incorporated into their family as my sister never was." Paolo's face filled with venom as he pulled a document from his coat and placed it on the table in front of Jeremiah. "We humbly demand that the Law of Nevia be enforced!"

Camille let out a cry, "*No!*" Valeria saw the horror on the faces of her family—including Alex's—as the gasps of the immortals echoed throughout the cavern.

Alex's face was lit with incredulity and horror. "*The Law of Nevia?*" He shook his head several times, momentarily speechless, and then glared at Paolo. "*Do you really hate us that much?* Because you know, you aren't just punishing me!" He clenched his jaw and shook his head in disgust. "You know that the Law of Nevia has no place in this discussion!"

"Alexander! You will address the council! Disrespect will not be tolerated!" Jeremiah demanded.

"What is that…that law?" Valeria asked, swallowing.

Camille didn't respond, but took Valeria's hand and held it tightly as if watching a train wreck, mumbling to herself in a near whimper, "Oh, Alex…oh, Alex. No! No, no…don't."

"Don't what?" Valeria cried, but was unable to get Camille's attention.

Grabbing Valeria's arm, Camille whispered, "Alex wants us to leave *now!*"

Valeria stared at her friend and felt tears forming in her

eyes, but she refused to let them fall. Shaking her head slowly, resolutely, she said, "I'm not leaving without Alex." She began moving toward him, but Tavish was quickly upon her, wrapping his long arms around her. She struggled, but with her long gown she couldn't break free.

"I am sorry, lass. I cannot permit that," he whispered. She turned toward him and his eyes looked almost as sorrowful as hers. "I could not bear to see the results to either of ya."

"Council, that petition requires two signatories and I only see one representative here! May I know the name of the other accuser?"

"You know the name!" Paolo interrupted. "And council, under the rules, my sister is not required to be present!"

Alex narrowed his eyes and began to clench and unclench his fists as he turned toward Paolo. Valeria thought Alex looked as if he was poised to hit Paolo. "You know where she is!" Alex said.

"If I knew where she was, I would not be here alone! My sister went into hiding because of you and your abhorrent behavior!"

"Kristiana isn't even recognized here! So I don't even know why we are discussing this."

Jeremiah interrupted, "Kristiana is a known immortal and we shall not argue her status. Paolo *is* recognized as an immortal. He has made charges and if Kristiana had wished to be recognized, I see no reason that would be denied. We shall proceed with the consideration that Kristiana is a recognized immortal in good standing."

Alex glared at Jeremiah for a moment and then resigned, he asked, "If Paolo hasn't seen Kristiana in 2500 years, then how is it that she signed this petition?"

Paolo glanced away. "It was delivered to me."

"May I see it?" Alex asked and Paolo nodded. Alex

approached Jeremiah. "This is an ancient scroll...at least a thousand years old." His raised a suspicious eyebrow at Paolo. "You've had it all these years?" He turned back to the council. "Council, Kristiana is not an oracle! This document must be a fraud!" he said, adding a silent prayer.

Jeremiah thought for a moment before responding. "Alexander, the fact is, that we have what appears to be a valid petition presented in the correct manner. We have no reason to question the validity. How do you respond to the charges?"

Alex's eyes were now desperate; he glanced back at Valeria before he continued. "Council, Paolo is right that I should have looked for Kristiana. I...I should have handled things...better." He gulped. "But we were all new then. We didn't know the rules of immortals. Cassandra was—is—my symbolon, and I believed her...I believed her to be gone when Kristiana came into my life. I did leave Kristiana to try to save the life of Cassandra as she had returned and I...I didn't know that was possible," he said, breathlessly. "I beg the council's understanding, but as discussed earlier, *there was no council* at the time of the marriage, nor its dissolution. And Cassandra should not be punished! Please council!"

"When you returned, did you attempt to reunite with your wife?" Jeremiah asked. "And I warn you, Alexander, you will testify on the stone of truth, if I believe you are lying to us!"

"No...no, council. When I realized that my symbolon had reincarnated, I went back to Kristiana in an attempt to dissolve the marriage amicably. When I saw that she had left, I established substantial investments for her, through Paolo, so that neither would want for anything for the rest of their existences."

"Except for her husband!" Paolo shot back.

"Council, there is no reason for the Law of Nevia! It is simply not appropriate here! Please!"

"Alexander! One more outburst and I will call for Erebos! Do you understand me?" Jeremiah commanded. Alex sucked in a breath.

"Do not do it, laddy, the lass is watchin'," Tavish said softly. Valeria saw Alex glance back desperately at Tavish, and she felt Tavish shrug as if to tell him that she wouldn't leave. She saw Alex take a deep breath, calming himself.

Lars went to stand next to Alex, ready to restrain him if necessary.

"I agree, definitely not worth it!" Ava said, as if in a discussion with Lars and Alex. Camille nodded.

Alex shrugged off Lars, in a way that said he was back in control of himself.

The council looked to Paolo who countered, "Alex states that he left my sister for his symbolon…and that Cassandra *is* his symbolon." Paolo smirked at Alex. "If that is true, then show the council that she bears your mark!" He glanced toward Valeria with a lascivious grin. "And remember, I have had the opportunity to search…every…inch of her body." Paolo winked toward her in an action that she was certain was more for Alex's benefit.

Looking down, Alex shook his head, attempting to control his emotions. "Council, I do not have evidence that Cassandra is my symbolon, other than my visions of her…other than our love for each other. I agree that I should have searched for Kristiana, but I felt that she would make herself known if she wished to be found. Today, my entire family has agreed to place all of our resources into locating her. But you know that this could be a very long-term process. I beg the committee to investigate the charges prior to enacting the Law of Nevia! We will delay the immortal marriage indefinitely until this is resolved. But there is no evidence that this is necessary! This is a private issue…it *only* involves Paolo and I. Please!" He turned to face Paolo. "Paolo! I beg of you—remove the petition! Not for me...*for her!"*

Involuntarily, a cry escaped Valeria's mouth. She didn't know what was going on, but she sensed that there was far more at stake than a wedding.

Alex continued, "Council, I also request that Cassandra be considered a mortal for purposes of our laws, until this can be settled with Kristiana—which I am certain it can be. Cassandra has never taken any action that justifies the Law of Nevia. She has not...we have not...consummated our relationship. Certainly, that proves her innocence! We would both testify to that, if need be." Alex glared to Paolo. "Also, please consider that Kristiana knew of Cassandra and knew that my first commitment was to Cassandra—always."

Jeremiah waved an arm. "You cannot undo what has been done, Alexander. You should have thought of the ramifications earlier. Now, it is too late. Cassandra is here as an immortal. That cannot, and shall not, be undone." Alex dropped his head a fraction, hanging on to hope. "As far as the Law of Nevia, that petition has been entered and signed by two immortals in good standing with this council. There *is* reason to consider this a valid complaint!"

"Council, I humbly beg you to consider delaying the decision on this matter until the next council meeting, when I am certain we can alleviate all of your concerns." Alex's voice was almost a cry that carried throughout the cavern.

Paolo stepped in front of the council, and his volume increased. "During that time, Cassandra will be further integrated into his family! No! Council, that is not adequate!"

Pursing his lips and narrowing his eyes, Jeremiah said, "Alexander, you attest that there has been no intimacy between you and Cassandra? I believe I will require details on what sort of physical contact there has been!"

"Council, please, may we discuss this delicate matter in private chambers?" Alex pleaded.

Paolo shrugged and smirked. "That is not necessary. I understand they have been living together for several months. My guess is that they share the same bed. But I am satisfied that Alex has not made love to Cassandra." He glanced back at Valeria. "However, the fact is that Cassandra has taken the place of my sister, not only with Alex, but with his family." Paolo narrowed his eyes. "And Alex has admitted to me that he has been unable to confirm that Cassandra bears his mark."

Jeremiah turned back to Alex. "Does Cassandra bear your mark?"

Alex glanced helplessly back to Valeria, with deep sorrow in his eyes. She could see he didn't want to answer. "I have not seen it, yet."

"It is unfortunate that Immanuel is not here to testify. Alexander, would her physician testify that she bears your mark?"

"I cannot answer for Mani."

"I could order Immanuel here, if necessary. Would he testify that she bears your mark?" Jeremiah demanded impatiently.

"No."

"Paolo, it is not often that I agree with you. It is a pity you were not forthright in your objection. You could have saved this council, and the parties concerned, considerable trouble." Jeremiah looked to Alex and Valeria.

Paolo shrugged.

The council rose and surrounded Jeremiah, as they began their deliberation. Alex looked frozen in a desperate plea. Moments later, Jeremiah waved his arms, ending the discussion as the council took their seats. Jeremiah rose.

"The council has decided that there is enough cause to

enact the Law of Nevia until the next council meeting. At that time, we will evaluate all of the information and make a permanent decision. That is all."

Alex almost fell to his knees, as if he had been slugged. The group began to disband as whispers ran across the room.

Within moments, the council rose and joined the other immortals, and then the room filled with laughter and music and gaiety, as if they had just decided something with as much importance as repainting a cross-walk.

Camille looked at Tavish, her voice flat. "We have to get Val out of here now!" Valeria saw both Paolo and Alex heading toward her.

"I'm not leaving without Alex!"

"Lass, we must!" Tavish whispered as he started to carry her towards the gondolas.

She turned her face to look at him with so much pain. "Please, Tav, I *need* to see him. Please." Tavish turned, as if a silent communication had come in from the family.

"All right, Lass." Tavish released her and, suddenly, both Ava and Camille closed in on Valeria, as Tavish moved rapidly toward Alex. Valeria realized that Alex was actually heading toward Paolo…who was headed for her.

As Paolo approached, Camille, Ava, and even Daphne formed a human shield, keeping him from her. "Bella, you must know that I did this for *your* benefit! Please, allow me to explain."

Just then, Alex grabbed Paolo and spun him. "Wasn't it good enough that you killed her the last time?"

Valeria broke around the women and, with Paolo momentary distracted, she ran into Alex's arms. Tavish and Lars formed a wall and blocked Paolo. Alex pulled Valeria in tightly and kissed her head.

She let out a cry, "Please tell me what's going on!"

She could feel his grip on her tighten. He was shaking. "It'll be all right," he whispered into her hair. "We'll get this straightened out."

Paolo looked at Alex in disgust. "You realize I could invoke the Law of Nevia for your actions now!"

Alex continued to hold Valeria. He drew a rough breath. "You wouldn't do that...*not to her*. You're too selfish for that!" He gulped. "You've done the damage. Can't you let that be enough?"

There was a stand-off between Alex and Paolo. She wasn't going to let go of Alex. He forced himself to relax and gently kissed her forehead. Then he whispered, "Please, Paolo. You don't have to do this." Paolo's expression didn't change. Alex tried again, "Paolo, she doesn't understand this. Please, I need time to," his voice cracked, "to take care of this. For her, Paolo...if you ever loved her, give me...give us...time."

Paolo spat, "You didn't offer that luxury to my sister."

Ava pulled on Paolo's shoulder. "Paolo." He glanced at her and then back to Alex. Ava's voice became a soft plea. "Paolo, you can give them that," she said, attempting to calm the situation. She moved in front of him and pulled his face to look at hers. "It won't do you any good to do otherwise. You will only instill hate. That isn't what you want. I think you want us to locate Kristiana. We can do that. But, come on..."

"One hour!" Paolo growled.

Ava brushed his face. "Come on, Paolo...one night." He put his hand to his forehead and brushed it with his fingers and shrugged, noncommittally. Ava nodded toward Alex and with his arm wrapped tightly around Valeria, he lead her to the gondola with the family surrounding them, protecting them.

CHAPTER 6

The ride back to the island home was somber and in total silence, except for the sound of the boat and the water. Valeria noticed the family appeared to be in serious, silent conversation.

Everyone looked war-torn. And she couldn't get Alex to look her in the eyes. He simply held her as if she would be ripped from his arms any minute. Finally, the boat pulled up to the dock and the family walked past her silently headed into the house.

Helping her out of the boat, Alex held her for a moment and then took her hand as they slowly followed the path to the house. She saw that the yard was now set up with chairs and tables for the wedding and reception. Twinkling lights had been run in the brush along the side of the property. She would have been so pleased to see the progress of the preparations, so excited knowing what the next day held for her. It was breathtaking, with the brilliant stars and the full moon casting its light on the dance floor; but now she felt only a profound sadness in the beauty of it. It was like a magnificent dream and now it felt as if it was only *that*…a dream.

Finally, Alex spoke in a strange, strangled voice. "So, beautiful…I was thinking that it's…it's a waste of this location for anything but a honeymoon." He pulled her around and kissed her and she could feel his grief through the kiss.

"Alex…" She couldn't seem to find her voice. "Will you tell me what happened? I know we need to leave tomorrow. But as long as I'm with you, I don't care where we go." She looked at him and saw the pain in his expression. "We aren't," she choked back a cry, "getting married tomorrow…are we?" He closed his eyes and held her to him. She knew the answer.

"Let's just go back to Morgana." She brushed his face. "I know that we can't have an immortal marriage…for now. But, that man, Paolo…he can't keep us from getting married!" she said with a hint of incredulity. "Don't worry…everything will be okay." But somewhere inside her, she knew that wasn't true and seeing the look in his eyes only increased her growing apprehension. "I guess…we need to find Kristiana before we…" She swallowed as her fears began to get the best of her.

He bit his lip and stared up at the star-filled sky and attempted to contain his emotion. "I…I am so…so sorry." He choked as he closed his eyes, battling the pain in his soul. "But, I never, never imagined…"

She clung to him as he looked out to sea trying to compose himself. He took a deep breath and then taking her hand, he kissed it and led her onto the patio. "You look…*so* beautiful tonight!" He stared at her with longing. She saw an ice bucket with champagne and two glasses sitting on the table next to them. "I've been saving this bottle…" He shook his head slightly, not finishing the thought. She suspected it was to have been for their wedding night. "I asked Caleb to put it on ice." He gulped back his emotion and then pulled her into his arms.

"We'll drink it tonight…and then…" He kissed her temple and whispered near her ear, "And then I want to make love to you until morning." He brushed his fingers through her hair.

She fought back the tears of apprehension that were building in her throat. "Alex, just please…tell me what happened tonight."

He broke their embrace and she could see the deep battle going on inside him. He pulled the bottle of champagne from the ice bucket and stared at the label with an expression that spoke of happier times. The longer the silence, the more frightened she became. She noticed he was still shaking badly. He popped the cork of the champagne and poured it into the two glasses. Then he passed her a glass and gulped down half of his, as if it might release some of his pain.

She took a deep breath and blew it out, in an attempt to calm her fears. "I didn't realize that Kristiana was immortal…I…would have liked to have known that," she said softly.

Alex looked out to sea again, momentarily emotionless. "Yes, I should have told you."

She took his arm and leaned into him. "Alex, I want to make love to you. I would have made love to you months ago. I love you."

Fighting her growing anxiety, she continued, "But you wanted us to be married first. You said that making love to me before we were married made you feel like you were…giving up on the dream." She fought back the horror of the revelation. She pulled his face, which was still emotionless as he looked at her. "But marriage is between hearts. Not by agreement of councils." The force of her emotions were drowning her. "Alex, with everything in me, *you are my husband.*"

He forced a half smile on his face and kissed her again and then downed the remainder of his champagne, refilled it, and swigged it down again, hiding behind the action. She continued, "I know it was important to you. But we can search for Kristiana and when we find her, this will all be resolved. She will see how much we love each other and she will grant you a dissolution."

"Yes."

There was a sound of doors opening and closing inside the house and then the entire family came outside with suitcases in hand. Valeria realized that a water taxi had arrived and she hadn't even heard it. She stared at the family, as shock formed a fog around her reality.

"What's going on, Alex?" She was trembling now.

"They wanted to give us privacy tonight," he said, woodenly.

Lars walked up first and hugged Valeria lightly, avoiding eye contact with her. "Goodbye, sweetheart."

Then Tavish looked at Valeria for a few moments and then kissed her cheek. "Lass," he said, and she noticed a tear in his eye.

"Tav?" She looked to Alex. "Where's Caleb?"

"He's in town already. Camille knew we would want to be alone tonight." He gulped another glass down.

Daphne gave Valeria a sad nod. Ava couldn't look at Valeria, but gave her a brief hug before walking quickly to the waiting boat.

Finally, Camille approached her. Valeria noticed Camille's eyes rimmed with tears as she looked down at the ground and shook her head as if trying to gain the strength to speak.

"Please, Camille, will you tell me what's going on?" Valeria said as a sob broke through the illusions she was clinging to and a few tears freed themselves from her eyes.

Camille hugged Valeria tightly, and stifling a sob, she hesitantly turned and left. Valeria could see Camille's body quivering with silent sobs. "Camille?" she called out, and heard a cry escape from Camille as she continued toward the boat.

"Isn't anyone going to say anything to me?" she cried loudly enough for the family to hear. She watched as Camille loaded her suitcases on the boat with the others. Alex sat down in the chair, again refilling his glass and immediately tossing down its contents.

The insecurities of her childhood, with the lack of love and the abuse, came back in full force as Valeria stepped toward the water taxi. "Please! Did I do something wrong?" she asked. "I'm sorry. I'm sorry for whatever I did!"

Suddenly, Camille climbed back out of the boat and headed toward them. Camille looked at Alex sorrowfully and he dropped his face in his hands. "I have to do it this way," he said, with the only voice that he could find.

"I'm sorry, Alex, but I just can't do it like that." She shook her head empathetically as a tear rolled down her cheek. "Please tell Val, she deserves to know." She moved up to Valeria and hugged her tightly. "Val, I love you like a sister!" she sobbed. Then, kissing her on the cheek, she turned and left without looking back.

Valeria's heart was pounding so loudly that it drowned out the sound of the boat motor starting up and pulling off shore. She held her breath, waiting for the news.

"Camille's right. I guess…" He sucked in a deep breath and refused to look at her. "I thought I could protect you from this for at least a little while…at least for tonight." His voice cracked as he stared off into the sea. He shook his head as if getting rid of the thoughts. He downed his glass of champagne before pulling another bottle out of a nearby cooler. Popping the cork, he refilled his glass and then slumped back into his seat, still not making eye contact with her. "I don't know how to say this." His voice came out as a cry and his face filled with grief.

Taking his hand, she sat on the cool ground in front of him and laid her head against his knee. "Just tell me."

Gently, he pulled her up onto his lap. She rolled her head onto his shoulder. "I made the biggest mistake of my life tonight...and I thought...it would be best to face it all in the morning. The family disagreed."

She touched his face. "Is that why they left?" She saw a slight turn of his head as if to say no.

"Why did they leave?" Her trembling deepened. She was certain that she didn't want to know, but something in her demanded the truth.

"Because...that was the decision tonight."

"They have to go back to Morgana?"

He reached for the champagne bottle and she put her hand on his arm to gently stop him. Then she pulled his face to hers. His eyes held no hope, only deep grief.

With his voice flat, he said, "You would think that the gift of immortality would only be given to the very good and the very wise. That's the way it should be...shouldn't it?" He shook off the thought, and continued, with no emotion in his voice. "Well," he continued, "I guess you have gleaned most of the story about Paolo and Kristiana." Alex swallowed. "I made an unforgiveable error."

Valeria kissed Alex. "I don't blame you for marrying Kristiana."

"Besides marrying Kristiana," he drew in a harsh breath, "I should not have requested an immortal marriage. It provided Paolo the opportunity to bring up old grudges." He looked down for a moment. "Honestly, I thought all of that was behind us. And the council has been...reasonable...in recent years.

"I should have known that Paolo and Kristiana would never give up. I should have married you when we had the opportunity." Alex shrugged. "I'm embarrassed to tell you that I risked *everything*—including your safety and happiness—because I couldn't bear the thought that Paolo might have you again."

"Have me again?" Valeria shook her head, incredulously.

Alex closed his eyes. "It was my jealousy…my need to…I don't know how you will ever be able to forgive me."

"How does Paolo know me?"

Alex avoided eye contact with her.

"Alex?"

He shook his head, attempting to will the truth into submission, and then said quietly, "You were married to him." The idea that she could have ever been married to Paolo, and never married to the sweet man who had loved her throughout her entire existence, was nearly crushing; and she saw the effect on him was magnified.

"I wouldn't have married *him!*"

Alex looked at her as if she were naïve. "You were fifteen. Paolo was able to charm your father…and you. But when it all comes down to it, you were sold."

She was speechless.

"You died a few years later with child." He drew another deep breath. "As time went on, I believed that Paolo and I had moved past all of that.

"When I saw Paolo at the airport, I knew…it wasn't over." Alex closed his eyes. "Still, I never imagined…"

"What is the Law of Nevia?"

He nodded, his pain visible. "Nevia was a Nymph who created a great deal of trouble with married gods. She tricked the families into believing that she was the actual wife. After disrupting several families, a law was put in place by the angry wives."

"Alex…what does it have to do with us?" Her trembling

was affecting her voice.

He closed his eyes and clenched his jaw. "Let's discuss it later."

Her fear had raised her tone several levels. "Alex, tell me." She knew she didn't want to know.

Alex fought back the sobs and took her face in his hands. He kissed her mouth and then cried, "It means that I have to...leave you."

"NO!"

"If I ever see you again, the council will spare no time or expense...we will be put to death!"

Her eyes widened in tormented disbelief. "How can this be?" she cried. "This can't be right. We have to fight this!" She stood, needing something to do.

He rose and grabbed Valeria as tightly as he could hold her and whispered into her neck, "There is no fighting this. It was the decision. Paolo gave us tonight. I have to leave you tomorrow morning." There was a long silence and then he whispered, "I can never see you again."

Valeria pulled away in shock. "Don't say that, Alex!" The realization of what was happening hit her and she stared at him. "Were you going to just leave me in the morning?" The horror in her eyes forced him to look away. "Alex, how can this be? How could you do that?"

He lowered his head to his hands and choked, "I can't! I can't do any of this. I can't leave. I couldn't even tell you. I thought...I guess, I thought," he looked at her, broken, "tonight...that's it."

"Please! Alex, there *must* be another solution! You said something about a dissolution. What about that?"

Alex slumped back into the chair and gulped down another glass of champagne. "Val, do you know how long we have been looking for Jonah? If Kristiana wants to hide, she can be gone forever."

"Let's go back to the council!"

Alex shook his head. "The decision was to address it at the next council meeting."

"Next year?" she said with a trace of hope.

"No."

"When Alex? When is the next council meeting?"

He couldn't look at her. "When is it, Alex?"

"Five hundred years from now."

She felt the despair building and she went back and curled up onto his lap. He held her tightly as she sobbed. Then he carried her to the bedroom and they curled together, while Valeria wept in his arms and hung on with all that was in her.

Finally, she spoke softly, hope creeping into her heart, "If Kristiana can disappear, so can we."

"No, my love." He shook his head sadly as he stroked her face. "It isn't just us; The Law of Nevia affects the entire family. Every member of our family will be put to death if we disappear. That's why they left tonight."

"I can never see them again?"

"It will be…as if we never existed in your life," he whispered, tormented. "Val, we cannot, under any circumstances, contact each other. No letter or notes. No phone calls. And no one in the family can reach out to you." He fought the pain. "Val, you need to know this. If I ever see you at a council meeting, I cannot speak to you. I cannot acknowledge you. But that is the only place I will ever be permitted to run into you. Do you understand?" She sobbed harder.

Suddenly, desperation took hold, and he kissed her with everything that was in him as he looked into her face, so lost. In a desperate plea, he whispered, "Make love to me tonight."

They hastily pulled at the silk and cotton that kept them

apart as their mouths and hands hungrily ripped at buttons and zippers and hooks and frantically wrapped around each other as the layers came off, still desperately desiring flesh upon flesh. Until, at once, a loud cry escaped her throat and her body succumbed to her grief. Alex held her tightly, unable to speak.

Finally he choked, "I love you, Val. I always will. No matter what...*no matter what!*"

They held each other until the first hint of daylight creased the sky. Valeria's sobs had worn down to trembling torments in his arms. She repeatedly traced the mark on his hand, while clinging tightly to him, until she briefly dozed.

When she awoke, moments later, she felt a sudden panic that he had left. Her cry rang out and he came to her, dressed in jeans and a T-shirt. She sobbed for a few moments in his arms and then he forced himself to release her and stand.

His face was ashen as he said, "I have to go." He swallowed, taking in the vision of her. "You can stay here at the estate as long as you want; forever if you wish." He swallowed again. "Or you can go back to the cottage...I built it for you."

She couldn't have this conversation. "The...the cottage?" Her voice was rough and foreign. "Are we...we're," she cringed, "we're *dividing things?*" With her voice flat, she said, "I guess...we have to." She began to weep. "But I couldn't be there...without you."

Numbness gave her a moment of reprieve. "But," she cleared her throat, still locked in this surreal world, "Alex...is it okay...can I go there to...to get my things?" She wasn't certain she could even bear it. But she couldn't stand the thought of never going there again either. She knew that, someday, she would have wished for that opportunity to be where they lived happily together for such a short, but glorious time.

"Take your time. Do what you need."

She heard her voice come out in a whisper, *"Please don't give up."*

He stood there, fighting back the sobs, and finally said, "There...there is no hope." Then he turned and started to walk out. He stopped himself in the doorway, his fists tightened as he battled the demons he needed to battle and clasping the entryway for a moment. He turned to her and said, "There's something I have to tell you."

His voice was breathless...his jaw clenched, as the sobs broke. "I don't..." He drew a deep breath. "Val, I don't want you to be lonely.... I know you will be...for a while. And..." He closed his eyes for a moment, gathering strength. "I'm so angry with Paolo, I could..." He nodded, realizing that what he was about to say was true. *"I could kill him."* He fought back the sobs. "But...I won't.

"Val, he *will* work his way back into your life. Paolo knows how to do that. And, well, the thing is..." His jaw quivered. He wondered how he could possibly say it. But he had to. "Paolo *did love you.* He could...be there for you, again."

Her stomach heaved and she ran for the bathroom as waves of nausea overtook her, but nothing came up. She sat by the toilet and sobbed, *"Don't tell me that!"* she screamed. "Don't tell me he loved me! He couldn't love me and do this." Her body shook violently and then she crumbled to the floor with a loud sob as dry heaves convulsed her body.

He pulled her into his arms waiting until the heaving stopped, and carried her back to the bed. "Val," Alex whispered through his sobs, "I know you can't hear this now. But it's the only chance I'll have...and, Paolo did love you. I think...I think he was a good husband to you. And I think you loved him." Alex shook his head. "When you died, he grieved deeply. Paolo and I mourned together. So you don't need to hate him. Live your life. Find a way to be happy. We both need to do that."

Alex kissed her forehead and then her mouth, memorizing it. Then he whispered hoarsely, through his sobs, "Be happy, my love."

And he left.

Valeria closed her eyes, knowing that her life would never be full or happy again. She had to block out the thought...pretend it wasn't happening. She grabbed his shirt that was lying on the bed next to her and pulled it on over her undergarments pretending that she would wake and he would be there. Because she certainly could never just let him walk away from her...*she could never do that.* Concentrate, she thought...make him here with you. This is a nightmare and you'll wake up and he'll be here and it'll be your wedding day and...*How could she let him leave?*

Then she heard the front door close...*Oh, God! It was real!* Her heart dropped into her gut, realizing she might never see him again. She ran down the stairs after him, terrified that she was too late.

He walked quickly, not trusting himself. Alex made a gesture to the driver before he reached the water taxi and the engine revved. He stepped onboard and stood facing out to sea—he couldn't look back.

She ran down the steps and the short hallway, racing out the door, just as the boat pulled away. With sheer desperation, she dashed down the walkway that was to have been her aisle, wearing only his shirt, not caring who saw her. She ran toward him as the boat began to pull around the corner and out of her view. Then the boat hesitated and she saw him signal for it to continue.

Tossing 500 euros at the driver, he said, through his agony, "No matter what I say, don't go back."

He couldn't look back, it was far more than he could bear. Tears covered his face as he wondered how he had searched for her for an eternity...*and now was just leaving her.*

As the boat edged the corner, she felt the sound that sprang from her gut in an agonized scream, *"Alex!"* She sprinted toward the dock and then collapsed on the lawn...unable to bear to see him turn the corner.

He heard the cry and he knew he shouldn't go back...knew he couldn't. Don't look...don't...he told himself. He would only have to leave again...how could he leave her *again?* The boat had rounded the corner and the house was now out of sight. He had done the unthinkable—the unbearable—he had left her...alone again in the world. Don't look, he told himself. Don't go back...

Within heartbeats, he gave the only instructions that he could and the boat pulled back toward the house. It was still five feet from the dock of his island home, the driver smiling happily with the thousands of euros that now laid on the dash, when Alex leapt onto the dock.

The steps to her were but a few sprints and then she was in his arms. He held her tightly, kissing her face, her forehead, her hair, her mouth. They held on to each other, as agonized sobs moved through both of them, both knowing it was truly for the last time.

He removed his dark gray jacket and lovingly wrapped it around her. He shook his head in agony, and they looked into each other's eyes. There were no words...no words... He stood and walked back to the boat.

She knew it was better if she didn't look. She knew that the last memory she would have of her beautiful life with him would be of him leaving. Unable to stop herself, this time she watched.

As the boat was about to go out from view, he turned to her. Even from the distance, she could see the haunted look in his eyes. And then he was gone.

CHAPTER 7

For Valeria, life stopped at that moment. She thought maybe she should have followed him. She thought maybe she should have forced Paolo's hand. Then the outcome might have been different. She thought about drinking too much. She thought about throwing herself into the sea.

After he left, she went down to the beach and laid in the sea with the cold tidal waters washing over her for hours in an attempt to numb the pain…until her ferocious shivers made her wonder what would happen if she died there. Then it occurred to her what it would do to him if he came back and found her like that. She couldn't bear to do that to him. She pulled herself up, wet and shaking violently from the cold water, and walked back to the house and up to their honeymoon suite.

It would be a relief to stop the pain with alcohol or drugs, but in the end, she just layed between the sheets where Alex had been with her. His clothes and all of his belongings were still just as he had left them. If she moved his things, her memory of the room would be of him gone…her world without him. She could still close her eyes and feel him moving through the room to her, and smell his wonderful scent. Maybe if she slept more, she would wake up to find he was here with her and it had all just been a nightmare. Oh, please God, make that be so!

There were a number of signs that life was going on outside of that bed. She was vaguely aware of the doorbell ringing several times. Valeria's mouth was dry and she pulled Alex's glass of flat champagne off the nightstand and drank it. She savored the feeling of being near him with that action.

There was a girl who was standing in the light from the window. It was late afternoon; Valeria could tell by the angle of the sun.

The young girl was speaking softly to her in another language encouraging her to drink a glass of green liquid that she held. Valeria turned her head, but the girl insisted. Deciding that she was thirsty, she drank the concoction. It tasted bitter, but it seemed to quench her thirst. Then she wondered, momentarily, if she had been poisoned or drugged and the pain would stop. The girl was encouraging Valeria to get out of bed. She shook her head, but the girl insisted, so Valeria got up, her sheets and clothes still damp from earlier. Following the girl into the bathroom, Valeria discovered that the tub had been filled, though she hadn't even heard it.

Normally, she would have wanted privacy, but she didn't care now. The girl helped her undress and Valeria stepped into the tub. The girl began washing Valeria's hair. It felt good and it reminded her that she was alive…at least a part of her was. She was grateful for this girl and at least made an attempt to fight the constant sobs that wracked her body. She stepped out of the tub and the girl wrapped her in a warm robe.

Wandering through the house, she felt its emptiness; there was the chair Lars had sat in reading a book on construction.

There was the counter where she and Camille had prepared a salad; Ava would pick up the mushrooms as soon as Valeria sliced them into the bowl, and Camille would occasionally reach over to slap Ava's hand and they had all laughed. Was that only yesterday? Tavish and Daphne had played chess at the table by the window. There was the spot, at the foot of the stairs, where Alex had stood with so much love and hope in his eyes, just one day before! This all haunted her now.

The girl seemed to be telling Valeria that she should go outside. Valeria took her purse and unzipped it to grab her sunglasses. She froze. Alex had stuffed her purse with a large amount of cash, at least 50,000 euros. It made her heart leap to see something he had done and made the quivers and sobs return. She wondered whether she should leave the cash here or at the cottage. But thinking was not something she could do right now and thinking about leaving either of those places was just too much.

Pulling her sunglasses on, she walked to the door and saw a white garment bag in the hallway. Something made Valeria turn to look at it, as she brushed her fingers over her mouth. She saw the tag from the shop in Venice where, just days before, she and Alex had purchased her wedding gown. Was today the day? She tried to think. Yes, it must have been today…her wedding day.

Slowly unzipping the bag, she saw the rich off-white silk-crepe and remembered the feel of it…how he had looked at her in it. She closed her eyes for a few seconds and then pulled the dress out of the garment bag. What life would be like if she were wearing that dress today for him! She stepped outside and saw the changes. The arbor was gone and the tables and chairs had been put away. All the help had been notified…efficient Camille! But somehow, the dress had gotten by. Valeria guessed that the assistant must have insisted on delivering it, perhaps hoping for another large tip.

Valeria took the dress and, rolling it up casually so that it didn't drag on the ground, she carried it with her outside. She walked on the patio to the wine cooler that had been stocked days earlier for the celebrations and took out a bottle of champagne. She walked barefoot across the lawn, carrying the bottle toward the shore.

The young girl didn't seem to want her to drink the champagne but Valeria didn't care. She went to the Adirondack chairs near the water, where she had sat curled up on Alex's lap the first night they were there. She could still imagine that he was there with her. She clung to her wedding dress while opening the champagne. It spilled on her dress and her bathrobe. When the girl tried to take the dress, Valeria was surprised to hear a fearful sound come from her own throat. Then she sat back in the chair and soaked in the warmth of the sun. It would have been a perfect wedding day, she thought. Then she fell back asleep.

When she awoke, everything felt very surreal. It felt like a nightmare that she couldn't wake from. Valeria knew she needed to pack up and move out of this family house and then go to their home in Trento...*their home*. How could she move out of the only real home she had ever known? Where would she go?

She thought of Florence. But that seemed too close to Alex and her family...the family, she reminded herself, since they were no longer *hers*. And she knew that if she was in Italy, she would not be strong enough...she would feel compelled to drive up to Trento sometimes. She decided that she would move back to her brownstone in New York. At least she liked it there, and it didn't remind her as much of Alex. Weege had been taking care of most things, so it should still be in good shape. All of these decisions felt cold and final to Valeria, like a death…hers.

When Valeria awoke again, she felt movement around her. Opening her eyes, she realized that it was now early evening…she would have been dancing with Alex, perhaps their first dance. Then she saw an older woman of sixty with a crop of short white hair and eyes of deep oracle blue. She was kindly directing the girl to bring something. Valeria saw a tray on the table next to them with cheese, crackers, and fruit.

"Hello, dear," she said in a friendly voice. "I'm Shinsu." She looked to Valeria. "I know. It doesn't sound Greek at all. Gosh I've gone most of my existence with people thinking I'm Chinese when they hear my name! Mother had very unusual likes and dislikes. But I guess it fits me. I'm a bit unusual…or, so I'm told."

Shinsu went on, "So! What a mess! The one council meeting I miss in millenniums and they make a decision like that!" She turned her head in irritation and then shook her finger. "I hold Jeremiah responsible! Sure, those boys get themselves into trouble. But come now—the Law of Nevia? For a nice girl like you? All they had to do was open their eyes to see that neither you nor Alex have a malicious bone in your body! You know that was the purpose of that law, for maliciousness!

"So, go ahead. Tell Su-su all about it." She signaled that Valeria should begin.

Valeria didn't answer. Her vision was blurry and she couldn't imagine someone was really there talking to her. It must be another dream.

"I guess you're not quite up to it yet," she said calmly. Then she shook her head in irritation. "What were they thinking leaving you alone here like this? As soon as I heard, I told Jeremiah that he may as well make use of her!" Shinsu eyed the young woman who was helping. "Thank goodness I found out when I did!" She shook her head again.

Valeria wasn't ready to engage in any conversation, but she wanted to know, "Alex?" Her voice felt awkward and strained. Just saying his name caused an enormous well of tears in her eyes.

Shinsu shook her head. "Alex is a mess." She looked at Valeria. "And you think you're bad off!" She rolled her eyes.

Looking down at the stained silk in her lap, Valeria again remembered Alex's face when she had tried on the dress and choked into soft sobs.

Shinsu leaned in matter-of-factly. "Yes. I heard about all of it. That must be the dress, huh? Pretty." She shrugged and said gently, "Well, you can't really marry someone when they are married to someone else." She looked off and rolled her eyes. "Unless you are Jeremiah and then, by God, you will find a way!" she huffed. Shinsu picked up the tray and looked at it unhappily, eyeing the young woman who had arranged it. She reorganized it and pushed it toward Valeria. "Here, eat some." Valeria didn't guess that Shinsu would take "no" for an answer so she took a cracker. She played with it, breaking it into tiny pieces, as she had learned to do in the foster homes she grew up in, so that no one knew how little she ate.

The girl brought Valeria and Shinsu something to drink and Valeria soon noticed the odd relationship between the two women. Shinsu said something directly to the girl in the Polynesian language that seemed to irritate the girl. The girl tried to argue and Shinsu shut down the argument in a very calm tone and then indicated that the girl could go.

"At least I have the title of senior wife." Shinsu rolled her eyes. "That's the least I should get after over a thousand years of marriage!" she huffed. "My one gift is that she'll look like she's a thousand years old in just a few decades." She sighed and then said something else to the girl.

Valeria's eyes narrowed in question and Shinsu seemed to understand the question.

"I know. Different rules for different immortals. Doesn't seem right does it? Well, rules—schmools. Don't let them fool you! The council does what they want to do! But don't you worry. It'll be straightened out at the next council meeting! I'll make certain of that!" Shinsu saw that she had upset Valeria by her comment. "Oh, dear! I know 500 years seems like a long time, but it's really not." She sighed. "Trust me! It'll be like a day or two when you are my age!"

Although Valeria wasn't in the mood for company or talking, Shinsu was a link to Alex and the family and she couldn't give it up. Shinsu got up and walked to Valeria. "Now, come on, dear. Hand me that gorgeous dress," she said and Valeria found herself handing the dress to Shinsu. "And that's not doing you *any* good!" Shinsu said, indicating the champagne. Valeria handed her the bottle and then Shinsu walked into the house with the bottle and the dress and returned with a blanket.

"So. here's the thing, dear. We have these bodies that are immortal, right?" Shinsu said, as she tucked the blanket around Valeria. "But here's the secret." Her eyes sparkled. "It isn't the body that is immortal!" Valeria looked at Shinsu in total confusion. Seeing this, Shinsu tried again. "Our bodies are like everybody else's. It's what *we oracles* do with them that's different."

This was too deep of a conversation for Valeria but Shinsu continued. "We all have the same carbon engines!" she said. "It's our spirit that makes us different." Shinsu studied Valeria. "I thought you should know that, dear. And here's the thing— Alex needs you to be all right. He needs your endowment of life force. So you need to pull yourself together, girl!"

Valeria felt like she was emotionally trapped at the bottom

of a well, with no way to climb out. Shinsu went on, "When you are ready, you need to get things done. You need to move your body." Shinsu lifted a finger toward Valeria. "And you will find solutions come to you, just like that!" Shinsu snapped her fingers. She brushed her fingers through Valeria's hair. "You know, time is just an illusion of motion." She shook her head. "I don't know why I'm telling YOU that."

Shinsu sighed. "Girl, you can't solve anything from where you are at right now!" She looked into Valeria's eyes. "Be the solver! You can solve this whenever you decide! But it takes you forcing yourself into someplace other than grief..." She narrowed her eyes. "Or apathy. Get angry. That's okay for now. Move the body some more. Look around. Get outside of that gorgeous head of yours! Just doing that will change your future!" Shinsu patted Valeria's leg. "You are considerably stronger than you think you are! I promise!" She winked and her eyes sparkled with life.

A soft breeze moved by her and Valeria closed her eyes, drifting off into a dreamless slumber. When she awoke it was night and she felt the coolness of the air. No one was there, except the girl in the house. The woman, Shinsu, must have been a dream or a hallucination. She noticed how brilliant the stars were from this part of the island. She could even see the Southern Cross. She had always wanted to see it. Valeria saw a brief picture of how this night might have been—the twinkling lights, the dance floor, her beautiful husband in her arms. Alex, her husband for eternity...in her bed, making love to her.

Pushing that dream back, she stood up with the blanket wrapped around her and walked to the house. The girl had prepared dinner for her but she walked past it. Her stomach wasn't ready for food. The girl brought her the green drink and again insisted that she drink all of it. Valeria decided that the sooner she did what the girl said, the sooner she would leave her alone. Then Valeria went back to the bed and slept, a dreamless night.

In the morning, Valeria got up and showered. She pulled her hair back into a ponytail and dressed in jeans and a T-shirt—the first time she had gotten dressed since that awful night. Now, somehow, it was almost two days ago. The girl brought her coffee and toast. It wasn't the perfect blend of coffee that she had become accustomed to, but it was good.

She packed only the casual clothes that she had brought. She couldn't bear to bring the rest of the things that Camille had purchased for her honeymoon.

She couldn't check flights with her cell phone since there wasn't internet or cell service at the house. She didn't want to go into the town of Gaios to see a travel agent because she didn't want to risk running into anyone—not the family and not the others. She knew she would not be able to control her reaction if she saw the men responsible for this. She thought how strange it was, given all the abuse she had endured as a child and a young girl, and yet she never harbored any anger toward the perpetrators. For this, it was different. She would not forgive them…*ever*. Valeria found a house phone and was able to make airline reservations to Venice and the following morning from Milan to New York. It was decided.

In the bedroom, she pulled out her toiletry case and tossed everything that wasn't Alex's in it, though most of his things had been moved to the other bedroom. She wondered if she should pack his things and take them to the cottage, but decided to leave them as they were. It did make her wonder where he was. Was he near? Was he wondering where she was? Would she always feel so very connected to him and, at the same time, so very isolated?

In the closet was the silk sweater he had worn the day before at the rehearsal. She pulled it to her face and breathed in. Oh, she hoped she would never forget his wonderful scent. Unable to stop herself, she laid down on the bed holding the sweater near her face. After an hour, she rose, put on his gray jacket, and slung the sweater over her shoulders, tying the arms in front of her neck.

The water taxi arrived and helped her with her bags. She kept her sunglasses on. They helped her from feeling like she needed to be social. Within hours, her flight was arriving in Venice. She recalled the balloon flight over the magnificent city just days before…when she was whole. She forced those memories to the back of her consciousness, wondering if there would be a day when she could stand to remember that extraordinary time in her life.

In Venice, she hired a limo. She wasn't up to driving…she wasn't up to anything. As she rode through the familiar hills, she tried to block out the memories—they were just too much. But closing her eyes only made it worse. This part would be over soon, she painfully reminded herself as the limo pulled onto their drive…she wasn't certain whether that thought made it better or worse, perhaps both.

Stepping precariously out of the limo in front of her beautiful cottage, she concerned herself with how she would keep herself together. If she broke down in front of the limo driver, would he think she was insane and leave her? Then what would she do? Pulling the fresh mountain air into her lungs actually soothed her. She took in the feeling of the coolness on her skin and the smell of the forest. There was no fire in the fireplace today. The place looked flat without the light that was Alex…that was them.

She wondered if it was a mistake to come here. She could certainly replace her clothes, but from somewhere deep within, she knew that if she didn't come back here one last time, there would come a day when she would regret it.

Her heart pounded nervously before opening the door. She closed her eyes and took a deep breath pushing back the tears that sat poised on the edge of her eyes and her heart. She recalled the first time she had come here, and how he had stood at the door anxiously wondering if she would like it. And perhaps a piece of him wondered if she would appreciate what he had spent centuries creating for her.

The door was unlocked and she stepped in. Their first kiss had been right there. She ran her hands over the library of leather-bound classics. *Walden* was missing. He must have come here! She wondered if he was still near. She saw that *Sense and Sensibility* was pulled out slightly, was that an invitation to take it? Or had he considered taking it himself. Next to it was *Wuthering Heights* and two open spaces. She remembered reading it under the gingko tree by the side of the house. The lines flashed into her head from the book, "If all else perished, and he remained, I should still continue to be; and if all else remained, and he were annihilated, the universe would turn to a mighty stranger." To Valeria, at this moment, the universe had become a mighty stranger.

Setting her purse on the counter, she removed the two books that she had brought with her for their honeymoon—*Pride and Prejudice* and *Shakespeare's Sonnets*—and replaced them on the bookshelf. Walking back to the bedroom, she stepped into their closet. Should she pack up everything now? Would it be more painful for him or less? Someday, he might want another woman. Her heart lurched in pain, and she held on to the doorway waiting for the waves of grief to settle. She decided that she didn't want him to be one of those people who held on to the clothes of someone who was no longer there. She would remove all of her personal items, so that he could move on. Though she held on to the doorframe, this time the wave wasn't as strong, and she was able to continue minutes sooner. *See, already I'm getting better.* And that thought brought her to her knees in an agonized cry. She didn't want to be *over him!* That time, she thought the sobbing would never end...but it did.

In the wine cabinet she pulled out her favorite 2002 Ladera Cab. She remembered Alex smiling as they had sipped it—he was so happy to please her. Valeria opened the bottle and appreciated the musical tinkling as she poured it into Alex's fine crystal. Taking a sip, she realized that his fine crystal made a difference in the taste of things. She would have to get some glasses like his...if she could bear it.

He had said that there could be no notes, no letters, nothing. Somewhere inside, she realized that she had held onto the hope that Alex would be here waiting for her to go into hiding someplace...but he wasn't. This time, she only cried lightly while packing. It was as if she was cried out. Valeria decided that beyond her clothes and toiletries she would only take the Limoges box that he had purchased for her on their first date, but leave everything else as it was—except the pictures. What would she do with the pictures?

In the great room she stared at the portrait over the fireplace as she sipped the wine from the glass held in her trembling hand. It had only been just over a month ago when they had stood together, sipping their wine, and admiring the portrait. If she took it with her, there would be a hole where it had been. She would leave it and he could move it when he was ready. She picked up the picture of her, Camille, and Ava making a snowman. She would take that one, and the picture of her and Caleb. In the bedroom there was the picture of her and Alex laughing. How could she leave it? She thought for a minute...how could she take that from him? Finally, she decided to keep the picture of Alex holding her while she slept, and she left him the one of them laughing. After his eons of mourning her, he needed to remember that there was a time when they had lived and laughed together...*and that she loved him.*

Valeria went back to the bedroom and packed the rest of her clothes. Her favorite sweater had been in the basket to be cleaned. Now it was gone. She glanced at his bedside table and there was the box that his watch had been in—the one she had given him two days before in Greece. She went to the bed and opened the box, wondering if she would find his watch there, but the box was empty. He was letting her know that he had been there.

In the end, they would both have to move on...eventually, she thought, attempting to be pragmatic. She looked down at the engagement ring Alex had given her. So beautiful, but to have the ring on without him...she knew she couldn't keep it. It would serve only as a painful reminder of what once might have been. She went to his drawer and pulled out the sterling ring box and slid the beautiful ring from her hand and placed it back in its metal box. Resisting the urge to write Alex a long love letter, she scribbled a quick note, "As much as I want to, it doesn't seem right to wear this now. Until we meet again. Please hurry back to me. Remember, I love you!"

Then she realized that he could end up reunited with Kristiana or someone else. She couldn't leave that message when that was a possibility. She crinkled her note up and threw it in the wastebasket and then hastily wrote one line on his elegant stationary and folded it. Valeria knew that the new "rules" forbid the note, but her heart felt too heavy to say anything less. Opening the envelope of cash he had left her, she pulled out 500 euros. Then remembering the kind Limo driver who was still waiting for her, she took another 1,000. She left the rest of the cash and the ring in the safe with a note that read, simply, "Until we meet again."

Looking around the cottage that she loved, she wondered if she would ever see it again. Without permitting herself to dwell on it, she left her beautiful cottage in the woods—her home where she desperately wanted to stay forever. Her heart was broken in half; as a symbolon—a heart divided in two, neither feeling complete until...she couldn't finish that thought!

The driver took her to a hotel near the Milan airport. As he pulled into the drive, Valeria's heart lurched again; it was the estate turned hotel where they had first stayed in Italy. She asked the driver to take her anywhere else but he had insisted, pointing repeatedly at his watch. She finally acquiesced, tipping him generously, and then spent the night crying before catching her flight to what would now be home. She remembered telling Alex that her home was wherever he was. Now "home" was someplace else.

The next morning, she thanked God, again, for sunglasses.

CHAPTER 8

The sound of his cane echoed loudly as it tapped on the stone floor of the dark hallway with each step he took. He saw her and cackled, with no joy in his eyes.

"Our exchange is complete. You have what you want...and I have what I want."

Toying with the crystal at her neck, the bronze-haired beauty glanced up and her eyes warily focused on Jeremiah.

"Are they still alive?" Kristiana asked, sitting on her battered throne in the cold grayness of her self-imposed prison.

The dungeonesque room spoke of another time with green velvet curtains, wrought iron candelabras, and rich tapestries that were now coated in thick cobwebs. Even Kristiana's tattered clothing looked to be of another century. Despite that, there was something tragically beautiful about her.

"Yes...yes, they are alive, for the moment—but surely, my dear, you don't believe that Alexander will be able to stay away from the girl."

"He will stay away from her because he wants her to live,"

Kristiana said, as if disinterested.

Jeremiah pursed his lips. "Alexander's impertinence almost cost him his life! He is fortunate that you and I have an agreement." His eyes narrowed. "Those damned oracles seem to believe that they are impervious to the laws of this council because they were once favored!" He shook his head. "I'm afraid I must agree with your friend Aegemon on this; we should have killed them all as soon as Apollo faded!"

"You and Aegemon could have cleared the world of the oracles...except that then I would not have gotten what I wanted." She sat up and widened her eyes dangerously. "And I *always* get what I want, because I don't care how long I must wait!"

Then her eyes looked down calmly as her fingers returned to the crystal. "Jeremiah, I will not have you speak of harming Alex. I will make that decision." She tossed her head to the side. "And as of yet, I have not decided."

"If Alexander shows disrespect to the council, I *will* call Erebos! Make no mistake of that!" Jeremiah pounded his cane on the floor as a decree.

"That was not our agreement, Jeremiah! Remember that you are in power *only* because of me." She swatted at imagined gnats.

She was most definitely mad, Jeremiah thought. Who else but the insane would spend century after century alone in a cold, dark room, existing only for their brief moment of revenge?

"Ah, but I am in power now, and it would be best for you to remember that!" Jeremiah said.

Her eyes narrowed and she was suddenly inches from his face. "As you recall, I have my ways. And if I choose for you to no longer be in power, there are those who will assist me!" She was back in her throne in an instant. She glanced at her short nails and picked at them. "There are those who want you gone."

He eyed her. "Our agreement was that—"

"Our agreement was that you were to take care of the girl," Kristiana bellowed. "And if not for my intervention, they would be married now!" She sighed, as the irritation left her voice. "Why must I do everything myself?"

"Do you suppose it was easy for me to ensure that Shinsu didn't know about the council meeting? That took almost a century of planning! I don't believe she will speak to me for another century; all for you, my dear."

A cynical smile touched her lips. "For yourself, Jeremiah! Remember that you have the council...and Shinsu, thanks to me and my visions."

Jeremiah hesitated for a moment and then his eyes narrowed again. "Tell me, my dear, how do you do it?" His voice quieted, enticing her trust. "After all, our secrets are our own. You may be immortal...but you are *clearly* not an oracle!" Kristiana glared and then looked away. Jeremiah, continued, "As I suspected, you do not carry the gift. You have fooled a great many—though your eyes are not the color of an oracle." He pursed his lips. "Your visions have dates...they are specific...there are only two oracles who are that powerful."

"*Were* that powerful..." Kristiana corrected, a wicked smile striking her lips. "Two oracles who *were* that powerful."

Jeremiah nodded and cackled. "Yes...yes, you are right!" He tapped his cane, he needed to know and he would play the game until she had given him the information he wanted. "And remember that *together* we handled the first...and soon the other will be gone." His eyes narrowed in sudden recognition. "Hmmm, Cassandra wouldn't have helped you." Rubbing his chin, he looked up and drew a breath in thought, narrowing his eyes. "It must have been Myrdd who gave you the events…Why would he do that?"

"Men are so easily controlled." She glanced down. "Still, I expected more of him."

"So this is about power…control! You see, you are not so different from me."

"Perhaps…at one time. But then," her face and voice suddenly softened, "I saw Alexander and how he…*looked* at her," she said, her words full of wonder. "It was long before I ever met him." A smile briefly lit her face and then disappeared. "I wondered…Jeremiah, do you wonder…" She tilted her head to the side, in a gesture that was more personal than she had been in eons. She laughed. "Of course you do! You only wanted Shinsu because she belonged to someone you envied. Or could it be that you saw their love," her voice became a whisper, "and you thought that if you were ever loved like that, your life might be different?"

Finding her honesty too much, Jeremiah cackled. "I believe you have too much time to contemplate, my dear! So, now I know. And Aegemon?"

She shrugged. "We have our agreements. But I don't expect that he will be chasing oracles any time soon. There is one more thing that you must do! I do not want to ever battle for my husband again—do you understand?"

Shaking his head, Jeremiah warned, "Be wise about what you demand now! I have done what I agreed. There will be no further price to pay."

Jumping from her position in her chair, she thrust her dagger toward him, and he cackled.

"You cannot threaten me with your daggers! I *will* take the next step. Not because you threaten me, but because I can…I do not want her there anymore than you do!" His face grew wary for a moment. "What will happen?"

Kristiana's eyes glanced up at the ceiling, pursed her lips

and then back down at the floor as she shook her head. "I'm not certain. He was going mad by then and the visions weren't as clear."

"Myrdd?"

She didn't respond to his question. "Still I have powers of my own now…powers that no one can take away from me." She fingered the crystal at her neck and glanced to the tome resting, with its pages open, on a pedestal across the room from her

CHAPTER 9

New York

Returning to New York was the right thing to do. It was a place where she could pretend that she hadn't lost the most important things in her life. She opened the door to the brownstone and remembered a time when she didn't expect so much from life, when this place had actually seemed like a home.

There were fifty-nine messages on her machine. But Valeria wasn't ready to listen to any of them.

∞

Three weeks had passed since she had returned. There had been many knocks on the door but she just wasn't up to dealing with it. This time the knocks continued; a pounding, desperate knocking, then the metallic sound of a key going into the lock. A gruff New York accent came through, "Lady? Lady?"

"I already told you I've been knockin'... Just cut the freaking chain!" It was Weege. The bolt cutters came through and cut the chain inside her door. Valeria watched it all, with nothing more than numb detachment. Then Weege walked into the apartment, as she excused the burly man in the wife-beater tank top and baggy pants.

She stalked through the flat in utter shock. Then Weege's eyes found her.

"Holy shit!" Weege shook her head. "What the hell did that asshole *do to you?*"

Valeria sat on the floor, now weighing less than a hundred pounds; she was pale and her eyes were still swollen. She couldn't even try to smile. The pictures of the family, who had been her only company, surrounded her; the one of her sleeping in Alex's arms was still in her hand.

Staring for several minutes, Weege was speechless and then regained her composure. "What are these?" She picked up the pictures and analyzed them. Weege stared at the picture of Alex holding Valeria. Weege's voice was hoarse. "Is that him? I see why you...uh..." She cleared her throat and then her face drew back for an instant as she stared into Valeria's eyes. "Val, are you wearing contacts?" Weege continued to stare. "Uh, I love the color, but honey, I don't know that you should be wearing them now."

"Thanks," Valeria said softy.

"But, Val, you gotta stop this crazy, friggin' diet...now!" Valeria offered Weege her closest imitation of a smile and hugged her. Weege continued, "Come on, we're gonna get you something to eat! I just found this new place; you're gonna love it."

Valeria decided that she needed to dress; she needed to find a way to at least pretend to be normal. She showered and changed into a pair of jeans, and realized that they were much too big. Yoga pants and a T-shirt would hide the actual weight loss better. Stepping outside onto the porch, for the first time since her return, wearing his gray jacket, the sunlight overtook her despite the fast moving clouds above that mostly blocked the sun. Covering her eyes with her arm and squinting, she frantically searched through her Louis Vuitton bag for her sunglasses. Finally she found them and scooted them along her nose.

She felt like a vampire, now exposed to the muted daylight of morning. Still, she was surprised that the cool air felt good; it made her feel something other than loss. Her legs felt a bit wobbly and she clung to the rail while she cautiously moved down the five steps that led to the sidewalk...and civilization. She noticed the buds forming on the trees along her street and recognized that it would soon be spring. Time was moving on without her.

As they walked up a block, bursts of steam rose through grates in the sidewalk. It was one of the oddities of Manhattan that Valeria loved. She felt her yoga pants sliding down on her hips. She reached for the waistband and yanked them up, hoping Weege hadn't noticed. There had been no momentous decision to stop eating. She simply wasn't hungry. She wasn't anything; she was simply a half of a whole...now incomplete. There hadn't even been a lot of tears since she'd arrived in New York—well, not the torrents like before. Now it was more like a constant drizzle.

Seeing Weege's physical response to her appearance had concerned Valeria. She didn't really see herself anymore. She didn't feel hungry. She knew her clothes were much too big. But she didn't care. Still, she had taken a major step...leaving her brownstone and going to breakfast with a friend. *Normal people* did that kind of thing...people who were whole, all by themselves. Valeria actually heard some of what Weege was saying and even responded a few times.

Reaching the main intersection, Weege hailed a cab and gave the driver directions.

"Ya know, Val, you need to find something to do with

yourself. Maybe you should write. I mean it's not like you're inexperienced at it. You've been writing your whole life—you know, your journals." Weege's eyes enlarged. "Hey! I know! You could write my life story! You could be…like a ghost writer. Now that would be a New York Times Bestseller—guaranteed!"

Valeria nodded, but didn't hear what Weege said. They drove around the north end of Central Park and a few oversized raindrops hit the windshield. As usual, Weege was shouting instructions to the cabbie, telling him how to get around the traffic that was slowing their progress. He occasionally glanced back with what appeared to be confusion but Valeria was quite certain that he didn't understand a word Weege was saying.

At last they arrived at their destination and Weege paid the cabdriver. Valeria didn't even think to object.

"Best breakfast place in Manhattan! I don't know how we didn't find this earlier. I guess there's one on the West side. But I haven't tried that one yet…and to celebrate your…uh…well, your return, I figured we go to the best! Right?"

They walked toward the green awning and Weege was smiling as she held the door open. There was something familiar that was gnawing at Valeria's consciousness…then she saw the name on the door: "Sarabeth's."

Suddenly, her mind returned to the previous fall. It was the morning when she had first met Alex. She remembered so clearly the look in his eyes and the sound in his voice when he said, "Have breakfast with me." It had been so sweet…so beautiful—a moment that, even then, had electricity and magic. He had held the door open for her and smiled at her in that way, that was now ingrained on her heart. Knowing Alex so well now, she realized how nervous he had been that day. But at the time he just seemed so cool…so charming…so Alex!

And now...*now*...she felt the panic building in her chest, the pain overwhelming her. Suddenly, everything became a blur. Valeria disconnected from it and saw Weege's expression become alarmed...Weege's mouth was moving...people were scurrying around her and in her face and talking to her. She could hear a sound, a wailing, and to her shock, she realized that the sound belonged to her. Then, suddenly, everything went black.

∞

There was a loud beeping that was getting rather annoying...and a pain in her arm. Valeria opened her eyes. She was in a small cubicle with a curtain and wearing a faded hospital gown with an almost visible blue pattern on it.

Weege was sitting by her side. "I want you to know that I gave that asshole a piece of my mind!"

Did something happen that she didn't remember? She wondered how she had ended up in a hospital.

"What are you talking about?" Valeria muttered.

"The asshole who did this to you! *That's who!*" How did Weege know about the council and Paolo? "Alex!" Weege said, as if his name were a profanity.

"What did you do?" Valeria demanded, trying to sit up; and then she weakly sunk back into the bed, but was just as suddenly hopeful.

"I told him that if he ever stepped within a hundred yards of you that I would kick his ass from here to eternity!"

"Alex? You spoke to Alex?"

"Uh, yeah! You didn't even tell me you were back. I had to hear it from him!"

Something definitely didn't make sense. Her head felt thick and everything seemed confusing. A nurse came in and smiled. "Feeling any better? You were pretty dehydrated! It took three nurses to get an IV in you!"

Valeria nodded at the nurse and then went back to Weege. Her heart rate monitor was showing a spike and the nurse looked at Weege in disapproval. "Let's keep our patient calm."

Waiting until the nurse left, Valeria jumped in again and asked, "You spoke to Alex? When..." She tried to calm herself. "How did he sound?" She was hungry for news of him!

"Yeah...well..." Weege's eyes narrowed accusatorily. "Hey, you aren't going to freak out on me again are you?" Biting her lip, Valeria shook her head. She wasn't certain she could control her reaction, but she had to know. "So this asshole—"

Valeria closed her eyes. "Please, Weege, *please*...don't call him that." Her eyes flooded with tears.

"Jeez Val," Weege said as hers eyes widened, nervously. "You know me...that's just my way." She looked away and swallowed and then continued softly, "It was the real thing, wasn't it."

Valeria closed her eyes tightly and swallowed back the emotion that was again overtaking her. Yes, it *was*.

The nurse marched in and, angrily, pointed an accusatory finger at Weege. "That's it. You're going to the waiting room!"

"*What?* I didn't do nothing! I swear it! Ask her!" But the nurse insisted and, finally, Weege shrugged at Valeria and patted her shoulder before walking out. "I swear that old biddy has it in for me! We'll talk more later," Weege whispered and left.

Within minutes of Weege's exit, the curtain pulled back again and the woman who Valeria had determined was simply a figment of her imagination appeared...the woman...Shinsu? Her eyes sparkled oracle blue, and Valeria noticed how striking they were with her white hair.

"Well, dear…" She shook her head disapprovingly. "This simply won't do! Do you suppose that this is doing *him* any good?

"Alex?"

Shinsu's face became even more irritated. "Well, *who do you think*, dear?" she huffed. "You are the one he loves more than life and you treat yourself like…" Shinsu lifted her hands.

"How does he know?"

"Well, there are rules! But then, as you know, Alexander Morgan isn't going to just leave you on your own."

"He's here?"

"No, dear. He can't do that! I thought he explained that to you. Alex is out of your life."

Tears welled in Valeria's eyes and she looked away.

"Ah, new love. You know after a few centuries, it really isn't such a big deal. After all, from everything I've heard, you don't even bear his mark. It isn't like he's your symbolon."

Valeria narrowed her eyes at Shinsu and, for once, anger welled inside her until she could no longer contain herself. "I don't understand how you can make that declaration so easily." Valeria's rage increased, and with every word, she was more certain of her statement. "Alex *is* my symbolon—*with or without the mark!* So don't you or any of your other council members dare talk to me about my heart or his! If you say that Alex and I aren't meant to be together then you simply don't know us!"

Pulling back, in surprise, Shinsu responded slowly, "I see." She thought for a moment. "I do remember my first husband—my symbolon. I remember how that felt." She pursed her lips. "Yes, I believe Alex may be your symbolon." She nodded. "But it won't change a thing until the next council meeting 500 years from now."

Shinsu continued, "So, dear, there have been several

urgent requests to the council from your young man. He absolutely insists that Immanuel be able to attend to you as a patient here. I happen to agree. You have some extenuating circumstances."

"Mani!" Valeria's face was hopeful. "I can see Mani?"

"Well, he is permitted to attend to you. You must understand that Immanuel must be cautious in his discussions with you so as to not violate our laws. Now...I must be on my way. I am going to leave you my card—I do agree with Alexander that you must have a fellow immortal to talk to. Call me or come to see me if you like." She handed the card to Valeria. "In the meanwhile, you simply must begin taking better care of yourself!"

"Will you tell Alex that I—"

Shinsu shook her head. "No, dear! I cannot tell Alex anything from you!" Valeria swallowed and nodded.

Just then, Mani walked in and she could see the pain in his eyes. "Valeria," he said softly. Shinsu nodded at Mani.

"All right, young lady! You have my card. Don't lose it!" Shinsu commanded, shaking her finger at Valeria.

As Mani approached her bed, Valeria threw her arms around his neck. "Mani! Is...everyone okay? How is he?"

"Valeria, please forgive me, but I cannot discuss...the situation. It places everyone at risk if I do." He shook his head mournfully. "Let's take care of business before we discuss other issues. Do you have any pain in your chest?" She shook her head, no. "Take a deep breath, please...thank you." The cold of his stethoscope moved from one side of her back and then to the other side. "Another?" She drew another deep breath. "Thank you." He moved the stethoscope again. "And once more...good." He breathed out in relief and stepped around to face her. "Valeria, I've already reviewed your chart and I don't see any sign of pneumonia."

He pulled the stethoscope from his ears and put his hands on her arms. "But you must begin to eat again. You are only making a difficult situation more difficult if you do not care for yourself."

Valeria nodded. She desperately needed to tell him how much she missed everyone…especially Alex.

"May I ask you a personal question? Not one about …" She swallowed and looked down. Mani nodded.

"Why didn't you come with us to…well, you know."

Mani thought for a moment. "This is not something I would normally discuss. But I believe it may be appropriate in your case. You see," he looked into her eyes intensely. "I *do* understand your situation, far better than you know!

"Valeria, this council, with Jeremiah, was not always the way it is. At one time, the council, led by Myrdd, was one who sought to expand understanding and reduce the prejudice between the immortals and the oracles, and to improve the world with our gifts, as Apollo had intended. Jeremiah was able to gain power with accusations that Myrdd had violated sacred agreements. As a result, he was executed."

"Melitta began a petition to remove Jeremiah as the council head. I was away when it was presented at the next council meeting, 500 years later. She was executed, along with all of the other petitioners. My name was on that list."

"I don't understand how they…I mean, they are—were—immortal. How did they…"

"I don't understand how they…" She gulped. "I mean, they are—were, immortal. How did they…"

Mani looked away and she could see that he didn't want to discuss it with her. Then he turned to face her. "They were beheaded." Suddenly, Valeria remembered Jeremiah's threats to Alex and Tavish's warning to Alex that she was watching. Valeria felt an eerie chill run down her spine.

His eyes narrowed. "Somehow, Jeremiah discovered that oracles do not recover if Erebos performs the…" He looked away and swallowed. "I've often wondered if it is because they bury their head and body separately." He shuddered.

Once she recovered from the horror of it, she brushed her hand over Mani's face. "I'm so sorry."

They sat silently for a few moments and then she asked, "That woman, Shinsu, isn't she on the council?"

"Yes, however, Shinsu is an oracle, and as such, she has been far more sympathetic toward us. She encouraged the council to reduce my supposed crimes to a misdemeanor. However, I will never return to Greece."

"How do you survive," she gulped, "without Melitta?"

Mani thought for a moment. "Are you certain that you wish to know?" She hesitated and then offered an almost imperceptible nod. He took a deep breath. "I believe it is easier now. But when you have been whole, the separation from your symbolon is a wound that does not heal." He looked into her eyes to measure her response and let out a deep breath.

"Valeria, the best I can do is to take care of myself physically and to occupy my mind with learning." He looked up and, with tears lighting his eyes, said, "And pray that, somehow, Melitta will return to me." He brushed her arm kindly. "You must find something to occupy your body and mind. You must eat and make your body strong. How do you think it would be if something happened to you? How do you think…*others* would survive? If you cannot do it for yourself, do it for *others*…who love you."

A tear escaped from her eyes. "I will take care of myself…*for others*. I promise that!"

Mani nodded and squeezed her hands. "I must go now."

A few hours later, Valeria was released and actually had a bit more energy because of the IV fluids.

∞

It had been over a week since she had been in the hospital and Weege was acting strange, as if Valeria was extraordinarily fragile…she guessed she could understand why. Still, she was feeling stronger but Weege insisted on picking up groceries for her every day. Valeria was certain it was so that Weege could peek into her refrigerator and trash to ensure that she was eating. Hearing the intercom ring, Valeria had learned just to hit the button to let her in.

Swinging the door open, she was stunned to see the boy at the door!

"Caleb!"

"Um, yeah…can I come in?" Somehow, Caleb looked older than when she had seen him just over a month ago in Greece.

"Of course!" He stepped into her apartment and she looked outside the door, realizing that she was praying that Alex was with him. He immediately wrapped his arms around her waist. She brushed his hair back and took several deep breaths and then gulped, needing to hold on to him probably more than he needed to hold on to her. After several minutes she was able to push back the tears and speak. "Caleb, did…someone…send you here?" She wasn't sure what she could say.

He released her and tramped into the living room where he threw his body down on the couch. "Boy, this place is small!" He peeled the clear gloves off his hands that protected others from being shocked. Then he noticed all of the family pictures sitting on the coffee table. Weege had tried to place them around the brownstone, but Valeria needed them close to her.

"Yes, it is small," she responded. Caleb picked up the picture of the two of them and the joy in their eyes.

Suddenly, she thought of the laws and couldn't bear to think of sweet Caleb being harmed. "Buddy…you do know that there are new rules." She would take Caleb and disappear and warn the others. Perhaps they would all join her and she could be with Alex! Of course, it wouldn't be fair to them, but she would die before she permitted Jeremiah to harm one hair on the boy's head!

He shrugged and gave a short laugh with none of the joy that was typical of him. "Yeah…well, I'm not an oracle. So, nobody cares about where I go…well, I mean outside of the family."

She breathed a sigh of relief and sat down next to him on the couch. "How did you get here?" She stroked her hand through his black, curly hair.

He swallowed sadly. "I get a new passport every five years. They think I'm 18 and still look like a kid. Once they see my passport, and my credit cards—no one questions my age."

"How did you find me?"

His face dropped, hurt. "I know that the rest of the family doesn't believe me. But I thought that you would! I'm here because I'm supposed to find you for Alex. I'm your compass, remember?" *That name!*

"Caleb, are you permitted to talk about…him?"

"I can talk about anything I want," he said casually. "It's only everybody else who can't talk to you." He slumped and pouted. "I *really* wanted to be a best man!"

Valeria swallowed and closed her eyes, breathing deeply. "Maybe someday…Caleb…how is…everyone."

"Mostly…sad." He thought for a moment. "Especially Alex." He swallowed back the emotion.

She tried to subdue a cry. Sweet, sweet Caleb…so sensitive!

"I've never seen Alex so sad," he said softly. "Lars told

me that Alex could never be with you again..." He stopped, noticing Valeria's reaction to his words. "Val..." His expression became one of pain. "I would hate it if that was true!"

After minutes of trying to find her voice, Valeria said, "Caleb, does anyone know where you are?"

"I left a note." Caleb's eyes evaluated her with such earnestness, that she wondered how she could hide her feelings from him. "Val?" She bit her lip to stave off the tears. "If Alex really can't ever be with you...well...I'm getting older all the time. I could be a man in a few more years, if you want. And...well, I don't probably know how to care about you like Alex does. But if you can wait a few more years, I'll be your friend...probably not as good a friend as Alex...but..." He sucked in his breath nervously.

She tried to smile, but broke down in tears. "Thank you, Caleb!" She closed her eyes, needing to change the subject. It took her five minutes before she could talk. He nervously rubbed her back. She selfishly wanted him to stay here. It was a reminder and a connection that proved that somewhere out there, that magical life really had existed.

Maybe, via Caleb, Alex and Valeria could communicate like George Bernard Shaw and Ellen Terry —"a paper courtship"—except never with their own words of passion that Alex and Valeria had written. Even if that would be permitted, Valeria would vehemently disagree with Shaw that a paper courtship was "Perhaps the pleasantest of all courtships." But at least it was communication with her beloved...her Alex. Then, just as quickly, she realized that she could not place her family in jeopardy for her own desires—regardless of how desperately she needed him. And it was unfair to place Caleb in that position. He was twelve and could touch only one person in this world. To permit his crush on her to continue was cruel.

"Caleb, you need to call Alex now. He will be worried about you." Had she really been able to say that without crying? She thought she sounded almost normal.

"My phone is out of juice."

"Where's the cord?" she asked.

He shrugged. "I guess I forgot it...well, kind of on purpose."

Valeria nodded. The trembling in her had taken on a new dimension. Caleb needed to call Alex...he would talk to Alex while she was next to Caleb. She might be able to hear his voice...he might hear hers. *Oh, to hear his voice again!*

She fumbled through her purse, and sat her cell phone on the table instead of handing it to him, so that he wouldn't see how clammy her skin was. "Here...call him. Tell him where you are." Her heart rate continued to climb, as she imagined what he might think when he saw her number ringing.

Caleb looked at her, hurt, and nodded almost imperceptibly.

She heard Alex's desperate answer, *"Val!"*

"No...it's me," Caleb pouted. She could hear a gasp on the other end of the phone. She turned away from Caleb so he wouldn't see her jaw quivering.

Then the tears began to roll down her face again and there was no stopping or hiding them. Valeria needed to calm her tears to be able to sit next to Caleb and hear Alex's voice.

"Oh! Caleb." There was a long pause. *"Are you...is she there?"*

"Yeah...yeah...Alex, she's really sad, too." Involuntarily, a sob escaped her mouth and she knew that Alex heard her. No one said anything for several minutes. Alex and Valeria both needed the connection—and Caleb seemed to understand it. She had to get control of herself. But to hear his voice was...a miracle...a gift!

"Caleb," she said, as she brushed the tears from her face and tried to find her voice, "please tell him that you will be home tomorrow."

"She's sending me home tomorrow," he said, reluctantly.

There was a long silence.

"Caleb, do you want...should someone come and get you?" she heard him say. Valeria knew how it would tear her heart out to fly Caleb home to Italy, only to reboard the plane without seeing Alex. She desperately wanted the connection but she couldn't do that to him. She dropped her face into her hands, working hard to ease the sobs.

"She's crying, Alex," Caleb said, sounding like he was ready to break down. She could tell that Alex was sobbing too. She couldn't tell him anything directly or even ask Caleb to deliver a message. That would violate the agreement.

At last finding her voice, she said softly, "Caleb, it would be best if Alex picked you up at the airport in Florence," she choked out. And then in a little more than a whisper she said, "And...I...uh...I..." a thought came to her. "Caleb, I'm going to give you a little reading assignment," she sniffed, her voice getting stronger. "Perhaps someone...back at Morgana could help you with it."

She could hear Alex's pained breathing...and then suddenly the connection was gone. They had been disconnected. It was better that way. Neither of them could have said goodbye...and Caleb knew it.

That night, Caleb was disappointed to discover that Valeria, *an American*, didn't have a TV. He had heard that everyone in America had at least one! But she bought him a charger for his phone and took him down to Times Square and even to a movie. It was so good to have his company. She needed to be strong. She needed to make her body strong. Before taking Caleb to the airport, passing him on to her beloved, she gave him his assignment to discover the author and full content of the passage she gave him. The passage read,

"Love is not love,
Which alters when it alteration finds,
Or bends with the remover to remove:
O, no! it is an ever-fixed mark."

Shakespeare's sonnets had become a favorite during her recovery in Trento, especially when Alex read them to her. This one was bookmarked on his shelf as her favorite.

Hugging Caleb tightly for about the tenth time, and probably embarrassing him, she finally let go as the sobs muffled her voice. Then she asked him to please take care of the people whom she loved, including himself! Then she watched as her twelve-year-old superhero carried his backpack through security. Several security people looked at his passport and then shrugged, permitting him into the terminal. He had to wear his anti-shock suit as he would be in close proximity to a lot of people but at least it wasn't visible. He turned once before he rounded the corner. Instead of the emptiness of the past month, she somehow felt that, regardless of the fact that it was temporary, Caleb was stringing a line across the Atlantic to that world with the beautiful cottage north of Trento.

∞

Finally resting in her bed, instead of restlessly dozing on the couch, Valeria sensed his presence and pulled his arms around her waist in her dream. His hands brushed along her fingers and then threaded and locked on hers. She pushed into the curl of his body as she dozed happily. Then she realized how vividly she could smell that wonderful blend of aftershave and soap—that was uniquely *his*. She felt his sweet kisses on her neck. Her eyes flew open as she turned and blinked twice. His extraordinary face was there, inches from hers. All she could do was stare at him, thinking it was a hallucination.

"Hi, beautiful!"

She threw her arms around his neck and drank in the feel of him. If she was dreaming, she didn't want to wake up. "How did you…?" she whispered into his neck. Alex pulled back and gently touched his finger over her mouth.

"I've been working on this," he replied. "It's not perfect…but it is better than the alternative!"

"Are we going to run away together?" she asked, clinging to him.

"In a manner of speaking." He stroked her face. "I decided that since we are spiritual beings, we should be able to master this tiny little problem." The corners of his mouth turned up in the way that she loved and then he gently brushed the hair from her face, looking at her intensely. "Here's the thing, Val. They may try to tell us that our bodies can't be together, but they can't control our minds, our hearts…our souls!" She smiled as the tears streamed down her face. He continued, "You feel it don't you. I'm with you always—just look." His eyes filled with great yearning. "Let me be with you."

"Always!" she whispered.

"I'm sending you some…well…some people whom I think can help us with this problem. You've already met them."

"I don't need anyone else, if you're with me."

His face got somber. "Val," he gazed up, "we need help." He shook his head. "This…is a lousy substitute." Then his eyes got playful as he reached for her hand, and said, "Now…let's play!" And then they disappeared into the blackness.

∞

He sat on the edge of the bed with her head cradled in his arms as his lips moved over hers and then brushed against her forehead. She felt no fear, no loneliness, no empty longing, only his love. She opened her eyes again and saw him smiling at her with absolute adoration and then sleepily, she closed them again and felt his hand brush her hair back from her face.

"Sleep," he murmured softly as his arms laid her head gently back on the pillow and his hand stroked her face. She sighed and turned her face to the side, kissing his hand. She barely heard him when he whispered in her ear, "I have to go now, beautiful. And you have things to do."

"No!" she cried, and bolted up in the bed. He was gone. She glanced over, but her door was closed. Still, she could smell his wonderful scent and she could feel his presence. Brushing her fingers over her mouth, she could still feel where his mouth had been only moments before. And then she remembered the Gretchen Kemp poem that he had shared with her when he proposed: "There's this place where your kisses still linger." It was the same quote that was engraved on the face of his watch. Could it have been a hallucination?

Expecting to feel slammed back down into the well of pain, she was surprised to discover that she felt strangely invigorated. She took a deep breath. It was time for confronting. She forced herself to get up and dress, then she ate some Greek yogurt that Weege had stocked in her refrigerator. It didn't have any taste to her but she forced herself to eat.

Then she put on her sneakers and walked out the door. The clouds were low and thick covering the tops of the skyscrapers. The pavement was wet from a recent rain, and it was cold enough that she could see her breath. Suddenly, she realized that every day when she avoided the places where *they* had been together, her life was that much smaller. She had to walk to the park where they met but, as she neared it, the tears began to flow...*hadn't they run out yet?* Then she began to run.

She ran down the path that she and Alex had walked over and over until she could do it without breaking down more than once. The cherry blossoms had started to bloom and she noticed that the man Alex had given money to was no longer there—as he had been every day for years before she had met Alex. Getting up her courage and strength, she ran down 5th Avenue where Alex had first saved her life.

Steam came off a nut vendor's machine, and she was surprised that it smelled good. She wasn't hungry, but she considered that major progress! Glancing at the spot where Alex had rescued her from the speeding red Mustang she recalled the feeling of his arms wrapped protectively around her as they flew into the air and then struck the sidewalk. Valeria glanced up to see the vendor who Alex had seemed to know. Her sobs lasted for only five minutes. And then she ran more. She ran until she couldn't catch her breath, until her sides stung and her legs trembled.

The next day she tried to walk into Sarabeth's. But the waitress, Katie, who had served her the only other time she had been inside, with Alex, came to take Valeria's order and she stood and left sobbing. She forced herself to eat at a restaurant a block down and had a veggie omelet and French pressed coffee. The food stayed down and she was actually able to walk home without any major tears. She did that every day for two months.

CHAPTER 10

The boardroom was filled with mostly corporate executives, and a few floral artists. Valeria wasn't crazy about the executives nor was she crazy about standing in front of them *or* wearing a business suit. But it kept her busy. And one day a week, it gave her something to do besides reread her favorite books and run…and avoid thinking of Alex.

She continued with the presentation, "That's a lot of data, I know. But what it all boils down to is that the success of The Secret Garden was because our artists felt free to experiment. I believe that Townsend Investments can best duplicate that success by creating a culture where creativity is not only embraced, but encouraged at every level!"

Suddenly, the glass door opened and in came Holly and Peg with a rolling cart topped with a birthday cake for Reggie Cotton. Valeria said, "Ahhh, isn't that nice," but her face revealed her true feelings.

Moments later, Valeria was briskly walking down the hall of cubicles when Weege joined her. Pointing an accusatory finger at Weege she said, "If you ever give Holly and Peg my birthday information—I will…I will disown you!"

Weege rolled her eyes. "It's just a party! What's the big deal? I mean, would anything be wrong with being just a tad bit social?"

Glancing briefly at Weege, she said, "Social? No thanks. I spent almost three years in foster homes—that was social enough for a lifetime! And let me tell you—after you understand true human nature, you know that it is just not worth it."

"Man, they really screwed with you, didn't they?"

Slowing her pace, Valeria shrugged. "No. Really none of it was a big deal. I just…I just didn't connect. I didn't understand them. They seemed so…different."

Weege pulled Valeria to a stop. "Do I seem different? Like them?"

Ever since Weege had seen Valeria's meltdown at Sarabeth's, she had been incredibly sensitive. Valeria tried to decide what to tell her friend. Certainly, Valeria was closer to Weege than to anyone outside of her new family, but not close enough to tell her about Alex.

Cocking her head to the side, Valeria smiled kindly at her friend. "No. You seem like Weege—my closest friend in New York!"

On the other hand, Valeria had never hesitated in telling Alex or Camille anything. As a matter of fact, she trusted almost everyone at Morgana on a different level from the rest of the world. Valeria shrugged to herself, thinking for the first time that perhaps she really wasn't such an emotional cripple. Maybe it was everyone else who was screwed up. She smiled at her thought—until she saw Holly and Peg heading toward them. They had taken the bypass around the building to cut her off.

"Hi, Val, we finally got the scoop on you!" Holly snipped. "I knew you were a Libra!"

Peg narrowed her eyes. "But probably a Capricorn rising is my guess." Holly looked to Peg, who nodded.

Leaning in toward Valeria, Peg added with glee, "I had no idea you were older than me!" Valeria noticed Weege about to pounce, Valeria held her arm out toward Weege, in assurance that this would be handled. Peg was most certainly at least ten years older than Valeria.

"Libra?" Valeria's eyes narrowed in thought as she looked at Weege. "Isn't that…hmmm isn't that…?"

"In the fall." Holly smiled, pleased with her secret knowledge.

Valeria shrugged, wide-eyed. "Well, I'm not sure where you got your information…What sign is the beginning of March? Isn't that Aries?"

"I told you, that's Pisces!" Weege interjected, playing along.

"Oh, yeah…that's right, Pisces." Valeria said.

Holly and Peg nodded, both obviously confused. Satisfied that she hadn't lied, but had thrown them way off track, Valeria continued walking. She smiled pleasantly, but as soon as they passed Peg and Holly, her glare turned toward Weege.

"I did not tell them a thing! I swear!" Weege continued, "They bribe Frank, in accounting. They keep a list of everyone and their astrological sign and who is older than them…well and then they lie."

They turned into the corporate gym and Valeria pushed open the door to the ladies' locker room.

"See what I mean, Weege?" She opened her locker and pulled out a water bottle with a thick green liquid. She took a long swig before stepping out of her heels.

Grotesquely eyeing the contents of the bottle, Weege

exclaimed, "What the hell are you drinking?"

"A kale and strawberry smoothie." Valeria set her drink on the wood bench and pulled her sports bag from the locker to change into her running clothes.

Sitting down on the other side of the bag, Weege rubbed her hands together anxiously. "So, what are you wearing tonight? Dress corporate okay? Looks hot on you. Looks," Weege looked down at herself, "decidedly not hot on me. But on you it's—"

"Got it." Valeria interrupted. "I'm wearing this." Valeria pulled jeans and a T-shirt from her bag.

Shaking her head, Weege said in disapproval, "Go for your run. Then take a shower!" Weege smiled, as if she had to say that to Valeria. "Then change into something sexy."

"*Oh, my God*, Weege! This is a set-up, isn't it?"

Shaking her head innocently, Weege continued, "You could show off your arms and wear a tank!" Valeria looked at her, irritated. "Well, if you feel the need to be covered, you could wear that gorgeous burgundy silk sweater you have in the front of your closet, the color's great," Weege thought for a moment, "although it's probably too big for you. Yeah…something more fitted would be good." Weege was talking about Alex's sweater so Valeria didn't even bother to respond. "I take that as a 'no.' Well, how about putting on some heels."

"I swear that if this is a set-up, I'm out of there without so much as a social response! Do you understand?" Valeria glared at Weege.

"Well…no. No. It's not a set-up." She cocked her head to the side. "No, not really. It's just some of us from corporate getting together."

"And?" Valeria asked suspiciously.

"Look, you don't have to like this guy. He's just a good

guy…and he's very sexy." Her eyes lit up at the words. "And I thought it would be a good fit. I mean, *you never know*—"

Valeria interrupted Weege, "I *know!*" she said, as she turned her face toward her locker so that Weege couldn't see the tears.

"Look sweetie, you don't have to do anything. You don't have to talk to this guy or even make eye contact for that matter. But I told him that you would be there. If there's no spark—nothing lost. Besides, this guy is golf buddies with my big boss. It would help me out a lot if you would just come with me."

"You are fortunate that I am such a good friend. I will go there with you. I may even say hello to this guy. But I will explain that I am not on the market. And if you do this again, I won't show up. Okay?" She finished tying her running shoes and then stood and loaded her clothes back into her locker.

"Okay. But, wear the heels, okay."

"I'm wearing what I have or else I'm going home for the evening." Weege rolled her eyes. Valeria picked up her sports bag. "Home or out?"

Weege shrugged, irritated. "Well, can you at least do your hair? Please don't just shower and throw it in a ponytail! Guys like a chick's hair down."

"I like it in a ponytail!" She tossed her bag back in the locker. "See you tonight."

∞

They arrived at Sardi's at 7:30 p.m. and it was packed.

"They're upstairs." Weege shouted as they worked their way around the crowded foyer and up the circular mahogany staircase that looked like it was from the Hollywood hay days. Following Weege closely, Valeria hoped this guy wasn't expecting her to be nice. She wasn't in the mood for "nice" tonight. In fact, she had to ignore the fact that this might turn into a set-up, because, frankly, it made her stomach feel weak. She really didn't want to think about anyone...but *him*.

From the staircase she could see into the dining room and although Valeria wouldn't know most celebrities even if they told her their name, she saw Dan Akroyd and Donna Dixon talking with an enamored tourist. In another part of the room was Kirk Douglas...*Kirk Douglas!* Weege and Valeria laughed at a couple of the cartoon caricatures that covered the walls.

Upstairs the bar was packed. She recognized a few faces from the negotiation of the sale of her florist shop and in her six month transition. She said hello, noticed all of them had wedding rings on, except for a few of the gay guys. They sat down at the bar and Valeria ordered a glass of chardonnay and Weege ordered an Appletini. After twenty minutes, Weege was getting concerned.

"Where is he?" Weege said, irritated, while continuing to scan the bar.

The thrill of it hit Valeria—she had been stood up! And by a guy who had gone to extraordinary measures to get a date with her. Chuckling to herself, she ordered another Chardonnay. The bartender was busy, but seemed to be ensuring that he was there for her. He winked seductively. What a game it was, Valeria thought with a laugh. Just then, Weege's phone rang. She looked at her phone. "It's him," she said. And then she covered her other ear so that she could hear over the bar chatter. "Yeah?" she said into the phone and jumped up and began looking around. "Oh! There you are! Yeah. Coming right over." She put her phone back in her purse. "He has a table for us." Damn, Valeria thought, she was about to head back to her brownstone.

She had to say that this guy had really blown it! Maybe he

had reconsidered and had decided that Valeria wasn't the girl for him. Or maybe he was slick and that was his intention; let her have a few drinks before he tried to pick her up. She decided she would be kind and explain to the guy that he should have been on time and purchased her drinks instead of hiding out like a coward....or words to that effect.

"You're going to be so impressed with this guy!" Weege was buzzing with anticipation. Valeria paid her tab, and then pulled her purse and sweater from the chair. As they approached the table in the back corner of the bar, she noted that he was sitting with his back to her. *What?* He didn't even stand up? Was he too good to come and meet her? Finally, he stood and pulled out a chair in the corner for her. Rude! He signaled for Weege to sit at the outside chair. This clown had a lot to know about being a gentleman. But then she had been spoiled by Alex...badly spoiled. She gulped back the thought. She preferred to be irritated.

As she pushed past him to the only other seat at the table, he moved to the right, effectively trapping her in the corner. She sat her wine down and pulled her sweater over her shoulder.

Having just turned back around, she heard Weege say, "Val, Paolo. Paolo, Val."

Valeria's jaw dropped in horror and then repulsion. Weege noticed but didn't seem troubled by her expression. "All right, well, I'm going to leave you two alone." She giggled and disappeared in the crowd.

The effect on Valeria's body was immediate and intense, a chill ran down her, and then just as suddenly, her entire body began trembling violently. Even if she could have found her voice, there were no words to describe what she felt.

She had to get out of there! He was blocking the way out. She would have to find another way. Leaning one hand on the wall and the other on the table, she crawled over the chair and table, almost dumping them—thank God she wore her running shoes!

Fighting her way around the chairs and tables, cocktail waitresses with full trays, and a large mass of people, she moved, for once, without an apology or an "Excuse me, please." From the corner of her eye she was certain she saw him following her. Suddenly, she was about to vomit! She covered her mouth as she broke into the restroom and pressed on stall doors until one opened, just as her stomach seized. It felt as if it would never stop, even though her stomach was mostly empty. Finally, the powerful spasms in her stomach ended and she went to the sink and rinsed her mouth. Then she realized, Oh, God…he would be waiting for her when she came out! She went back to the stall and locked the door.

How could she speak to someone who had robbed her of the only people she loved in this world and *the one person who she couldn't live without?* He had plotted and planned and then just as she was about to have everything that she could desire in life, he had ripped it from her grasp the night before her wedding!

Earlier, she had been certain that she would not be able to stop herself from hurting him if she ever saw him. Now, here she was! Oh, God! She hadn't actually cried since Caleb had left and she was determined that she wouldn't cry now. How could he have the nerve to try and meet with her? *She would never speak to him.* She wished she was the kind of woman who could slap a man. She wanted to hurt him, to humiliate him for everything he had done…and instead, coward that she was, she hid in the bathroom stall.

The bathroom door opened. "Val?" It was Weege.

"Tell him to leave!" was all she could say.

Knocking on the door to the stall, Weege said softly,

"Honey, open up. Okay?"

"Tell him to leave! Just do that! Just tell him to leave!" She felt herself getting hysterical.

"Okay. Okay, honey," Weege whispered. "I don't know what happened with you and Alex, but, Val, Paolo is right outside the door and he can hear everything you say.

"I explained to him that you just went through a rough break-up. He says he just wants to make sure you're all right." Valeria didn't know how to respond. "Honey, did Paolo say something that upset you? He says he didn't even say hello before you took off." Weege knocked again. "He's really a nice guy, he said—"

Valeria felt the hysteria take over. She screamed, "You tell that son-of-a-bitch...you tell him that I will *never* want to see him. Never! Get rid of him! You tell him to get the hell out of my life!"

Nausea overtook Valeria and she turned and vomited again. Weege knocked on the door to the stall. "Okay... It's okay. I understand. This is about Alex. It's probably just too soon. No problem. Come on out, okay, honey?"

Something snapped in Valeria. She realized that she wasn't a coward...and she certainly wasn't afraid of Paolo! She opened the door of the stall and pushed past Weege and the five women holding out in the restroom waiting to witness the event. She rinsed her mouth and washed her trembling hands then splashed some cool water on her face, all while Weege stood looking helpless. She patted the water from her face with a towel. The other women in the restroom continued to watch, trying to pretend to be engaged in other activities, like lipstick application, obviously afraid they would miss the action when Valeria went postal on the man outside. That's all right—she was stronger now. He had already taken everything she loved. There was *nothing* else he could take from her now!

She pushed open the bathroom door and marched directly past him without even looking at him. If he touched her, *he would regret it!* She walked around the front of the bar and down the stairs with Weege following her to the door. "Val, wait! I need to get my purse!" But Valeria wasn't waiting. She bolted, running past the Shubert Theater and then up 8th Avenue. She ran two blocks and then stopped, choking on a sudden sob that held her hostage. She leaned down on her knees as one long sob went through her and then she pushed it back. She wasn't going to cry anymore.

When she finally stood back up, Paolo was behind her looking concerned. Valeria looked at him and, again, no words would come from her mouth...and then something that was angry and animal arose in her. *She would make him hurt!* The street was still crowed with tourists when she swung her purse at his head, hitting him in the face, then she began punching him with her fists and kicking him. The tourists stared at her like this was just the sort of behavior they expected from a New Yorker. Then the tears started flowing, increasing with each punch or kick, becoming tears of rage and then pain. He didn't defend himself. He didn't need to. He wasn't hurt by her efforts.

When she realized that fact, she shook her head and said quietly, dangerously, "If you ever come near me again, I will kill you! I don't care if I spend the rest of my life in jail. I'm already dead!" She turned and began to walk down the street, feeling empowered, and a little less dead than she had felt in months!

Finally, he spoke with no anger or charm. "Bella, I had to do what I did. You would do the same thing for your family." Valeria ignored him and flagged a cab. One angled in, and she waited until she was in the seat and the door was closed before giving the cabbie her address.

It was silly. If he could find Weege and set-up this elaborate scene, he knew everything he needed to know about her. He had prepped Weege well. The set-up in the bar was perfect so that she was forced to see him. He knew she would attack him. He was prepared for that, too.

An hour later, Weege showed up at Valeria's. But Valeria didn't want any company—except Alex. She *needed* Alex. But he didn't come back to her. She had lain in her bed and willed him to come to her night after night, with no response. Now she was certain that it must have been a dream or a hallucination.

Still, sometimes she had the feeling that his lips were there, inches from hers. And sometimes, she felt like he was thinking about her, especially when she was running. Didn't he know that she needed him now? If it had been real, and it *had* to be real, she needed him. Weege kept pounding and apologizing until one of the neighbors started yelling at her to shut up. Now, Valeria listened as Weege and the neighbor had it out verbally. But Valeria had gotten her keys back from Weege and just didn't want to talk. She hoped Weege would leave. How could she explain all this? Then she realized that she couldn't.

In her bed, she tried over and over to recreate the moment when Alex had come to her. She drifted again into a restless, dreamless state.

∞

The next day, Valeria drank her coffee and then went to Zabar's for groceries. She wore her sunglasses as a protective mechanism—she wasn't in the mood to talk. She picked up kale, strawberries, more coffee, and cream and then walked back to her brownstone, sighing with relief after seeing no signs of Paolo.

Maybe she could get a restraining order. Valeria wondered if there were any complexities in getting restraining orders against immortals...she didn't even know his last name. Did he even have one? Back at her brownstone she blended the kale and strawberries and drank it down.

Why didn't Alex come back to her, like he did that time? That was real...she had to believe it was real! Maybe she had gone insane, like Cassandra. Valeria changed into her running clothes. She ran to the park and around the reservoir. Everything was in bloom. She realized that no matter the time of year, there was never a time when she didn't love the view of the skyscrapers about the rich green foliage. She could feel Alex's love and then she remembered something that he said, "I'm sending you some people who I think can help us with this problem. We need help!"

Had Alex intended to get help from Paolo? No! But then his last words to her in Greece were that Paolo had loved her. Alex had to know that she would *never* be with Paolo. But maybe Paolo had something that could help them resolve this. Maybe he knew where Kristiana was. Alex had to know that Valeria could never violate her loyalties or even pretend that she had anything but repulsion for Paolo. Still, maybe there was a way to get what she wanted. Maybe Paolo could understand how she felt about Alex. If Paolo had ever loved her, maybe he would drop this ridiculous petition.

Valeria ran to the Bow Bridge overlooking the pond. She stopped to stretch, throwing one of her legs on top of the wrought iron rail, while glancing down at the rowboats in the narrow pond below. She heard his voice from behind her.

"Bella?"

She froze. Finally, she lowered her leg from the bridge and turned. "Why are you following me?" she asked hostilely.

He stepped forward with a shrug and she sensed his nervousness. "Bella…Valeria, I know you are very angry with me. But I did what I had to do. You would do the same."

With no recognition or evaluation of the statement, she slapped Paolo with all of her might. His face turned from her effort. She noticed with pleasure, the red, angry mark on his face. She had finally made an impression!

She glared at him with venom in her eyes. "What do you want from me?"

Paolo looked down. "I want to make it up to you."

"There is only one way you can even begin to make it up. And until you are willing to do that, we have nothing to discuss." She turned and started to walk away.

"Yes…you are right." He spoke with no hint of the arrogance that she had heard before. "That is what I am offering." Valeria stopped. Was this a trick? Of course it was.

She didn't turn. "If that's what you were offering, Alex would be here. Not you."

"It's a proposition."

Valeria turned around. "Go on."

Paolo knew better than to reach for her. He evaluated her. "Maybe we should discuss this over lunch. You have lost too much weight."

"My weight is none of your business!" She glared at him. "Besides, you ruin my appetite. It's here or nothing."

Paolo nodded. "I think I like you better like this than the sweet, young girl I married."

"Yeah, and I liked you better when you were *gone!*" She took a few steps toward him, "You need to understand this— you may have taken advantage of a fifteen-year-old girl who looked like me, but *don't you ever*, for even one moment, think that you can talk to me that way now. Do you understand?" Paolo looked down and nodded. "Get to the point," she demanded.

"I want to see you."

"Not in your dreams!" She started to walk away.

"I will allow you to see him." It stopped her in her tracks as her heart suddenly lurched into her throat. She turned to look at him and felt her heart pounding heavily in anticipation. *Oh, God, what she would do to see him!*

"I don't believe anything you say," she said cautiously.

Paolo looked at her and his eyes softened. "You have my oath on it." She felt her heart rate increase and she feared her emotions would overtake her if she didn't remember that he was a con man.

"What? I have to whore myself out to you and in exchange…" She gave him a look of vile disgust, but inside she knew that she would do anything for five more minutes in Alex's arms.

"No, Bella. There are many opportunities for me, if that was all that I desired. I want you to spend time with me." She rolled her eyes in disbelief.

"What's the catch?" she asked suspiciously. A breeze suddenly moved through the greenery around the bridge and she thought she caught that blend of aftershave and soap on the air. Was it because they were talking about him?

"No catch." Paolo shrugged. "I believe that if you spend time with me you will get over your affliction for Alex. I am certain that you will realize that it is you and I who belong together."

Releasing a short, caustic laugh, she rolled her eyes. "That will *never* happen!"

"That is a risk I am willing to take. Of course, if you are too afraid to risk the possibility that you and Alex are not meant to be together…"

"I'm not afraid of you. I hate you." The only emotion she

felt at that moment was a well-hidden desperate desire to see Alex…and her obvious hatred of Paolo. "There is no risk for me, except that you won't perform as agreed."

"Oh, I always perform." He winked seductively. "Well then," Paolo smirked, "I will see you this evening."

"Not so fast. What's the agreement?"

He looked up as if he was calculating but she knew that he would have considered all of this long before he arrived. "I will see you two weeks a month for a year and then you can see him for one day." She calculated quickly.

"You think I would do that? I will go out with you for a month one time a week, four dates, and then you withdraw this ridiculous petition!"

"I cannot withdraw the petition. That would require a scheduled council meeting. Besides, it is in defense of my sister. But I can amend it. So eight months spending every weekend with me and then I will let you see him for eight hours."

She narrowed her eyes and shook her head. Truly she was willing to do anything she needed to for any time with Alex. And she knew that Paolo also knew that. "Three months, one date a week. Then you give me a weekend with Alex."

"I cannot give you overnight visits or I have violated our laws. Your visit can be no more than a day."

Leaning on the bridge, her eyes tightened as she had seen the attorneys do in negotiation. "Last offer: I see you for three months, two dates a week. No physical contact. At the end of the three months, you permit me twelve hours with Alex."

"Yes. But just so that you understand, I will not be offended if you wish to have physical contact with me. But I cannot permit you to have any physical contact with him."

A chance to see Alex, in three months! Valeria was certain her face flushed. "All right. I won't ever want you. But I insist on seeing Alex alone."

"I agree to all of your terms, except again, it would be a violation for you to be alone with him. You may, however, be with him in a public place," Paolo said, and she gave him a slight nod. While they both displayed a level of seriousness, inside they were both doing a victory dance...for very different reasons. "The first date is tonight. Be ready at six."

CHAPTER 11

Paolo hadn't asked for her address or what she would like to do. Still, the intercom rang at precisely six p.m. She didn't let him into her building. In fact, she didn't even answer the intercom. Instead, she came down the stairs and met him outside. Paolo was dressed immaculately in designer silk pants and a button down light blue shirt, opened at the collar. She, on the other hand, wore her yoga pants, a T-shirt covered by Alex's gray jacket, and flip-flops, with her hair in a ponytail. He had flowers for her. She knew her flowers and this was a very expensive and beautiful design. She momentarily appreciated them then shrugged and tossed them into the trash can on the street.

The car took them to a nearby marina on the Upper West Side. He offered his hand to help her out of the limo. She completely ignored his hand and stepped around him, avoiding eye contact.

"I thought we would go out on my yacht." There was a forty-five-foot sailboat named "The Isabella" in the marina. "I named it for you."

"I don't like the water," she said flatly. "And that's not my name."

Paolo ignored her comments. "I think you will like this, bella. It is a beautiful evening."

Shaking her head, she muttered, "It's just one down, twenty-three to go." She boarded the yacht.

"Bella, three months, two dates per week is twenty-seven." He lifted an eyebrow. "I expect you to pay in full!" he said.

Her eyes narrowed; she knew the math. "Understand that the bargaining points are as discussed. There is no contract that includes physical contact."

The yacht pulled out into the Hudson and she had to admit that the temperature was delightful on the water.

"We will eat now, I think," he commanded.

She sat at a table in the rear of the yacht that was set with white linens and china; a man in a white-tailed tuxedo brought out a bottle of fine wine. She was repulsed by just the idea that she was on Paolo's yacht. She tapped her fingers anxiously on the table. *Would this evening ever end?* Oh, how she wanted to be any place but here! Still, the results were that she would get to see Alex. She had to keep her mind on the prize!

Paolo nodded at the label on the wine and the server opened it smoothly. Just as Paolo was about to taste the wine, Valeria's face suddenly lit up. "May I see the bottle?" she asked the server.

"Bella, I did not realize you were a connoisseur." He nodded to the server to show Valeria the bottle.

Eyeing the label for a moment, she said, "Nice vintage." Not that she would know a good vintage from a bad one. Frankly, she didn't even know what a vintage was—except she had heard Alex say that occasionally.

Then, to the server's horror, she took the bottle from him.

Taking a quick swig from the bottle, she rose and lumbered down the stairs, through the interior hallway, opening each door until she had located the bathroom. She glanced back, expecting to see Paolo raging; instead, saw that he was actually shaking his head in amusement. He wouldn't be so amused after she spent the rest of the cruise in there! She locked the door and swigged the wine, feeling quite pleased with herself! It was just the sort of thing David, her ex-boyfriend, and the rest of his diplomatic crowd, would describe as vulgar. After ten minutes, Paolo knocked on the door.

"Bella…"

"Don't call me that!"

There was a beat and then he said, "Valeria, is it all right if I call you that?"

She thought about it for a while. She really wanted to say, *Don't call me anything! As a matter-of-fact, don't call me at all!* But instead, after a few moments, she said softly, "Okay."

"Valeria, we are moving into the harbor. I thought you would like to eat while we circle Liberty Island. We can stop there if you like…or perhaps you would like to see Ellis Island?"

"I prefer the company in here."

"Valeria, if you stay in there you will be seasick."

"I'll take my chances," she retorted and rolled her eyes as she took another swig.

He sighed, "Bell—Valeria, you are not spending the evening with me. If you stay in there the rest of the night, I cannot count this as part of our agreement."

Immediately, she opened the door and pushed past him. "Alright," she sighed deeply, and then turned to him, lifting an eyebrow. "Do I owe you an additional ten minutes? Or can we count your invasion of my privacy earlier today?" He began to answer but she turned away from him and continued to the deck. "And while we are at it, are there any other rules I should know about?" She walked past the elegantly set table to a cushion on the back corner of the yacht and sat down.

The yacht circled the Statue of Liberty and, looking back across the blue harbor, she could see the deep green of Battery Park and, further north, the skyscrapers of Manhattan. It really was quite magnificent. Valeria had drunk less than a quarter of the bottle when she asked for a bottle of water. Paolo instructed the crew to serve dinner. Valeria's sat untouched.

"The sea bass is delicious. You really should try it, Valeria," he took another bite of his dinner, "especially if you insist on drinking heavily."

She had eaten before they left so that she would not be forced to eat while looking at him. "Don't worry; I may get drunk, but not drunk enough to ever forget who you are and what you did."

The cruise ended with Valeria refusing to eat any of the food that Paolo's staff had prepared. Despite that, he continued to be gracious. He took her home in the limo and even walked her to her door where she put her hand out toward his chest, holding him at arms distance. "Trust me, you don't want to try anything with me!" He sighed as he nodded and took a step back from her.

"I plan to pick you up at seven a.m. tomorrow."

Valeria looked at him as if he was insane. "It's two dates a week and you need to schedule it with me in advance!"

"Can I see you tomorrow morning at seven a.m.?"

She thought about it. The faster the subsequent twenty-six dates were over and done with, the sooner she could see Alex! She shrugged. "I may as well get it over with and then I don't have to see you the rest of the week. But I want this clear—I am not spending all day with you. Maximum date length is four hours."

"Five hours. Seven a.m. tomorrow?"

Valeria shrugged again before turning to run up the flight of stairs, quickly unlocking her door. She flew into her flat and slammed the door shut, as if blocking out her memories, and then threw the deadbolt. Leaning against the door for a moment, she fought the mounting emotion. She went to her bed, her eyes filled with tears. "Alex, where are you?" she choked.

She arose at six to go for an early morning run and by seven she was showered and dressed in sweats. He picked her up and had coffee waiting for her in the limo, but she refused— a first for her, especially considering that she had barely had one cup, let alone the two cups that she allowed herself each morning.

They drove to a field in New Jersey where hot air balloons were being filled. Her heart lurched; the memory of her only time in a hot air balloon flooded into her mind and, for a moment, she allowed her memory to take her back to Venice. She bit her lip hard to keep from crying. *How could she balloon with Paolo?* Hiding behind her sunglasses, she turned her head to look out the window in attempted nonchalance, knowing that her nose had turned red from the threat of tears.

It was a beautiful morning but Valeria remained in the limo, studying her cell phone as if there was something on it that was actually of interest to her. When Paolo came to join her, she got out and engaged a group from another balloon in conversation.

Once they were ready to launch, she climbed into the basket, with Paolo behind her; as the balloon rose, the pilot offered her some champagne. She took the bottle, thanked him, and slid down to sit on the floor of the basket so that she couldn't see anything. She would not, and could not, enjoy the view with Paolo. She didn't want to remember the last time she had been in a balloon. Sitting, she could concentrate on the bottle…and that's all. She would never permit herself to enjoy anything with him.

Two days later, a messenger delivered an invitation for the following week, Wednesday at six in the evening. Valeria marked it, "Okay, that will be three down, twenty-four left," and sent it back.

They went to dinner at an outdoor restaurant near Battery Park, called Gigino's, with an extraordinary view of the harbor. Valeria wore jeans and a T-shirt this time.

As soon as they were seated the waiter asked if they would care for a bottle of wine and Paolo tilted his head to the side. "The lady typically prefers her own bottle. Valeria, would you care for a glass this evening?" He raised his eyebrows, with a glint of humor in his eyes.

Slightly embarrassed, Valeria rolled her eyes to the waiter, as if she didn't know what Paolo was talking about. "Of course, I would like a glass." Then she bit her lip lightly and hid behind her menu.

Paolo ordered a bottle of wine and when it arrived, she heard the waiter say, "2002 Ladera Cabernet."

Her heart froze; it was her favorite wine from Alex's collection. "No. Please…can we have something else?"

The waiter had already begun to open the expensive bottle of wine. Paolo eyed Valeria for a moment. "Certainly. I apologize. Valeria do you have a preference?"

She pulled the menu up higher and shook her head, unable to speak for a moment. Paolo spoke to the waiter, "Please take this bottle back. Valeria, would you care to try the 2008 Louis Martini Cabernet?" She offered a nearly imperceptible shrug, still hiding behind the menu.

During dinner, he allowed her the space to recover, and while she appreciated it, it would have been much easier if he had been a jerk. By the time their coffee had arrived, she had completely recovered and decided it was time to further antagonize him.

Four men were seated behind her, and she turned around to talk to them. As soon as she turned, the men began flirting with her, and she shamelessly flirted back. She even scooted her chair closer to theirs, while Paolo just watched pleasantly and sipped his coffee.

The men bought her a pomegranate martini and she sipped it gratefully. It was good! She even offered two of the men her phone number, telling them she would go out with whoever called first after she left. Of course, she gave them both the wrong number. Except for Alex, Valeria had never flirted before, and it made her feel ridiculous.

A Latino band began playing in the park next to them. The food had been very good and the music fantastic. Paolo asked her if she wanted to listen to the band and Valeria sighed as if bored, but the fact was that they were great. With the sun setting, the first stars and planets bejeweled the sky next to the crescent moon as the sky was painted with brilliant purples and blues with just a hint of yellow, orange, and red. She sipped her martini as a masted yacht strung with colorful lights cruised toward Liberty Island, just as she and Paolo had done only nights before. It was breathtaking and she found it interesting that in all of her years in Manhattan, she had never been down here to enjoy this. The wonderful smells of the food filled the air along with the Latin music. Couples began to salsa to the band, while families played on the lawn beside them. She found herself enjoying the evening despite her insistence that she would not.

The next day he took her on a private backstage tour of Wicked and then they attended the musical in box seats. Valeria found that she was embarrassed to be in her jeans.

Afterward, they went to Sardi's and had champagne and hors d'oeuvres.

She refused the next several requests, saying that she was busy. Although she realized that each date brought her closer to Alex, she didn't want to be enjoying herself. *Where was Alex? Didn't he love her anymore? Had he moved on? Maybe he had reunited with Kristiana.*

The following week, Paolo invited her to lunch at Tavern on the Greene. Valeria agreed, but said that she would meet him there. When she arrived, Paolo was wearing jeans and a silk shirt. She was dressed in slacks and a blouse. She wore her hair down and had actually put on a bit of makeup. They sat outside in the beautiful garden setting.

Paolo's eyes sparkled. "You look beautiful."

"Thanks." She shrugged without meeting his eyes.

After they had eaten lunch, Paolo seemed particularly excited. "Bella—Valeria, I have something for you. I hope you like it." He smiled nervously.

Gifts from Paolo…as if they would mean anything to her! She shrugged, knowing she would reject it as soon as he presented it to her. Still, surprisingly, she had witnessed a vulnerability in him with this gift and she didn't want to be cruel; and, to her own shock, she realized that she didn't want to hurt him. Paolo had taken whatever cruel comment she had thrown at him and responded with kindness and consideration; well, *except for the part* where he had destroyed her life and taken any piece of happiness she might ever have, and threatened the lives of everyone she truly loved! *Aside from that,* he was starting to grow on her. Despite it all, she knew that she would reject this gift. There was only one purpose to all of this…*to see Alex!*

Paolo lifted his napkin to his mouth and rose to cross the patio. He stepped behind a tall hedge that led to Central Park, returning in moments with a small, tri-colored puppy with floppy ears and big brown eyes. For the first time she saw someone other than her enemy. Paolo's expression was so excited, so sweet and vulnerable. A couple at the next table watched as if it were the most romantic gesture that they had ever seen. The waitress even told Valeria how fortunate she was to have someone so sweet!

Valeria felt nauseous. She had to get out of here! Paolo proudly held out the puppy to her and, in response, the puppy wagged its tail wildly, smiling at her with a silly grin nearly matched by Paolo's. Paolo looked like someone with a heart—not the man who had ripped hers out only months before. Were there any depths he wouldn't stoop to?

"What is this?" she demanded, ignoring the puppy. Paolo tried to hand the puppy to her. But she jumped up. "*I don't want a dog from you!*"

"Valeria, just pet him, he's very gentle...and smart! I taught him a trick...allow me to show you." Paolo set the puppy down. "Valeria, just watch!"

She jumped back, and her throat tightened. Tears were threatening to spill, and she certainly wouldn't—couldn't—permit Paolo to see them. She turned and hurriedly began walking away from him. Valeria felt the puppy at her heels and prayed that Paolo would have the good sense to come and get it.

"Valeria, what is wrong?" Paolo yelled.

She kept walking out onto the sidewalk of busy Central Park West. The puppy was trying to keep up with her as Paolo yelled after her, "Bella, please take him!" She began sobbing. She didn't want something he had given her. She simply *couldn't* care for anything Paolo had given her.

"Bella! Please pick him up!" Valeria could see the innocent puppy out of the corner of her eye, distracted by the traffic. She was desperately afraid that he would run into the street and she wished she could pick him up. She simply couldn't do it. If she picked him up, she wouldn't be able to set him down again. It would be as if she accepted this life—or half-life—away from Morgana and her family. *Away from Alex.*

Finally, she heard the words from Paolo that changed everything, "Alex asked me to give the puppy to you."

Valeria froze. She knew she couldn't trust Paolo. He would lie in a heartbeat to get what he wanted.

Paolo came closer. "Alex was worried about you being too alone. He said there was a puppy you liked in Trento."

Valeria remembered the day she walked with Alex through the streets in Trento and had spotted a dog, just like this one. She had played with the puppy for almost an hour when Alex had suggested that after they returned from their wedding festivities, they should get one.

Immediately, she dropped to the sidewalk and pulled the puppy into her chest as her body convulsed in an attempt to rid itself of the emotion. She would not cry. No more tears, she promised herself. No more tears, she chanted. If one fell, others would follow. *Alex hadn't forgotten her!*

Paolo knelt by her, while she drew in deep breathes as a bulwark against the tears. "He said you would like this kind of puppy. He sent him to me to give to you." Paolo put his hand on her shoulder and she ignored it, her attention was focused on the puppy and Alex. He looked away and said, almost to himself, "I swore to myself that I would not tell you the dog was from him." Then he looked directly at her. "You know that I should not have told you."

She put all of her efforts into loving the puppy, instead of hating Paolo. Holding the puppy close as he happily licked her face, she whispered, "Thank you for telling me." She petted him. "He looks like a Charlie," she sniffed.

Rising, as if she now had the most precious gift of her life in her arms—and a reason for living—she began walking back to her brownstone.

"Valeria," Paolo said, as he petted the puppy and smiled at him. "Charlie needs supplies. I can drive you home and then bring over his supplies."

She wiped her face. "No, I think we'll walk."

"But Charlie should not be left alone and there are so many things a puppy needs. May I at least bring them to you?"

She nodded. "All right."

"I will see you shortly."

An hour later, she buzzed him into her brownstone and he stepped in loaded down with numerous bags of puppy supplies—a doggy bed, a leash, toys, dog food, dog bowls— and a bottle of wine and flowers for Valeria. She took the dog supplies and wine.

"Thanks, Paolo." Then, taking the flowers, she shrugged and tossed them into the trash can. They both smiled. After drinking a glass of wine with her, Paolo said goodnight and left without fanfare.

That night, she laid in her bed with Charlie asleep in her arms as she silently pleaded for Alex to come to her.

CHAPTER 12

It was Memorial Day and Central Park was packed for the concert. Valeria sat on a tan blanket feeding Charlie, the puppy, leftover pieces of the barbecued chicken she had brought from Daisy Mae's—her favorite barbecue in Manhattan. Charlie gratefully lapped up the remainder of the barbecued chicken from her fingers. The temperature was eighty-two degrees and it felt perfect on her skin. Weege watched Valeria with interest for a few minutes. "You're happy, aren't you?"

Valeria looked at Weege and realized that Weege had never seen her when she was with Alex. The only measure that Weege had was from Valeria's life before Alex, and her deep despair after losing him. So comparatively, she was considerably happier than she was either of those times, especially knowing that Alex was somewhere in the world. And looking at Charlie reminded her that he was thinking of her. But she wasn't about to discuss all of that with Weege.

"I'm okay," Valeria said, laughing at Charlie's expression

as he finished the last bites of chicken. When she failed to give him more, he dropped his head on the blanket and gazed up at her woefully...evidently emotionally decimated by the lack of more barbecue.

Glancing at the grass next to them, Paolo was playing bocce ball with a few of the kids in the area. Weege's new beau, Kenny, was watching him and looked like a fish out of water; he was an overweight truck driver wearing shorts, revealing his very white legs and knee socks. Paolo looked like a male model or pro-athlete...which only increased the comedy of Kenny's appearance. Kenny's hands were lodged on his hips as he watched Paolo, as if at any minute Kenny might jump in.

"Kenny doesn't know whether to throw a line at it, tackle it, or have it for lunch!" Weege laughed. "So, Val," she smiled smugly, "I always knew you and Paolo would end up together."

Valeria shook her head, no longer upset by Weege's constant comments about Paolo. "We aren't together."

"Well, did you notify your face? Because girlfriend, you look happy for the first time in a very long time."

"Yeah, well, you thought I was happy with David!" Valeria offered Weege a critical glance. She really didn't want to hear that she was "happy" now. She just wasn't in agony.

"Well, duh! David was a diplomat!" she teased, scrunching her nose. "Still, with Paolo—"

Valeria interrupted in irritation, "Weege! I'm not *with* Paolo!" Valeria glanced toward him and lowered her voice. She really didn't want to hurt him. She just saw him as a means to an end, which would seem cruel except for the fact...she shook her head. She needed to find another path!

"Weege, Paolo is just a friend. I'm *with* Alex!" Valeria rolled her eyes. She noticed as Charlie hunched down slightly as if he was in trouble. She pulled him tightly to her chest. "I wasn't talking to you, buddy! I was talking to Weege." Charlie recovered and licked her neck in forgiveness.

She had never told Weege about what happened with Alex or who Paolo was. Weege had never asked about what happened that night at Sardi's, but Valeria was certain that Paolo had somehow justified her extreme reaction. Still, she had always been curious.

Glancing casually at Weege, Valeria asked, "I have been wondering how this whole set-up with Paolo happened." She played with Charlie, pretending to be only mildy interested.

"Oh, I guess he must have seen you at the office." Weege looked at Valeria. "I told you this, right?" Valeria shook her head no. Weege went on, "Well, he saw you and the next thing I know, Orin fricking Taylor—as in CEO, Orin Taylor," Val nodded and Weege continued, "is calling me and telling *me* that a friend of his is quite taken with you. I assumed it was some computer geek—or worse, a flower freak!" Weege shrugged. "Then Orin says the guy wants to come by and introduce himself so that I know he isn't some weirdo."

Weege turned to Valeria. "Can you imagine?" Valeria shook her head. "So, Paolo comes by five minutes later and I think he is just about perfect for you! Then he said I should keep the meeting very casual. He also said that the two of you may have had a misstep during the transition..." Weege rolled her eyes. "Misstep! Huh! I still don't know what happened with that!" Valeria shrugged as if it wasn't worth discussing and Weege continued, taking a bite of a carrot stick. "Well, anyway, Paolo said he wanted another chance to not screw things up with you...or something like that. Oh, and he asked me not to tell you who he was until he could clear it all up."

Valeria glanced at Weege and shook her head. "*Clear it all up?* Is that what he said?"

"Something like that." Weege thought for a moment, as

Valeria anxiously waited to hear what words Paolo had used, feeling herself getting riled up. Weege glanced up. "Oh! I remember. He said that he would appreciate an opportunity to show you that he wasn't the guy who you met before." Valeria sighed. "He said that he would appreciate it—and so would Orin." Weege sighed. "And you know the rest." Valeria twisted her neck in tension. "Val, you must have had some fight with him, huh?"

"Don't remember him." Boy, she had gotten adept at lying, but she had needed to in order to survive the past few months. Valeria glanced down. "I'm going to take Charlie for a walk. I'll be back."

Valeria hooked him up on his leash and Charlie started wagging half of his body in response. She smiled and then noticed Paolo watching her. Despite her anger toward him, he had grown on her, although she really didn't want that. She wanted to hate him forever. But he had been a friend in a time when she felt very alone—albeit because of him!

Still, she found that she looked forward to their meetings although she refused to call them dates. Only six more weeks and she could see Alex. Her longing for him had not waned. There was this emptiness in her gut that nothing seemed to fill...except for him! One thing she felt certain of, Paolo would not permit her and Alex to meet if Paolo felt any threat that Alex would win. The meeting with Alex had to feed Paolo's plan, not Alex's.

Her mind had gone wild in the months with nothing from Alex to let her know that he was thinking of her. It was definitely a curse of her well-honed imagination! She wondered what he would say. Did he still love her? Would he tell her that he had reunited with Kristiana? Would he let her down easy? Valeria shook her head attempting to free herself from her thoughts. Still, she felt like she was in the best shape of her life, physically. And emotionally, she was doing better with her sweet Charlie. Alex would love Charlie. In her mind, she could see Alex playing with Charlie in front of the fire at their beloved cottage.

The first anniversary after her twenty-seventh birthday was in just over four months, the birthday that she had been cursed to die on for eons. Was she immortal now? Or had they just delayed things a year, as Tavish had questioned? She felt a cold chill run down her spine. She didn't want to be away from Alex on that day. Perhaps they could meet on the anniversary of their first meeting in Central Park, when he had saved her life. She felt a tension of yearning in her gut. No, she couldn't wait that long.

She imagined that they would hold hands—maybe that was permitted—and talk. Regardless of any rules, Valeria would tell Alex how much she missed him. He would tell her that they had made great progress and they wouldn't have to be apart much longer. Or maybe he would surprise her early and tell her that everything had been resolved and they would walk off into the sunset—Alex, Charlie, and her.

The walk back to the group was a lonely one—wondering if she would ever hold Alex again. At least Charlie's wagging tail and smiling brown eyes made her feel a little less alone. She watched as a couple kissed over Bow Bridge. To be feeling that feeling again, so loved, so protected...so unalone. She had waited night after night for Alex to come back to her, but now she decided it had all been a dream or hallucination.

At the blanket, Kenny was making his way through half of a pie that Weege had brought. Paolo saw Valeria and jumped up in concern. "Valeria! I was about to go looking for you." She shrugged.

"I was just walking." The world smelled of grilled hot dogs.

Paolo looked at her critically. "You are sad."

She didn't answer. Those thoughts were best kept in her head. Weege and Kenny were in their own world. Paolo started playing and laughing with Charlie. She noticed that Paolo's eyes sparkled when he laughed and, despite the fact that she did not want to notice, it was hard to ignore how attractive he was. Paolo would never replace Alex, but his company was still oddly and surprisingly comforting to her.

She laid back on the blanket and stared at the sky, noticing its intense shades of blue, wondering why life had taken her down this path. Why had she met Alex, only to be left alone without him? She closed her eyes, not wanting to think about it. The sun warmed her and she listened to nearby children laughing and playing. It was such a joyful sound. She imagined Alex there with her and breathed deeply, relaxing finally. She felt Charlie curling into her and she wrapped her hand around him. Thinking how the world would be perfect with Alex sitting next to her, her fingers moved through Charlie's fur and then she felt Paolo's fingers as he attempted to lace his fingers through hers...the way she would do with Alex. Her eyes flew open in shock as she immediately pulled her hand back and jumped up.

"I'm going home. You all have fun without me." She straightened her top and grabbed Charlie's leash. Paolo looked at her with concern.

Weege looked mildly upset. "The concert hasn't even started!"

"I'm just not in the mood for a concert. Besides, I think Charlie is overwhelmed with all the people."

Paolo stood. "I'll walk you home."

"No." She shook her head. "Thanks."

Paolo kept walking with her. "Did I do something to anger you?"

"I'm just tired. I'll see you next week," she muttered.

"I had a thought," Paolo said, and she could hear his concern. She tried to keep her thoughts about Alex to herself, although it didn't seem as if he cared anymore. She kept walking briskly and Paolo easily kept up as he said, "I thought perhaps we could go away together."

"No. Sorry."

He pulled on her arm to stop her. "What is it, Valeria?"

She turned to Paolo. "Do you talk to him?" she blurted out, without thinking.

Considering his answer carefully, Paolo finally said, "Yes, sometimes."

"Does he," she gulped, "ask about me?" Tears welled in her eyes.

Paolo considered for several minutes and then looked down and nodded almost imperceptibly.

She swallowed and said almost in a whisper, "What do you tell him?" She knew she was crossing the line but she felt she had a moment where she might hear the truth from Paolo. A few kids on bikes rushed by them and Valeria pulled in Charlie's leash, but otherwise she didn't move.

"I tell him how you are." Valeria looked at him as if the answer was a cop-out. Paolo drew a fast deep breath, knowing he needed to give her more. "I tell him that you are doing better every day."

"Does he know about…the arrangement?"

"He is aware that there is an arrangement." Paolo continued to keep his face down.

Valeria drew a shaky breath and touched Paolo's arm with a plea in her eyes. "I can't wait another six weeks to see him. Will you let me see him sooner?"

He looked away.

"Please, Paolo." She swallowed back a tear. "*Please,* let

me see him sooner?"

Evaluating her critically, he finally responded. "Valeria, we have an agreement." He thought for another moment, analyzing her expression, and his face softened for just a moment before he nodded. "All right, I have something I want and you have something you want. If you go away with me for a week, I will consider that as a fair exchange. But, be warned. I do not know if Alex can rearrange his schedule. So, please, do not take my word that he will be able to see you any sooner."

She touched his arm. "I won't sleep with you."

He jerked back, angrily. "You think I do this for sexual pleasure?" His eyes clouded. "There is much more at stake for me. I know for you it is just the price to pay so that you can see a man who is married to another woman. For me, it is having my wife back."

For half of a second, perhaps less, Valeria felt sorry for him. But then she remembered that Paolo was the cause of so much of this devastation in her life.

She took a deep breath. "Separate rooms. Separate baths. No midnight visits." Paolo nodded and smiled. She went on, "And then, I want to see Alex."

She turned from Paolo and walked away without another word.

CHAPTER 13

The flight climbed through a clear New York sky and over the Atlantic. It was the first time Valeria had flown since her return to the States and she had vowed that she wouldn't let herself get melancholy. Instead, she would focus on this trip and attempt to enjoy it and then, hopefully, she would see Alex when she returned!

Paolo was drawing a lot of attention from the flight attendants and it was getting on Valeria's nerves. She rolled her eyes at one of the flight attendants who had been unprofessional enough to begin giving Paolo details of the Mile High Club initiations with a hint of invitation in her voice. Paolo smiled subtly and Valeria guessed that he had already conducted his fair share of initiations.

As soon as the flight attendant left, Paolo's face lit in amusement as he turned back toward Valeria. "You are a jealous one." He tapped her nose. "I remember."

Pulling away, she wondered why men thought it was appropriate to talk to women like they were little girls—so condescending! Alex would never talk to her like that.

"I am not jealous of anyone who chooses to flirt with *you!* Or do anything *else with you* for that matter! For all I care, she can have at you. It's just, whatever happened to professional conduct? Those women don't know that we are just friends. I could be your wife for all they know."

"You were my wife!" he said, with a glint in his eyes.

Leaning into the window, she huffed, "Well, I'm not now."

They landed at the airport in Frederiksted, on the island of St. Croix, a few hours later. Valeria had watched the shades of the Caribbean change from deep sky blue to azure, to an incredible turquoise that she had always believed had been enhanced on Photoshop.

But the area around the airport was disappointing. It was flat and desert-like and surrounded by refineries. Paolo saw her expression as she looked out at the island. "Valeria, St. Croix is one of the most majestic of the Caribbean islands. You will not be disappointed!" Then he winked at her in a way that reminded her of Alex.

As they walked out of the open air terminal, there was a rum stand and the woman signaled them over. "I don't think I like rum," Valeria said.

"You must try it!" Paolo led her to the stand. The woman poured several different types of rum in small thimbles. Valeria had expected it to be like shooting vodka. But to her surprise it was delicious! After a few tastes, she nodded to Paolo that she was done and they climbed into their limo.

Sitting in the backseat, Valeria watched with horror as their driver pulled out on the wrong side of the road. Then she relaxed as she realized—thank God—that the other cars were also driving on the "wrong side" of the street! They headed toward the center of the island, winding their way over the crest and through a small rainforest, and then they came to an overlook that revealed a remarkable view of the north shore of St. Croix.

As the limo looped through the coastal town of Christiansted, Paolo had the driver pull over. They strolled along the waterfront with its wood buildings and narrow alleys with small, but elegant, tourist shops framed by palms. In a jewelry shop, Valeria fell in love with the simple elegance of the Croixian bracelet. It was a sterling silver band with a hook that latched in a U.

Paolo tossed his card on the counter to purchase it for her, and Valeria shook her head disapprovingly. She wasn't going to wear any jewelry purchased for her by any man, except Alex! She handed the jeweler her own card and then asked him to wrap a gold Croixian bracelet as well. She would give the gold one to Weege for taking care of Charlie. Valeria would have loved to purchase one for Camille also. But Camille, the sister of her heart, her closest friend in the world, could never see her again...because of the charming man whom she was vacationing with.

Valeria wished that she could hate Paolo forever, but she seemed to be incapable of holding anger or hate in her heart for any length of time. It just wasn't within her. And, frankly, he was growing on her. Still, she would never forget what he did! She was certain that a part of her acceptance of him in her life was that those sweet months in Italy seemed almost like a dream, almost like it had never happened, except for Paolo's presence. She had to know that it had been real! The purpose of this trip, and the only reason she agreed to see Paolo at all, was for the chance to see her beautiful Alex. Just the thought of Alex caused her heart to jump as tears briefly rimmed her eyes. Then she remembered the promise to herself and she shook off the tears. She had spent enough of the past few months in mourning.

They strolled along the wharf and stopped at a seaside restaurant. While eating her salad, Paolo struck up a conversation with the bartender, who convinced Valeria to taste a few more flavors of Cruzan rum; it tasted good and went down like juice!

They were joined by a very charming sailor, known as "Black Beard," who had an extraordinarily long beard—though it was now white. Captain Jim, as he was known by the locals, told Valeria about sailing to Buck Island and how magical it was. She explained to him that she was afraid of the water, but with Valeria's courage artificially amplified by the rum, she agreed and Paolo booked a trip that left within the hour.

Realizing that she hadn't even brought a swim suit, she went into the dive store. To her disappointment, they only had bikinis in her size. After searching through their meager selection for a few minutes, she finally found a black one that covered a little more of her than the others had. She purchased that and a white cotton cover-up and wore it and some flip flops out of the store. Paolo was wearing swim trunks and a white polo shirt. She had to admit that he looked good. Soon, they saw a catamaran with a sail that had a caricature of a jovial sailor with a long black beard.

They boarded and Paolo encouraged Valeria to sit on the netting, but the memories of the netting of the catamaran from last fall made her nervous. Paolo ordered her a rum punch and that loosened up her fears and, soon, she easily went to the front of the boat with him. As the catamaran moved its way out toward Buck Island, Paolo pulled off his shirt. Valeria noticed several women eyeing Paolo. She also noticed that Paolo was fully aware of his affect on women and completely enjoyed it—knowing exactly how to play it so that all eyes were on him. Paolo leaned back against the incline of the cabin in front of the boat and moved his arms so that they flexed and then rubbed lotion over his chest and shoulders as several of the girls' jaws hit the floorboards. Valeria rolled her eyes and, with a smirk, looked off in another direction.

"What?" Paolo asked, with mock innocence. Valeria just continued to shake her head in mild amusement. *"What?"* he asked again, both of them fully aware of the game being played.

As they approached the island they were surrounded by dolphins that swam synchronously in front of the catamaran, crisscrossing in front of them. Valeria's face lit in absolute delight!

Twenty minutes later they pulled between the reefs near the deserted island. Captain Jim explained that Buck Island had been named a National Monument by JFK who had sought to preserve the reefs. The air smelled of coconut oil and rum punch. Paolo tried to encourage her to snorkel with him. Evidently, there was a path through the reefs that surrounded the island. But there was no chance she would do that. Paolo went off...followed by a half dozen young girls.

There was a little boy who was terrified of the water. She knew how that fear felt! But with the help of the rum, Valeria found herself attempting to lure the boy into the water with her. As she climbed down the ladder into the warm Caribbean, she noticed something moving toward them in the water that was disc shaped. She decided that it must be a ray. While everyone on the boat clamored into the water to swim with the ray—or with Paolo—Valeria sat in the very shallow azure waters of the deserted Buck Island. It felt extraordinary, like bath water!

She had finally convinced the little boy to join her, and they sat on the very edge of the water as they happily built a sand castle. The ray seemed to agree with their location and joined them. She saw it approaching and, somehow, with its shape and the soft sand, it moved swiftly and smoothly underneath them. If she hadn't seen it, she wouldn't have known he was there.

While excited for herself that this shy creature had decided to join her, she knew that the boy would not be so pleased. When the boy looked through the two inches of water in front of him and realized there was an eye in the sand, if he could have walked on water, he would have. Fortunately, he didn't have that far to go. Valeria worked to hide her giggles. Why was it that every other person there had attempted to draw the ray to them, but it chose the one person, the little boy, who wanted to avoid it!

The crew started a fire on the island and grilled fresh fish and vegetables. Paolo retrieved two large plates and they sat on the warm sand while they feasted. She had to admit it was delicious and that she was enjoying herself. After lunch, Paolo returned to the snorkeling trails, while she laid back, catching color for the first time in...well, she thought, probably the first time!

He would return now and again, encouraging her to try to snorkel. He did convince her to put a snorkel in her mouth— though she refused to put something in her mouth that had recently been in someone else's mouth and then hastily rinsed in a tub. Her gag response would kick in. So he washed it thoroughly for her and then she kneeled in the shallow waters near the shoreline and floated. He held on to her and she wanted to push his hands away, but frankly, even though the water was only a few feet deep, she was afraid. There was a moment though—with her face covered by a mask, where she watched the sun lacing through the water onto the white sand, being lulled by the cool water lapping over her sun-warmed back, and feeling the gentle current rocking her—that she actually enjoyed herself.

As she dried in the sun after her brief swim, Paolo returned from the boat with a creamy brown drink.

"What is it?"

"It's called a 'Nilla Killa."

She took a sip of it. "Hmm! Delicious! Thank you."

"You need more lotion!" He grabbed the sunscreen and, before she could object, he was moving it over her shoulders and back. His thumbs ran over her neck and she leaned into it. It did feel good. She knew that he was spending far more time working in the lotion than was required. She also knew that she should inform him of such.

Finally, she pulled forward and said, "Thanks, I think that's plenty." Paolo immediately stopped.

"I'm going back in," Paolo said abruptly, as he rose and disappeared into the water.

Laying back on her beach towel, with her drink and the sun and cool breeze, felt good. She hadn't felt this good in a very long time. Granted, much of that was due to the rum, but it didn't really taste like there was much alcohol in her drink. Suddenly, Paolo stood up in the waist deep water, looking comical with his mask over his face and the snorkel dangling from his mouth.

"Valeria, come quickly! You must see this!"

"Thanks, but I'll pass."

"Come, Valeria. I promise, you'll be very glad you did!" he encouraged.

Resigning herself, she reluctantly grabbed her mask and snorkel and joined him.

"You do not need to swim this time," he said as she began to slip her mask on. Suddenly, a pod of dolphins began swimming around her. Her jaw dropped in wide-eyed amazement.

"Dolphins!" She stood watching them as they circled them

and played. They were so close she could touch them! She got her nerve up and brushed the back of one of them.

For nearly ten minutes, the dolphins played around her. The look in Paolo's eyes was just as amazed. Soon, other tourists were trying to video the event and pushing their loved ones near Valeria to get a picture. Paolo offered to hold the camera so that a father could be in the shot with his children. Then, just as quickly as the dolphins had come, they left.

Valeria heard the blow of the conch shell, announcing that it was time to return to St. Croix. During the trip back, she comfortably laid on the front of the catamaran and sunned herself. The breeze and the cool air from the sea were delightful, and the crew kept the rum punch flowing.

Paolo glanced at her. "You are turning pink. You should roll over."

With a shrug, she rolled onto her stomach and adjusted her towel.

"You need more lotion." He immediately began massaging the warm lotion into her skin and, this time, she simply enjoyed the feel of his skilled hands on her back and neck.

Everyone on the boat was still talking about the dolphin's behavior at Buck Island. The crew went on and on about how they had never seen the dolphins circle someone like that before.

"Valeria, do you know why the dolphins came to you?" Paolo asked as he added a stroke of sunscreen to her shoulders.

"I think it was just luck."

"No," he said softly, and she turned to look at him. He leaned back against the incline of the boat so that his face was not far from hers. "You know it is said that Apollo once disguised himself as a dolphin." Paolo folded his hands behind his head. "I believe they came to you to say welcome." Valeria smiled. Although she had seen visions about her life with

Apollo, that part of her existence was simply not real to her. Paolo closed his eyes. "I'm sure Alex could tell you more." Realizing what he had said, Paolo abruptly stopped.

Yes, Alex would be able to tell her more about it. He would have kept her interest, and he might have even gotten her to snorkel.

They arrived back at Christiansted and waved goodbye to Captain Jim and the crew. Their limo drove east along a winding coastal road with spectacular views and the occasional home. After only a few miles, it pulled into a plantation, turned resort. The sign read, "The Buccaneer."

As they wound along the long entry road lined with palms, she admired the lush greenery and orange and red tropical flowers. They drove past a large cone-shaped structure with a flat top, made of stone which the driver told them was an old sugar mill. Arriving at the great house of The Buccaneer, with its burnt pink buildings covered in fuchsia bougainvillea, her mind flashed back to Gaios where she and Alex were almost married. If things had worked out she might—she forced that thought away.

The open air lobby sat at the top of the hill providing spectacular views of the grounds and the Caribbean. While they waited for keys and a bellman, they strolled around the lobby, which merged seamlessly into the restaurant and was completely surrounded by large pink arches that seemed to encapsulate all the pleasures of the Caribbean with its colors and temperature and smells. Shell wind chimes were hung throughout the lobby and every few seconds made sweet tinkling sounds with each soft wave of the breeze. Paolo pointed out a tiny spot of white and green in the sea of blues and told her that it was Buck Island.

The bellman escorted them to a golf cart and drove them down the steep winding road to a villa on the water. Valeria saw that it looked like they were going to a single room. She looked at Paolo sternly, but he patted her arm. "We will only have adjoining balconies." He smiled seductively. "I will only enter your room when you invite me."

"Well then, it'll be a while." She stepped out of the now stopped golf cart and removed her foot from her flip-flop, tapping it on the pavement. "Ground's still warm." She raised her eyebrows and looked at him over the top of her sunglasses. "I don't believe hell has frozen over, yet!"

Still, Valeria found herself enjoying Paolo's company and she realized that the rum and sun had affected her to a degree. She had the sudden knowledge that if she hadn't known Alex, she probably would have fallen for Paolo. But not now....*definitely* not now! Still, something stirred in her and made her very uncomfortable being this close to him.

Her suite was extraordinary; it overlooked the sea, with wood slat walls that allowed the sound of the sea into the room, along with the wonderful Caribbean breeze. The temperature was delightful. He knocked on the door to her deck and handed her another rum punch. She didn't want to be rude, so she took it. Besides, she was certain that it had to be weak, because otherwise it would have affected her by now.

As they sat on the deck, enjoying the setting sun, Valeria wished that she had insisted that he stay in another building. She had briefly thought about doing that but felt that it would have been silly. Adjoining decks weren't a big deal...but if that were true, then why was she suddenly so uncomfortable? As she glanced over, she noticed that he was, too.

Paolo asked if she was ready to go to dinner and, suddenly, she realized that she was famished! The salad and fish and vegetables hadn't been enough with all of the sun and activity...and the rum. They went their separate ways to dress for dinner, and something about it all just felt a bit too intimate.

In the shower, the warm water ran over her newly sunburned shoulders, stinging just a bit. It was strange to think about it, but sometimes, Paolo had this child-like sweetness, such as his excitement over Charlie or the dolphins. Then other times, he was just infuriating! But she was surprised to discover that she now enjoyed her time with him. In fact, they might someday be friends. She would have been good friends with him if he hadn't done what he did. She shook that memory away; if she thought about it too much, she wouldn't be able to be here with him and she would do anything to see Alex! But enjoying her time with Paolo created a conflict in her that felt like a betrayal.

With her sundress on, she pulled her wet hair into a ponytail, and went out the front door and down the steps. Paolo was waiting for her on the lawn and, as usual, he was immaculately dressed. He offered his arm and, for once, she took it as they walked up the winding hill to the arched outdoor restaurant overlooking the Caribbean.

The sky turned various and magnificent shades of pink and blue as the sun set. A guitarist played romantic music while the Caribbean breeze gently kissed them. The food was extraordinary. Valeria wished she was there with Alex. But it didn't seem like he thought about her anymore.

After dinner, the hotel manager sent over special rum drinks. Valeria and Paolo drank and laughed and enjoyed each other's company. An elderly couple came by and observed, "You must be on your honeymoon."

Valeria jerked away from Paolo. "No! No it isn't like that with us," she said, but when she turned back to Paolo she realized that he was looking at her with love in his eyes.

He ordered more flavored rum shots. But the rum didn't seem to affect her like wine did. She sipped it and it just tasted so good and felt oh so wonderful. It took the edge off her other thoughts.

A steel band started up.

"Come. Dance with me, Valeria."

"I don't think I can dance to this."

"If a woman has a good lead, she can dance to anything."

"I see," she said with a cynical smile, but then she took his hand.

As they started to move to the Caribbean beat, with the views and the stars, she had to admit, he could dance. Weege always told her to never trust a man who knew how to dance. In this case, it was certainly true. But then again, Alex was a great dancer, too. Oh, how wonderful it would be if...she closed her eyes and imagined that it was Alex who she was here with...Alex who was holding her. She felt his arm tighten around her waist.

She thought about Paolo's words that he didn't know if Alex could meet her and it made her wonder, what if Alex refused? If Paolo told her that Alex wouldn't meet her, could she believe it? No, she couldn't. If Alex had moved on, he would never leave it to someone else to tell her. Then she realized something; wasn't that the message he had given her that last night—that they both needed to find a way to be happy? She shook that thought away.

Tonight was too pleasant to think of Alex rejecting her. Instead, she would imagine that she was here with him...she leaned her head against Paolo's chest as she stared out across the water to the flickering lights of St. Thomas...and just behind that, St. John. She noticed that Paolo smelled good...not good like Alex, but pleasant.

The longing for the man she loved increased and Paolo sensed it and pulled her tighter into him as his mouth brushed the top of her head—not a romantic gesture, just a comfortable one, she justified.

They danced and drank more and then walked back down the hill in the brilliant star-filled night. They continued past the stairs to their rooms and Valeria realized she wasn't quite ready for the evening to end. It had been so long since she had felt good that the evening was a relief. She slid her shoes off and felt the soft, cool sand under her feet as she moved toward the water. The gentle tide lapped at her ankles.

"We could go for a swim," Paolo suggested softly. Valeria ignored him. She knew that she was being more relaxed with Paolo than she should be. He did have feelings for her and it was unfair to allow him to think that she had any interest in him.

She saw something in the sand and knelt to dig at it as the light rolls of the tide hit the bottom of her dress. She pulled out a heart-shaped head of coral.

"Look at this! Paolo, I wonder if I can keep it."

Paolo helped her pull it out of the sand and they stood there, with both of their hands on it.

"It's a sign, bella."

"Do you think so?" she said, hopefully.

His face softened. "Yes."

Realizing that they were thinking completely different thoughts, she decided that she needed to set the record straight. "Yes! It's a sign that I'm going to see Alex soon!"

Suddenly hurt and angry, Paolo took the coral and tossed it into the water. The splash covered most of her face and dress as he turned and walked away.

Drunk, she yelled at him as she wiped the water from her face, "Oh, come on, Paolo. Don't be a bad sport." It was so nice out here on the beach, under the billion stars. She could even see the Southern Cross.

Turning for a moment, Paolo stopped and his eyes narrowed for an instant as he glared at her in her now wet sundress. Then he began to move toward her, his eyes focused with an intensity that she hadn't seen in him before. There was something dangerous about the look. She saw his chest rise and fall rapidly. She knew he was battling anger and...something else. He grabbed her by the waist and instantly his mouth came down on hers.

She pulled back and opened her mouth to speak, but he kissed her again, pushing his tongue into her open mouth. Now stunned, she realized that she was kissing him back. It felt good to be held, to feel something other than pain. His hands began to run over her in a way that Alex never would have...before their marriage anyway. It was seductive and sexy and the way that he touched her was...intoxicating. She felt her heart beat pulse through her entire body—knowing she should end this. *She should end this!*

"Make love to me," he whispered in her ear.

She was instantly transported to a few months before in Greece, and it was Alex who was there, loving her, wanting to make love to her. And it was so...luxurious, the feeling of being loved and wanted. His hands found the hem of her dress, her hips beneath it, and her bare back.

"Say my name, Bella. Tell me you want *me*," his voice was silk in its gentle urging. And then, with a sudden shock, she realized—this wasn't Alex! Oh, God, what was she doing? She pushed back, but Paolo pulled her in even closer.

"Stop it! *Now!*" she cried, slamming both of her hands into his chest. Stunned, Paolo released her and she fell back hard onto the sand. Paolo knelt to help her up, but she pushed him away.

"I am sorry, bella. I did not mean to do that yet."

She was angry with him—but mostly, she was angry with herself. She used the emotion to lift herself back on her feet and completely avoided his hand. With her jaw grinding angrily, she brushed past Paolo and back to the grassy edge of the beach where there was a spigot. She briefly rinsed her feet, while battling her thoughts of what had just occurred. Paolo approached her, looking sheepish.

"Please forgive me, bella! Alex would not be angry with this...he would not."

At that, her heart rate sky-rocketed, realizing that she had harmed the only person she loved more than life. A few tears escaped, but she fought to hold back the flood of emotion that sat lodged in her throat. She finished washing her feet, grabbed her shoes, and marched up the stairs, occasionally staggering slightly. Then she turned to Paolo and losing her battle against her emotions, she said, "Please, get another room far away from me. I'm not sharing a balcony or anything else with you!"

"Yes. I know, bella. It was too soon. I'm sorry, bella."

∞

There were repeated knocks at her door with the sun shining through the slats on the wall. Her movement on the sheets scratched her and she realized that she had sand all over the bed.

Finally, she rose, still wearing the semi-damp dress from the night before, her head aching and her body stinging from sunburn. It was the maids. She asked them to come back later. She wanted to doze a bit more. Instead, she forced herself out of bed and staggered into the bathroom so she could vomit; then she showered, put on her running clothes, and stepped out the door. Everything in her ached as she began her fast pace up the steep hill toward the great house and lobby. Despite the fact that she desperately needed a coffee, she passed the dining room. Then, fighting the dizziness and aching joints, she ran down the long entrance road to the hotel, turning on to the dirt shoulder of the coastal road.

The cool breeze of the day before had vanished and in its wake was an oppressive heat and humidity that blanketed her in misery as she battled a monumental headache and nausea. She stopped a few times to vomit, but forced herself to continue...a penance, of sorts. Finally, an hour later, she returned to her room, showered again, and ordered fruit and coffee from room service.

She sat on her balcony, still in the hotel robe, brushing her hair and staring out over the turquoise blue waters, her head pounding. Accusations repeatedly ran through her mind. What was she thinking going away with him when she was so lonely? How could she have let this happen? She shouldn't have danced with him and certainly shouldn't have done any shots!

There was a knock at her door. She had hung the 'do not disturb' sign and assumed that in a suite of this expense, they would leave her alone. The knocking stopped, but then in front of the deck she heard Paolo calling her from down in the grass below. He looked as though he hadn't slept and his voice was full of the regret that she felt.

"Please allow me to come up and apologize. Please, Valeria," he pleaded.

She ignored him for a few minutes and then quietly she said, with no emotion, "I'll meet you in the dining room in an hour." She continued to sip her coffee and then casually went in and packed her bags and walked up the hill.

When she arrived, Paolo was sitting at the same table with the spectacular view where they had eaten dinner the night before. It was the best view overlooking the Caribbean. He still looked awful.

"Valeria, please believe me that was not my plan last night. I...I saw the way you looked at me and...I believed that you wanted me…and then I felt you kissing me back and I…I know it was too soon. Please, forgive me." Paolo looked down and shook his head, mournfully.

She knew what he was doing; he was reminding her that it was not all his fault. She didn't need to be reminded! She knew. The guilt engulfed her and she fought to push it back. But to admit to Paolo that he was only partially to blame—which she was certain he was waiting for—was dangerous. If she did, he would know that she was vulnerable.

"I've been thinking about some things. How we all ended up…here." She narrowed her eyes. "And I have a question for you."

"Anything, bella. Ask me anything."

"I'm wondering how it is that while Alex receives visions of me, you somehow found me first and married me?" She needed to understand how Paolo had ever worked his way into her life, all those lifetimes ago. If he hadn't, she would be married to Alex now.

Paolo drew a deep breath, grateful that she was speaking to him. "Bella, I did not find you first. Alex did."

Valeria drew her brows together. How could that be true? Alex was there first? "Why is it that I wasn't married to Alex then?"

"That you must ask Alex, although I have often wondered. Perhaps you can discuss that when you see him!" Valeria's mind was slow today so she needed to concentrate. "I want to make things right with you," he said nervously. Valeria continued to stare out into the Caribbean. "Alex has agreed to meet with you."

Her heart felt as if it stopped. Alex! "In New York?" She felt tears of hope rimming her eyes.

"No, Alex is here today!"

She felt her heart jump into her throat. She was going to

see Alex! Her heart filled with joy—the day she had dreamed of for what seemed like an eternity! Then, suddenly, she realized...*today, of all days!* She dropped her face into her hands. This wasn't the way she wanted to see Alex—hung over, away with another man at a romantic Caribbean resort, *having just kissed that man.* This was not the way she had pictured it at all!

"Did I make another mistake?" he said, as if hurt by her response.

"What time will Alex be here?" she said flatly.

"His car is on its way. He will be here very soon."

Valeria swallowed and then stood to walk away.

"Bella, where are you going?'

She sighed. "I'm going to shower and change again."

In her room, she wrapped herself in a towel as she dried her hair and then drank a shot of rum to try to kill her lingering hangover—the first time that she had used what her father had called, "a hair of the dog." She put on her best dress and makeup. At least her slight sunburn hid the green of her hangover! Then she walked back up the hill.

Entering the lobby, she twisted her hands, wondering when he would actually arrive, feeling that desperate need filling her heart again. Suddenly, her heart stopped for an instant; he was there in the lobby! Her heart began pounding so hard that she thought it might leap out of her chest! She saw his expression, a mix of so many emotions—pain, desire, anguish, and relief—as if the anchor that had concealed those emotions had just been released. He had lost weight. But it was her Alex!

Running to him, she began to throw her arms around his neck, but softly he took her wrists and held them, keeping her from the embrace they both desperately needed, as tears filled their eyes.

She was certain that his grasp on her arms was as much to

keep him from holding her, as it was for her benefit. And she remembered, *there were rules*...and people died if she didn't follow them. His grasp on her arms tightened in longing as he closed his eyes and his jaw tensed, while he breathed deeply, keeping his grasp on her arms, trying to get control of himself.

Despite being ageless, Alex looked older. He looked tired and sad, and nervous. He took her hand and it was paradise. For a moment, he smiled, wistfully, as her thumb traced the symbol on his hand. She looked into his beautiful face and saw the pain and the emotion that he fought to hold at bay as she swallowed back the tears so that she wouldn't waste their time crying. They went, without asking the hostess, to a seat by an open air arch.

"How are you, beautiful?" he asked, in a voice that was foreign to her.

"Without you," she choked softly. She forced herself to breathe—in-out-in-out. "How are you?" she asked with concern. He didn't look like he was doing well.

He shrugged and bit his lip as he closed his eyes.

"And everyone else? Camille? Ava?"

He answered like he hadn't slept since the last time she had seen him all those months before. "They miss you."

"I miss them, too," her voice cracked. "I miss you." And a sob lurched from her throat, and then she got control again. She took another deep breath. Now was a time to soak in every moment together and she would not waste one instant of it sobbing. "The search...has there been any luck?"

He looked away. "Kristiana went into hiding."

She reached over and touched his arm and he grabbed her hand and she could feel the intensity of emotion in that touch. "Alex, don't give up hope."

His face said it all; there was no hope. He attempted a smile and a nod, but there was no joy in his eyes. He looked around. "Do you want to…can we go for a walk?"

She stood up and they wandered down the long, winding road toward the beach.

He looked down at the ground as they passed bright pink bougainvillea covered walls. Then he glanced toward her briefly. "You look beautiful. You've been doing something right."

Unable to stop herself, she turned to him and her hand moved to touch his face. His eyes closed again, as if storing her touch as a memory. "Alex…I will never stop loving you. And I will never stop hoping." He removed her hand from his face; they had already crossed the line.

Glancing at his arm, she saw that he wasn't wearing her watch. But the white line around his wrist indicated that he had been wearing it recently.

"Never is a long time for an immortal." He looked away and swallowed as his jaw clenched again. "You know, I don't have very much time here."

"No!" she cried, feeling a lurch in her gut. "I thought we would have a full day together. He promised me that!"

"Val, I have to leave in just a little while."

"That wasn't the agreement!" She felt the tears beginning to overwhelm her, but she fought even harder. Alex closed his eyes hard, fighting the quivering in him. Then he pulled both of her hands into his and up to his heart. With her throat tight with tears, she asked, "Leaving early, is that your choice?"

"It's the only way it can be," he said flatly. Then he drew a deep breath. "But we have some things that we need to discuss before I go."

She didn't like the way that sounded. He led her to a table on the beach and glanced around to ensure that they had privacy. She wasn't ready for this kind of conversation, especially when they had so little time together. But she didn't ever want anything between them.

"I have to tell you something."

"Whatever happened…" Then he glanced down for half a second, shedding the hurt, before his brilliant blue eyes looked directly into hers. "I understand." *Paolo had told him!*

"Alex…" Her heart pounded even louder. "I was thinking of you, and I," she gulped, nervously, "I kissed him." She breathed out. "There was too much rum and I am just so…so angry at myself for allowing myself to be in that position. It will *never* happen again. Not ever!" There she had said it.

She saw the momentary flinch, as if she had hit him, but then he recovered. "It's okay. I understand. I…" He looked away, and then into her eyes, hurt, but trying to hide it. "Beautiful, you share something with him that you and I never have."

"What are you talking about? You and I share something that I will never have with anyone but you! I don't share anything with Paolo!"

He looked out to the sea again and then swallowed before saying, "Intimacy. You—"

"Is that what he told you?" she said, ashamed. "*No!* We…it was just…"

Alex stopped her by placing his finger on her mouth, and his eyes softened, attempting to ease her guilt. "Beautiful, I meant in the past." He swallowed again. "You have a memory of love and intimacy. Especially with recent events, you need to feel," his jaw clenched again, "loved. Val, I don't want you to feel guilty. " Tears rimmed his eyes. "He does love you."

She couldn't hear this, especially now. Then, with a hint of hesitation, he turned to her, the pain on his face overwhelming her.

"Before I go, I need to show you something." He swallowed and took her hands in his.

The transference began and she felt the flow of energy and the pictures. She saw her beloved cottage. It looked a bit different. Then there was a view of a bedroll and boots from another time and Alex's hand with his mark—the triquetra. From behind him, there was a sound and he turned, it was giggling laughter that Valeria recognized as her own.

Through the thick greenery of summer, Valeria saw a very young version of herself, half dressed in corsets and silk. Paolo was seducing the fifteen-year-old version of herself, in a location where Alex would be certain to see it all.

Hearing the girl laughing and sighing with Paolo's mouth covering her and touching her, Valeria was horrified to be watching it…horrified that Alex had seen it!

"Oh, Paolo! Sei tutto per me!" The girl whispered the passionate oath. Paolo's face looked sweet and full of love. Valeria knew that phrase, Alex had used it; it meant, "You are my everything." Valeria shuddered at the vision…and at the idea that Alex would share it with her.

Whatever Alex's reason for showing this to her, she had seen enough! She tried to pull her hand away from his to end the transference. But his grasp tightened.

"Signore Alex?" the young girl asked Paolo, looking toward the cottage.

Paolo waved his arm, obviously reassuring her that they were alone. Then Valeria saw what Alex wanted her to see— Paolo's face turned directly toward Alex and, with a petulant glare, he ran his hands over the girl in ownership.

The vision ended. Valeria sat not knowing what to say. She felt dead. "Why did you show that to me?"

"I thought you should see what I see," he swallowed and looked down for an instant, and Valeria sensed Alex's embarrassment.

"Are you giving up on me, because I was once a foolish

girl?" Alex looked at her with so much love, it overwhelmed her again.

"No, Val. No! You were a girl in love. I want you to know that you can be happy again."

The anger and hurt rose in her until finally she cried, "You think this is okay? You think that after everything that we had that I can just forget and be okay again? Well it's not okay and I will never be happy without you! Not *ever!*"

Valeria tried to go into his arms and he took her hands and squeezed them, halting their embrace. A cry escaped her mouth, but she stopped the sobs again. Then he looked behind him and removed his hands, leaving them where he could stop her, should the need arise. Paolo must be watching.

"I need you to remember that there are others whom you can talk to. Remember?"

"Who?" she asked, and then her face filled with repulsion. "*Paolo?*" she asked in disgust.

"I have to go." She heard the ache in his voice.

"No!"

"Yes, beautiful," he choked. "I have to go."

He turned for a moment and looked up the hill. Her eyes followed the line of his glance as she focused on the lone figure on the grassy hill. It was Paolo and he was most definitely watching them. Valeria caught something in Alex's eyes and attempted to quickly analyze his expression but the only thing she seemed to be able to focus on was that he was leaving her again, and probably for the last time.

"Did Paolo tell you that you have to leave?" Even from the distance Valeria could see Paolo attempt to look like he wasn't watching every glance and touch between them.

"Val, I'm so sorry, about all of this." Alex squeezed his eyes shut…she could tell that in his mind he was holding her. His hand brushed over her face for an instant and then he rose with a brief and painful sob. Turning from her, he began walking briskly up the hill toward the lobby.

She started to follow him and then, in a desperate attempt to keep Alex from leaving, she ran up the grass toward Paolo and screamed, "I'm supposed to have a day with him! What did you do?"

Now Paolo nearly sprinted to close the distance between them. Once he was within arm's length of her he said, "I'm sorry, bella, he did not have a day for you." He shook his head sadly and reached out to soothe her. "I have tried to please you."

"You..." She pulled back from him and narrowed her eyes. "You played us both, didn't you? What did you offer Alex?"

A breeze picked up off the Caribbean, and Paolo shook his head. "No, bella. I called him last night after you became upset. I explained your feelings of guilt. Alex had very little time, but he did not wish for you to feel guilty about what you may be feeling for me. Please understand that he did not have more time for you."

Her voice came out as an angry shriek, "*You're a liar!* He would make time for me!" She coldly glared at Paolo. "You *will* give us ten more minutes without you there! *You will!* Do you understand me?" Paolo looked away.

She chased Alex up the hill. He had already entered the lobby and his car was waiting for him. She ran to him and wrapped her arms around his back, savoring the moment. She felt his breath hitch several times, before he took her arms, ending their embrace. Valeria grabbed his hands and he squeezed them for an instant. It was another moment before he looked down at her, with tears in his eyes.

"What did he offer you?" she whispered.

He shook his head. Valeria brushed the side of his face.

"You aren't going to tell me, are you?"

Moving his trembling hand to her face for a brief moment, he winked without a hint of joy. "You're a smart girl. You can figure it out." Despite everything Paolo had done, Alex wouldn't violate his agreements.

"You know he's double dealing," she said, still hanging on to his arms as she breathed in deeply, drinking in his wonderful scent.

"I know Paolo." Alex looked down into the eyes that he adored and his jaw tightened. "I can't stay," he breathed. "Val, I don't trust myself to stay on the island with you and to stay away." He forced another breath. "I hope you understand." He ran his hand over her hair and then whispered, "I have to go." He choked again. "Remember who you are." Then he turned and walked out of her life...again.

CHAPTER 14

Valeria marched to where Paolo had been standing on the grassy area above the sand. She grabbed his arm and pulled him to the table where, moments before, she and Alex had been sitting.

"What did you offer Alex so that he could see me?" she demanded. Paolo winced as if injured from her accusation.

"What have I done to make you so suspicious of me?" He cocked his head. "Did Alex say something?"

"No. He wouldn't. Despite all of your lying and cheating and double dealing." She shook her head. "He wouldn't violate your agreement."

"Bella, I have only tried to please you."

"You gave him only thirty minutes. What was the exchange?" she angrily blurted out, her face red with rage and her whole insides shaking.

Despite that, his eyes looked painfully innocent. He reached for her. "Bella—"

She slapped his hand and pulled back. "Don't you touch me! Just answer my question." Then sadness moved in and she leaned toward Paolo and said softly, "Please, don't play me. Just tell me the truth." Her eyes begged him. "Paolo, what did it cost Alex to see me?"

He looked up and his face momentarily hardened and then he acquiesced and shrugged. "The vision." He rubbed his face. "I wanted you to know that you could be—that you were—very happy with me once."

Valeria nodded as she drew a deep breath. "Makes sense." She swallowed, hurt that she had been taken. "I want more answers."

He held up his arms innocently, as if he had nothing to hide.

"You said that you weren't the only signatory on the petition. Was Kristiana the other?"

Paolo looked away and then at her. "Yes."

She shook her head. "Don't lie to me, Paolo! How could she have known that we would be requesting an immortal marriage?"

He stood and walked for a few moments. "I do not know what I've done to cause you so much distrust!" She glared at him. "Bella, I have had the petition for some time—you were there when I explained this to the council. It was delivered to me after you...after my Isabella died."

Valeria shook her head in disbelief. "I don't believe you!"

Paolo shrugged. "How would she know that Alex and I would be married?"

"I believe that was an obvious assumption...to most of us."

"Is Kristiana an oracle?"

His eye twitched, as if it was a sore subject. "No."

"Then how would she know that we would go to the council? How did she know that you would stand up against us?"

Paolo looked up. "I don't know, bella. I only know what she told me in the message."

"What did the message say?"

"She said that there was an opportunity to set things right so that we could both have what we wanted, if we were patient."

"How could she have known that, Paolo? Doesn't it appear to you as if she knew what would happen?"

Paolo shook his head, and she knew that it was as much a mystery to him as it had been to Alex. "The only thing I do know is what must happen next."

"What?"

Paolo looked off into the distance. "You will find the message in your room."

∞

From St Croix, Valeria flew to Puerto Rico. She knew that Alex was flying out of St Croix as well and she prayed that she might have an accidental meeting with him on the flight—although it wasn't the wisest choice.

She was still wearing the dress from her brief meeting with Alex and if she concentrated, she could smell his wonderful scent. If she concentrated even harder, she could feel her arms wrapped around him; the feel of his chest. He had lost weight too. Valeria knew that she should have changed into something more comfortable, but she couldn't bring herself to do so.

The flight landed in the very loud city of Puerto Rico—the major thoroughfare back to Europe. Alex had to be near. She watched closely as she exited the airport. She passed a stand where a woman beckoned Valeria to sample the free rum. Shaking her head no, Valeria turned the other way, jumping into a nearby cab.

At the hotel, she checked in and then immediately went downstairs and sat in the lobby that also doubled as a lounge, sipping a glass of wine. Pulling out the envelope that she had found in her room in St. Croix, she brushed her fingers across her name written in Alex's beautiful script.

Then she removed the card, with the name, address, and phone number in order to study it again. She watched every person who walked through the lobby. What would she do if he was there? She wouldn't risk everyone's lives, but in the end, it didn't matter; she didn't see him. Finally, Valeria gave up and went to her room, attempting to sleep, and needing to dream the only dream that could console her.

Was he near? Perhaps he wasn't sleeping either. She finally drifted off only moments before her wake-up call. She showered and dressed before heading out to the airport. She got a cup of coffee, but after only a few sips, she grimaced and dumped it out. She would wait until she arrived at her destination.

The early morning Lufthansa flight to Florence, Italy, left on time. She would be there by the afternoon, where she hoped to get some answers. Studying the envelope again, she wondered, had Alex been in her room or had Paolo left it for her? Was the envelope with the business card a part of Alex's price or was it truly a message from him? She remembered Alex telling her to remember there were people with whom she could talk. Was that what the card was about? Why hadn't he said more?

After landing, she gathered her luggage and boarded the train to downtown Florence. It felt almost like being home! A taxi was sitting by the curb and the driver jumped out and placed her suitcase in the trunk. Valeria handed him the card and the driver began to loudly complain. She ignored his tantrum and, eventually, he pulled out toward the address she had given him. A few minutes later, he pulled over, less than a mile from the train station.

Evidently, even with his miniature vehicle, he couldn't make it down the narrow road where the flat was located. He dropped her off, continuing to berate her in Italian. She smiled at him and gave him a nice tip. He rolled his eyes and then, finally, smiled back.

She walked down the narrow cobblestone street with ancient earth-toned buildings, pulling her suitcase behind her. She carefully watched the building numbers and attempted to match it to that of the card she clutched in her fingers. She had transferred the information to her cell phone, for fear of losing the data, but she preferred to touch the card that could change her future and gave her hope.

The road was only wide enough for bikes and pedestrians. She could hear families talking to each other just a tad too loudly…but their voices were like music to her. She was home, back in Italy! She breathed in the wonderful Italian smells of coffee beans and fresh bread baking from a nearby restaurant and could hear someone playing Puccini. Italy...home! For how long, she didn't know. But there was something that needed to be done here and, for that, she was grateful.

The narrow road opened up into a piazza, or square, with five narrow roads extending from it. On her right, she saw the restaurant where the smell of rich Italian herbs became more distinct with each step. But her eyes lit up as she saw the familiar Italian sign across the square, "Patisserie"—a pastry shop. It certainly wasn't a pastry she was after...patisseries had *real* cappuccino!

In the shop, Valeria ordered and paid. The woman filled a demi cup of espresso and topped it with foam. It had been many months since she had enjoyed an addictive Italian cappuccino! The rush of energy was almost immediate. She decided that she shouldn't show up completely empty-handed. Opening the pastry case, she removed two cold tomato pizzas, each the size of a Danish. She wanted to bring groceries, but there was no time—she was desperate for answers! Valeria wanted to order another cappuccino, but she didn't need to be jittery, just awake.

The flat was located off another narrow street lined with tall stone buildings that had pretty green shutters. She pulled the suitcase into the dark hallway and began to climb the ancient stone steps that had been rounded by time. With the buildings proximity to the Medici Castle—the Palazzo Pitti— she imagined that Michelangelo, Galileo, and Di Vinci might have also climbed these ancient stairs.

She lifted the rustic knocker and dropped it against the wooden door. It left a sound far louder than she had intended. A few minutes later, she saw Shinsu's bright eyes and crop of white hair.

CHAPTER 15

Shinsu's sparkling blue eyes were a welcomed sight. "You made it, dear! Come in!"

Valeria stepped into the relatively small flat. Elegant furnishings occupied most of the well-used space and the ceilings were high and beamed. The entry was used as a combination of formal living and dining room. Straight ahead, and to her right, she saw the tiny, but efficient kitchen with shelves above and below the counter stocked with every kind of gourmet food device known to man, as well as colorful ceramic pots and bowls.

"You'll be staying in here." Shinsu headed toward what appeared to be the only bedroom, with a four poster bed and antique armoire, but turned to the left as they entered an enormous family room with numerous couches.

The wall in front of them was adorned with four open windows that were almost as tall as she was and swinging out from the windows were the green shutters that she had admired from the street level. From this level, she could also see the flower boxes bursting with rainbows of impatiens. She glanced beyond the flowers and saw the piazza and restaurant down below, as the wonderful smell of fresh herbs wafted into the flat.

"Here's where I entertain, most of the time. Though, in Florence, why stay in when there is so much to do! Leave your suitcase in here, dear, and let's go have some tea, shall we." Shinsu pulled some linens out from an armoire, set them on a couch and then did an about face heading briskly past the mahogany dining table that seemed to sit in what might have been a walkway into the kitchen. "There isn't much to my flat here but it suits me just fine when I'm in Florence." Valeria appreciated the addition of fresh flowers in every room.

In the kitchen, Shinsu pulled out a stool from a counter and began preparing the tea. The door to the deck was open and Shinsu walked outside, cut some herbs and then came back in. The enormous deck had been converted to a garden with potted flowers around the edges of the deck and vegetables in the center. Beyond the deck were the spectacular rooftops, domes, and steeples of Florence. It was breathtaking with the pinkish mist of early evening.

"Cup of tea?" she asked. Valeria nodded and Shinsu moved the bright pot onto a gas stove and then frowned. "Nap or talk?"

"Let's talk, please! Shinsu, I almost thought you were a dream."

"I'm not surprised! You were in rough shape in Paxos and at the hospital." She pulled her Persian cat onto her lap and petted him. The cat looked at Valeria, seeming to size her up. "Apollo, go find a mouse, Valeria and I have things to talk about!" The giant Persian jumped off her lap as if he understood. "You do prefer to be called Valeria, don't you?"

Valeria nodded and then looked at the cat critically.

"Apollo? Uh…that's not…uh?" She felt silly even thinking it, but her point of reality had shifted in the past year.

Glancing at the large gray cat, Shinsu shook her head. "*Apollo?* No, dear, that's a cat!"

A bit embarrassed, Valeria shrugged. "I have a lot of questions. I guess the first one is, why did I find your card in my hotel room in St. Croix?"

"I don't think that's why you just spent a day flying almost halfway around the world. Let's jump right to the primary questions." Shinsu placed tea bags in the cups and signaled toward the dining table. "Let's sit in here—more private." Grabbing a small tray she asked, "What do you take in your tea, dear?"

"Just plain, thank you." Shinsu returned to the kitchen to catch the squealing tea pot, and once it was silenced, Valeria asked, "How do I get things back to where they are supposed to be?"

Shinsu smiled from the kitchen, carrying the now full tea cups. "Now that's a good question!" She busied herself with bringing in spoons and biscotti. Then biting into a biscotti, Shinsu indicated that Valeria should take one. To please Shinsu, Valeria picked up a biscotti and pretended to be interested in it while awaiting the answer. When Shinsu didn't respond Valeria asked, "What's the answer?"

"Dear, why are you asking me?" Shinsu leaned back and set her biscotti down on her saucer.

"I thought you could help me. I really don't mean to be difficult. But can you?" Valeria was getting frustrated.

"Dear, when you phoned me from St. Croix yesterday, you told me what happened with Alex." Valeria nodded. Shinsu went on, "Do you remember what he told you?"

Valeria tried to recall their phone conversation. "Alex said that he knew Paolo would double deal with us." Shinsu frowned as if that was not what she was looking for. Valeria thought some more, but her energy was lagging and her mind was not as sharp, despite the cappuccino. "Well, Alex said that he didn't trust himself to stay on the island with me." Shinsu nodded, waiting for the next bit of information. Valeria thought for a moment. "He said for me to remember who I was and then—"

"Exactly!" Shinsu's eyes sparkled and she pulled her hands back onto her lap, expecting Valeria to have a major realization, which didn't come. Shinsu leaned forward. "Well? What does that mean?"

"I don't know. I guess he meant that I should remember I don't have to put up with that lying—"

Shinsu shook her head irritated. Valeria thought. "I'm..." She looked up. "I don't know...remember I'm the woman who loves him?" They were both getting frustrated. "I'm Valeria Mills. I'm, I guess I'm an oracle." Shinsu nodded, excited with Valeria's answer, but, clearly, she wanted more. "I guess I'm also Cassandra."

Shinsu held up her finger. "And *who is* Cassandra?"

"She was...I don't really know what you are looking for here."

Shinsu rolled her eyes and then was suddenly distracted by Apollo getting into trouble. She jumped up and went into the kitchen pulling Apollo's paws from her trash bin. "Apollo, not now. Go on." Shinsu looked back at Valeria. "Who wrote the Sibylline Oracle?"

"The Sybils."

"Those were created by...well," Shinsu rolled her eyes and then crossed her arms. "I'm talking about the original. You! You wrote the original! You are the last oracle and you are the most powerful! You are the one who can solve all of this! And Alex and the others need *your* help!" Shinsu slammed the lid on the trash bin and returned to where Valeria was.

"I can't help them. I don't have any power now. I don't..." Shinsu got irritated and began removing the items on the table. Evidently, social hour was over. In the kitchen she dumped the plate of untouched biscotti back into a clear glass container.

"Dear, I don't have time to listen to you invalidate yourself! I certainly hear enough of that out there." She signaled, indicating outside on the streets. Then she grabbed a hand towel and picked up the dishes on a drying rack, wiped them dry and put them away. "I am on the council; I can't tell you how to solve this. I can tell you that as long as you are perceived as a threat to the relationship of Alex and Kristiana, the family—*your* family—and Alex cannot work with you to solve this and they will need to stay clear of you, except for brief meetings agreed on by the immortals who filed the petition." Shinsu looked at Valeria. "And they *need you*, far more than you need them!"

"What do you mean 'perceived as a threat'? I don't intend to be a threat to Alex's relationship with Kristiana." Valeria drew a breath. "If he wanted to be with her, I would never stand in his way!"

Shinsu cut her off with a cynical, "Yes, dear."

"All right." She bit her lip. "How would the council, or maybe Kristiana, consider that I was no longer a threat?"

Satisfied that this was now heading down the right path, Shinsu smiled. She walked back in and sat down next to Valeria with interest.

"Is there a statement I can make? Or..." There was a knock at the door.

"Someone's here." Shinsu grabbed her purse and dramatically threw a beautiful flower wrap around herself. "You two chat until I get back." And with that, Shinsu opened the front door to a very nervous Paolo. She gave him a frown and said with mock sternness, "Now, I expect you to behave yourself!" With that, she whacked him on the behind and was gone.

Feeling betrayed, Valeria walked straight into the family room and pulled her suitcase toward the door, without making eye contact with him. Paolo stepped in front of the door and put his hand on her shoulder.

"Valeria, I have been forced to realize that it is only a matter of time until you find yourself in very serious trouble."

She pulled away from him. "You put this all in place. You can stop it."

"As I said before, I was not the only signatory on the petition. I did not even originate it. I cannot simply cancel it, and even if I could, it would have to be taken to the council at their next scheduled meeting, which is not for another 500 years."

She had heard enough lies. "Are you even capable of telling the truth? I know that's a lie! I know there is a way to solve this! Alex was able to arrange a council meeting in less than a month to get approval for our engagement. If he can do it, so can you."

"Yes! Exactly!" Paolo looked up and then with a pretentious smile said, "*That* is exactly how we will resolve this!" Valeria felt confused by Paolo's seeming change of attitude.

"Resolve this? Paolo, no more games!"

He narrowed his eyes. "This is not a game, Valeria. And I need you to understand that, regardless of my assistance, I am not resolving this so that you can interfere with Kristiana's marriage to Alex."

Rolling her eyes, she retorted, "I don't really care what you want or expect. I know that you never do anything if it doesn't benefit you!"

He went on as if he hadn't heard her, "I am willing to help, if you will allow me. I believe that I have a solution." He leaned forward. "I have arranged for your family to join us for a celebration."

"My family?"

He nodded and took her hand tentatively. "Our engagement celebration." She pulled her hand back in disgust.

"You're dreaming!"

"Valeria, it solves many problems. It allows you to speak to your family which also permits you to help locate my sister. With Shinsu's assistance, I have retracted the Law of Nevia so that your family is no longer included in the petition." He continued, "I have submitted a request to the council for an emergency meeting to approve an immortal marriage. This can be done in days. Immortals are romantics!"

"I will never marry you. There must be another way."

"Bella, I can think of no other solution. We need a council meeting." His eyes pleaded. "Do you know how very close all of you were to being executed when you were hospitalized?"

She lowered her eyebrows. "You know about that?"

He went on ignoring her question. "*I saw* what very nearly occurred." Paolo gave her a painful glance. "That was never my intention, bella!" He swallowed.

"Alex wanted to come to me in the hospital?"

"You know him well. What did you expect he would do? Why do you think Mani and Shinsu were there by the time you awoke? They arrived within hours of your admittance. Do you even realize what everyone went through for several hours! The emergency plane and helicopter transports. Yes, Valeria, it was very serious...*is* very serious."

Her jaw dropped. "I had no idea," she said softly. And then she shook her head. "Paolo, you caused this. You can resolve it."

"No, I cannot do that alone. I have taken the only steps that I am permitted. With the exception of Alex, the remainder of the Trento Family has been removed from the petition. But you must understand that The Law of Nevia still stands between you and Alex! The only other thing I can do is permit you a brief meeting with him. Those are the only actions that the council and the law will permit. Any further amendments to the petition will require council approval...at a council meeting.

"Valeria, there is only one possible way that this can be resolved soon." She glared at him suspiciously. "But you must understand, bella, that this is an engagement between immortals. The cost of betraying the council is death. They do not tolerate trickery or lies. If it is found that you violated agreements with me or the council, if you were to have secret meetings or secret communications, if there were any...*further* embraces, it would certainly be discovered. If anyone suspected that this engagement was not real in every way, it would be very dangerous."

"Is this a trick?"

Paolo looked at Valeria, steeled in his response. "No, it is an engagement."

Valeria considered for a moment. "And my family is coming *to celebrate?*"

"Representation from your family will be arriving in Florence."

Still suspicious, her eyes narrowed. "Representation?"

"Alex may not attend, of course, without council approval." He gulped. "You may ask your family. They will tell you the truth."

"And what is your plan? We get engaged and then what?"

"I wish to locate my sister. You could help. If we combine our efforts, perhaps we could find her sooner."

"Why are you doing this, Paolo? Just tell me!"

He got up and walked to the window overlooking the piazza. Valeria stood by the door and finally huffed and walked in to hear his response. She stood behind him silently waiting.

"Why should I try? You do not believe a word I say."

Valeria glared at his back. "Tell me!"

He finally turned and looked at her critically. "You began to care for me. I could see it in your eyes. I felt it when we kissed. You enjoyed it."

She shook her head in disgust. "I was lonely, *because of you*, incidentally."

"You started to believe you could be happy with me. You will deny it. But I know it to be true." Paolo turned to her. "When I kissed you—"

She put her hands over her ears and walked away, but Paolo followed her back into the kitchen and put his hand on her shoulder so she would look at him. She brushed off his hand, and glared at him.

"Valeria, you asked me what I want!" Paolo's eyes were intense. "I am aware that by following other's...rules, I have made a mess of things. I have been forced to realize that I must fix this, before people I care for are harmed." He looked up. "I am angry with Alex for the life my sister has had. But I would never wish him gone. And I would never wish that for you."

"Well, what *did* you intend out of all this pain that you caused, besides gloating rights?"

"I wanted you," he said, and then shrugged. "And I wanted to gloat." He looked down at her. "Valeria, I would probably do it this way again. Because if I had not interrupted your marriage to Alex, my sister would have lost, and she does not deserve to lose that way, abandoned as if she were nothing of importance. And you would be his, without choosing. You should choose."

She nodded, feeling that, for the first time since Alex's transference, Paolo was capable of telling the truth. "I will always choose Alex!"

"Alex is married. Valeria, there are not many immortals who are related by blood. My sister and I are very close. She has made some decisions that I do not agree with. But I love her and I want to find her. When Kristiana is found, if she does not perceive a threat from you, she and Alex can decide what they are to do, without you as a factor. It is right. It is fair."

"There has to be another way."

"Yes. We can continue with Alex and your family barred from your life until Kristiana is found. Regardless of what you wish to believe, Kristiana has a special connection to Alex and she knows what will happen—especially when it comes to him. Do you think she will be found, simply to be discarded?"

"When this is over, the engagement is over." He shook his head. Valeria glared at him. "I would never marry you! Not in a thousand years!"

Paolo looked into her eyes and spoke softly, calmly. "If our engagement was discovered to be a pretense, we would be charged with Frivolous Abuse of Council Time, as well as being charged with Council Deception. And the Law of Nevia might be enacted against those who were believed to be involved in the deception. Valeria, I could not accept a false engagement, and neither can you!"

Her eyes moved around the room. She couldn't think. What if this was another trick? How could she agree to marry Paolo? Could she pull off any affection for him? She had. She had felt affection for him.

"I'll have to think about this."

He nodded.

The door opened and Shinsu walked in with a loaf of bread and a bag of produce. She looked at Paolo critically and he shrugged. She nodded and sighed. "Paolo, I think it is time for you to give the girl some space." She winked at Valeria.

Paolo didn't move. Shinsu gave him a slight smile, but her voice had power, "Now!" He nodded, dejected, and slipped out the door. She went to the dining room table. "One thing we must always remember is that trickery and lies are not tolerated by the council. As a council member, I would never permit myself to be in that position." She looked at Valeria, ensuring that she understood. Valeria nodded. She went on, "Good. Now, did anything happen while I was gone?"

Valeria thought for a moment. She wanted Shinsu's input. She *desperately needed* Alex to tell her what she should do. She needed Camille and Ava and Lars and Mani; *she needed her family.* Valeria didn't really know Shinsu well enough to know if she could trust her in this decision. She felt that she could. But who had sent for Shinsu? The first visit, Valeria had assumed it was Alex. Now, she wondered if it had been Paolo.

"Paolo asked me to marry him," Valeria said flatly, watching for a reaction. Shinsu's eyes sparkled.

"I see. And have you made a decision?" Shinsu said, unpacking the produce and bread.

Valeria got up and went into the kitchen. She needed to see Shinsu's face. "What do you think?"

"Well," Shinsu said, as she leaned over the counter between them. "I have known Paolo—and Kristiana, for that matter—much longer than I have known Alex and his family." She looked to the side. "For such a small group, it's amazing how long we can miss people in our own backyard, as Trento is."

Shinsu took Valeria's arm and led her to the couch. "Do you at least like Paolo?"

Valeria thought for a moment, she had to be careful how she worded things. "I was growing to like him. But Paolo will never —"

Shinsu raised her hand. "Dear, be very careful with the word 'never.' You put into place postulates that are difficult to change, and I believe beings *can* change. People can be positively influenced by others. I do know Paolo has some growing up to do. I'm sure that is your concern." Shinsu looked at Valeria squarely, waiting for her to acknowledge the comment.

"Yes. I have a concern about that." Valeria jumped on the opportunity to ask what she should not. "What if Kristiana and Alex dissolve their marriage?"

Narrowing her eyes, Shinsu stepped carefully, "I know that you were in love with Alex only a few months ago." Valeria noticed that Shinsu used the past tense and that left a pain in her heart. "But if all goes as expected, you will be on the right path for you. It's a different path, but it may end up even more exciting. Life can always change directions! Look at me; not so very long ago, I practically drooled when Jeremiah looked at me. Of course, that would be ancient history to you!"

Valeria's face fell; she didn't want to hear that someday she wouldn't care about Alex. There were plenty of examples of love that survived time and trial—though most of her examples were fictional. Still, there were enough live examples, particularly Alex's absolute devotion to her!

Shinsu smiled and squeezed Valeria's hand as if she saw her thoughts and continued, "Right now I'm concerned about *some people* being so alone. I don't think that's good for *anyone*. I think it would be better if you had your family back, and they need you, as well."

"What about Alex?" Valeria wondered if Alex had been included in the "all." Was Shinsu considering how this news would affect the only person who really mattered in this whole conversation?

"Alex has created a situation that needs resolution." She spoke slowly and deliberately. "But I think this engagement can help resolve many of the wrongs and set you on the right path." Valeria nodded, uncertain of what Shinsu perceived as the right path. "Dear, I can tell you what I think. But remember *who you are*." She tapped Valeria's arm and winked.

CHAPTER 16

Shinsu walked to the door, again picking up her flowered wrap, and threw it dramatically around her. "This time of year I still get chilled. Come, dear. You haven't seen much of Florence yet, have you—at least not this visit." She winked as they walked out the door.

They stepped down the rounded stone steps, and then crossed the piazza with its restaurants now serving wine and appetizers. They passed the small patisserie where Valeria had purchased the cappuccino earlier that day.

Walking rapidly down an alley wide enough only for pedestrians or bicycles, they arrived on a main street. A swarm of colorful Vespa motor scooters, driven by beautiful women in business suits, moved around the corner. Valeria stepped out of the way. Shinsu didn't even blink and crossed the road between the swarm causing no upset at all. On the south side of the road was an ancient brick building with little architectural interest, an oddity in Florence.

Shinsu smiled. "It looks like a prison from here. But

inside, it is marvelous." Then she looked at Valeria and said casually, "Well, you know."

Valeria studied the building, but none of it was familiar.

"It's Palazzo Pitti. Palazzo means palace. The Medici's purchased it from a man named Pitti." Shinsu smiled. "We must find time to have a glass of wine in the palazzo's Boboli Garden. It is really fabulous!"

Glancing sideways to Shinsu, Valeria thought that, although she liked Shinsu, she still wasn't completely certain she could trust her. They continued along the street, with the Palazzo Pitti next to them as they approached the Ponte Vecchio, a bridge across the Arno River.

The bridge had multiple stories, with numerous shops and several arches in the center, providing an ideal view of the beautiful, gently flowing Arno. "You know, Cosimo Medici— oh he just adored you, by the way—Cosimo had a walk-way built from the palace over the Ponte Vecchio, to the Uffizi gallery. You can still see it!"

They stopped below one of the arches with a particularly fantastic view of the river. It was evidently a Florentine lover's lane and several couples were taking advantage of the view. Shinsu looked at them in a way that said "move" causing two of the couples to cross the road to the other side. The other couple walked along the bridge, offering them privacy.

The water gently flowed through the center of Florence. Shinsu leaned on the rail of the bridge and took in the view. There were other bridges that Valeria could see from her vantage point on the Ponte Vecchio but this location seemed special. "You sense it, don't you, dear?" Shinsu said. Valeria looked at her quizzically. "When the Nazis left Italy, they didn't want to leave all of these roads across the Arno. The Ponte Vecchio has existed since Roman times and is the only original surviving bridge. Of course, they rebuilt early in the

Renaissance." Her face lit up. "What a wonderful time that was to be in Florence!"

Shinsu stared at the river and said, "Dear, it is important for you to understand that you don't have to communicate everything you think. Do you understand?"

"I'm not sure."

"If someone were to ask you how you felt about certain individuals, it would be important that you knew how to answer that question without causing concern. Do you understand?" Valeria thought for a moment and then shrugged. "You know about transferences?" Shinsu asked.

"Yes. I've had three of them with Alex and Mani. And I gave one to Jeremiah. He wasn't very pleased."

"Yes, well, pleasing Jeremiah is..." Shinsu stopped, muttering something to herself as she rolled her eyes. "I did hear about it. Dear, you will most definitely be required to give at least one transference. You may even need to testify via transference to the council. It is important that we don't," Shinsu sighed, "waste council time. So I thought perhaps I could work with you on this." Shinsu narrowed her eyes narrowed with significance. "Here is the important thing. You must learn how to only answer the question that was asked and place a wall around everything else." Shinsu paused and stared into Valeria's eyes to see if she got the point.

"I just don't think I'm very good at that."

"Well, you simply *must* become very skilled at this very quickly! There may be some who have concern about approving your marriage. We want to deliver information that needs to be transferred, but there is no need to deliver all of the information you have, especially regarding recent events. Do you understand?" Valeria shrugged. She didn't want to marry Paolo.

"I'm..." Valeria wondered if she should say this, but the

words came out of her mouth before she could evaluate it. "Shinsu, I'm concerned about Alex."

"We all are, dear!" Shinsu's voice got quietly intense. "How long do you think it will be until Alex violates the rules? Months? Years? Do you believe that on your birthday he will feel comfortable trusting that this curse has been removed?"

Shinsu took a breath and calmed herself. "Alex is a good boy. But he needs to focus on his situation and he must get it handled." She pulled Valeria around. "Do you understand, dear?" Valeria nodded and Shinsu smiled and winked. "Paolo said that you were a very bright girl!

"So, dear, let's…let's try something, with far less charge on it." Shinsu frowned for a moment and then lifted a finger to her. "All right, tell me about something important that happened when you were a child."

Valeria thought for a few minutes and then shrugged. "There wasn't much that was important."

"Was there something you decided you didn't want anyone to know about?"

"No. I'm pretty much an open book."

Shinsu took Valeria's arm and spoke sternly, "Dear, you must listen to Su-su! You must *not* be an open book!"

A little frightened by Shinsu's expression, Valeria mumbled, "All right."

"So think of something that you don't want anyone to know about."

Valeria looked down the Arno. It was breathtaking with the pinkish sunset over fantastic rooflines. She remembered living at the Wilson's home. "All right. The time I lived with the Wilsons was…interesting."

"When you say interesting, do you mean bad?"

Valeria only nodded.

"All right, dear, now take what you don't want to convey

and put a wall around it. Only think of the nice things about the Wilsons. Focus very hard on the good things about the Wilsons. Don't permit your mind to wander anywhere else. Do you think you can do that?"

"I think so."

Shinsu nodded and took her hands. "Now, look me in the eyes and think very clearly only about the good things from the Wilsons. Think about the energy of that travelling from you to me."

Instantly, Shinsu pulled her hands back in irritation. "Well, dear, we are going to have to work on that!" She shook her finger at Valeria. "Those boys! Someone needed to..." she huffed.

Embarrassed, Valeria looked away. "I don't know if I can do this."

"Let's try it again. Think of the good things about the Wilsons."

Focusing for a few moments, Valeria said, "Okay. Let me try again."

She again took Shinsu's hands. And again, Shinsu yanked her hands back, stopping the flow as she cocked her head to the side. "Dear, I know you have the skill and the talent. What is it? Why are you unwilling?"

"I...Shinsu, I'm..." Valeria gulped. "I want to do what you say...but I guess it feels like I'm lying if I wall in some memories." Shinsu took Valeria's arm and steered her back toward her flat along the Ponte Vecchio and past the Palazzo Pitti.

"My darling girl, this is not about lying; this is about you choosing what you want to tell." Before returning to the apartment, Shinsu turned to Valeria and took her arms. "Dear, you need to master this. This is very important. You need to learn how to transfer some information, but not all information.

Can you practice that?"

"I'll try."

When Valeria and Shinsu returned to the flat, Paolo was there. He glanced at Shinsu and she nodded and winked at him. Valeria noticed that Shinsu did not have the sparkle that she had before. They all knew the lesson had not gone well.

Valeria avoided eye contact with Paolo. She didn't trust him and she was angry with him.

Shinsu sighed. "Paolo, you should go and take care of those details. Valeria needs to take a nap. Then the two of you should go to dinner."

It normally would have been irritating to have her evening dictated, but Valeria was too tired to think about it. Shinsu guided her to a nearby chair and Valeria slid into it and dipped her head into her hands. Valeria wondered how it could be that she was even considering marrying someone other than Alex. It was wrong on so many levels! How could she even consider marrying someone who had caused so much pain in her life and threatened the lives of all those she loved? And then there was the issue of trust…how could she marry someone she didn't trust?

Still there had been moments when Paolo had seemed tender-hearted, like at the park. There was something in him that could be very sweet, but to be married to him and not to Alex was an overwhelming prospect. Why did it need to be resolved now?

There was one thing that both Shinsu and Paolo had said that had a significant impact on her; how long could she stay away from Alex? How long could he stay away from her? But with a council approved engagement, that would end the threat. At least she could talk to him then. At least they could see each other. They wouldn't be exiled from each other's lives. The real question was, could she marry Paolo and stay away from

Alex? Was that even the plan?

The door closed and Valeria realized that Paolo had left. She was weary and her hand wandered over the arm of the chair and something fell. Valeria bent to pick it up and immediately recognized the stationary and the beautiful script. It was more than simply the business card from before…it was a letter from Alex.

She took a deep breath as the tears formed. She held the letter to her heart. Shinsu looked at Valeria. "I need to attend to my garden. Some things are private and should remain so." Shinsu's hand rubbed across Valeria's shoulder with a soft pat, before she walked outside to her balcony and closed the door.

Valeria opened the letter.

Beautiful,

This is some mess, isn't it? I want you to know that my deepest regret in life is the pain that I have caused you over the past few months! Because of my carelessness, you were left alone in the world again. I would have never chosen that for you. I wish the situation was different.

Paolo and I don't agree on very much. But we do agree on this; you must take the next step. The family is eagerly awaiting the reunion.

Until we meet again,

Alex

She took the letter and ran into the bathroom. She pulled the lid down on the toilet and sat down, holding Alex's words closely to her heart as silent tears rolled down her cheeks.

∞

Once Valeria had finally dried her eyes and kissed the letter again, she discovered that Shinsu had left a message stating that she would be gone until late. Valeria saw that the large living area had been converted into a bedroom for her. She was certain that it had been planned to keep her in the flat, where everyone involved could keep a close eye on her.

The note said for Valeria to have a glass of sherry, and that Paolo would come in a few hours, so she should rest and then dress for dinner. Shinsu had hung up Valeria's clothes, which would have been presumptuous from anyone else except Alex or Camille, but for some reason, she didn't mind.

She closed the door to the family room and lay down, waking later to a knock at the door to her room. It was Paolo. She let him in, without pretending to be cordial; she wasn't unfriendly, she just wasn't about to make any pretense of her feelings.

"I have made reservations at my favorite restaurant. It is only a few blocks from here on The Oltrarno, this side of the Arno, where there are fewer tourists."

They walked down along the Palazzo Pitti and then turned at the Arno. He offered his arm and, after a few near mishaps in her heels, she finally accepted his assistance. Still, Valeria's mind was a hundred miles away, in a cottage north of Trento. She wondered if it would always be that way.

The restaurant was called Mamma Gina's and the waiter clearly knew and liked Paolo. There was a special table in the back reserved for them. Paolo ordered in Italian and various dishes came out. Valeria had no interest in eating but she had learned long ago that there were ways to placate those around her.

They sat at a candle lit table for two. Paolo seemed nervous. She just went through the motions.

"Valeria, I believe this is the finest minestrone in all of Firenze—or Florence, as you call it. Try it," he encouraged.

She sipped the Chianti instead. It was nine p.m. and the restaurant had just opened for dinner only an hour before.

Dinner lasted several hours and she had somehow managed to answer questions by the server and occasionally even responded to Paolo, even looking him in the eye.

After the bill had been paid, he steered her onto the Ponte Vecchio to the overlook of the Arno where she had stood with Shinsu earlier that day. The lights of Florence were reflected on the river in various shades of yellows and white. He placed his arm around her waist, but she pulled away, and he awkwardly pulled his arm to his side.

"Valeria," he tapped his elegant forefinger on his cheek as he drew a deep breath, "Shinsu spoke to you. You know that now, right now, we are making memories." He glanced out at the river and drew a nervous breath before reaching for her again. This time she permitted it, although her body went rigid.

"Why is it their business? I'm going to do this. Isn't that enough?"

Paolo looked out at the Arno again and pursed his lips for a moment. "No. It is not."

Her face flushed with anger. "Well that's just too bad."

"Valeria, how I proposed will be an important part of our life. Our memory of this must be…special. Something…you remember. It will be very important."

Understanding what he was trying to convey, she rolled her eyes. "They can only kill me once." She thought for a moment and shrugged. "Or so…" Paolo heard the joke and smiled. It almost made her smile. "All right, Paolo."

With his arm around her, he pulled her toward him. She caught a hint of sweet vulnerability in his eyes. He brushed the hair from her face and Valeria forced herself to not push his hand away.

Nervously, he reached into his pocket. "Valeria, I know it

is too soon after everything. But I want you to be my wife." He pulled out a small ring box from his jacket. All Valeria could think of was the night Alex had proposed while they were in bed in their wonderful cottage. Paolo opened the box and there was a ring with a large diamond in the center surrounded by emeralds and rubies. It was two rings wrapped together.

"It's called a Gimmel Ring." It was beautiful. Still. Valeria found herself comparing it to Alex's simple but elegant ring.

"Pretty," she said flatly. Valeria noticed ancient engraving on the side of it. "You must have spent the afternoon with antique dealers."

"No. This was your ring...when you were my Isabella." She wondered why she felt bad. He continued, "I took the ring from your finger before you—before she was buried." He took a deep breath as if that were a deeply painful memory.

Glancing down at the ring she saw an inscription, a Latin phrase that read, "In meo corde aeternaliter." Valeria looked away. She did not want to care about him. "So, what does this inscription say?"

He stared down the river, and then whispered, "Forever in my heart."

"That probably meant a lot, considering you didn't even know Isabella before she was sold to you."

"The inscription was added after...her death..."

Valeria rolled her eyes, now she felt as if she had just been dancing on the grave of his dead wife and child. She looked down, irritated with herself for even caring. "Okay. What do we have to do here?"

He looked at her critically. "Do you accept?"

There could be worse things in life than marrying Paolo. Her heart would always be with Alex. But what if that meant certain death for them both? She nodded and Paolo twisted the rings so that they disengaged. He took one of the rings and slid it onto her left finger and placed the other back in the case and into his suit pocket.

"We should kiss. That is what people do now."

She shook her head ever so slightly. "I'm not ready for that." She swallowed.

He looked away and then back at Valeria. "If you are to become my bride, you must behave as my bride. There can be no other way."

He waited for her and she leaned up to kiss the side of his face but he brushed his fingers through her hair and stopped her with that action. With his other hand he pulled her into him and held her face inches from his. Then, as he saw her relax, he leaned down and softly pressed his lips to hers. It was a tender kiss...a first kiss of sorts. Valeria was surprised to see that there was emotion behind it—on both sides. It wasn't the same feeling she had when kissing Alex. But it was definitely better than kissing David.

Thinking for a moment, she realized that, not so long ago, she had been willing to marry David. And recognizing that Paolo was far more interesting, she decided that perhaps she could pull this off and Alex would be safe. He allowed the kiss to end, without the driving passion that had been in the kiss in St. Croix days before. But this time, there was no guilt from it. She could honestly admit that it was...pleasant.

Paolo smiled, seeing her acceptance of him. "Good." He took her hand in his and they walked back to Shinsu's.

∞

The daylight shined brightly through the shutters. For the second night she had struggled to sleep, drifting off as the sun began to ease its way over the horizon. She glanced at the clock in the room. Nine a.m. At least she had slept for a few hours. Then she heard the voices on the other side of her door. She slipped on her cotton kimono over her T-shirt and cotton yoga pants. To her surprise, it was Lars and Camille! Lars put his arms around her and spun her around in a tight embrace, as tears ran down her face—oh how she had missed her family!

"We've missed you sweetheart!" He nuzzled into her ear. "Ava would have been here but we thought, for now, it might be best if it was just Camille and I."

Valeria leaned back and brushed her hand over Lars' face. "I've missed you. And please tell Ava how much I've missed her!"

"Soon, you'll be able to tell her yourself."

And then it was her turn to hug Camille—the sister of her heart! She felt soft sobs run through both of them as they hugged. Paolo entered the room from outside with a cappuccino for Valeria. She thanked Paolo and shot it down while catching up with Lars and Camille; just having them with her improved her mood dramatically.

Camille took Valeria by the arm and led her to the deck overlooking Florence. It was such a breathtaking view. And the air was perfect.

"I can't tell you how much I've missed you!" Camille said. A tear formed in the corner of her eye.

"It's been a wild ride, that's for sure." Valeria's face got serious. "Not at all the way we planned, is it."

"No," Camille said wistfully, turning away. "Val, you aren't really in love with Paolo, are you?"

Valeria wasn't sure how much she could tell Camille. "Oh, well, he kind of grows on you."

Camille's eyes narrowed in sudden understanding. "It's been tough, I know. Val, I want you to know that none of us are going to judge you for this! We all know that you have your reasons." She shook her head. "But I have to tell you that, as much as I love you, I just can't plan your wedding to, " they both glanced in through the glass toward Paolo, "*him.*"

The men were engaged in conversation. Lars seemed to be hiding his distaste for Paolo quite well.

"I can't either." Valeria tried to laugh, but it sounded more like a cry. "I suppose we will figure it all out when we have to." Her eyes filled with concern. "How is he really?"

Camille shook her head and closed her eyes. "You know he never loved Kristiana. Never! That relationship spelled disaster from day one!"

Valeria felt the tears building. "I'm sorry, Camille. I really can't talk about Kristiana and Alex, yet."

Gulping, Camille said, "Well, I will be here for you. I will be there tonight for your engagement party and at the wedding—whenever it is. You know I'll do whatever you need, so if you really want me there, I'll stand up with you for this…this marriage." Her tears returned. "I will, if you need me there for you," she said.

Valeria shook her head and smiled weakly. "No. I wouldn't ask you to do that. I haven't thought about any of it. But I'm definitely not interested in anything like…well, like before."

Lars and Paolo stepped out onto the deck, both looking concerned. Paolo had a note in his hand. "We have the notice. Jeremiah will join us tonight for the engagement party. If he approves, tomorrow we will fly to Paxos for presentation to the council."

Fear clouded Valeria's eyes. It was all happening so fast. Still, she thought, it would be easier to do this quickly. If she had time to think about it, she would not be able to go through with it.

Shinsu joined them, still in her flowered wrap. "I just got the news."

Lars glanced at Shinsu. "We need to postpone. From everything I've heard, Val needs more time...to adapt."

Shaking her head, Shinsu said, "There is no postponement. This girl must be prepared by tonight!"

CHAPTER 17

The engagement party was in Carrara, at Paolo's family estate. Valeria packed up her bags and drove with Camille, while Lars rode with Paolo.

"Val, have you really thought about all of this?"

Uncertain as to how much she could tell Camille, Valeria said, "It's what I have to do." Then she smiled softly. "At least I get all of you back with this deal."

"I just don't trust Paolo. Alex seems to, but Paolo has just done too many questionable things for me to believe him at this point."

With a slight grimace, Valeria nodded. Still, she was glad to hear that Alex truly supported this plan. Even while reading the note, she had wondered if Paolo was pressuring Alex into writing it.

The drive was through rolling hills with occasional views of the Mediterranean. Valeria wondered if there would ever be a time when she would return to that wonderful life with Alex. It had been a dream life and just to have a snippet of that life had been a gift. Maybe that's all people really got—just snippets of their ideal life. For her, it was painful enough, but to think of Alex waiting eons for her only to see her married to Paolo brought tears to her eyes.

Paolo had asked them to meet in Pisa. The town still had the ancient walls and they parked near the Leaning Tower. It was truly beautiful, but most of that was overshadowed with her thoughts of what was about to happen—she was actually going to marry *Paolo*.

When they left, he insisted that his fiancée ride with him for the last hour. Valeria stared out the window as they rode in silence. Paolo punched the gas pedal and left Lars and Camille behind as soon as they entered the highway. She shook her head; it was so like Paolo to show off the speed of his Aston Martin! Nearly an hour later, Paolo slowed slightly and now Valeria could see Lars' black Mercedes on the road about a mile behind them.

"Valeria, there are some things that require…attention," he said, oddly pre-occupied with something in his rearview mirror.

"The transference?"

"Yes, but first, I would like some time alone with you." She winced; she had hoped that intimacy would not be required until they were married. Still, she remembered how sweet and gentle Paolo had been with her the night before. "I thought perhaps we should have some time to ourselves before this evening."

"And the other?" she questioned. Paolo glanced at her, puzzled. "You said there were *things*…plural."

"Oh, yes." He nodded. He seemed nervous and distracted. "Yes. You will be required to provide Jeremiah with a transference this evening and I have an idea that may assist you in providing him with more pertinent information."

248

She glanced at him awaiting the details. Instead, Paolo hit a button on his steering wheel, and immediately she heard a phone ringing over the car speakers.

"Yeah, Paolo." It was Lars.

"Valeria and I are making a stop. We will meet you in Carrara at the bar in the Hotel Michelangelo."

"Alright, well, we'll see you two there." Valeria heard Lars say. She could also hear Camille beginning to object, when Paolo disconnected the phone. There was a row of sycamores that ran along both sides of the road and tall bushes that ran behind the trees. Paolo seemed to be watching Lars' car in the rearview mirror and then signaled as he slowed to a crawl. Valeria wondered what Paolo was up to. It almost seemed like he wanted Lars to see whcre they were going. Then Paolo turned the car down the dirt road about thirty feet and stopped.

Seeing the empty field, Valeria realized that Paolo was looking for privacy and she began to panic. He quickly walked around and helped her out of the car.

"Paolo, I don't know what you have in mind, but it will not involve—"

"No—no rum," he interrupted. "But we must toast our engagement. This time I promise not to ply you with too much alcohol." Paolo was playing a role...creating a memory. He opened the trunk, and removed a blanket and spread it on the ground next to the car. Then he opened a basket and removed a cold bottle of champagne and two glasses, handing them to her. Without wasting a minute, he pulled her onto the blanket with him and then opened the bottle. While Valeria held both glasses, Paolo filled them and then set the bottle down. Nervously, she took a sip of champagne remembering that the last time she had any was the day after Paolo had ruined her life.

"I have an idea." He leaned in toward her, and she started to block him. "I am your fiancé, allow me to…" Paolo took her glass and sat it next to them. Then he leaned into her and his hand gently brushed her face. His lips pressed against hers as his arms went around her, tenderly lowering her onto the blanket. Struggling beneath him, she realized that she was pinned. Panic began to overtake her. Would he force her into intimacy?

His voice was soft, "Do not fight me, bella," he cooed into her ear. "I know that you would prefer to wait until our wedding night."

"Then, please…" She started to choke, but his mouth went back to hers, prohibiting her from finishing the sentence. Just then, she heard the sound of Lars' approaching car. Could she signal to them? Camille would certainly be watching to make sure she was all right. But would they stop? She was engaged to Paolo now. To even think that she could be engaged to someone other than Alex was painful.

Just then, she heard the honk of the car. As soon as they passed, Paolo's head popped up, watching until they were out of sight. Then he sighed as he sat up and offered his hand to help her up. His eyes darted around and then shaking off some emotion, he smiled as he picked up the champagne glasses and clinked them in a toast and then downed it. She didn't drink.

"Valeria, let's see what we can do with a transference." Her heart was pounding. His lips brushed hers lightly and she nervously took his hands. Within a few seconds, Paolo nodded. "Good."

He sat next to her on the blanket as he continued to sip his glass of champagne. She wondered what this was all about. She closed her eyes. It was really sinking in; she was marrying a man other than Alex! She tried to hold back the tears.

"It's time to go now." Paolo leaned over and kissed her

again. She guessed that she would need to get used to it. Still, there were worse things than kissing Paolo.

They arrived in the ancient hillside town of Carrara and wound their way along a narrow road, stopping in front of a medieval building with a sign that read, "The Hotel Michelangelo." They walked hand in hand across the lobby and straight to the bar where her friends sat. It felt odd and unnatural for her to be holding hands with Paolo, and Camille seemed concerned. In response, Valeria offered her a weak smile as Paolo offered to take them to lunch.

They walked through the tiny town and Valeria thought that it had probably not changed much in thousands of years. It was lodged on a hill between the bustling Carrara port and the Apuan Alps, surrounded by tall grass and wild flowers. She noticed that the white mountains that rose in the distance were occasionally missing a peak, and instead, had a square gash from mining. The mountains were covered with white, although it seemed late in the year for snow.

Seeing Valeria's expression, Paolo said, "That is powder from the marble quarries."

Lars asked about visiting the quarries.

"The roads up to the marble quarries are very dangerous." Paolo pointed out the hairpin turns moving up the mountain. "It is not uncommon for trucks, loaded down with marble, to roll off the mountain and on to the lower roads."

Camille piped up, "Well then, I'm out." Valeria nodded to Camille in agreement. Then Camille leaned into Valeria, and said, "Besides, we need to talk!" Valeria knew exactly what Camille wanted to talk about.

"The town's water supply." Paolo waved at a water fountain with a beautifully carved lion in the town center. Valeria wondered if that was last year or a hundred years ago.

They crossed the cobblestone street to enter an upscale

restaurant. The owners were ecstatic to see Paolo and hugged and kissed him. Paolo introduced Valeria as his fiancée and she winced again, but accepted the hugs and kisses of the owners. They ate lunch and then drove back into the country to Paolo's home.

From the road, there was a large white marble carving of a mermaid, and a sign that read, "Bella Vida." Valeria wondered if there would be a day when she would think of this as her home. Caterers and service people bustled around the estate, with fountains, flowers, and boxes of supplies.

The home itself was a traditional stone villa with at least twenty rooms and she guessed that it was as old as the town. There were servants busily preparing for at least two hundred guests.

Paolo went into control mode with the servants, but Valeria felt that perhaps his need to dominate the servants was to compensate for his nervousness. He guided her up the stairs to a room at the end of the hall. He opened the door and it was exquisitely detailed with furniture that one might expect in a palace. The windows looked out over both the mountains, and the gardens below, where the party would take place.

"Paolo? When am I going to practice doing transferences? Jeremiah wasn't very happy with me the last time. And then with Shinsu…"

Looking up for a moment, Paolo narrowed his eyes, selecting his words carefully as he sat on the edge of the bed. "You must not worry about that, bella."

"But Shinsu said—"

Paolo shook his head to interrupt her sentence. "The truth will speak for itself." Another memory, Valeria thought. Paolo took her hands in his. "I do not want you to concern yourself with this." His eyes held such earnestness and sweetness that she wanted to believe him. "I have not always deserved your trust. There were times that I have been…" He shook his head. "Valeria, you must trust me, now. Please trust me."

She didn't have a choice.

Paolo rose, ending the conversation. "I need you to focus on being relaxed…and beautiful." He crossed to the huge armoire and opened the door, revealing a sky blue silk gown. She took it out of the armoire and examined it. It had a haltered top, and a very low back—far more risqué than she was comfortable with. Good thing she hadn't eaten much in the last few days!

"It's beautiful, Paolo. But I thought I would just wear one of my dresses."

"This is a formal event and you will need a formal gown. I need your dress to be distracting." He pulled her face around and said softly, "Many problems can be hidden by the right…clothing."

Still, she was concerned. "Paolo? What will happen tonight?"

He came behind her and held her shoulders, looking at her in the mirror on the door of the armoire. "Do not worry." He kissed the back of her neck and this time she didn't fight it. "Your mind is going a million miles a minute." He glanced at her knowingly. "That is a lot of pictures." Paolo turned to walk out.

Anxiously, she cried, "Will that work?"

He turned back to her. "Bella, please trust me, there are many people worried enough for both of us."

How different her life would be here than at her home in Trento. It was beautiful, but it wasn't *her home*. Still, she could imagine a life here. She clamped her eyes shut, breathing deeply. The truth was, she didn't want to think about living here.

Their *engagement party* was tonight. She wondered how

this could be happening. Then tomorrow, she would return to Paxos. How could she return to Paxos so soon? Still Valeria thought it might be easier to go there without so much notice; less time to think about it.

∞

It was evening and she examined the dress in the mirror. It was exquisite. Paolo knocked on her door and she let him in. He looked quite handsome in his tux, but she could tell he was nervous. He escorted her down the stairs where she was presented to the guests.

A band was playing music on the lawn as Paolo grabbed two glasses of champagne. She felt a bit naked in her gown and began to tense. Then she saw that Jeremiah had arrived and was heading toward her. This was the moment she had been dreading. Her life and Alex's depended on her handling this well. Paolo noticed and immediately excused himself, leaving her alone as Jeremiah walked toward her while leaning heavily on his cane.

"You don't waste any time, do you!" he cackled, with no joy in his eyes.

"Yes, well," she gulped.

"So, young woman, you have a very interesting history with this council. I'm here to ensure that the council is not led astray, again."

"Alright. Well, anyway that I can help."

"Let's get on with this!" Jeremiah led her to some chairs, and sighed. "I hope you've learned a bit more than last time!" he snapped. She was stunned to be by herself. Alex would have never left her alone at a critical moment like this. Jeremiah's eyes salaciously drank in her body and she repressed a cold shudder of repulsion, as well as the urge to wrap her arms around herself. Instead, she kept her shoulders back and her arms down. Then she heard a familiar voice.

"Jeremiah, I expected to see you on time tonight," Shinsu admonished.

Seeing Shinsu dressed in a beautiful silver gown, Jeremiah's eyes lit with new appreciation. "Shinsu, you're speaking to me!" They kissed each other on both cheeks. "Well, I must say, you look absolutely charming tonight, my dear!"

"Jeremiah, don't bother with a transference!" She shook her head in dismay. "I did one earlier and it will take a week to evaluate what I saw. But everything looked fine, just fine."

"Well, I'll take my chances." Jeremiah laid out his hands, and Valeria nervously went to grasp them. Just then, Paolo took her hand and pulled her up and into his arms.

"I apologize, Jeremiah! This is our song!"

Paolo and Valeria moved onto the dance floor both attempting smiles that barely hid their nerves.

"What are we going to do now?" she asked.

"We are going to give you," he drew a deep breath, "a lot to think about."

Valeria looked at Paolo confused. Then he pulled her into a corner and said, "Make it good, bella." He pulled her into an embrace and his mouth skillfully worked with hers. His hands moved across her bare back and down around to the edges of the dress. Then his lips and tongue caressed her neck, as his hands began to move where they should not. She would have fought him. She wanted to fight it. But she clung to him, helplessly. The longer she was with him, the longer it was until she had to sit with Jeremiah. Paolo caressed her ear with his mouth and whispered breathlessly, "Very good." Then he kissed her mouth again, lightly.

At that moment, Jeremiah rounded the corner, and Paolo

jerked his hands back to more modest locations, but continued to kiss her, and then pulled back so that they were nose to nose; she saw that he was evaluating the look in her eye. She noticed him nod slightly and release her. At that moment she realized what the plan had been; she had a lot to think about, and her blush and increased heart rate were real.

Paolo led Valeria to a seat and Jeremiah faced her. She reached over, nervously, and took Jeremiah's hands as Shinsu, and now Camille and Lars, watched. While attempting to feel some level of affinity for Jeremiah, she also focused on the feel of Paolo's mouth on hers, and the feel of his hands on her skin, and her blush deepened.

Finally, Jeremiah dropped her hands and said, "You have made quite a fool of me!"

Paolo laughed, like he knew what Jeremiah might say, but for once, Valeria could see beyond Paolo's façade. Everyone seemed to draw a breath.

"You know, I was certain that I was going to discover a ruse! After our last attempts at this, I believed that the girl had no ability to focus whatsoever." Jeremiah chuckled, and lifted a finger toward Valeria. "Frankly, I believed you to be quite a scatterbrain!" He shook his head and cackled. "Well, young lady, evidently you do have the ability to focus—when you are with the right man!" He offered Paolo a congratulatory slap on the shoulder and then continued, "Paolo, allow me to offer some reassurance—this girl thinks about *nothing but you*! It will be *some* honeymoon!"

Jeremiah's words hit Valeria hard, *"With the right man..."* and *"This girl thinks about nothing but you!"* She had won but, instead of relief, she felt absolute devastation! Her jaw slackened and she was unable to speak as the tears flooded her eyes and the trembles deep inside her gut began to overtake her. She could barely breathe. Somehow, she kept the smile almost pasted on her face, while her eyes betrayed her terror and heartbreak.

Noticing Valeria's expression, Paolo covered by engaging Jeremiah in male banter about the honeymoon that she might have found in very poor taste…if she could have even listened. Paolo made eye contact with Camille, who had also noticed Valeria's expression.

"Gorgeous dress!" Camille announced loudly. "Let me take a look!" Camille continued to speak as if Valeria were actually engaged in the conversation, taking her hand and slowly guiding her so that she no longer faced Paolo and Jeremiah. Camille nodded, seeing Jeremiah leering at the low back of her dress.

Valeria wondered how it could be that all Jeremiah saw were her feelings for Paolo. Was she so hungry and desperate for that kind of relationship…was she *that kind* of girl? She thought of Alex hearing about this…*and he would!*

She felt the panic rising within her. After all the years of holding herself above the girls she had roomed with who had just wanted sex…here she was in love with one man, and the only thoughts Jeremiah could find were her elicit thoughts about another. *What was wrong with her?* Was she so shallow and needy that only one kiss from Paolo had made her forget the only man who had validated her entire existence?

Camille continued, "Jeremiah, very nice to see you. Paolo, excuse us." Camille leaned in as if to whisper, but her voice carried the required volume, "Valeria is having a little issue with her dress that we need to fix." Camille smiled at Jeremiah cordially, and placed her hand on Valeria's trembling back as they began walking toward the house.

Immediately, Lars was there with an artificial smile. "What's happening?"

"She's having a meltdown," Camille said.

"What's the quickest escape?" Lars asked.

Smiling pleasantly, Camille waved at immortal acquaintances, and then whispered, "I think the kitchen."

By this time, Valeria was loudly hyperventilating. Lars and Camille continued to laugh and greet friends as they moved rapidly across the massive lawn toward the kitchen. Lars blocked the view of Valeria from the front, while Camille hung onto her arm, blocking the view from the side. When they entered the kitchen all smiles dropped.

"Val! What happened?" Valeria's eyes rolled in devastation. "Focus, Val! What happened?" Camille demanded.

"I..." Valeria quivered, and Lars removed his jacket and put it around her shoulders. "I don't seem to think about Alex anymore." Both Lars and Camille sighed with relief.

Lars said, "Camille, tell you what; I'm going to check in with Jeremiah and make sure it all went as expected. Can you go back out and run damage control? If anyone asks, tell them she ate something that didn't agree with her."

Camille nodded. "Val, will you be all right here for a few minutes?"

"Okay," Valeria said, completely uncertain that she would ever be all right. And then the doors closed and she was alone in the kitchen.

Then her eyes focused for an instant and she saw the Aston Martin keys hanging from a hook. She took them in her hand and walked out the opposite door to the garage.

∞

The car seemed to be on auto-drive as it wove along the foothills. Valeria forced herself to think of nothing other than her destination. Each moment brought her closer and felt more right.

It had been over three hours since she had abruptly left the party, without a purse or phone. She knew that if she permitted herself to think too much, she would turn around and somehow, despite what should be, she would end up married to Paolo forever. She thought about Camille and Lars and even Paolo and was certain that she had worried them. But right now, she could do nothing else. She saw the large droplets on the windshield and searched for the windshield wipers, eventually finding them.

It was a shock to suddenly see the familiar drive and her heart began pounding. The rain obscured her view of the road, but she could tell, despite the darkness and the rain, how much thicker the foliage was. Then a heavy downpour obscured her view of the road. She flipped the switch to turn up the windshield wipers but accidentally turned them off and was forced to stop and locate the controls.

In that moment, she suddenly wondered if this was a mistake. Nerves suddenly took hold of her and she wondered if he was even there. The road was so black that she suddenly doubted it. She hadn't brought her purse or a phone—how would she refill the gas tank?

If he was here, would he be angry? Her actions had risked their lives. How would he respond? *Was he even here?* She couldn't evaluate it right now, if she did she might never see him again.

Incapable of turning around, she continued as her heart began pounding so loudly that she could hear it over the loud splatters of water on the car. She rounded the curve in the road and there she saw it…their cottage was lit with the glow from the fireplace.

She barely stopped the car and leapt from it into the pouring rain. She saw the beautiful, cedar doors, with the oversized Cs carved into them; they opened hesitantly and then, *he was there*, on the porch. Her heart lurched at seeing him, but he seemed frozen.

Immediately, she was certain it had been a mistake. Perhaps he had someone with him. Of course, it was a mistake—she had just signed their death warrants! Would he speak to her? He didn't move. She remembered him peeling her hands off from his chest in St. Croix. Now she was certain he would be upset with her. She stared at him, as tears streamed down her face. Then she saw in his eyes not the anger, and certainly not the pain and anguish as before, this time his face was filled with what could only be described as gratitude!

It took him only a few steps and she was in his arms; he kissed her hair, her face—their emotions a mix of tears and tremendous joy. His mouth came down on hers with the passion that wiped away all of the months of agony, as if erased by the pouring rain. In an instant, she felt the magnitude of her love and desire for him. It was then that she knew that regardless of what anyone said or thought or felt, being with her symbolon was another plane well above what most could even imagine—and very few had experienced. This level of love and desire *could never* be compared to another; she felt loved and she loved…and she was whole.

Finally, Alex guided her into their cottage. They were both dripping, and a pool of water formed around the base of her dress. They laughed through their tears and he went to the bedroom and returned with several towels and a blanket. As he dried her hair, he said softly, "Let's get you near the fire so you can dry off a bit."

Immediately, she noticed the family portrait still there over the fireplace. And then she saw on the coffee table, right in front of him, next to his glass of wine and the book of

Shakespeare's sonnets, the picture that she had left for him. It was the first picture that Camille had taken of them, laughing and so much in love…it was the picture that she carried in her heart. She felt the blaze of the fireplace, but it was his love that warmed her heart.

He brought her a glass of wine and then wrapped her in a blanket, holding it in place with his arms and warming her…loving her. Finally, he led her to the sofa where, covered in the blanket, she curled onto his lap. She held his hands and then, seeing his mark on his hand, she traced it several times and then laced her fingers through his as he kissed the top of her head.

She laid there in the comfort of his arms where time melted into an eternity. Neither spoke, knowing that if they did they would have to talk about what was happening, what had happened…and neither could. They stayed in the moment, surrounded by their love. Alex stroked her hair, now almost dry, and stared lovingly into her face.

Finally, she leaned into his shoulder and kissing his neck, she whispered, "Let's disappear."

"We already have…for a little while anyway." He continued to stroke her face, and said softly, "They will be here shortly and you'll need to go with them." Sighing, he pulled her in closer. "I don't need much more in life than you in my arms. But I do need you to be alive."

"Have I caused too much trouble tonight?"

Alex shrugged. "We'll figure it out."

∞

She looked at his arm and he was wearing the watch that she had given him. She brushed it and smiled.

"I always wear it," he whispered softly.

"Not in St. Croix," she said as a question.

He nodded. "I couldn't wear it there."

She wondered what he meant by the comment, but she was too comfortable to ask him.

Hours later, there was a hint of light beginning to show to the east of the now star-filled sky, when Lars' black Mercedes pulled in front of the cottage. She had been fighting sleep, despite her exhaustion, trying to be there every moment in this wonderful dream. Two car doors opened and closed. She snuggled sleepily into Alex's chest, breathing him in. The door of the cottage opened and Lars and Paolo stood there looking somewhat relieved.

Alex kissed her head and gently said, "Time to go, beautiful." She shook her head slightly. He picked her up and carried her to the door as she pulled in even closer to him. Alex walked by Paolo and Paolo held out his arms as if to take her. Alex offered him a cold wink. "Nah, I've got her, pal."

The rain had stopped and the ground showed only a hint of dampness. Alex set her on her feet by the passenger side of Paolo's car and they held each other tightly for a few minutes, ignoring Paolo and the rest of the world. She started to tremble again and Alex pulled her in tighter, as Lars brought her another blanket from the backseat of his car. Alex took the blanket, his eyes never leaving hers, as he opened the passenger door and helped her in. Then he wrapped the blanket around her with so much tenderness that it overwhelmed her. Paolo stood outside the car, looking helpless. Finally, he climbed in behind the wheel and stared blankly straight ahead.

Alex touched Valeria's face memorizing every detail. He started to pull out of the car when she pulled him into a passionate kiss.

Lars interrupted with a pat on Alex's back. "We need to get going before the guests begin waking."

Paolo started the Aston Martin and she heard Lars close the door to his Mercedes behind them. Alex kissed her again, softly. Then he stepped back and closed her door. The car pulled away from what she knew would always be her home...*and her love*. She watched Alex as he stood alone in the driveway and her heart began aching, again.

They drove for hours in silence along the countryside, with the sun rising behind them. Finally she asked, "Why didn't you tell Jeremiah?"

There was a long silence. He took a deep breath.

"Alex was my best friend and..." Paolo focused on the road, unwilling to complete the sentence. His voice sounded pained and exhausted.

"And?"

"And because I have loved you since the first moment I saw you."

She nodded and closed her eyes.

CHAPTER 18

Valeria opened her eyes abruptly to see that it was now early morning and Paolo had pulled off into the same field where he had stopped the day before. His face was more serious than she had ever seen it.

"I think it will be best if we alleviate any questions," he said.

Rubbing the tension out of his neck, he seemed to be thinking and then with an exhausted sigh he said, "We do not know who will see us. Hopefully, the guests will still be asleep. I instructed the caterers to open my finest champagne and to pour liberally but we cannot risk a meeting with any of them."

She noticed that Paolo was unbuttoning his shirt. "What are you doing?" she asked, alarmed.

"There will be questions if you are seen in your dress. You will wear my shirt so that other assumptions are made."

He removed the cuff links and pulled off his shirt and then handed it to her. He immediately jumped out of the car and opened the trunk. He came back a few moments later with two bottles of champagne and one glass. Paolo faced away from the car to allow her privacy while he opened both bottles.

Taking a drink from one of the bottles, he then filled the single glass and dumped out most of the first bottle.

"Are you dressed?" he asked.

"Yes," she said softly, as she buttoned the last button and scooted his long sleeves up to reveal her hands. Then, she picked up her dress from the floorboard of the car, and started to fold it. Paolo got back into the car and handed her the glass. Then he took her dress, crumpled it up, and tossed it into the back seat.

He joylessly clinked the near empty bottle against the crystal flute that she held, and then took a large swig. Noticing that she only took a sip of her champagne, he said, "As we say in the clubs, alla goccia—drink up!" He put his hand at the bottom of her glass to assist. His eyes trailed down her chest as some of the champagne dripped down the front of his shirt she was wearing. Nodding, his eyes evaluated her for a moment. He reached over and unbuttoned the top three buttons of the shirt, so that the shirt was open almost to her navel. She took a large gulp of her champagne and started to push his hands away, but something in his eyes told her that she needed to comply. He scrutinized her appearance and then ran his hands through her hair messing it up a bit more. Satisfied with her appearance, he said, "We need to get into my room without questions."

"Your room?"

Paolo started the car as he handed the almost empty bottle to Valeria. "Hold this, please." And then she noticed that his hands were trembling. He turned the car around, as he spoke, "My room is on the ground floor. Do not speak to anyone, not even Camille. Drink bella, remember, you have had too much champagne." His normally velvet voice was now marred with exhaustion and worry.

As they pulled up the drive of his home, everything looked quiet. Paolo stopped the car short of the house at an odd angle. He drew a deep breath and then reached over and grabbed the near empty bottle of champagne. Climbing out of the car, he chugged the last of it before sauntering around his car toward her door. He pasted on a lusty smile as he opened her car door. She popped out holding the glass and the other bottle of champagne. Paolo pushed the full bottle up to her mouth and she tried to drink, but it mostly spilled and went up her nose.

He grimaced. "Sorry."

Glancing at her feet, he said, "Take your shoes off."

She kicked her heels so that they flopped off into the car and he tossed them onto the backseat, along with the blankets. Then he grasped her hand and wrapped it around his waist.

They headed down the drive toward the back of the house. As they rounded the corner near the door to his room, some guests walked into the garden.

"If they speak to us, they will suspect all is not as we..." He swallowed. "We must make them *very* uncomfortable." He pushed Valeria into the wall and, this time it was a kiss of duty, not passion. As they heard the giggles from the guests, Paolo pulled the shirt off her shoulder and it was only his chest that kept her covered. Wondering if they would ever leave, Valeria reached around and grabbed Paolo's behind; to her delight, the guest's snickers grew even louder. Finally, Paolo grabbed her leg and pulled it up on the side and she wrapped her leg around him. The amused snickers became embarrassed chuckles, but the guests remained in the garden.

"Ask me to make love to you."

"No," she whispered.

"Please, Valeria...loudly."

She moaned, "Paolo, make love to me."

"Wrap your legs around my waist." She did as he asked without questioning him, and he kept his mouth on hers as he carried her through the French doors into his bedroom. Paolo turned his head toward the guests and offered them a wink.

In the bedroom, he carried her straight to the bed and sat her down, pulling the shirt back up on her shoulder before releasing her and then he drew a deep sigh.

Walking back to the French doors, he closed and locked them and then slid the forest green curtains shut causing the room to instantly darken. Then he slumped into a gold and green upholstered chair and placed his face in his hands.

"Paolo?"

"Yes." His response was abrupt, as if he was upset with her.

"I'm sorry for all of the trouble."

"You need to try to get a few hours of sleep. This is not over."

"I had to go."

Paolo sighed and ignored her.

"Paolo?" Valeria asked softly.

"What?" he said in frustration.

"Thank you."

∞

A light mist outside of the cottage rose with the sun. With her eyes still closed, she listened to the melody of the songbirds in their celebration of summer and then breathed in that wonderful mix of fragrant jasmine and that extraordinary blend of soap and aftershave. Valeria felt Alex's kisses before opening her eyes, just as she sensed his smile, before seeing his beautiful face. Everything was right with the world.

"Good morning, Mrs. Morgan!" His eyes sparkled and she

felt the thrill of his words.

"Good morning, Mr. Morgan!"

His eyes filled with desire as they disappeared under the covers.

A knock woke Valeria from her dream…the first dream she could recall, except for the hallucination, since she'd been away from Alex.

"Val?" It was Camille.

"Hmmm…come in." Valeria looked around and remembered that she was in Paolo's room, not the cottage.

Camille closed the door and sat on the edge of the bed. She looked like she hadn't slept well. "Do you know what you put me through last night when I came back to get you and you were gone?"

Valeria felt bad that she had upset her friends, but she was not sorry that she had gone—the trip had renewed her soul. Looking into Camille's eyes it was clear she had not slept. Valeria was certain that neither Paolo nor Lars had slept either and no telling who else. In fact, she was certain that of all of them involved, including Alex, she was the only one who *had* slept; although, according to the clock, it had only been a few hours.

"I am so sorry," Valeria said, reaching for her arm. "I would never want to worry you." Valeria wondered if Camille knew where she had been. It didn't matter because Valeria couldn't withhold her joy. "I knew that if I talked to anyone, I wouldn't go." She closed her eyes. "And *I needed to see him.*" Her eyes filled with tears of joy, remembering the feeling of being back in Alex's arms.

"I'd have done the same thing." Camille's eyes shined with interest. *"So?"*

Valeria's smile said it all.

"Ahhh! And you know, he needed to see you, too."

Camille shrugged. "Surprisingly, Paolo handled it well. When we finally had to tell him that you were missing, we both expected that we would have to tie him up to keep him from doing something really stupid. But he was just...more concerned about you and about the others discovering that you were missing."

"He was actually pretty amazing last night...with the whole situation."

Walking toward the window, Camille pulled back the sheers and peeked out. "You should have seen how he handled your disappearance with the guests this morning." Camille went on, "And the empty champagne bottle on his car—great touch!"

"Camille? Could you bring me the blanket in the back of Paolo's car?" She thought for a moment. "Oh...and you don't need to tell Paolo about it."

"Sure, I'll get Alex's blanket for you." She looked down at her watch. "I know you've only slept for a few hours, but right now, my job is to get you ready to head to the airport. Most of the guests have left. We are keeping you completely out of sight until the last guest is gone. So I'm going to pack for you. Don't worry about a thing."

Rising, Valeria hugged Camille as they heard a knock at the door. Paolo entered and Valeria noticed the dark circles under his eyes.

"Everyone has left, Valeria. I have brought your robe." She was still in his shirt from the night before. "You can go to your room and dress. But we need to leave within the hour." She hugged him as she left the room. The surprise came when Camille hugged him too.

While Camille packed, Valeria showered and dressed. Then they grabbed their bags and loaded up for their drive to Milan and the flight to Corfu.

Valeria walked toward Lars' Mercedes, obliviously happy. But he stopped her. "Sweetheart, I think after last night it would be best for you to ride with Paolo."

"Oh, alright." Valeria turned and just as happily strode toward Paolo's car and slid into the passenger seat. She realized that her nerves were significantly calmer than the rest of theirs. She wondered if there was more to this than she knew. But she opted not to think of that, and instead, decided to indulge in the memories from the night before. Paolo seemed absorbed in his own thoughts, so there was no forced conversation.

If she permitted herself to think about returning to Paxos, she was certain it would have caused a nervous reaction; but having had time with Alex, Valeria felt almost serene. She was a natural optimist. And while the past months had taken the wind out of that sail, last night had given her back the outlook she had somehow, always before possessed. Alex still loved her! She would go through the actions she needed to. She could marry Paolo if she had to. But at night, when she closed her eyes, her mind would be with Alex. She sensed that Paolo now also knew that, and she suspected that was part of his pain.

They drove along the coast for some time, weaving along the colorful cliffside towns overlooking the Mediterranean on their way to the Milan airport. She would have liked to have been able to spend time here with Alex. But now, that would never happen. She was marrying another man.

Landing on Corfu, she was plunged back into memories of her last trip. She remembered the visit to the mayor's office, and the rehearsal. She remembered her beautiful wedding gown and briefly wondered what had happened to it. She remembered the romantic evening, hours before her world had crashed...and she almost remembered returning to Corfu, alone.

At the ferry dock in Corfu, Valeria saw a sight that immediately caused her to smile: Caleb! She glanced at Paolo and she ran to hug her young superhero. Caleb was especially excited to show Valeria his new trick. Tavish had made a miniature fan that ran off the power of his finger tip. She noticed that he seemed slightly older, which would be no big deal for a normal child, but Caleb was far from that.

She was grateful that their ferry bypassed the beautiful harbor leading to the town of Gaios, and then passed the southern boundary of the island of Paxos, continuing almost a mile to the tiny island of Anti-Paxos. While Paxos was covered with olive trees, a family had planted vineyards covering most of Anti-Paxos. For a moment, Valeria imagined that she was coming back here to marry Alex. That felt considerably more real than the idea of marrying *anyone* else.

Lars, Camille, and Caleb had decided to stay with them at Paolo's estate. While Valeria was thrilled to have them with her, she was certain that the intention was to ensure that she didn't disappear again.

It was the end of June and the temperature was fantastic. Despite his obvious exhaustion, as soon as they arrived at the estate, Paolo changed into his swimming trunks.

Sitting by the pool, she sipped her kale and strawberry smoothie as she held a book that almost had her attention, *A Room with a View*.

Paolo glanced at her as he carried two oars down to the dock. "Valeria, if you refuse to come in the water, then you should sleep. Tonight may be difficult, and it is important that you have your wits about you."

She had no interest in partaking in any water sports. She had snorkeled only once in her life, and look how that ended up—she was now engaged to Paolo. Still, she knew that she should rest as she had slept no more than five hours over the past few days. But she just couldn't. She wanted to think about every detail of the night before while it was still fresh in her mind.

Caleb was only too anxious to fill the void and play in the water, although he had to wear a wet suit so that Paolo could help him. They intended to kayak and snorkel, and Paolo said maybe even do some scuba diving. Valeria didn't know what the rules were in Greece, but she wasn't really comfortable with Caleb scuba diving when he wasn't certified. Paolo promised he would take good care of the boy. She was surprised that Caleb and Paolo seemed to have an instant camaraderie. Occasionally, Valeria would hear an echo of Caleb's joyful laughs coming over the sound of the surf. Paolo and Caleb were gone for almost five hours before Paolo conceded that he needed to get some sleep.

∞

That evening, while Caleb played a video game, Camille, Lars, Paolo, and Valeria loaded onto the trog, the low boat that would take them into the underworld. Valeria was reminded of that momentous evening, now almost four months ago, that had changed her happy future.

Because she hadn't gone shopping, Paolo had arranged another dress for this evening. He had selected a white Grecian style one-shoulder gown with a gold cord that wrapped around her. This gown was as beautiful as the one the night before and she decided to wear her hair up.

The mood was far more somber than it had been on the previous trip. Everyone except Valeria seemed nervous, particularly Paolo. "Remember, bella, you must not offer the council more information than necessary."

She remembered. He had said the same thing three times

in the past hour. Still, she didn't know what to expect. They all hoped that she would not be required to testify or answer questions. Two of the council members were already convinced that she should marry someone other than the man whom she truly loved. Hopefully, that would be enough. She attempted unsuccessfully to keep her mind from wandering to the "ifs": If the marriage was approved, could she end the engagement and go back to Alex? Or, if the marriage was refused, could the Law of Nevia still be removed? She didn't suspect the answer to either question was yes.

The boat turned off its lights as it approached the east coast of Paxos and continued just off the rocky cliffs. They laid their seats back and Valeria was reminded of Alex sitting next to her, with the wind blowing through his hair, his champagne glass coolly in his hand. That thought swelled her heart.

The driver throttled the engine to position the boat toward the steep cliffs where, hidden from view, there was an opening into another world. She heard the familiar gunning of the engine timed in between the swells, as they headed for the cliffs. Still, the view caused her heart to pound.

"Valeria, I'm certain that you recall that you must remain reclined," Paolo warned.

The driver revved the engines and headed toward the cliffs. Moments later, they were in total darkness and the only sound was that of the surf crashing on the entrance to the cave behind them. Valeria felt Paolo's hand on her arm. He must have sensed her anxiety.

Finally, she felt the boat stop and heard the sound of a match being struck as the cave filled with light. They stepped onto the ledge and she watched as the trog used a thick rope that ran along the cave's edge to retrace its journey and then disappeared. Then Lars held the torch, leading them along the path. She heard a loud creaking sound as the bridge was lowered.

They transferred to the gondola, with a drib gondolier. The pale, skull-like faces of the dribs still frightened her. Their boat glided smoothly into the Delos chamber and pulled up to the landing. They crossed the foot bridge, this time without fanfare.

She could not help but remember the last time she had been here and, with that thought, she was forced to also remember who Paolo had been to her that night—the enemy. She again worked to block out that thought.

As Jeremiah approached, Valeria pasted on her sweetest smile—she had a lot more practice hiding her real emotions now. A server came by and Paolo lifted two glasses of champagne from his tray and handed one to her. Jeremiah leered at her with a raised eyebrow. "A hair of the dog?" She smiled, without saying a word.

Glancing down at her, Paolo kissed her cheek. "You look ravishing." He glanced at Jeremiah. "Would you excuse us, Jeremiah? I would like to introduce Cassandra to some of the immortals."

As soon as they had turned, she could see Paolo relax slightly. He walked her to a table laden with exquisite food. "Valeria, please excuse me, there is business that I must attend to."

Valeria realized that for the first time in months she was famished! She took a plate and loaded it with a few slices of beef wellington. She was certain that Paolo hadn't eaten and it made her feel a bit guilty that she had an appetite and he, evidently, had none.

There were a group of immortals in the distance who laughed and her ears suddenly perked up. Could that have been Alex's musical laughter in the mixture? She scanned the crowd and saw a man leaving the group. There were too many people between them but it looked like Alex! He passed behind others, so she moved to get a closer view. Was it him, or was it merely wishful thinking?

It was probably just that she was thinking of him or about the last time she had been here—her heart lurched—she couldn't think about that now. The man passed another group and she lost sight of him; but, peeking through the crowd, she thought it looked similar to his dark blond hair.

Now stepping around the table, she began to follow the man. Through a group of people, she saw the flash of his oracle blue eyes for just an instant. *Was she imagining things?* She knew she shouldn't follow him, but now she was drawn and completely incapable of stopping herself. She saw the man step behind a stone wall along the edge of the River Styx.

She peeked around the wall and the man was facing away from her, picking something up—or setting something down—then he quickly stood and turned toward her. *Alex!*

"You look breathtaking!" His face lit with his brilliant smile.

She held out her arms but he put up a hand to block her advance. "Sorry, beautiful! Not here. Not now."

"I didn't realize you would be here," she said, beaming in his presence.

"I was summoned."

She looked critically at Alex. "Is that bad? Why were you summoned? It wasn't because of last—"

He interrupted her, "No. I received the summons yesterday afternoon. Frankly, I was planning on coming anyway." He looked into her eyes. "Any chance to see you."

"What will happen?" she asked, now concerned.

He sighed and shook his head, but both of their moods were lighter than they had been in months. "I don't know."

She offered a small laugh. "Some bunch of oracles we are,

huh?" She glanced down, wishing she could hold his hand.

"We had better get back with everyone." He winked at her.

Suddenly, Paolo came around the corner. Without a word, he took Valeria's arm and guided her to the front of the room.

The gong sounded, and this time, all nine of the elegant chairs were occupied.

Jeremiah began. "Paolo has a request. A rather interesting request considering what occurred here several months ago."

Paolo glanced down momentarily and something in his expression caused her to wonder if he had changed his mind. If he did, what would happen to her and Alex? She glanced toward Alex and he looked away.

Pulling her into the spotlight, with less affection than she typically expected from him, Paolo said, "I have proposed marriage to this immortal, and she has accepted. We request council consent for our marriage. And, as my last petition involved Cassandra and Alex, I would like it withdrawn."

One of the council members said, "I really don't understand how this all shifted so quickly. Paolo, was this the design of your actions here a few months ago?"

Paolo looked as if he had expected this question. Shinsu gave him an emotional nod.

"No, council. I was married to an incarnation of Cassandra—there is a prior emotional connection. However, my actions at the previous council meeting were only to protect my sister's interests. My sister requested that I join her in signing the petition and that I deliver it to the council.

"Since that time, the Trento Family has provided substantial resources in the search for Kristiana and they have promised a continuation of those efforts. It is also evident that with Cassandra's extraordinary gifts, we may be able to locate Kristiana more rapidly. Lastly, Cassandra and I have spent considerable time together and, with the support of her family, she has come to recall the depth of her feelings for me," Paolo took Valeria's hand and kissed it, "as Jeremiah confirmed last night."

She thought it odd to hear talk of her great gifts. She had no evidence of any special gifts.

Several council members nodded. Then another council member spoke up. "Was Cassandra aware that you were going to withdraw the petition?"

"Not initially. However, we did discuss it the day of our engagement. I wished to invite her family to our engagement party and so informed her of my plan."

"Do you believe that Cassandra intends to be a good wife to you Paolo? Is it possible that her purpose in agreeing to the marriage is so that the council would agree to remove the petition?"

Paolo shook his head, but Valeria could tell he was nervous. "Cassandra has been a good wife to me in the past. We share affection and many similar interests. I believe we could have a successful marriage."

Shinsu spoke up, "Paolo, just months ago, you accused Cassandra of malicious misconduct. What has changed?"

"I witnessed her behavior over the past several months and they were not those of someone intending to interfere in a marriage." Valeria thought Paolo's response sounded a bit rehearsed.

Another council member turned to Valeria and she felt Paolo's grip tighten on her hand. "Cassandra, do you now love Paolo?"

"I care for Paolo."

"That wasn't the question."

Shinsu interrupted, "The girl has answered the pertinent question. She cares for Paolo. That's more than many of you had prior to your marriages."

Jeremiah narrowed his eyes. "Yes, Shinsu. But because the girl was accused of maliciousness only months ago, I believe that this council has a responsibility and right to question this marriage more stringently. It is our responsibility to approve only marriages that are most likely to be successful." He pursed his lips and glared at Valeria. "I would like to know if you intend to be a good wife to Paolo."

Valeria wanted to ask Jeremiah if he considered himself a good husband but good sense kicked in and she decided to leave her sarcasm outside of the cave. "I'm sorry, but I'm not certain what a good wife is. Are you asking if I'll cook and clean?"

The council looked upset and Paolo leaned down to her. "You must answer 'yes,' bella."

She knew she should do what Paolo said, but he did say that she needed to be truthful. "I'm sorry, but I really can't answer the question truthfully if I don't know what you mean by being a good wife."

"Will you have extra-marital affairs?" Jeremiah asked, now irritated.

She looked down to hide the sarcasm that now flooded her face. Paolo sensed her mood and tightened his grip on her hand. Valeria glanced toward Alex but he looked away again.

"No. I would not have extra-marital affairs."

Jeremiah glanced toward Alex and back to Valeria. "Would Paolo be first in your heart?"

"I would place my husband's needs above others."

Jeremiah continued, "All others?"

Paolo pulled Valeria close and kissed her neck whispering, "Please let me help you." Paolo spoke up, "Council, please! I don't understand the purpose of this questioning. Cassandra has never been one to cause trouble. That would not change."

Jeremiah leaned forward in his chair, tapping his cane on

the floor for emphasis. "You say that now, but several months ago, you said something quite different! Paolo, it is our responsibility to investigate this! I believe there is a problem!"

"And last night you received a transference that demonstrated that she only thinks of me!" Paolo challenged.

Shinsu gave Paolo a look that said she did not approve of his disrespectful tone and then said, "Jeremiah, though I do not approve of the way in which Paolo stated his concern, he does have a valid point. These questions were all answered last night. And now let's just get this business done with and enjoy ourselves," she huffed.

Jeremiah glared critically at Valeria and then toward Alex again. "I believe that there is more to this than is being said." He clasped his hands over his cane as his eyes locked on Valeria's. "Last night you disappeared." Valeria blushed and shrugged, but out of the corner of her eye she could see from Paolo's expression that this was going badly. "You must speak the truth to this council, do you understand."

"I don't lie." But she knew that she would have to find a way to answer the next question. "I am not a public person. I needed time away from the crowd."

"Have you seen Alexander since the last council meeting?" Jeremiah demanded. Valeria looked at Alex and saw him close his eyes. She knew this expression, it was the same one she had seen when Paolo had entered his petition four months before.

"Yes."

Paolo interrupted, "Yes, and as the petitioner, I am aware of these meetings."

Jeremiah very nearly smiled as he leaned toward her. "Was last night one of them—the evening of your engagement party to Paolo?"

Paolo sighed heavily, and then Valeria could have sworn

she saw a flash of intense pain in his eyes. He squeezed her hand and then turned to look at her with a combination of love and loss. For an instant, she could see the man that had lost his Isabella and she wanted to touch his face and tell him that it would be all right. He closed his eyes and when he opened them, his face was filled with something new that she couldn't identify. She wondered what had changed.

"Council, I would like to respond." Paolo drew a deep breath. "I know that it is your responsibility to ensure that the marriage is right, and I must admit that—since last night—I *have* had some reservations." Valeria suddenly felt concerned. Then she felt Paolo's grip tighten on her hand, again, and then he released it. "Last night, Cassandra did disappear." He looked down and then glanced up toward Alex. She saw their eyes meet for an instant. "Lars and I discovered her in Trento and in Alex's arms."

Of all the things she was prepared for, betrayal was not one of them! She glared at Paolo with a mix of stunned shock and outrage as angry tears formed in her eyes. *She had trusted him!* Trying to catch her breath, she realized what his betrayal meant. She recalled Alex telling her that there was only one punishment dispensed by this council: death. *She would be beheaded tonight!* Had this been Paolo's plan all along? Had his betrayal been a plan that he and Shinsu had concocted months ago to get even? The room got dim as she realized what was to come.

Then she realized that Alex would watch. She couldn't bear to think of that! What if Alex was found guilty? *Oh, God, what had she done?*

Jeremiah almost smiled in glee. "She violated the petition? Why didn't you inform this council?"

Paolo sighed. "She returned with me and confided that she felt remorse for her actions."

Now Paolo had lied. Her ears began to loudly ring and she could barely hear what he was saying. *What was his game?*

He continued, "Last night, I believed Cassandra when she told me that she required time to say goodbye to Alex. Then tonight, I discovered them alone again." Paolo refused to meet her eyes.

Alex's voice rang from his position near the back of the room. "You bastard! You promised to protect her!" He raced near them.

"ALEXANDER!" Jeremiah roared. "I warned you months before that this council will not tolerate your outbursts! You shall treat your fellow immortals and this council with respect! Anymore outbursts and you will be dealt with before the present issue is concluded."

Alex's face was red with rage. But there was something else. She wondered, was it fear?

Another council member spoke up, "Cassandra, did you go to Alexander twice?"

"Council! May I speak?" Alex requested.

Jeremiah raised a finger. "Alexander, you will be permitted to speak when you are asked."

Her voice was breathy and nervous. "Yes. I...I went to him. Alex didn't know that I would do that. It was my fault. And then tonight, I followed a man...I didn't know if it was Alex until I was alone with him. It was not a planned meeting." The council shook their heads in accusation. "Truly, Alex didn't do anything to encourage me. He has followed your rules. I was the one who broke them, only because I couldn't bear..."

Jeremiah's voice rang out, *"Bear what?"*

She had to answer it, but how could she without further incriminating herself? "I couldn't bear to marry someone else without first telling Alex, without knowing that he was all right with it."

Paolo's face became enraged. "Our laws are our laws! They are both to be punished!"

"Paolo we will require your testimony!" Jeremiah demanded.

Shinsu stood. "Excuse me, Jeremiah, but I have known Paolo longer than most of you and he has developed a skill that permits him to manipulate his testimony. This was a well known fact by my late husband. Paolo, this council will require witnesses to your very serious allegations!"

"Who do you think could have taught me that skill, but an oracle? Alex showed me many of his tricks when we were in Carrara!"

"Alexander, Paolo, are there others who might testify? Paolo you mentioned that Lars was with you last night?"

"Yes. Camille also witnessed my fiancée's disappearance." Paolo glanced toward Camille as she hissed a curse under her breath.

Jeremiah nodded. "Lars and Camille, please give your testimony."

They both stepped forward, looking devastated. Camille glanced toward Valeria with tears in her eyes, and placed her hands on the quartz plates. The council glanced up at the screen and saw the events unfold from Valeria's transference to Jeremiah and then her disappearance. They also saw the conversation that Valeria had with Camille that morning, confirming that she had been with Alex.

"Thank you, Camille." Jeremiah nodded. "Lars?"

Lars looked at both Alex and Valeria with great sadness as he placed his hands on the quartz. The council saw Valeria disappear and then saw her with Alex. Lars removed his hands and walked back where Camille was standing.

Jeremiah nodded. "Camille and Lars, you are pardoned

from any wrongdoing here." Jeremiah spoke to Paolo and said, "Paolo acted admirably. Alexander, as much as I disagree with many of your actions, this council finds only Cassandra guilty of violating the laws of this council."

This fueled Paolo's anger. "Alex betrayed our agreement and caused Cassandra to doubt my love for her. Last night I found her with his arms around her."

She turned to Paolo glaring incredulously. *"Who are you?"* She took the engagement ring off her finger and threw it at him. It struck him in the face and he closed his eyes as the ring rolled down to the ground. Paolo glanced down at the ring but refused to pick it up. She saw a hint of pain in his eyes but she was unable to feel any compassion for him. He had just signed their death warrants!

"Young woman!" Jeremiah's voice echoed throughout the chamber. "You have committed crimes and now you have crossed the line with your disrespect! I will have you bound and gagged for the rest of the proceedings if necessary."

Paolo turned back to the council. "She would not have gone to Alex unless he had indicated it was all right."

Valeria stepped forward. "That is not true! Alex didn't know I was coming!"

Paolo spat, "I saw him kiss her!"

She could see her family looking as if they were witnessing a murder. Valeria looked toward Alex, but she couldn't read his expression.

Jeremiah asked Valeria, "Do you deny this?"

"Alex did nothing wrong. I was the one who went to him last night. I was the one who followed him tonight. Please, I am the only one who should be punished," she said, knowing that it made no difference now.

Jeremiah nodded. "I tend to agree young woman! You have caused this council considerable trouble in less than a year." He lifted his arm, and called, "Erebos!"

A giant of a man wearing a green silk toga stepped out from the shadows behind the council, carrying an ancient, double-sided axe.

Alex stepped toward Paolo. *"No!"* His eyes filled with rage. "You did this to us! If you had not filed that ridiculous petition, Valeria and I would be married now!"

"Alexander I've warned—" Jeremiah started, but was interrupted by Paolo.

"She wanted *me!* Ask Jeremiah!"

"Alexander! I will not tolerate anymore—" Ignoring Jeremiah, Alex turned toward Valeria for half of a second, and then his fist raised and slammed into Paolo's jaw.

Stunned, Paolo brought his hand to his face as a caustic smile lit his eyes.

Jeremiah's voice boomed, "Alexander, you are in violation of this council's orders!"

Valeria was suddenly thrown into a nightmare she never even imagined. She couldn't catch her breath. She and Alex would die tonight. Alex pulled her into his arms. "Don't worry," he whispered in her ear.

Four dribs approached and pulled them apart. The man with the double-sided axe gave her a frightening smile. It was happening now! These were her last minutes on earth. At least she was going first. She couldn't bear it if it was the other way around. Valeria was dragged by her arm and hair to a stone block and forced onto her knees as her head was pressed onto the cold stone. The room went gray as she struggled to maintain consciousness in the face of the threat. She heard Erebos's rough, low breathing and then a terrifying sound that resembled a laugh.

Her eyes met Alex's and she saw his pain. She tried to focus on him. The room was in absolute silence.

"Alex, I love you," she choked. *"I will always love you!"*

Suddenly, a familiar and joyful laughter echoed off the walls of the cave. The guards released Alex and Valeria as they went back to investigate. Alex pulled Valeria from the ground and into his arms, brushing the side of her face. He whispered in her ear, "I'm so sorry for all of this, Val," he said, his voice filled with remorse.

"Wow! Hey, this is cooool!"

Valeria looked to Alex. "Caleb? How did he..." Valeria remembered that Caleb had been kayaking. He must have followed them in.

Alex continued to hold her, not responding to her question, but intensely watching the scene. "Oh, Alex! I don't want him to see what's going to happen!" She pushed her face into his chest and he ran his fingers along the back of her neck.

One of the council members yelled, "Who is that? Isn't that the boy who lives with the Trento Family?"

"Yes," Paolo responded.

Two dribs moved toward Caleb who was wearing cargo shorts and a T-shirt. One of them tried to grab Caleb. "Oh, dude, I wouldn't!" Caleb said sympathetically. But the guard reached for him anyway and was instantly shocked. Caleb looked at him apologetically. "Sorry." But then Caleb's laughter escaped. This caused the guard to try it again. And, again, the guard was shocked. Caleb apologized once more, but continued to laugh heartily.

Valeria could do nothing but try to grasp what was going on. She started shaking and Alex rubbed his hands along her arms. She hated that because it made her feel weak. She didn't want to be weak. She wanted to have the words to end this. Somewhere, there were words that would end this!

Lars approached Caleb, concerned and totally baffled by the boy's appearance in Delos. "Caleb? How did you find this place? What are you doing here?"

Caleb shrugged. "I just wanted to see where you guys were going. I followed in my kayak." He looked around wide-eyed. "And this is so cool!"

Jeremiah and the council members shook their heads. Shinsu spoke up, "The boy is not an immortal."

Lars responded, "We aren't certain if Caleb is an immortal. He's lived over 2,000 years. But I can assure you that Caleb would not divulge this location or this council."

Jeremiah said, "We do not have the luxury of allowing foolish children into our sacred grounds. I'm afraid that the boy must join Alexander and Valeria."

"No!" Valeria screamed. "Caleb *is* immortal! He has simply not been recognized!"

Alex raised a hand. "Please, council! I'm certain that satisfactory evidence of Caleb's immortality could be presented by Mani within days." Jeremiah's eyes became wary.

Shaking her head, Shinsu added, "Jeremiah, you know full well that we cannot punish the boy without a hearing."

Paolo spoke up for the first time since Alex had struck him. "I would be willing to fund the expenses incurred for a delay in the proceedings in order to ensure justice for the boy."

"Lars, can you provide evidence in two days time that the boy is immortal?"

"I'm certain I can provide adequate evidence," Lars breathed, in a sigh.

"We obviously cannot punish these two," Shinsu pointed to Alex and Valeria, "with the boy here."

"What do you suggest, my dear," Jeremiah asked.

Shinsu placed her hand on her neck and stretched it, to relieve the tension. "Jeremiah, I suggest we hold off until we can make a determination on the boy. After all, what does it matter if we wait a day or so? I am certain that Erebos will be all too pleased to oblige at any time." She sighed. "Besides, there has been enough business tonight and the council is getting impatient—particularly me!"

Valeria breathed for the first time since she had received the death sentence.

Caleb's eyes grew wide, and then he broke out into his full, joyful laughter. "Do you have like a dungeon? That would be too cool!" He glanced toward Valeria and saw Erebos and the double-sided axe. "Sweet! Don't you call that a labrys? Is it sharp?" He started to walk over to check it out, but then glanced at Alex, who closed his eyes and subtly shook his head telling Caleb that it was not a good idea.

One of the other council members spoke, "Jeremiah, Shinsu is right! This has dragged on long enough. What is the harm in delaying everything a day or two?" The guards attempted to grab Caleb again, but failed, and by this time, Caleb wasn't paying attention to them. "Perhaps with a little investigation, the boy could be declared an immortal. But it is late and there is no evidence to make that decision now."

Jeremiah thought, and then declared, "We will delay the decision." The council members nodded. "The council will reconvene in two nights. At that time, if the boy is found to be an immortal, Lars will escort him home and we will proceed with the business that was at hand. If the boy is not found to be an immortal, he will join Alexander and Cassandra."

A guard grabbed Valeria's arm and wrapped it around her back. She was stunned by the deathly cold feel of his hands on her and he didn't seem to be aware that he had her arm twisted further back than necessary to control her. He forced her to walk toward the place where she and Alex had stood less than an hour before...before it was decided that they would be beheaded. She glanced briefly at Alex as another guard grabbed him and cinched his arm behind his back, walking him in the same direction.

Caleb asked, "Can I go with Alex?" Jeremiah nodded, irritated with the situation.

Valeria was hauled down a narrow path that wove along the River Styx. The guard grabbed a lit torch and continued down the trail with Alex and Caleb being escorted behind her. They were moving fast enough that she worried about tripping in her heels, which would easily dislocate her arm or, even worse, make her fall into the river and be carried to hell. As the cave narrowed, they passed a large dug-out in the cave with steel bars in front of it that served as a cell. One of the dribs opened it but she was forced to continue.

"Hey wait!" Alex shouted to the drib that held Valeria as he pushed out of his cell. "Wait! Can't we all be in the same cell?" Neither guard responded as Alex was thrown into the dug-out. Valeria almost cried out to Alex and instead risked a backward glance to him and thought that she saw something in his eyes…something he wanted to say to her.

Caleb smiled. "Can I go with Val?" The drib pointed to the cell with Alex and Caleb happily obliged.

She was dragged past a bend in the river where the cave narrowed even more. The guard opened the door to another cage and she stepped in. The cell was at least seven feet high, but only four feet deep. There was a bit of a ledge built into the limestone and she sat down. She was shaking already and the coolness in this part of the cave was making it worse. Then the drib sealed her door and left, taking the only light source with it. Valeria realized she would be left in the cold until they came for her. And then it was dark and she was alone with her nightmares.

CHAPTER 19

In the total absence of light, Valeria began to imagine faces and shapes. For a moment, she was certain she could see the boney face of a drib in her cell—his face inches from her own and she let out a small scream. Alex, instantly alarmed, called to her through the depths of the darkness, "Val?" She heard clanking as if he was struggling to get to her and then silence.

She waved her hands in front of her to fight off the face that she knew was only in her over-active imagination. Now her imagination had placed him in the corner, mocking her.

"I'm sorry. I'm okay." And then she added quietly to herself, "I guess." She gulped. "Are you okay?" she shouted...hoping the drib really was her imagination, though she could see him smiling at her, if she focused.

There was a hesitation and then she heard the quality of Alex's voice and volume changing as if he were turning away from her and then turning back. "Yes...don't worry. Okay?" His voice sounded like he was busy...not like he was sitting in a cave, like she was. Perhaps Caleb was scared and he was trying to handle it.

Valeria thought about his words, *don't worry.* How could he say, "Don't worry"? They were sitting in cold, dark cells waiting to be executed. She heard the clanking sound again and Valeria took a breath. Were they coming for them already? She had hoped to have time to think about this. Her heart rate increased in step with her rising panic.

How could she bear it if they took Alex and Caleb first? She simply couldn't. To know that either of them had been harmed because of her was so much more than she ever thought she could take...a few tears broke free and she swiped at them.

She remembered the line in *Wuthering Heights,* "If all else perished, and he remained, I should still continue to be; and if all else remained, and he were annihilated, the universe would turn to a mighty stranger." That line took on an entirely new meaning now and she prayed that the universe would not turn to a mighty stranger. If it did...she would throw herself into the river of death. Hell fire would be nothing compared to the pain that would remain in her heart for eternity.

If they took Alex and Caleb first...God, she couldn't bear the thought! But if they did, she would run toward the water. That would be better than witnessing what they intended to do to them. Somehow, she would have to be able to tolerate the idea of being in the water...but, without Alex, nothing mattered.

Her ears perked up, she thought she heard movement along the narrow walkway. Valeria could hear her breath and feel the trembling in her gut. She wondered, if they came for her first could she throw herself in the river? What if the council had changed their mind? No, she would wait.

Then she was certain that she heard movement—was it an animal? She backed into the corner of the cell as her gut forced a labored breath, but she was determined not to scream again and frighten Caleb. Poor Caleb!

It wasn't her imagination! There was definitely movement near her cell now. This time a small cry escaped her lips. Then she heard Alex's calming voice, almost a whisper…was it her imagination? "It's all right, Val. We're here."

His voice was right outside of her cell. She must be hallucinating! "Alex?" she said frightened.

"Yes, beautiful, we're here."

Then she heard Caleb giggle. Alex whispered, "Caleb remember—we must be very quiet."

"Sorry," Caleb whispered from outside Valeria's cell. She still couldn't see anything.

There was the clinking sound again and she drew a deep breath as the door squeaked open. A moment later she thought she saw a shape and then felt the warmth of his arms. She fell by memory into his chest, as he wrapped his arms around her and immediately noticed that he wasn't wearing a shirt.

"Val, I'm sorry we don't have much time to explain. You are going to need to change into this quickly." He handed her some material that she realized was a bikini.

"But Tav said she was just going in her underwear!" Caleb whispered.

Alex's voice was quiet, but commanding, "Caleb, you need to get busy."

"How can you see?" she asked.

"Night vision goggles."

She nodded; blind in a seeing world, she began to unzip her dress, when she heard Alex's voice say sharply, "Caleb! Turn around."

"Sorry," Caleb snickered under his breath.

Valeria paused. "Alex, is," she gulped, "is it okay to change now?"

"Yes, it's fine, but hurry! We're going to have to snorkel out of here."

Feeling very self-conscious, Valeria pulled up the skirt of her dress to shed her underwear and then pulled up the swimsuit bottoms underneath her dress. Then, feeling shy, she turned toward the wall. Alex's hands grasped the zipper and his fingers brushed along her skin as he unzipped her dress. They lingered at her waist for just a moment before his lips brushed across her shoulder. Then his attention was diverted again. "How's it going, Caleb?"

"Almost done."

Valeria pushed the dress off her shoulder and it dropped to the ground. Alex handed her the top. She pulled it over her neck and it caught on the hooks in her hair. He adjusted it and set it around her neck and then he reached around the front of her grasping the straps, pulling them around to her back as he hooked it. He whispered into her ear, "Sorry this suit was the most I could risk bringing in with the other required supplies."

As Alex fastened the strap she asked, "I don't understand, I thought the current would take us downstream."

"It's going to be a bit interesting. Caleb, is it together yet?"

"Almost have it," Caleb answered, quietly serious.

"Caleb has a motorized propeller to give us a few knots to combat the River Styx and get past everyone who's still here. He's going to use it to push us. I'm sorry, beautiful, you are going to have to do this in the dark. But trust me, both Caleb and I will have you the whole way out. Okay?"

Her mouth instantly went dry; she was going to be underwater with a snorkel…not just any water, but the river to hell, and all in the blackest of black. Valeria didn't know how she would control her fear.

In a loud whisper, Caleb said, "Okay. Ready to launch." Valeria heard Caleb moving out of her cell. "Can I throw her dress in the river? That'd be cool to see."

"Actually, that's a good idea," Alex said. Valeria felt the whir of material flying past her and heard it light on the water.

Then she heard a nervous hesitancy in Caleb's voice. "Alex? You don't really think it's true about the monsters in the river, do you?"

Alex's breath caught for a moment before he responded, "I'm certain that's a myth."

There was a whirring sound and then the sound was submerged and quieted. "All right, time to get into the water."

While her heart pounded wildly, Alex brushed the curls from the edge of her face and then pulled a wide plastic band over her head. "This is the snorkel. Here, this goes in your mouth." She felt his fingers moving the plastic around toward her mouth. "Good. Now practice breathing a few times." Sensing her hesitancy, he added, "It's all right love, I bought this snorkel for you and washed it myself."

Thinking for a moment, she wondered how he knew about her aversion to publicly used snorkels. But then she realized that he just knew her better than anyone in the world.

She bit down on the plastic. "Breathe through your mouth," he said. She tried but it felt like she couldn't get enough air. She took it out of her mouth.

Alex spoke again, "You're doing great. Just relax. Now, if you get any water in the top of the snorkel, just use a little breath to clear it, okay? Caleb, show her what it sounds like."

She heard Caleb give a strong breath out from his snorkel. "Yes. But when we get into the Council room, it will need to be a bit softer than that, all right? We'll be stopping there for just a moment and you'll both need to be completely silent then."

Spitting the snorkel out of her mouth, she reached for Alex and he pulled her into his arms. She could feel his quick breaths and she knew that he was nervous as well. She leaned her head against his bare chest...a rare treat! And, this time, she knew it was not desire, but fear that caused the thundering of her heart.

She wasn't certain that she could do this at all. Alex continued to hold her close and she realized that he was wearing swim trunks. She clung to him and then he pushed her away. "We have to go, beautiful." He took a few steps, but she didn't move.

"Alex, where did all of this stuff come from?" She knew she was delaying the inevitable by asking about something she should ask later. But just a few more seconds could help her relax.

"We'll talk about that later." Grudgingly, she stepped out of her heels and with Alex carefully guiding her, inched her bare feet along the cold ground. She was terrified that at any step she might fall into the river. "There's a bar you need to step over." Oh, they weren't even out of her cell yet. She drew a deep breath and let it out, feeling the bar with her foot. She remembered that there was at least three feet to the river from the edge of the cell. The ground seemed warmer as she inched her way to the edge. Her trembling was getting out of control. "Okay, love, you're at the edge. Now sit down on the side and put your feet in the water."

He helped her sit and as her feet touched the river, she shuddered and then pushed her legs into the water. She could feel Caleb floating next to her.

"All right. Now I've got this hand," Alex said holding tightly onto her left arm. "Now, with your right hand grab onto Caleb's arm and slide in."

"Val, it's fun in here!" Caleb added.

"Beautiful, we have you. Slide in. The water's deep so you won't be able to stand. I'll hang on to you until you are secure." She couldn't bring herself to budge. She felt Alex begin to lift her toward the water and she wanted to beg him to give her a few more minutes. But this was about all of their lives. She had to be brave. Bringing his hand to her mouth, she kissed it and then blindly plunged into the black warmth of the river. Despite the warmth, her shivering worsened and she felt herself near terror. She clung fiercely to Alex's and Caleb's arms.

"It's warm," she said between shivers, attempting to reassure them that she was okay.

"Caleb, do you have her?"

Caleb gripped her arm solidly. "Got her." Valeria frantically clung to both of them.

"Val, I need to let go. Caleb has you." While he held on to her wrist, her fingers desperately fumbled along the edge of the river so that she clung to Caleb and the edge. She groped along until she found Caleb's left hand and noticed what many would not…he was wearing the rubberized covering on both hands.

She heard Alex sliding into the water next to her and felt his body next to hers. It was a shock to find that despite her terror, his body next to hers was still such a thrill.

"All right," Alex said softly. "Are you both ready?" She felt him turn toward her and then his hand slid her snorkel into place on her face. "Okay? Let's try it out." She nodded and he gently pulled her underwater. She immediately fought him and rose.

"I don't think I can do this," she said frantically.

Alex's hand stroked her face. "You can do this!" She shook her head violently in disagreement, forgetting that he could see her every movement. Alex took her face in his hands. "Yes. Yes, you can." He swallowed. "Beautiful, it's okay. Just feel the snorkel." He took her fingers and led them along the length of the tube.

"Feel it?" he asked, as he huffed out water that had flowed into his mouth. "The snorkel is long enough for this depth—we'll need to be that deep to get by the others. We're going to stay along this edge where the current isn't so strong. I'll have your hand and Caleb will be pushing both of our feet." He held her close and kissed the top of her head. "I want you to bring your knees up and just float here for a minute. I'll hang on to you." Valeria put her face in the water for an instant and, faced with the blackness, immediately pulled it back up. "Good," he whispered. "Try it again." This time she was able to actually relax a bit. Then she came up. "Very good! Now, I want you to put your head down and get water in the snorkel. I need you to breathe the water out, like you heard Caleb do just a few minutes ago."

"It's easy!" Caleb added as she heard him taking in air and huffing it out.

Alex heard a sound and she could feel his alarm. "I think we're out of time. I'll try not to get you too deep for your snorkel, but if I do, quickly…let me hear you blow out on the snorkel." She blew out. He sighed, then said more softly, "All right…so if you start to get water in your mouth just breathe out, okay?" he repeated nervously.

Her shaking had increased to a level that she could barely speak. "Okay."

"Just relax and imagine we're home, in front of the fire. Imagine we're listening to Jason Mraz on the stereo and you're sipping the Ladera Cab that you love. Can you imagine that?" She nodded slightly. "Good…what song would be playing?"

"Umm…*Sleeping to Dream*," she mumbled.

"Perfect." Alex drew a deep breath. "Caleb, let's go."

Valeria grabbed his arm. "No, wait! How long will this take?" She knew it was only another delay tactic, but she couldn't help herself.

"To get out of the River Styx, I hope about ten minutes."

"Okay...well then, *Song for a Friend*...that's over ten minutes."

"Good. Beautiful, we're going now." He leaned over and kissed her and she felt the goggles brush her cheek.

"On three...one, two, three." Then Alex dove holding on to her arm. She left the safety of the wall and suddenly felt something on her foot. She kicked and pulled her face out of the water.

Caleb whispered, "It's okay, Val, it's not a monster, it's just me. I need to have your foot to push you."

She spit the snorkel out of her mouth. "Oh, okay." He grasped her feet. Alex lifted his head out of the water as they started to move.

"Beautiful, put your snorkel back in." He helped her replace it. "Good. Now, head down." She reluctantly complied as they continued to move. Then he wrapped his arm around her waist and she clung to his arm like a life-preserver. She closed her eyes and tried to breathe calmly. Alex squeezed her for an instant and she was at once overwhelmed by the blessed feeling of him next to her. The emotion began to choke her and she worked to minimize that thought for the moment. She needed to feel like they had never been apart. She could feel him using his other arm to guide them along the edge of the river.

Although his arm had a tight grip around her, his fingers gently stroked her waist. With the feeling of the warm water gently moving over them and his arms around her, she began to relax. She noticed that he pulled her down deeper and this time she permitted herself to go. It meant being closer to him.

Through her closed eyelids, she could sense increasing light but she didn't want to open her eyes. She was afraid of what she would see. She felt their progress slow down and she felt her head touch the surface when Alex tapped her. She prayed that they were finished being in the water. But she knew that was too much to hope for. She saw Alex pull the goggles down around his neck and, glancing at her, he touched his finger to his mouth with a slight wink. She could see the tension in his eyes even though he was attempting to hide it from her. They were in the Council Room!

The smooth sandstone ledge rose up almost two feet. She watched as Alex grasped along the shoreline for something—she realized that this was where she and Alex had been right before the meeting...when Paolo had found them.

Then she heard Shinsu's voice, "I apologize, I simply wanted to discuss this while it was fresh..."

And then another voice, most definitely Jeremiah's, but she missed what he said.

Valeria looked into Alex's eyes and, at that moment, she knew without a doubt that she would do *anything* for him! He winked again, replaced the snorkel in his mouth and they dove back into the water. Valeria relaxed into the feeling of his arm as the water surrounded them.

They continued along smoothly until Valeria felt Alex's sudden jolt, and then she sensed Caleb responding to something as well. A monster? She didn't want to look. Fortunately, they continued and then it got darker again. At last, Alex rose out of the water pulling her up as well. They were in the cave entrance to Delos, where the large boulder sat and they had loaded onto the gondolas. She watched the rough water from the sea roll past them, barely affecting them while they were behind the boulder.

"You did great," he whispered. Valeria noticed that Alex looked upset.

Caleb looked excited. "That was cool! Did you see—"

Alex gave a very brief shake of his head. Caleb nodded

into silence.

Looking around in the light, Valeria could see that both Alex and Caleb had the goggles around their neck. She could see some light shining down from the Council Room. It would have seemed mostly dark, except for the extreme darkness they had just left. They had successfully passed the remaining council members and guards! Valeria glanced down the inlet to the cave, wondering if she would see the trog that was going to come and get them.

"Where's the boat?" she asked.

Alex shook his head. "Sorry, love. There is no boat. Right now, we have to get across this water way. That's the tricky part—or one of them. They confiscated Caleb's kayak. So right now, we need to get across here, there's a rope attached to the cave wall. The boats guide themselves in and out with it. We're going to use it to get out of here. Caleb? Do you have the hook?" he asked.

Caleb dove down and came back up, handing Alex a line of cord with a large hook on the end. Alex threw the hook toward the base of the railing on the other side of the cave. The hook splashed into the water. He pulled it back in.

"Alex can't we just lower the bridge?" Valeria asked.

"We can't risk having someone hear or see it. Sorry." Tossing the hook a second time, it latched on to the railing. "Okay, Caleb. Do you have it secured on this end?"

"Yep," Caleb answered. Valeria could tell Caleb was enjoying this.

"Okay, beautiful, I'm going over to the other side. Watch how I move. Then you are going to cross. Okay?"

Valeria nodded.

Carefully placing his hands, Alex started to move along the cord and then immediately turned back and pulled his goggles around to the back of his neck and signaled for Caleb to do the same. Then he moved across the rushing tidal water clinging to the cord and struggling to hang on until he finally reached the other side. He looked at Caleb.

Caleb nodded. "Alex just told me to tell you that I'm supposed to tie you in." Valeria glanced at Alex and realized he had passed Caleb a silent communication. "He says the current is too strong for you." Caleb took the cord and hooked it securely around her waist. "Alex says it's pretty rough, but it will only be a couple of minutes and then he'll have you."

"Okay." This was far less worrisome to her than snorkeling in the dark. But she wasn't excited about it either.

"He says he's sorry about this." She shrugged and grabbed hold of the cord as Alex nodded, and she discovered that she was shaking again. Immediately, the character of the water changed to brutally rough and cool. She was instantly rolled underwater and tossed downstream and then a moment later her face broke the surface and she caught a breath before being dragged back under. Then she felt Alex pull her out of the water and she was in his arms. His eyes looked particularly tense. "We're about out of time here!" He tossed the cord back to Caleb, who tied it around his waist as Alex pulled him across.

"Val, we need to hide in the water. We need to wait for them to close the adamantine gate. But I'm going to stay right with you!" They walked deeper into the cave and then he said, "I think this will work." He glanced toward where they had been and nodded. "We may need to dive down a couple of times."

Then she heard Shinsu and Jeremiah arguing loudly. "If I am to be the senior wife, I insist that the girl treats me as such! Simply because she is your favorite consort is no reason for such disrespect!"

"Shinsu, you know full well that she is not a consort! The

issue is that the girl feels that you dislike her."

"I *do* dislike her! She is disrespectful! You certainly would not tolerate the insults that she lavishes on me."

Alex pulled Valeria toward him and hugged her while tying the cord around her waist again. On each end of the cord was a clip. "I'm sorry, love. You will probably have rope burn but it's the best I can do." He finished with the knot.

Then he knelt by the water and hooked the rope around the railing while clipping the other end around his waist. "In the water," he said, as his eyes darted toward the boulder and the approaching gondola. She lowered herself into the water and wrapped her arms and legs around him as he clung to the cord and railing. The bridge began to lower and they could hear Shinsu and Jeremiah continue to argue.

"Jeremiah, I will never understand how you justify this lifestyle!" she snorted.

"I have told you, my dear, it has *always* been our way to abide by the rules of the society that we live in."

"And how long did it take you to discover this society?"

"Why are we always arguing the same point?"

They had crossed the bridge, while Jeremiah carried a torch. The bridge rose back up and there was an incredibly loud screeching noise and, as if by magic, the boulder at the gate of the River Styx began to move and seal the entrance to Delos. Jeremiah and Shinsu walked down the walkway as a boat trog pulled into the cave.

A light from the boat shined near Alex and Valeria. "Go under, now!" Valeria was plunged under the water as Alex wrapped himself around her like a cocoon, protecting her from the violent pulls of the rope and sea. A moment later, the boat turned off its forward lights and they lifted their heads out of the water. "A few more minutes," Alex whispered to her. Valeria felt movement and was certain that it was Alex and

Caleb replacing their night vision goggles. Then, Jeremiah and Shinsu were gone, and they were back in total darkness, except for the last burning embers of Jeremiah's torch.

Alex lifted her onto the ledge and then he and climbed out. "We can relax here for a couple of minutes," Alex said.

She was glad to be out of the water; there was just something about water in the dark that she really hated!

"Caleb, where's the bag?" Alex asked. She could hear Caleb splashing around in the water and then there was something urgent about his movements. She heard the panic creeping into Alex's voice, "Caleb?"

Suddenly, Caleb breathed a sigh of relief which echoed through the momentary silence of the cave, until the next surge of water came through. "Good," Alex said and she could hear him rummaging through something.

A moment later she heard a flick and a small flashlight came on. Caleb handed it to her, while leaving the goggles over his eyes.

"Thought you might like to be able to see," Alex said.

Her face showed relief and she kissed his neck. There was a band attached to the small flashlight and Alex pulled it over the top of Valeria's head and adjusted the angle of the flashlight. He stood and helped her up; then he picked up a large white mesh bag, evidently the one that Caleb had been searching for. Then, Alex said, "Let's go."

"Where are we going?"

"We are going to walk along the ledge until it ends. And then—I am sorry to tell you this—but, beautiful, we have to swim out of here. If we had requested a trog to pick us up, it would have alerted Jeremiah and we couldn't think of a way to hide a kayak."

They walked along the edge of the water until the ledge ended in the spot where the troglodyte had let them off.

Alex sat the mesh bag on the ground and opened it. He pulled out three sets of flippers and three bright yellow cans with mouthpieces that were the size of a large can of hairspray.

"Okay, you'll need to put on the flippers."

Valeria looked at the current. "Alex, I can't swim against this."

"We won't be swimming for a while. But you need to be ready. We'll have to swim out of the entrance. We'll wait for the outbound wave and ride it out. But there'll be another wave behind it pulling us back in. That second wave is the dangerous one. We can get trapped miles down the cave where there is no rope to hang on to.

He lifted one of the cans. "This is air. So on the second wave, you'll put this into your mouth and breathe slowly. We are going to dive low to avoid the heavy currents and catch the undertow away from the shoreline. With the way you're breathing, you'll only have two to three minutes of air if you're lucky, so I want you to practice slowing your breathing, okay?" Valeria nodded as Alex continued, "Once we get to the entrance, we're going to take three deep breaths in and out." He demonstrated. "And then we'll dive down and out until we are safely off shore. Okay?"

She nodded. She didn't want to do that but it was the only way out. The mesh bag converted to a back pack and Alex pulled the straps over his arms. He checked the cord around Valeria's waist. "Caleb? We're ready for you." Caleb stepped around her and grabbed the other end of the cord, ran it around the thick rope on the cave wall and clipped it to his waist. Then he slid into the water.

"Ready?"

She thought, *No,* but she grabbed the rope; she realized with disgust that it was covered with a slimy algae. Alex strung his end of the cord around the rope and then clipped the cord around his waist. She clung to the rope and crawled into the cold water, with Caleb in front of her and Alex behind her constantly encouraging her forward movement down the rope. She was splashed in the face several times and stopped. Alex tried to keep her moving.

Every ten feet, the rope was attached to the cave wall and, when they came to the first attachment, Caleb unclipped the cord around him and was about to refasten it on the other side when a wave came and threw him violently into Valeria. Alex tried to move her, but Caleb's elbow slammed into her face, hitting her and zapping Alex. Caleb frantically clung to the cord and then was able to grab the rope and clip his line back into place.

With a panicked look, Caleb glanced over as Alex turned Valeria around to see if she was hurt. "Are you all right?" She was shaking so bad from nerves and the cool sea water that all she could do was nod. She really didn't know if she was hurt; she just felt numb.

She wanted to reassure Caleb, but she just couldn't do anything but hang on and shiver. Alex nodded to Caleb.

"It's okay, buddy. Next time, we'll wait until the inbound wave passes before the transfer."

Caleb nodded, obviously upset. He took a deep breath as Alex grabbed Valeria around her waist. After the third stop, her flashlight was already starting to dim.

"It was supposed to last for hours!" Alex took it for a minute and tapped it in his palm and it brightened.

She dreaded moving back into the darkness and tried not to think about the slime on the rope. Then the light dimmed again and died, leaving her in the pitch-blackness again. Despite the occasional wave in the face, she was calmer now; especially with Alex so near, her shaking became less fierce.

This continued for almost an hour. The strength of the

current slowed their progress significantly. Finally, Alex pointed out that they were not far from the opening, and then Valeria saw the momentary reflection of the moonlight, as the sound of the crashing waves became thunderous. Her gut tightened in fear—swimming out terrified her.

Alex pulled off the mesh backpack and took out the cans of air, handing one to Caleb and attaching one to his snorkel band.

"Okay, we are going to wait for the outbound wave and swim. When I say dive, I need you to take a deep breath and dive with me. Put the snorkel in your mouth." He attached the yellow can to the strap on her snorkel and then leaned his forehead against hers. "We're almost done here but if we're going to get out of here alive, you're going to have to do exactly what I say. Okay?" She nodded.

"Caleb, are you good?" he asked. The boy nodded.

She could almost see Caleb as he turned to face her. "I know Alex will help you. But I can help you too." She shivered and gave Caleb a hug.

A large crashing wave came through and, as it passed, Alex unclipped Valeria from the rope on the cave wall and clipped the cord around his own waist. "Swim!"

She let go of the slimy rope and struggled to figure out how to swim but instead ended up kicking Alex with her fin. She couldn't move her arms and Valeria realized she was just a weight to him and he was unable to use his right arm or leg. With her fear mounting, she pulled the snorkel out of her mouth and sucked on the canned air.

Immediately, Alex turned to her. "We need to go back!" he yelled, and she could hear the panic in his voice. The next wave was building and she remembered what he had said that a wave could trap them at the very back of the cave.

Fighting the swift outflow of current, he struggled to get

them both back to the side of the cave wall. She watched with horror as the next monstrous wave built strength and was about to crash through the opening of the cave. Just as it struck, she heard the deafening crash and felt Alex frantically reaching for the rope. She saw his hands on it. But he couldn't maintain his grasp with the strong current. He kicked even harder and his hands once again slid off the slick rope; finally, he got a hold of it and was able to latch the cord back around it. Once secured, he pulled her back into his arms just as the wave hit with much more fury.

Alex winced. "That didn't work too well. We'll figure this out." He glanced around and then nodded, as if he received a non-verbal communication. "Caleb made it out."

"Let's see." He took a deep breath. "Val, drop your fins. I think it will work better with you on my back. Wrap your arms around my neck and your legs around my waist. Then I can use my arms and legs to get us out of here."

It all sounded frightening to her but she nodded. Alex adjusted the cord and she wrapped herself tightly around him.

"Remember, we are going to dive as the next wave comes in, so I'll tell you to take your breaths and then put your mouth piece in and breathe slowly," he said. "When I tap you, if you are okay, give me a thumbs up. Okay?" Through her shivering she managed to give him a thumbs up.

She heard the crash of a large wave and knew they were about to head back out. "Ready?" He started swimming and she clung to him while attempting to keep her face up out of the water. But it was almost impossible. She opened her eyes so that she could at least see the waves, and then realized that they had made it to the cave entrance as she looked up at the moonlight and stars in appreciation.

"Take your breaths now. One, two, three. Ready?" She nodded. "Can in your mouth. Are you good?"

A wave splashed her and she fumbled nervously, but finally, she got the can in her mouth and did a thumbs up. He dove deeper into the water, and she clung to him with all of her remaining strength. She kept her eyes closed and just breathed. Using his arms and legs, Alex took long, deep strokes downward.

She could feel the violent turbulence of the wave above them and wondered if they had been pushed back into the cave. Her own breathing and heartbeat drowned out most of the sounds. She remembered she was supposed to slow down her breathing but when she tried, she felt breathless and it seemed like she just couldn't catch her breath. She prayed that they would surface and soon! Alex must have sensed it and patted her thigh. She shook violently, but forced herself to give him a thumbs up. He kept going.

Laying her head against his back soothed her, and finally, they rose and broke the surface. Immediately, she spit the mouthpiece out, but a large wave was heading right at them.

"Going back under." Alex dove before she could say or do anything. She fumbled and finally got the can back into her mouth and breathed deeply. Alex had patted her thigh several times and, again, she forced herself to give him a thumbs up and laid her head against his back.

She noticed that she was having to suck on the mouth piece to get a breath from it. She wondered if it was psychosomatic and worked to relax her breathing. She wondered how to tell Alex that she wasn't all right. They hadn't talked about that. But what could he do? He couldn't risk rising and getting them thrown back into the cave or slammed into the rocks.

Then the can completely stopped giving her air. She hung on as long as she could but now her lungs ached and *she had to breathe!* She let go of Alex and waved her limbs violently, trying to get to the surface. The current caught her and started to jerk her back toward the cave. Alex grabbed her foot and tried to pull her back down as her lungs were about to explode. She fought him…needing to breathe. She was out of time and she knew she would die as he held her tightly near the bottom. Then he forced something into her mouth and she realized it was *air!*

She breathed deeply and stopped struggling as he held her tightly. He tapped her and she gave him a thumbs up and climbed on his back as Alex kicked all the harder.

At last they broke the surface, and he drew several audible gasps for air. Valeria pulled the can from her mouth and let out a whimper as he yanked off his goggles and pulled her around in front of him.

"Val! Are you alright?" He was out of breath and it was her fault. She tried to nod, but felt the quivers begin. "Look," he said, as he pointed to the shore. "We made it past the breakers. No more diving!"

Glancing around in the moonlight, he finally located Caleb quite a distance from them and saw him lift a thumbs up. When Alex responded with the same, Caleb continued snorkeling.

Alex kissed her. "Just a little further. I'm going to hold your hand. You can help by kicking your feet. It's all easy going from here!"

She knew that she *should* be okay. But she couldn't bring herself to say it. Still, she put the snorkel back into her mouth, placed her face in the water, and held Alex's hand as she kicked.

After a few moments he stopped. "Look, Val, that's where we're going."

She felt a shudder of relief as she saw Caleb climbing onto the small motor boat. It would be Lars or Tavish…maybe Ava. Despite her exhaustion, she kicked even harder and in minutes they were there. She was grateful to see the hand reaching down to her, and clasped it. She was nearly in the boat when she glanced up and—to her absolute horror—realized *it was Paolo!*

In a sudden panic, she struggled to free herself from his grip and fell back into the water, her face plunging under, before she rose and screamed out, "No!" Valeria turned in terror and splashed and kicked trying to move away as Paolo tried to pull her onboard. She tried to scream a warning to Alex, but instead, she breathed in water and then frantically began swimming back out to sea.

Alex tried to catch her but, in her near hysteria, she thought it was Paolo taking her back to Erebos. Finally, Alex wrapped his arms around her. "Val! Val! It's alright!"

When her vision cleared, she flung her arms around his neck with muffled sobs. He stroked her back. "It's alright, beautiful," he murmured in her ear, holding her tightly. "Paolo's helping us." She had reached her threshold and shook violently as the sobs tore at her. "I'm sorry, Val." He blew the water out of his mouth. "I should have warned you. It's okay. It's okay." He rubbed her back as he kicked his feet to bring them back to the boat.

This time, Caleb reached down for Valeria. "It's okay, Val. Really, Paolo's okay." In her current state, she couldn't understand what was going on. She thought her mind must have shut off. Was the plan for her to go off and marry Paolo? Or was Paolo now going to take them back into that cave where Erebos could finish the job?

She couldn't permit herself to think about it, and gave Caleb her hand. Not that she had much of a choice! She really couldn't stay in the ocean. Her shaking was now violent; her sobs continued as Alex climbed on board. Seeing her tremors, Paolo tried to wrap her in a blanket.

"Don't touch me!" she screamed.

Alex moved to the middle of the boat with her and pulled her into his arms, and then wrapped the blanket around the two of them.

She glared at Paolo as she leaned into Alex. She would *never* go back to Paolo! "I'm not going to marry you! I don't care what anybody says! I'm not!" she wailed. "I would rather die than to be with you! Do you understand?" Alex stroked her back, lovingly.

Paolo looked down. "Yes, Bella, I know." His voice was soft, as if he were afraid of his own words.

She watched Caleb talk to Paolo like he was his best friend and it upset her. But then Caleb hadn't witnessed Paolo's betrayal. What made it worse to her was that it wasn't Paolo's first betrayal, or second. And, yet, Alex seemed relaxed about the whole situation...more so than even the night before at the cottage.

"Alex, I'm staying with you...no matter what. I don't care what he says! I don't care what they say! I'm never leaving you again! *Please, don't send me back!*" she pleaded.

He looked at her, emotion rimming his eyes as he adoringly stroked the side of her face. "Yes, beautiful, you are staying with me," he said, tenderly pulling her in closer, and whispering, *"forever!"*

With that, emotion flooded every part of her and the sobs overwhelmed her...tears for the pain of the past, tears for the joy of the future, and tears for the pleasure of right now, with her Alex, her symbolon—whole once more.

The motor started and they were off.

CHAPTER 20

The boat putted along through the water. Valeria was almost relaxed feeling Alex so near.

"How's the jaw?" Alex asked Paolo.

Moving his jaw back and forth, Paolo shrugged. "Alright."

Paolo leaned toward Alex. "You may use my yacht. I had it moved not far from here. Or, there is a plane waiting on a private strip on the mainland. Which would you prefer?"

Valeria looked at Alex. "Please, let's go on the plane." She was still shivering slightly and thoroughly convinced that Paolo had another trap awaiting them.

Kissing the top of her head, Alex smiled softly. "Val, it's been a tough night and I haven't slept in days. I don't trust my flying skills right now and we can't get a hotel on the mainland, we are too close. We have to make time and the best way we can do that is on the yacht. We'll sleep tonight and as soon as we are able, we'll get on a plane. Okay?"

She could see that it had been an emotional and exhausting couple of day for him, too. She nodded. Paolo turned the boat to the west and headed a few miles off shore. They approached a large yacht and settled next to it. Paolo went about securing the lines and a ladder was dropped. Valeria noticed that this was not the same ship that she'd been on in New York. It was much larger, with multiple levels. Then she saw the name painted on the side, *The Kristiana.*

The moonlight lit the rope ladder as she shed the blanket and began the climb with Alex right behind her. Once onboard, a man in a white naval suit handed her a warm brandy. The liquid went down smoothly, heating her up from the inside. Another man handed them all dry blankets. Caleb grabbed one, while Alex took the other two and wrapped one around her. Then he sipped his warm brandy and watched as Caleb immediately tossed off the blanket and began exploring excitedly.

Paolo turned to Alex and Valeria. "I apologize about the name of the yacht. On such short notice, this was the most comfortable and accessible."

Alex nodded but Valeria refused to meet Paolo's gaze.

"Valeria, I could not remove your belongings from the island house without being questioned but you should find everything you need in your state room.

"Alex, there are clothes for you and the boy as well. I've left a case with money and passports. I also took the liberty of purchasing brown contact lenses. I suggest all three of you wear them until you have some distance.

Glancing down, Paolo's eyes filled with sadness. "Bella, please don't hate me. Alex, will you tell her?" Alex nodded, but Paolo appeared unconvinced. "Will you tell her everything?"

"Yes, I'll do that."

Paolo continued, "You are welcome to use the ship as long as you would like."

"Thanks, pal. We'll need it less than a week. Contact Lars and he'll arrange for you to be reimbursed."

Swallowing back his emotion, Paolo said softly, "I must get back. I must be seen tonight."

Alex winced and shook his head. "I don't know, Paolo, I think you had better disappear for a while."

"I do not have your gifts with money. I cannot walk away from it."

Paolo started to leave and then paused. He turned hesitantly toward them. "I will give you this gift...this wedding gift." He looked at Valeria with more love than she thought he was capable of, and he started to reach toward the left side of her face, but she jerked away from him.

Seeing her repulsion, he retracted his hand and sucked in a quick breath. "Valeria, I believe you will want to know about this. It's about—" She turned her face into Alex's chest.

Sympathetically, Alex placed his arm on Paolo's. "Sorry, pal, maybe another time."

"But, Alex, please allow me to—" Alex shook his head and Paolo stopped and clenched his jaw as he looked down.

When he looked back up, there were tears in his eyes. "Yes. Another time, then." Paolo stared off into the sea and she noticed that he wore her engagement ring on his little finger. Then, without another word, he walked to the ladder and climbed back down. The engine started up and then he was gone.

An officer came up and introduced himself, and asked, "What is your destination, sir?"

Alex looked at Valeria and his face glowed with love. "West, for now."

"Sir, please allow me to show you and the lady to your quarters." Alex nodded as he slipped his arm around her, holding her closely as they followed the officer down some stairs to the front of the yacht. The officer opened the door and Alex and Valeria entered. The enormous stateroom had a king-sized bed and luxury bathtub surrounded by candles.

At the end of the bed was an upholstered bench, with a large Louis Vuitton bag, a locked metal case, and a sports bag. Alex pulled clothes out of the sports bag: two pairs of jeans, a pair of slacks, three polo shirts, along with various socks, shoes, and underwear.

"I think I'll put these away," he said, and took them into the walk-in closet.

Valeria's brain was on slow motion and she was still shivering, though only slightly now. She couldn't quite put together how everything happened, only that she was here. She opened the Louis Vuitton bag and found jeans, sweats, shorts, several dresses, and an inordinate amount of lingerie—including a silk negligee and matching robe—and all the accessories including jewelry.

She was looking at the French lingerie when Alex returned. He had shed the blanket and was now there in just his swim trunks. Her heart lurched and then she saw his slow smile as he eyed what she was holding—lace underwear. They both laughed for what felt like the first time in a long, long time.

"I'd like to see you model this collection!" He stepped toward her, as if in a dream, and kissed her lightly. Then he ran his hands around her back as his other hand brushed the edge of her face. She touched his chest, as he again kissed her softly, and then leaned back, a dreamy look in his eyes. "Beautiful, why don't I give you some time to warm up in the bath?"

She wrapped her arms around him. "Only if you join me." She kissed his chest.

Alex pulled her to him, overwhelmed with feeling. "Tempting," he murmured breathlessly in her ear. Then he shook his head, returning to reality. "Actually, I need to go check on Caleb and make sure he's settled, too." He kissed her forehead. "Besides, you need to eat something and you look exhausted."

He kissed her neck, running his lips up to her ear in a way that made a shiver run clear down to her toes. Now her heart was pounding. "I...I need to shower before we..." she said dreamily.

He leaned his nose against hers, and kissed her again. "And I need to check on Caleb. I can also try to round up some food for us while you shower." He drew in a deep breath and shook his head. "Looking at your eyes, my guess is that you'll be asleep in less than twenty minutes."

"No! I am going to enjoy every minute with you tonight!" she said. He winked as he closed the door behind him.

Stepping into the bathroom, she reached into the glass-block shower and turned on the water, adjusting the temperature. She stripped out of her cold swimsuit and moved under the relaxing warmth of the shower's spray. She shampooed her hair and shaved her legs. Then she wrapped herself in a lush white towel, brushed her teeth, pulled on the silk negligee, and finally crawled under the covers.

There was a knock at the door and Alex announced himself before coming in. He had a tray of cheese, crackers, and vegetables and carried a bottle of wine. He glanced at Valeria in bed and smiled before looking away to pour them both a glass of wine. "Caleb is doing fine. He's up with the captain." Alex leaned across the bed and clinked his glass against hers.

"Reunited, at last!"

Valeria looked at him with pure adoration. "Forever!"

He took a deep breath, his eyes taking in the silk negligee *and her*. He sipped his wine, and then reluctantly said, "I need to get cleaned up, too. Promise me you won't fall asleep before

I get out of the shower?"

"Oh, no worries about that!" She smiled, and then noticed that his mouth had turned up in his charming smile as well. She lowered her eyebrows and said, "I do remember *that* smile of yours! So, tell me...what are you thinking?"

His smile broadened. "I will leave that to *your* imagination!"

Her eyes sparkled. "Hmm, I think you want to...skip the shower and jump under the covers with me!" He laughed with delight and nodded his head almost imperceptibly.

"You need to eat." He narrowed his eyes as if he was contemplating her offer. "And I do want to clean up *first.*" Then he cocked his head to the side. "Although, I suspect you have...oh, I'd say no more than ten minutes until you're asleep."

"I'm not falling asleep!" she protested, as she picked up a cherry tomato and popped it into her mouth. Then she realized how hungry she actually was! "This is good."

In truth, she didn't taste anything, not the wine, nor the cheese. She was certain that it was good, but her mind was preoccupied.

"Just don't fall asleep before I get out, okay?" He smiled as he grabbed a pair of boxers and went into the bathroom and, for the first time ever, he left the door ajar so that she could hear him brushing his teeth and shaving. Then her heart stopped as she got a brief glimpse of him stepping into the shower.

She imagined having the nerve to go into the shower and step inside with him. He would turn and wrap his arms around her in surprise and then they would make love...there.

Feeling the blood move from her face down to her belly, she shook her head, attempting to clear the delicious fantasy. She sat up and decided that she had to get her nerve up. Then she frowned when she heard the shower turn off. She pouted for a moment and then leaned back against the stacked pillows behind her head. The shower fantasy would have to wait...*until next time*. She smiled and felt her heart pound against her chest.

Then he stepped out and, by the time she saw him, he was already wrapped in a towel. But his eyes met hers for a moment, and she saw that smile that she loved. As an intense blush moved across her face and neck she forced herself to look away.

A moment later he came out of the bathroom, wearing the silk boxers. She preferred the previous view. He slipped into the bed and glanced at the tray, noticing she had only had a few bites, and he looked teasingly displeased.

"Val..."

She sat up. "Alex..."

Staring into his eyes, she said, "You know, the only thing I want right now is to make love to you!" He jerked his head back in surprise. She moved her mouth to his and remembered how she loved the feel of his lips on hers.

He pulled back and the corners of his mouth turned up in mild amusement. "By the way, you were wrong earlier." She raised her eyebrows. He smiled and this time a slight blush moved across his face. "I mean, yes, the bed was my second choice, but my first choice was the shower."

"Oh!" she answered, completely startled by his response; then she felt the warmth run from her throat, exploding within her belly, and then continued down again until her toes curled.

He pulled her into a deep kiss and then drew a breath. "Let's get rid of this," his eyes sparkled as he took her wine glass, "for a while," he whispered breathlessly.

Her smile deepened as he took her glass and she wrapped her legs around him, thrilled that tonight she would finally make love to him. She leaned her face against his chest and kissed it, while Alex moved the tray of food to make room for the glasses of wine on the bedside table.

She noticed a rope burn on his side and brushed her fingers along it and felt him shudder. It was so comforting…so comfortable to feel him next to her! She closed her eyes for a moment.

When Alex turned back toward her, she was asleep. He gave a small chuckle, still amazed that he was here with her. Then, brushing the hair back from her face, something caught his eye. He leaned in and his jaw dropped.

∞

The sun peeked through the curtains in the stateroom and Alex kissed Valeria. "Good morning, beautiful!"

She stretched, realizing that she had actually slept! She felt revived and alive and the world felt right, finally! She whispered, "Never leave me again." She kissed his neck and chest.

Alex pulled her into him in a way that was more sensual than she had expected. She felt the sudden electricity of the moment, as his fingers brushed her hips and pulled her legs up around him.

Leaning his nose against hers, his eyes filled with love. "You may get tired of me."

She shook her head vehemently in objection. "Never!" she whispered. He moved his mouth the short distance to hers, pulling her closer into him, and then brushed her negligee off her shoulder. His mouth and tongue moved down her neck and caressed her shoulder as he slid his hands under the crisscross of the silk in the back of the negligee. His hands were on her and it was thrilling!

A moan escaped her mouth and she pressed his head against hers. "Make love to me…now."

"Yes," he said, his voice husky with desire.

"Oh, Alex," she whispered, "You are already my husband." She pressed into him and, instantly, she realized the error of her words as she suddenly sensed his hesitancy.

He lifted his head and said as he bit his lip. "Sorry, I got caught up in…you."

Seeing her disappointment, he continued, "But…we are on a ship. And there is a captain. I'm certain he'd be happy to marry us. Hell, if we asked, he might even perform the ceremony right here, right now." Then Alex sighed and rolled on to his back, laughing as he shook his head. "But I don't know, Val, it's difficult for me to believe that after waiting 3,000 years, I'm going to marry you, *and finally make love to you*, on Paolo's ship and—"

He moved his nose back to hers as they said in unison, "On a ship called *The Kristiana!*" They laughed the long musical laughter of happiness.

"Point well taken!" she said, as she curled into him and pulled his arm back around her. "But let's not wait long. I don't want anything else to ever come between us!"

"I agree!" Alex leaned down and kissed her head, and then something caught his eye on Valeria's side of the bed.

She turned to see what he was looking at and stunned, she said, "It's one thirty in the afternoon!"

He rolled back on top of her. "Do you know what is so amazing about that?"

She massaged his shoulders. "How time flies when we're in each other's arms."

"That *is* pretty amazing!" She thought about how much she loved the beautiful sound of his voice. It sounded so free of anxiety, so…happy.

He laughed. "I guess I am just going to have to say it."

She tilted her head to the side, awaiting the revelation. "You haven't had any coffee!" He winked.

Then, in mock horror, she dropped her jaw, and recovering, she smiled flirtatiously. "I would have guessed it right the first time, if you hadn't distracted me." The corners of his mouth turned up in a playful smile.

"We need to resolve this oversight immediately!" He sat up, which initiated a cry of protest. He patted her arm, as he picked up the phone with his other hand.

"What does a guy have to do to get some coffee around here?' He turned back around to her. "Any chance we can get some good French press with cream?" He listened and then said to Valeria, "He says that they also have Italian style cappuccino."

She thought for a moment and then shook her head, indicating she preferred the French press. "French press, the lady says, in the cabin, please. We'll have breakfast on the main deck in about an hour." He looked at Valeria, with a hint of mischief in his eyes. "Oh, could you please bring the item that I requested?" He winked at Valeria. "Thank you." He hung up the phone.

Alex kissed her forehead again. "We do have some business to take care of. I made a promise to myself and to Paolo that you would know everything—the sooner that business is over with, the better." He popped out of bed. "I'll shower first, so that I can go check on Caleb and make sure he isn't getting into trouble."

Valeria knew that Alex was concerned about having left Caleb alone for so long. There was a knock at the door, and she got out of bed and threw the silk robe on over her negligee.

A woman in a white uniform handed her a tray with a coffee press full of coffee and two cups. Valeria felt like she should tip her but she disappeared, after almost bowing, as soon as Valeria took the tray. She set it down and poured the cream in her cup and could smell the quality of it. Then she took a sip and savored the flavor.

Alex came out of the bathroom fully dressed in jeans and a polo shirt. She looked at him appreciatively and then shook her head, tears coming into her eyes again; she was so very grateful that he was here with her. "Did I ever tell you how incredibly handsome you are?"

He smiled *that smile* and then kissed her. "Good coffee?" She nodded. "Good! I'll see you up on the deck when you're ready." He kissed her again, grabbed his cup, and headed out the door. "Don't be too long."

She showered and changed into jeans and a white silk blouse. The clothes that Paolo had selected fit nicely, as expected. Paolo even had makeup in the bag and she put on a touch of mascara and lip gloss.

On the deck she saw Caleb absorbed in an electronic game. She messed up his hair when she walked by and he turned slightly sideways and said, "I'm on level five." He gave a little laugh and turned back to his game and shouted, "Paolo has really cool games!"

Alex was leaning over the rail, looking off into the sea. There was no land visible on either side of the yacht and the sky was a soft, misty blue.

She wrapped her arms around his waist tightly.

"Do you know how good that feels?" he said, as he raised his arm to pull her in front of him and glanced at her. "Nice clothes."

Breakfast was being served on the table. "Caleb, did you eat?" Valeria asked.

"Yeah! Level six, gotta concentrate!"

They sat down to frittatas, sweet potato hash, and fruit.

Then the chef came out and set a green drink in front of Valeria.

She glanced curiously from the chef to Alex. The chef stated, "Kale and strawberries, just as the gentleman requested."

She held it up, it looked perfectly green. She nodded to the chef and then gave Alex a quizzical glance. "You? You ordered this?" Alex shrugged a single shoulder with a wink. "Alex, how did you even know about this?" She hadn't started drinking it until she had returned to Manhattan.

Leaning across the table, he said, "Do you honestly think I didn't spend *every single day* thinking about you?"

She smiled as she lifted the drink. "Have you tried this?"

He scrunched his nose and shrugged. "A bit like drinking grass clippings." He shook his head distastefully.

"It's all in the blending...needs three minutes, at least!" She took a sip, and then realizing that the chef was still there, she nodded approvingly and he left.

"Just the same, I think I will leave the kale shakes for you," he said.

They finished their breakfast and the dishes were cleared. Valeria hadn't realized how hungry she was. Then she noticed Alex's expression. "What's so serious?"

He shook his head. "I told you that I needed to fill you in on the rest. Val, I'm not proud of all of it. But I promised myself, and Paolo, that you would know everything that happened over the past few months."

"Whatever it is, I know that you are nothing but honorable."

He kissed her hand. "Reserve your thoughts for later. You don't know how often I've lied to you since the previous council meeting. You don't know how selfish I've been. So much of this awful situation was because of me—not Paolo."

She wondered what he could have possibly lied to her about.

"Val, this all happened...the misery, the pain," he lifted a brow, "the fact that you were almost killed—several times—all because I couldn't bear the idea that if you weren't immortal, that Paolo might win your heart again." He gulped. "If I had just...trusted us, and been willing to take the chance, none of this would have happened."

"Alex, I do have a question about how I ever ended up married to Paolo in the first place." He glanced up at her. "I asked Paolo how it was that he found me first, when you have your visions. Paolo said that you did find me first."

"Yes, that's true."

"Then how was it possible for Paolo to...negotiate marriage. But you didn't?"

A light breeze moved by them, and the sun provided a wonderful warmth. "I found you when you were seven. I became your tutor, so that I could protect you. It was not wise, because it prohibited me from being in a social class that might marry you."

Nodding, as if she was now satisfied, she said, "Paolo wouldn't tell me that part, of course!"

"Val, there is more to it." He glanced up at her and took her hand. "I very simply could *never* bring myself to...to buy you!" He shook his head and looked down. "Again, my pride has gotten in the way of everything." He stared out to sea, unable to meet her eyes. "I always hoped that if I was near you, you would see me...know me...love me."

The ship rocked gently and she pulled her chair closer to his, kissing his cheek and then holding both of his hands.

Alex went on, "So, about the lies...that night after the first council meeting, I was up all night running scenarios to resolve this. I knew that Paolo, despite our differences, would not have placed this petition over us if he understood what it would do to you—or to me, for that matter. For him, this was all a simple game to see who would win you. He also wanted to help Kristiana, but I don't think he knows what to do to help her."

"What's wrong with her?"

Alex shook his head. "She...well, she is having difficulties." Valeria knew that was all Alex was going to say on the subject. "But with regard to me, I handle their finances, providing them the wealth to do whatever they wish. You don't kill off the golden goose."

Valeria pulled back in shock. "I don't understand. Paolo has a fleet of yachts! If Paolo is this wealthy, then why aren't you?"

It was Alex's turn to be taken aback. Then he asked, "Would you like a fleet of yachts?"

"No. I just had no idea. I guess I knew you had money. I just didn't imagine it was that much."

Alex shrugged. "Money's easy." He continued to stare out to sea, unable to meet her gaze. "That first night, after the council meeting, I knew the first target had to be to get the council to meet within a few months. Although the target date was delayed once you became ill."

Shaking off the emotion, he continued, "I could think of only one possible solution to get the council to meet and address the petitions in the near future, and that was for Paolo to submit a proposal of marriage to you. That way, he could remove the original petition and get approval for marriage. After that, if the engagement ended a few days later, we would be out of this mess."

"It would have been good to know the plan!"

Alex shook his head. "And I would have liked to have been able to share it with you! But if you did know, the deception would have been quite obvious to Jeremiah!" He sighed. "So, that was plan A. We also knew that we might need witnesses to prove that your relationship with Paolo was real. Neither Lars, nor Camille, knew about any of this. That was the reason for the scene in the field, after you left Pisa—that, by the way, was Paolo's idea. Not mine!" Valeria winced, realizing that Alex knew about it. He drew a deep breath.

"Plan B was basically what we experienced. It was in case anything went wrong. Because Paolo had seen the plan, he couldn't testify. If it appeared that he might be required to testify, he had to go on the offensive."

"Yes, he was pretty offensive."

Alex continued. "We suspected that Jeremiah might use this engagement as a way to get rid of you."

"Why would he do that?"

He shook his head. "I don't know. But we are quite certain that Jeremiah arranged for Shinsu to be gone during the first council meeting. If she had been there, Paolo's petition would have been thrown out or at least under investigation until the next council meeting. Someone knew about the petition before it was filed and worked with Jeremiah to ensure that Shinsu was away when it was presented."

"And you don't believe that it was Paolo?"

Alex raised an eyebrow. "No. Paolo didn't know about our engagement until the emergency council meeting announcement. But someone knew about it long before I even had the vision of you last year! That points to an oracle— though it wouldn't have been anyone in the family!"

"I don't think so either. But what about Daph?" she asked.

"I've known her almost all of my life. I just can't believe that she would set this up!"

"And you really don't believe that Paolo had anything to do with it?" Valeria asked, still suspicious of him.

"Paolo wouldn't have helped us if he had been involved! It

was probably Kristiana...maybe Aegemon." Alex continued, "Shinsu's job was to ensure that I was charged with a crime and that Paolo was not forced to testify. Plan B would be enacted if the council suspected that there had been a violation of the petition, or if Paolo was going to be forced to testify. We hoped for plan A, but expected plan B.

"As I said before, we also required enough innocent witnesses. That's why Paolo suddenly became friends with Lars and Camille. Both of them would be beyond reproach. Shinsu had some input in the plan but she would never be questioned. Most of all, you had to play your role. You did so beautifully."

Caleb yelled over, "I did good, too, didn't I?"

Valeria and Alex laughed, and they both said he did great. Caleb went back to his game.

"Caleb was very important in plan B and C!"

"Plan C?"

"Yes, that was if everything went poorly, Caleb was to wrap his arms around you and put you in his kayak and leave and not turn around until you were both safe."

"If it went poorly?" Valeria asked.

"If Paolo was forced to testify, it would be damaging. Caleb was involved but he couldn't testify, even if he was a member of the council and he also couldn't be searched. If necessary he was also a weapon that could protect you!"

"Yeah! I got to be the superhero again! That was so cool!" Caleb lifted an arm in victory before returning to his game.

"If we had gone to plan C, how would you have gotten out?" she asked, concerned.

He shook his head. "If Paolo had testified, both he and I would have certainly been put to death!"

Valeria shuddered. "Then why would Paolo do that? For the gamble?"

"Paolo was more involved than you know! He and Caleb set up all the supplies for the escape."

"Paolo?" she said in surprise. "I don't understand how this all came about! If you planned this, how could you testify?"

"A transference—which is what we use in testimony—doesn't show what you thought, only what you sensed externally." Alex brushed his hair back and rubbed his thumb over her hand and then laced their fingers together.

"I don't understand how you came up with all of this and were able to tell Paolo?"

"Let me show you." Alex took Valeria's other hand in his and she felt the rush of energy.

Valeria saw Alex approaching Paolo in an Italian restaurant. She could see Alex's mark and his white knuckles on his clenched fists. She immediately knew that Alex wanted to hit Paolo.

"You know you may have just signed her death warrant. Is that what you wanted?" She heard Alex say angrily.

"What is done, is done." Paolo's eyes were wary.

"Why did you do it?"

Paolo shrugged, unwilling to answer him.

"If we don't work together to fix this, we will be burying her again."

Glancing off into the distance, Paolo shook off his thoughts and without looking at Alex said, "I have always intended to withdraw the petition at the next council meeting."

"That's just not good enough. Do you have any concept of the pain you have caused her?"

"She will recover."

"I have always believed, deep inside, that you truly loved her." Valeria sensed that Alex was working to curb his rare temper. "If you did, you never could have done this to her. She's alone now. Ask Shinsu how well she's recovering—she nearly drowned herself in Paxos!"

Paolo flinched. "She needs time to…recover from your influence."

Alex nearly exploded in rage. "Well, she may never recover! Are you willing to win even if she dies? Even if you're causing her pain? Are you willing to win at the cost of her life?" He took a deep breath, attempting to regain his composure. "Were you aware that Mani and I were working on ensuring that the curse is resolved? But it takes testing."

"The curse is gone! Her eyes have changed back."

Alex looked up in frustration and then glared coldly at Paolo. "You're willing to take that chance?" He shook his head. "If you would have believed me last time, you might still be married to her."

"I read Mani's report, she's immortal!"

"My reports are that she has stopped eating. She won't leave her flat. I am going to need to contact someone to break into her apartment." Alex's voice was almost a cry. "I don't even know if she is still alive."

Placing his face in his hand, Paolo's voice softened. "There are no other options."

"There is another option."

Reaching into a pouch, Alex pulled out a notebook of drawings and slid it over to Paolo. "This is…an idea. Take a look. I'm certain it will be acceptable to you."

Alex pulled his hands from Valeria's, effectively ending the transference.

"What was in the book?" she asked.

"I had to find a way to communicate to Paolo without having a discussion. I couldn't see any details, or discuss it, so I typed it out on a keyboard and printed without permitting myself to look at it. That way there was no recorded memory.

"Paolo was aware of Caleb's rare gift. So when Caleb

returned from his wayward adventure to New York, I had Paolo pick him up so that they could begin planning.

"I typed out my concept of the propeller that had to be invented by Tavish for Caleb. It had to be waterproof, work off of Caleb's power, and we had to be able to completely break it down so that Caleb could wear it into the Council Room. Paolo and Caleb both already knew how to dive, but Caleb needed a brief lesson in snorkeling and kayaking—especially in that treacherous cave!

"Actually, the St. Croix trip was planned to get you into the water," Alex said.

"You planned that trip?" Valeria asked, startled.

"It was the only way I could think of to move things along."

"Move things along? Alex, that kiss...on St. Croix...with Paolo. Please tell me that wasn't—"

"No!" Alex's eyes got wide. "No, Val!" He shuddered. "I would never plan something like that! As a matter of fact, Paolo and I had quite the discussion on appropriate behavior. He knew better than that. His hormones just got out of control, with a little help from the rum."

She pressed her hands into his. "Alex, I am so sorry about that and I hope you know—"

He smiled softly. "I know." But she could still see the pain in his eyes.

"Alex? That wasn't all of your conversation with Paolo, was it?"

"You really don't need to see the rest."

"Is it something about you and Kristiana?"

"No! No, Val." Alex swallowed and then nodded as he took her hands in his and looked into her eyes and she again felt the rush of energy.

Paolo smiled slyly. "I agree to this on one condition,"

Paolo said. "On plan A, if the council approves the marriage, Valeria must tell me she doesn't love me and wants to marry you. I will not end the engagement unless she tells me so."

"Pal, she will never want you. She loves me."

Smiling smugly, Paolo said, "Without you in her life, she will need someone who knows her past. She will be angry with me at first. That's to be expected. But then she will realize that I am a link to you." Paolo sipped his wine before continuing. "Then one day, she will realize she enjoys my company. Soon, she will become afraid of her feelings for me and realize my...skills. She will insist on seeing you. You will come...I think with that redhead, Daphne? Yes, I think she would be suitable."

Valeria's face turned flaming red. "That bastard!"

"Well, that bastard saved our lives. So in the end, I'm grateful for him. To be honest, I did want to kill him but I needed him in order to resolve this. Fortunately, he loves you enough to repeatedly risk his life to set things right."

Her anger with Paolo was on several levels; the fact that she had responded exactly as he had told Alex was upsetting.

"Alex, if you had come to St. Croix with Daph..." Valeria knew that she would have believed that Alex had moved on. She would have given up and probably run straight to Paolo's waiting arms. That thought gave her a shudder!

"Yes." He looked down. "That's why I refused that one request." He looked her in the eyes. "Still, I hated what I did in St. Croix, giving you the additional vision of Paolo lying to you. I did that because I was feeling insecure. But it was wrong. We might have been able to proceed with plan A, with no need to place your life at risk, if I had just kept my agreement with Paolo. And I am so sorry about that!"

She pulled his face to hers and kissed him. "Hey!" He looked up. "You know that I would never choose anyone but you!"

He offered her a weak smile. "I will admit that I had my doubts in St. Croix."

She ran her hand over his cheek. "I'm so sorry."

"I understood the situation. I didn't like it, but I understood. And, beautiful, I never blamed you. It was a situation that I created. Actually, it was the result that we needed. Val, you went through so much over the past few months. I only regretted that I couldn't be there and that Paolo could, and that you were forced to turn to him."

She kissed Alex, again.

"The night after the council meeting has haunted me through this whole ordeal. Having to plant the seed for a relationship with Paolo was bad enough." Alex shook his head. "I didn't know if I could do it. I didn't know if I could make it believable. But if I didn't, I knew there was a chance I'd never see you again."

Alex cleared his throat. "But there is something…there was a lie that I cannot live with another minute."

Valeria suddenly wondered if Alex had fallen into someone's arms…Daphne's? Kristiana's?

She stroked his face. "Just tell me." He looked away, ashamed; it must be bad, she thought.

He gulped. "The night that I left…" He drew a deep breath and looked out at the horizon. "I told you…" Tears came to his eyes and he closed them.

"What? Just tell me!" He had an affair, she concluded.

"When Paolo submitted the petition, all I could think of was…*how can I solve this?*"

"Of course!" Oh, her poor, sweet Alex!

"That last night on Paxos, I laid there with you in my arms…" He bit his lip and pulled her into his chest. "I couldn't imagine what life might be like for you. I was haunted by it.

Tormented."

"Yes." She let out a cry.

"And finally, I knew that Paolo had to resolve it. I knew he would and the only way that would work is if…" He broke into a silent sob.

"What?" She clung to him.

"Beautiful, you have to know that leaving you was the hardest thing I have ever done."

"Just tell me…you found someone else?"

Alex looked at her for a minute stunned. "No!" He let out a small laugh and raised his eyebrows. "No, Val! There is no one else for me."

"What has you so upset, Alex?"

He closed his eyes and clenched his jaw. "It was the last things that I told you before I left. You asked me and I looked you straight in the eyes and lied to you." Tears flooded her eyes. "I told you that I had given up and that we both needed to move on. I said that there was no hope of us ever seeing each other again and it nearly killed me!

"But, Val, you must know—you need to know," he shook his head in agony, *"I would never give up on you! EVER!"*

"Yes, somehow, I knew that." She held him, while she brushed his hair back. "Alex, I love you and you love me. And no one is *ever* going to force us apart again!"

He looked relieved.

"Alex, what were you doing at the edge of the river when I first found you?"

His mood suddenly lightened as he shook off the previous memories. "I almost forgot!" He reached in his pocket. "I needed something to signal Shinsu that we had left." He brushed his hand across something in his hand. "I made this after we were forced apart to remind me of who we are."

He took out a shiny metal triquetra that was mounted on a

thin leather cord. "My plan was to give this to you until we discovered your mark." She took it in her hands and kissed his cheek.

"It's beautiful! I'll wear it always!" She pulled up her hair and he hooked it around her neck.

"But then last night…"

"What?"

He shook his head and narrowed his eyes for a moment. "Come with me!" He took her hand and led her back to the bedroom. In front of the mirror, he pulled her hair back from her face.

"What is it? A gray hair?"

"Hardly!" he laughed.

She looked in the mirror as he kissed a spot behind her ear and looked at her knowingly. She leaned in even closer and then she saw it, on the edge of her hairline; the tiny mark that told them that they were meant to be—the triquetra, the mark that Apollo had given to them alone—as symbolons.

∞

Caleb, Valeria, and Alex stood at the Barcelona airport looking at the outbound flights with their sunglasses on. She was wearing a dress and heels that Paolo had bought her—and her new necklace from Alex—and looked quite the jet-setter. Alex wore slacks and a polo shirt. They all wore their brown contacts.

"So, where to?" Alex asked. "The only stipulations are that it has to be more than two thousand miles from Paxos, preferably a bit unpopulated, and probably nothing in Europe for a while; too many of us here."

Caleb said, "Can we go to Disneyworld? Then we can go snorkeling and scuba diving and deep sea fishing!"

Valeria shook her head. "Can we delay that trip? I've had enough water for a while."

"How about Africa? We could go on a safari!"

She shrugged. "I could do Africa."

Glancing back up at the scheduled departures, Alex nodded. "We'll need to stay put for at least a month or more. I'm fine with Africa as long as we can find a preacher or Justice of the Peace." He winked at Valeria.

She nodded and hugged him.

"Africa it is!" As they started toward the counter, Caleb tapped Alex and Valeria, wearing his fully insulated body suit.

"Val, doesn't anyone know who I really am?

"Sure they do!" She smiled and brushed her hand through his hair. "You're Caleb, the superhero with the magic touch!"

His smile brightened, as he said to himself, "Cool!"

She walked ahead of them to the water fountain and suddenly began to wonder who Caleb really was, and if she was supposed to know. Behind her, Alex and Caleb watched her appreciatively.

Caleb bit his lip in thought and after a moment turned to Alex. "Hey...I know you were upset with me for going to New York and all to see your girl. But...um, well, I wouldn't have really stolen Val from you. I guess I just figured she could be my girlfriend until you could have her back." He glanced nervously at Alex. "I just wanted to make sure we're cool on that!"

Just then, Valeria headed back toward them and Alex's mouth turned up in an amused smile that brightened the room. Barely glancing at Caleb, Alex's eyes locked on her...his symbolon.

"I appreciate that, buddy! Yeah, we're cool." Then his smile expanded into the one Valeria knew so well. She wondered for a moment what he had in mind and glanced around her, suddenly noticing an alcove by the water fountain. His smile continued to broaden, in their secret smile.

As she reached him, she took his hand, tracing the symbol on it without looking and then their fingers laced together as the three of them walked to the ticket counter

Epilogue

Known opportunities were running out. She sat on the step of her throne, her elbows perched anxiously on her knees with her hands balled into fists, as she clenched the dagger tightly. She had knowledge that all had not gone as planned. She could feel it—that gift had always been hers and she didn't have to rely on anyone else for it!

Jeremiah's footsteps were more hesitant than usual. She listened impatiently to the chink of his cane and then the slow clunk of his steps. His news was not good and she could not wait for him to make his way down the hallway.

"YOU FAILED!" she screeched as she ran her thumb across the crystal that was bound around her neck.

Waving an arm, Jeremiah continued toward her. "Now, now, my dear, calm down! All is not lost. There was no way for them to escape." His eyes flinched as he glanced around the room avoiding her glare "They are most likely in Tartarus!" He offered a weak cackle—but he didn't believe it either.

Her eyes became giant saucers, wild with rage. "They

swam out, you fool—right in front of you and his wife!"

"His wife?" Jeremiah asked.

"Myrdd! Myrddins's wife! That's his name, you know—Myrddin." She stood and began pacing as her arms flew about, occasionally catching on cobwebs—although she didn't seem to notice and kept muttering to herself, barely coherently. "I told Myrdd that Alexander was mine. I wanted him and he must help me have him. The girl, she doesn't love him! Myrddin said, people had to decide their own path and his path was already designed and he belonged with the girl! But I told him, I could change history. Myrdd *told me* he would give Alex to me and then he told me that I couldn't have him because he could never love me. But *I wanted him!* And so Myrdd should go away and I said, I can arrange that." She laughed, softly, like a child. "But he is already dead. Alex must die, too! But where has he been all these years? Why does Paolo love her, too? Alex used to call me...no...it was... Why does everyone I care about love her more? If she was gone, then they would all love me again. But Myrdd, he has to help me with the boy—I told him it was his responsibility...the boy. He must have told his wife..."

She glanced at Jeremiah. "Who are you?" she asked, her voice now confused. For once, Jeremiah was truly afraid. Typically, he was able to control her with rational conversation. Now, he doubted it.

He tried to find his voice, clearing it before he spoke. "I am Jeremiah. And Shinsu is *my* wife. Myrdd is dead, remember?"

"You aren't Myrrdin!" she pronounced.

"Uh...no. No, my dear, I'm your friend, Jeremiah. I helped you and you helped me." He tried to smile.

Kristiana sat back down. "Of course! But you have not..." She swallowed. "You permitted them to escape. Now what are we going to do?"

"Do?" Jeremiah asked.

She shook her head, weary of his portion of the conversation. "There are only a few more opportunities."

Jeremiah's eye twitched. "Then we will take advantage of those opportunities."

"I do not require your assistance anymore. You have failed me time and time again. I asked only for a simple thing. Now, I must take matters into my own hands."

"But, my dear, if they have both swam in the River Styx she should be immortal now. All of them would be. That means that there is only one way to rid ourselves of them."

Pursing her lips, Kristiana thought for a moment and then said, "It doesn't matter, I will find them...I have been shown how I will." She sneered and swiped her knife at something imaginary as her expression turned into rage. "I will show him what it feels like to lose the only thing you love! And then I will take his heart...and keep it with me always!

Personal message from Delia Colvin

I hope you enjoyed The Symbolon! As much as I enjoy writing, I enjoy hearing from readers. If you enjoyed this or any of my other books, it would mean the world to me if you would send me a short email to introduce yourself and say hi. I always personally respond to my readers.

I would also love to add you to my mailing list to receive notifications about future books, updates, and contests.

Please email me at deliajcolvin@gmail.com so I can personally thank you for trying my books.

Delia

Titles by Delia J. Colvin

THE SIBYLLINE TRILOGY

The Sibylline Oracle

The Symbolon

The Last Oracle

Acknowledgements

A VERY grateful thank you to those special people whose kind words and encouragement served to "talk me off the ledge" of insecurity! Writing is so very personal and your support has made a tremendous difference for me!

Irene Enriquez, absolutely FABULOUS notes on story! Rosanne Eskenazi, for your wisdom, enthusiasm and encouragement! Sandy Rudiger for your wonderful support, friendship and marketing! The sisters of my heart: Mary Jo Palmer, for all your fantastic promotion support and friendship and Pauline Lagana, my wonderful new friend from Melbourne!

My very extraordinary previewers: Emily Kubat, Al Hatman, Bernadette "Bibi" Berrios, Sandy Rudiger, Pauline Lagana, Paddy O'callaghan, Irene Enriquez, Dave Khanoyan

And the wonderful people that have supported me in this precarious adventure: Jo Anthony, Dewitt Wilcox, Fran Bartlett, Marv Halbakken, Patty Tully, Dave Khanoyan, Laurie Linfoot Brown, Karen Ang, JJ Upton, Jennifer Mansfield, Cindy Abell, Kim Perry, Krissy Wright, and Joyce Wallace and Leslie Vanderwilt

Significant contributions were made by: Jen Youngs in so many areas, website (and repair after I "tinker" with it), concept and design of the covers, story and editing, marketing and organization of events; Randy Colvin in his phenomenal support and marketing; my editor David Gregory and Natalie Quinn, graphics designer extraordinaire.

Lastly a special thanks and love to both Jen and Randy! You were both the first to read the rough drafts. Words cannot express what your phenomenal support network for me!

About the Author

DELIA J. COLVIN

Delia has lived all over the country from Fairbanks, AK, to Huntington Beach, CA to Knoxville, TN. but considers Danville, CA home. She currently resides in Prescott, Arizona, with her husband, Randy and their two Cavalier King Charles dogs.

She has worked as an Entrepreneur, Sales, Advertising, Air Traffic Control and as a Russian Interpreter.

For more information and contact information go to: www.DeliaColvin.Com or email DeliaColvin@gmail.com

Made in the USA
Charleston, SC
21 September 2013